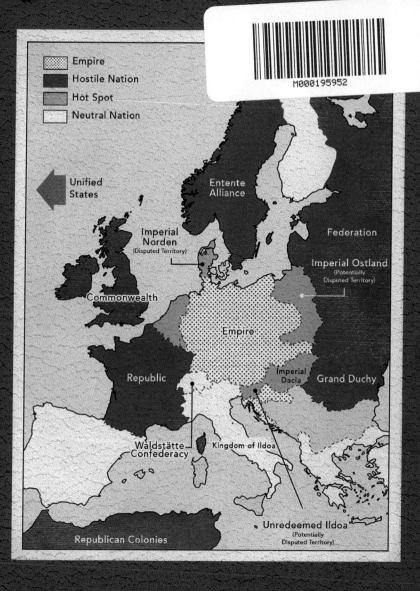

Empire
Hostile Nation
Hot Spot
Neutral Nation

Unified
States

Entente
Alliance

Federation

Imperial Norden
(Disputed Territory)

Imperial Ostland
(Potentially
Disputed Territory)

Commonwealth

Empire

Republic

Imperial
Dacia

Grand Duchy

Waldstätte
Confederacy

Kingdom of Ildoa

Unredeemed Ildoa
(Potentially
Disputed Territory)

Republican Colonies

In Omnia Paratus

THE
SAGA OF TANYA
THE EVIL

THE SAGA OF TANYA THE EVIL

In Omnia Paratus

[8]

Carlo Zen

Illustration by Shinobu Shinotsuki

YEN
ON

New York

The Saga of Tanya the Evil, Vol. 8

Carlo Zen

Translation by Emily Balistrieri
Cover art by Shinobu Shinotsuki

YOJO SENKI Vol. 8 In Omnia Paratus
©Carlo Zen 2017
First published in Japan in 2017 by KADOKAWA CORPORATION, Tokyo.
English translation rights arranged with KADOKAWA CORPORATION, Tokyo, through
TUTTLE-MORI AGENCY, INC., Tokyo.

English translation © 2020 by Yen Press, LLC

Yen On
150 West 30th Street, 19th Floor
New York, NY 10001

Visit us at yenpress.com
facebook.com/yenpress
twitter.com/yenpress
yenpress.tumblr.com
instagram.com/yenpress

First Yen On Edition: December 2020

Yen On is an imprint of Yen Press, LLC.
The Yen On name and logo are trademarks of Yen Press, LLC.

Library of Congress Cataloging-in-Publication Data
Names: Zen, Carlo, author. | Shinotsuki, Shinobu, illustrator. | Balistrieri, Emily, translator. |
Steinbach, Kevin, translator.
Title: Saga of Tanya the evil / Carlo Zen ; illustration by Shinobu Shinotsuki ;
translation by Emily Balistrieri, Kevin Steinbach.
Other titles: Yōjo Senki. English
Description: First Yen On edition. | New York : Yen ON, 2017–
Identifiers: LCCN 2017044721 | ISBN 9780316512442 (v. 1 : pbk.) |
ISBN 9780316512466 (v. 2 : pbk.) | ISBN 9780316512480 (v. 3 : pbk.) |
ISBN 9780316560627 (v. 4 : pbk.) | ISBN 9780316560696 (v. 5 : pbk.) |
ISBN 9780316560719 (v. 6 : pbk.) | ISBN 9780316560740 (v. 7 : pbk.) |
ISBN 9781975310493 (v. 8 : pbk.)
Classification: LCC PL878.E6 Y6513 2017 | DDC 895.63/6—dc23
LC record available at https://lccn.loc.gov/2017044721

ISBNs: 978-1-9753-1049-3 (paperback)
978-1-9753-1050-9 (ebook)

2 4 6 8 10 9 7 5 3 1

LSC-C

Printed in the United States of America

THE
SAGA OF TANYA
THE EVIL

In Omnia Paratus

contents

Prepared by the Commissariat for Internal Affairs

Federation

General Secretary (very respectful person)

    Loria (very respectful person)

[Multinational Unit]

Colonel Mikel
(Federation, commander) ————— First Lieutenant Tanechka
(political officer)

Lieutenant Colonel Drake
(Commonwealth, second-in-command) ————— First Lieutenant Sue

Kingdom of Ildoa

General Gassman
(army administration) ————————— Colonel Calandro
(intelligence)

The Free Republic

Commander de Lugo **(head of the Free Republic)**

Relationship Chart

Empire

【General Staff】

Lieutenant General von Zettour
(Service Corps, inspector of the eastern front) ——— **Lieutenant Colonel Uger**
(Service Corps, Railroad)

Lieutenant General von Rudersdorf
(Operations) ——————— Colonel
von Lergen

Salamander Kampfgruppe (aka Lergen Kampfgruppe)

203rd Aerial Mage Battalion

Lieutenant Colonel Tanya von Degurechaff

└─ Major Weiss

├─ First Lieutenant Serebryakov

├─ First Lieutenant Grantz

└─ (replacement)
First Lieutenant Wüstemann

Captain Ahrens (**Armored**)

Captain Meybert (**Artillery**)

First Lieutenant Tospan (**Infantry**)

The Lergen Kampfgruppe...?
I saw them once, a long time ago.

——————— Andrew, WTN special correspondent ———————

The words *operation*, *military campaign*, *pitched battle*, and *decisive battle* instantly bring to mind images of hard, brutal fighting. And certainly, any situation described this way will undoubtedly involve combat.

But on the eastern front, it was a slower trickle of blood that drained the two opposing armies.

When veterans talk about the eastern front, they think of the infinite skirmishes that occurred in the massive theater of operations where major maneuvers simply didn't happen.

It was the same on the Rhine.

That was another place where towering piles of corpses lurked behind the words *nothing to report*.

Those minor engagements don't appear in history books and are hardly ever remembered. But there is no doubt that much of history was decided in these moments, and now those who gave their lives sleep in silence.

My name is Andrew.

I am one of the embedded reporters who visits these forgotten battle-grounds no one speaks of.

I took up my pen intending to write a memoir, but my preface has gotten awfully long. Maybe I'm too much of an empath.

Or perhaps by telling my story, I hope to escape my past?

I wouldn't say I'm particularly keen on running away, but the young man who lived through those years came back a world-weary scoundrel... In any case, I would not describe them as happy times.

Still, I was a witness.

It's difficult to say how much insight I have to offer or if I can even be considered a reliable observer. To be quite honest, there's little chance that I accurately remember everything I saw. Moreover, I was inexperienced and didn't truly grasp what was going on in the Federation.

But by a quirk of fate, I was permitted to work as a reporter embedded with the multinational unit established by the Federation and the Commonwealth. (At the time, the Federation and Commonwealth could do friendly things like that. Do younger readers know that rather than curse rivaling ideologies, the heads of state back then extolled each other as precious brothers-in-arms?)

The reason a young reporter would be given such an opportunity was—paradoxically—*because* I was young.

To Federation authorities, who angrily glared at most journalists, someone unseasoned and ignorant was the perfect candidate.

The majority of the other embedded reporters were also my age. I recall that any older reporter I encountered on the scene usually turned out to be a crazy—apologies, I meant "passionate"—Communist.

But maybe I should be grateful that this experience allowed me to make longtime friends.

Anyway, we're getting off topic. Apparently, when you get older, your stories start to meander. Maybe there are just too many memories.

Memories, yes. Memories.

For me, there's the Toad Offensive, a series of operations that took place around the same time as the Imperial Army's Operation Andromeda. I even saw a unit that might have been the phantom Lergen Kampfgruppe. When I realized what a devious enemy we were up against, I penned a bitter article that the censors latched on to immediately.

Back then, the censors must have had a hard job dealing with a multinational unit of Federation and Commonwealth troops. The two sides had such conflicting ideas on what should and shouldn't be written that it was impossible to not fall afoul of one rule or another.

The result ended up being a good reference for learning how to properly interpret a newspaper article.

To all the young readers out there, I recommend you take newspapers from that time period and study them alongside your textbooks. How different the history books are from the newspaper stories!

What should have been fact-based reporting often wound up reading like accounts of a mission to the surface of the moon. I hope you'll understand the reasons for all the nonsense that made it impossible to find out what really happened without reading between the lines.

Still, sometimes hard truths that couldn't be swept under the rug would surprisingly appear right on the front page.

I myself learned of "Zettour the Terrible" on the eastern front, and that general truly was…a terrifying being.

Even now, I don't think there's anyone who can give a full account of everything he's done, but as a simple citizen of the Commonwealth who saw him with my own eyes, I think summing up his existence is simple:

Curse the Imperial Army General Staff for sending that lunatic to the eastern front.

Overall, it could be considered a disaster for the Imperial Army. Perhaps I should celebrate that, as someone who hails from the Commonwealth. But as one of the people on that eastern front, I have to say that it was none other than Zettour who made our lives hell.

His presence can't be described as anything less than a nightmare.

As an embedded journalist, I must admit our situation was rather ideal. We never ran out of material for stories, and you couldn't ask for a better environment to dig up scoops. In the end, though, we got too used to the daily body count.

We special correspondents were praised for our wonderful articles, but…something must just have been wrong with the times.

I often wrote special dispatches featuring our comrades and brothers-in-arms from the Federation as they fought on the vast eastern front against the "railroad" mages who piled up mountains of corpses. People in the home country couldn't get enough of these tales about the fierce battles.

I'm sure there was something wrong back then.

And that's why I want to know.

I'm not looking for judgment, censure, or revenge.

I just want to know the truth.

"What do you think of my new manuscript, General Drake?"

"…It's your memoir. Write whatever you want. I appreciate you showing me, since we're old friends, but honestly…are you asking me to censor it? Go find a Commie for that."

We're discussing the manuscript of what I suppose you could call my chronicle. But the reaction of the gentleman who took time out of his day to sit at this café and read it is brusque.

Unconcerned and indifferent.

I suddenly feel like cradling my head in my hands. I more or less anticipated this reaction, but he's even more uncompromising than I expected.

Considering that this was only the first hurdle, I find it difficult to feel optimistic.

"What a harsh reception. Wouldn't it be more enjoyable to simply reminisce together? Isn't that one of the old standbys of retirement clubs?"

"Thank you for your fascinating opinion, Andrew."

There it is. I brace myself.

Regardless of what the colonials might say, if someone from back home has a cup of tea in one hand while he describes something as fascinating, there's no way to interpret that as anything other than scathing sarcasm. He might as well have declared *Are you an idiot?* to my face.

"That said, I don't believe I've lost my edge in retirement just yet. If it appears that way to you, I can't deny that I'm disappointed. How about we reconsider your proposal once we've lost all trace of backbone and reason to go on?" Channeling the John Bull spirit with his biting remarks, Drake casually reaches for his tea. His stance hasn't changed since the old days. In other words, he doesn't intend to say anything else.

Very well. I steel my resolve.

I'll show him the difference between a self-styled journalist—who merely tries to do their best without prying too much—and myself, a true professional.

"I've gotten on in years. So many things have become a hassle."

"Hey now, Andrew. You're younger than me."

Though he's practically a retired veteran, I can't help but wince at the words of this general, whose posture is so ramrod straight, it's as if his body has stiff canvas sewn into it.

What Drake said is true if you're counting years, but I can't help but think of the words *physical age*. Even a body that could take a beating when younger inevitably mellows with age.

"Then I'd appreciate it if you'd act more like an old man, General. Couldn't you take our dear friendship into consideration? How about giving me a peek at your soft underbelly?"

Honestly, I'm jealous of his energy.

I've heard that aerial magic officers who survived the war either died young from the tremendous strain of using too much magic or wind up living to a bizarrely old age… Drake must be one of the latter.

"Ha-ha-ha." Seeing him laugh so brightly, it's clear he's a stranger to the concept of wasting away in retirement. "My 'soft underbelly'? All right, then. I'll tell you something I've been saving. Back when I was a young magic officer in the marines, I telegrammed my lover—"

"If you'll excuse my interruption, General, I want to hear about the eastern front."

After furrowing his brow for a moment, displeased, he sighs heavily. It's an utterly natural gesture… He seems genuinely offended at being cut off, but is that truly the case?

This is where things get interesting. I feel like I'm making real progress.

"…Andrew, you want to talk about that? Really?"

"Well, yeah."

"What is it you want me to say?"

"Hmm." I smile wryly and confess. "I want to be able to tell future generations about things I didn't understand myself at the time."

I saw it.

I heard it.

But I didn't comprehend it.

The sad truth is that merely being present at the time didn't bring understanding.

"You're an awfully persistent chap."

"It's the spirit of journalism."

"Spirit, eh? Well, I suppose that's a good enough reason." Drake shrugs and takes an elegant bite of his sandwich. His good upbringing reveals itself in the strangest moments, just like it used to back in those days.

"Let's say you couldn't resist and gave in to my persistence. Today

would be a good day to finally learn about General Habergram's role on the eastern front. I wouldn't say no to hearing the story of Mr. Johnson, either."

"Sorry, but I don't know."

"I beg your pardon, but…," I cut in quickly. "What about the record of Intelligence deploying your marine mage unit in secret? Though it's circumstantial evidence, the findings of a recent survey conducted by several researchers makes a strong case that your unit participated. Besides, it happened in the very same Federation territory where we first met, General."

"I have no idea what you're talking about. As you can see, I'm not the type who did well in school. I have no idea what the academics are writing."

Only a second-rate amateur would fall for that confusion in his voice. I know for a fact that Drake saying he hated school is a bald-faced lie.

"The very man who shaped the comprehensive officer education curriculum into what it is today claims to detest school? I'd like to tell *that* to the kids being put through the grinder right now."

"I was simply following orders and doing my duty. It's not as if it was my choice to work on education."

"…That's a very different story from what I've heard. In any case, let's get back to the original topic. Please tell me about the secret operation."

"Are you forgetting what my rank was at the time? I was only a lieutenant colonel, for crying out loud. What exactly do you think I was privy to?"

That telltale gesture he favors whenever he feigns ignorance really brings me back to the old days. It's no wonder countless young journalists misread the dashing marine magic officer.

But I'm not about to make the same mistake again.

"'Only a lieutenant colonel,' you say—yes, I was once green enough to buy that excuse. How nostalgic. I occasionally think about those days, even now."

"Nostalgic…? I have complicated feelings about hearing that from someone who was also there on the same eastern front."

"In that sense, thinking of Colonel Mikel makes me nostalgic, too."

0

For a moment, I catch a glimpse of conflicting emotions on the general's face, but sure enough, his mask of innocence is solid as steel. Nodding with a wry grin, he proceeds to change the topic. "...That's a name I haven't heard in a long time. You're a crafty one. We're living proof that there was actually a time when we called Federation soldiers allies, huh?"

"Wouldn't you like to leave something behind while you're still alive?"

"How about a story, then? I can't talk about what I don't know. But, well... Do you mind if I smoke?"

"Not at all."

As the mellow smoke of his cigarillo fills the air, he flashes a bitter smile. "...Those were truly strange days, Andrew."

》》》   **JUNE 8, UNIFIED YEAR 1927, THE EASTERN FRONT,**   《《《
                          MULTINATIONAL FORCES HQ

"...Haaagh, I made it," I murmur softly. Even as Andrew, the *WTN* correspondent who learned the ropes on the Rhine lines, I feel terribly uneasy entering the Federation.

Honestly, I'm surprised my credentials didn't get in the way. Even before war with the Empire broke out, the Communist Party papers were calling my homeland "a den of bigoted reactionaries."

Nothing short of the grace of God could have saved this plan to allow dozens of journalists from a capitalist state to cross the border.

As a result of the aberrations caused by the monster known as politics, a miracle occurred.

Yesterday's enemy became today's ally. *Commies and Limeys together at last*, quipped the imperials of the outlandish alliance, but the result was that these mortal enemies, Communists and capitalists, would unite to fight a common threat.

Even if it was only on the surface, that change became an opportunity for potential breakthroughs on everything that had been previously considered nonnegotiable. It was only natural for relations between the Federation and the Commonwealth to improve dramatically. Thanks to this elevated level of cooperation, the Communist Party allowed a group of Commonwealth reporters to enter their territory, even if it was only because they were accompanying the expeditionary force.

The Federation traditionally barred the vast majority of foreign press. It really was a miracle that reporters were allowed in any shape or form.

This was an unprecedented chance. Veterans of the industry began fierce negotiations to secure the limited slots. Some leveraged their breadth of experience or emphasized their proficiency in Federation language. There were also those who boasted their extensive knowledge of history. None of these skills was something that could be acquired overnight, so needless to say, it was hard for a small-time journalist to compete.

Though I had experience reporting from the Rhine front, I was one of the younger reporters at *WTN*. I was self-aware and objective enough to realize that I had little chance to be picked over my seniors.

Honestly, when my boss told me I'd been chosen to go, I immediately suspected an ulterior motive.

But the moment I set foot on the ship bound for the Federation, I understood I hadn't been picked because the higher-ups thought I could do a better job than my colleagues.

Why did *WTN* choose me? The explanation is extremely simple: The only possible answers are my age and my lack of experience.

One look made it painfully obvious. With few exceptions, the press corps was made up of youngsters from each publication.

I'll also mention here that ours was a small industry. Right or left, I'd at least heard the names of the more polarizing thinkers.

With numbers so skewed, even a child could grasp the Federation's intent. Just a list of the members would have been enough to figure it out. One glance told me they had handpicked a biased group of rookies who hadn't made a name for themselves yet alongside a handful of veteran Red sympathizers.

I'll admit that the young journalists seized the opportunity and made up for their lack of experience with zeal; the moment we hit the ground in the Federation, we began sending reports of everything we saw and heard back to our offices. To be blunt, greedy baby journos, eager to rack up achievements and starving for any scoop they could get, sallied forth to the front lines to make their fortunes.

Granted, we had a degree of education and maintained a veneer of civility…but you needed some serious ambition to be willing to come all the way to the eastern front.

After all, I also came here with the intent to jump-start my career.

First thing I set my mind to was implementing a few safety measures I picked up during my time on the Rhine lines, such as familiarizing myself with the vicinity of my lodgings to burn the lay of the land into my brain. I did this while trying my best to get a feel for the unit we were attached to.

My first moves were, if I'm being honest, complete failures.

Although some loosened up to questions about their hometowns and their lives back there, these consummate marine mages wouldn't spill a word about anything important. When I tried to interview the former Entente Alliance volunteer mage unit, a political officer from the Federation Communist Party immediately got in my way. After several more attempts to sound people out, I got the sense that they were determined not to let any significant news leak.

But if all I did was forward the official statements to Londinium, there would be no reason to pay my salary. If I was going to return empty-handed, I would have to be prepared to not have a job anymore by the time I got home.

When the need arises, people get creative. My plan now was to secure an interview with the commander of the Commonwealth unit dispatched to the Federation, Lieutenant Colonel Drake.

While memorizing the lay of the land, I shrewdly scoped out the places the higher-ups liked to spend their time. Having filled a thermos with tea, I cruise around the garrison until I find my target.

Pretending as though it was a coincidence, I take out my thermos and say hello. "You're Colonel Drake, right? Funny meeting you here. Would you fancy a cup of tea?"

"Thanks. Andrew, was it? So what's this about?"

"Come again?"

"You're a journalist, no? I don't imagine you're the good-natured type who would serve free tea to a public servant you just happened to run into."

I cock my head at him in a show of confusion, but in my mind, I click my tongue. Journalists always pay for the tea, and things tend to get hairy when the source figures out exactly how much it'll cost them.

"...What's wrong with having at least one kindhearted journalist around?"

"Ha-ha-ha. Then how about we spend all day chatting about the weather? Or maybe I should recite the official lines about the beautiful cooperation between the Federation and the Commonwealth like a broken record?"

"Anything but that, I beg you."

Between the shrug he gives in response to my complaint and the casual way he pretends to be hiding nothing, Drake proves to be bizarrely impervious to the ministrations of mass media.

"If you don't mind me asking, are you part of some frontline public affairs unit, Colonel?"

"No, as you can see, I'm a rough-and-tumble marine mage."

Oh, come on. I sigh, figuring it's a bit—well, more like quite a bit—of an overreaction. I try to rattle him.

"So you're saying a mere marine magic officer... Oh, no offense."

"None taken. You're a civilian, not to mention a dirty journalist. You have the right to say what you think."

"...I'm honored, Colonel."

All I learn from trying to provoke him is that unfortunately he's a cut above me. He wasn't angered by my rudeness, and he doesn't opt to ignore me, either; I don't have any more moves to make if he's just going to come back at me with sarcasm and a smile.

He can see every card in my hand.

Respecting journalism is all well and good, but this is undoubtedly an officer who knows how things are done. It would be extremely difficult to get him to say anything I might want to hear.

"Come now, Andrew, there's not much point in two fellows from the Commonwealth stealthily trying to probe each other. Why don't we compromise? First, tell me a bit about yourself and your career."

"Uhhh, I think my résumé was attached to my application to come here."

Applying for the visa at Londinium's Federation Embassy had been a nightmare. It got so bad that I was tempted to ask if they were trying to create a set of rules governing the rules that governed the rules.

"I had to fill out a ton of paperwork for both countries in order to get authorization to come along as an embedded reporter. What else was I supposed to put in there?"

"I mean, I did take a look at your documents. Alongside the paranoid Federation chaps."

"You say they're paranoid?"

"Oh, are you a Red?"

"I may not be green anymore, but that doesn't make me a Red."

Apparently, my attempt at a witty remark impresses the lieutenant colonel. He doesn't ridicule me for putting on airs—on the contrary, he nods in satisfaction.

"…Then you have my apology. I guess I've had a lot on my mind lately."

"Could that comment be…you throwing me a bone?"

Is he hinting at struggles working with the Federation? There's no denying that this grinning lieutenant colonel is a tough customer. Anyone's interest would be piqued if an officer directly involved in Federation-Commonwealth joint operations hints at such news.

If I want to hear any more, I'll have to play by his rules. I make it clear I understand and nod.

"Allow me to reintroduce myself. Special correspondent Andrew from *WTN*, a poor journalist who, after being embedded on the Rhine lines, covered Entente Alliance refugees and was then, through some irony of fate, told there were scoops to be had on the eastern front and thrown out here."

"Thrown?"

"*WTN* would have preferred to send veterans. Curiously, it seems all the papers only managed to get young people admitted to the Federation."

It's becoming hard to tell who's interviewing whom, but…if I can draw Drake out this way, I'm more than happy to play along. Whether I'll be able to uncover some real news and not just pick up whatever he feels like sharing comes down to my skill.

"Ah, well, journalists do make the Federation fellows nervous."

"…I've noticed. I mean, they're so considerate of even a greenhorn like me. I get both a 'guide' and an 'interpreter.' Frankly, it's all a little overbearing."

"The thing is, Andrew, and maybe you aren't aware, but their hospitality can go even further."

"Oh?"

Is he finally going to tell me something worthwhile?

Drake chuckles to himself in satisfaction in response to my eagerness. However, when I look more closely, I notice the smile never reaches his eyes.

"You can ask them for tea, snacks, or anything as long as it isn't film or a telegraph. They'll gladly accommodate any reasonable requests."

Ah. I nod. "So the Federation soldiers want to look good for the press—propaganda... Honestly, though, this isn't my first time reporting on the front lines, so I wasn't hoping for any special treatment."

"By which you mean?"

"If I can sleep in a military cot, that's good enough for me. Colonel Drake, I'll have you know I was on the Rhine lines. Naturally, that means I reported from the trenches."

It was a terrible experience, but most educational ones usually are. One day holed up in the trenches with Republican troops and not much will shock you anymore.

With the guts I cultivated living through that, I'm confident I can make it anywhere now.

"I've had my share of 'delectable meals packed with nutrition' that turned out to be a tin of corned beef and some moldy hardtack, so I'm used to the military's brand of hospitality."

Drake just shakes his head at this. Is he amused because I misinterpreted his grin?

"Ah, Andrew, you're so pure."

"Huh?"

"In this area where the multinational unit is deployed and this area only, the Federation Army's supply problems have all been mysteriously solved. I think you really can get anything, as long as you ask."

"Like scones and tea and cucumber sandwiches?"

"An elegant afternoon tea like back home? I bet they could make that happen."

Right as I'm about to laugh while thinking he has to be joking, I notice Drake nodding with a completely straight face.

"I beg your pardon, but that seems utterly impossible in a war zone... Are you being serious?"

I nearly scream. Is he really telling me that even though there's a war on, the Federation military is willing to serve journalists a luxurious high tea?

"It may be difficult to believe, but I suspect it's quite possible."

"This is the forward-most line, for goodness' sake."

"The cucumber may not be fresh—probably pickled—but they'll do whatever it takes to fulfill your requests, two hundred percent."

"...Wait. There must be a catch, right?"

No matter what kind of pretext we came under, embedded reporters are unwelcome interlopers here. The best we would normally hope for is being treated as such, especially considering how we're eating for free.

But if what the colonel said is true, such a gift would be far more costly than the cup of tea journalists regularly offer.

"Is it for propaganda...?"

"That's level one." Drake's grin disappears, and he suddenly looks tired. "It's also likely you'll find yourself running into plenty of chances to have a fiery romance with pretty girls or whatever sort of companion you prefer all over the eastern front, so be careful."

"H-h-hold on a second!" I shout in spite of myself, unable to gloss over that.

After glancing around to make sure there are no Federation people here...I finally remember that we're talking outside with no one nearby. I panicked so hard that I completely forgot.

There are rumors about the exact thing the colonel just mentioned, the sort that manifest as jokey gossip over drinks. Of course, they aren't the type of stories you can just take at face value. Or so I thought.

"That really happens?"

"I like to joke around, but I would swear on my rum that this is true. If I could, I'd warn everyone."

"...I've heard the rumors, but it's really that bad?"

"It's awful," he mutters. "I have been making a point of telling everyone in private...though your Red pals really lit into me for it." He shrugs with an exasperated mutter. His expression is one of utter exhaustion.

It's clear he's fed up with it all.

"In their defense, the Communist Party is desperate, too."

"You mean they're at the end of their rope?"

"Not quite." Taking a moment to consider how to best explain, Drake falls silent briefly before continuing his thought. "They say their party is perfect, but it's barely hanging in there. That's why they'll resort to pretty much anything at this point to keep up appearances."

I have no idea what he's trying to say, but it seems awfully significant. I must be missing something. It's frustrating to not have all the pieces I need.

"Well, I've shared quite enough for one day. We got pretty into it for a single cup of tea. Any more will cost you extra."

"Then next time, I'll bring a cigar."

"…That's a tempting invitation, but as a marine magic officer, I prefer my old friend alcohol—easier on the lungs. I already have some rum, so my request is a nice scotch."

An unexpectedly pricey request.

Will the returns be worth it? Still, if I don't invest, there won't be any returns at all.

There's no choice but to commit.

"Understood, Colonel. I'll have it ready before your next operation. So…"

"You're saying I should tell you when the next operation is? You know I can't do that, Andrew. Just find a bottle and keep it handy."

He got me. It's my loss. I didn't think my ploy would work, but you can't blame me for trying… And sure enough, the colonel knows how to spot a trap when he sees one.

On top of that, all I got in return was a verbal promise, but I still take him up on it. Since I said I would make it happen, I can't very well tell him I won't have it in time. Nothing is more despised than the promise of a journalist who can't keep their word.

I'll have to hurry and procure a taste of home somehow.

"All right, Colonel. I'll have it for you in time for your operation."

"Oh? Then if you don't mind…I'll take that bottle right now."

"What?"

I'm bewildered as Drake smiles in amusement and places a hand on my shoulder.

"Andrew, I'm giving a briefing for a joint operation with the Federation today. In the large lecture hall at 1700. Looking forward to that scotch."

He won this round, no doubt about it.

After luring me in with a roundabout conversation, he's managed to get me to make a careless promise, too. As a journalist, the moment you recognize that you've let your source get the better of you, there's nothing to do but feel ashamed.

"Colonel, this isn't very sportsmanlike. You fight dirty."

"Consider it your tuition, young man. Now then, the clock's ticking. You're going to prove to me you're not a lying newshound, right?"

>>>　　　　THE SAME DAY, THE LARGE LECTURE HALL, 1700　　　　<<<

I figure the Federation Communist Party must be ventriloquists. Maybe the shocking headline could read, *An Amusing Puppet Show: Even at War, Federation Maintains Sense of Humor and Tradition.*

When someone tells me the interpreter at the press conference will be a woman, I'm surprised. My initial reaction is that, in at least one way, the Federation can be quite liberal. I admit I'm impressed.

But the moment I hear her title, any favorable impressions—or perhaps pitiful notions—get obliterated by heavy artillery fire. The fact that it's a political officer who's taking the stage to lead the conference proves the Communists have a very poor grasp of public relations.

Officially, a Federation Army colonel named Mikel will lead the conference, but since he isn't fluent in the language of the Commonwealth, this political officer is supposed to serve as his "interpreter." Of course, I understand the need to overcome the language barrier. It's natural to have an interpreter.

But sending a political officer to do the job makes for an awfully explicit statement.

"All right, it's time, so I'd like to begin. I'm First Lieutenant Tanechka, and I'll be interpreting for the colonel today."

The pair speaks in turns.

Everything must be following a preset program. You could call it an indescribable jumble of a theatrical production—third-rate performers acting out a fourth-rate script.

Is Lieutenant Tanechka interpreting? Or is she the only one truly speaking? I can only assume the latter.

"The colonel will give a rough outline of the upcoming joint operation that will be conducted by Federation and Commonwealth units."

Commonwealth language in a strong Russy accent. For one of those notorious political officers, her pronunciation is actually quite good, but should I praise her or request a proper interpreter? This is a problem.

I've noticed how she chooses her words carefully.

I expected propaganda would be involved in any press conference where foreign journalists are invited to cover the multinational unit's plans to launch a counterattack. Still, it's a mystery why the Federation doesn't understand that having a political officer interpret will have the opposite intended effect.

I change gears.

There aren't any other *WTN* correspondents present. I can't afford to get distracted and miss something. The news desk back home frightens me more than any Federation Army political officer ever could.

I scribble furiously in my notebook, noting the main points of the slightly difficult-to-follow briefing.

"The situation is as thus: The Federation Army, who must repel the invaders on behalf of the people, will work alongside the Commonwealth Army and other allies and comrades to initiate a major counterattack."

A tidy explanation. Perhaps they have some knowledge of media relations after all, but there's still too much extraneous material for it to be truly easy to understand.

After removing the empty words included for dramatic effect, wouldn't *We're going to counterattack together* suffice?

"The ultimate goal is to retake the land of the people. Our main objective will be to drive out the invaders, who are none other than the Imperial Army."

As far as I can tell, after peeling back all the overwrought phrasing, it seems like a straightforward plan. They want to contain the Imperial Army, establish a bridgehead, and secure a path that would be a prelude to future operations.

Chapter **I**

"That is all. Are there any questions?"

Allowing time for Q and A seems rather progressive for the Federation. Would posing critical questions to a political officer be considered a breach of etiquette? …I feel conflicted in spite of myself, but for better or worse, my ambitious colleagues seem unconcerned.

One brave soul thrusts a hand up.

"I'm with *East-West News*. I heard that the Imperial Army is gathering in the south. I'd like to hear the Federation Army's thoughts on that situation."

"As you pointed out, the Imperial Army is threatening cities to the south, but we're already digging in for a defensive battle. While keeping imperial forces pinned down there, we'll counterattack here. Imperial lines should be pushed back substantially as a result."

A faint sigh escapes the press corps. It's the sound of disappointment at hearing an answer that seems proper at first glance but actually says nothing. What everyone wants to know is whether the Federation thinks they can defend the cities or not.

Are people in the Federation just not very eager to please? The political officer onstage got us all excited but then refuses to give a straight answer.

Having apparently abandoned the customary restraint when questioning women, the insistent *East-West News* correspondent looses a second shot.

"How likely is the defense to succeed? The imperial units are massing rapidly, so is there any truth to the rumors that the southern lines are in trouble?"

"I'm unfortunately not at liberty to discuss the movements of our forces in detail due to operational security concerns, as per the colonel's earlier statements."

She adds the bit about quoting the colonel at the end of her reply as if it was a complete afterthought. This Lieutenant Tanechka could have at least pretended to confirm that with him…but the colonel simply had a blank look on his face. Does he even understand the Q and A proceedings?

Perhaps only God knows for certain, but the entire press corps is already treating it as all but confirmed.

"I'd like to hear directly from the colonel, if that's all right. If you don't mind, could you give even a general answer?"

"Apologies, but the colonel doesn't speak the language of the Commonwealth."

She requests that he hold back any similar questions in a tone that's mild while also being a firm nonresponse. Even though she could have just as easily checked with the colonel.

What's going on? Right as I start worrying, a man puts his hand up.

"I'm with the *Times*. Would it still be an issue if I speak the Federation's language?" The moment after the nice chap says that, he fluently belts out a stream of words that must be Federation language—a brilliant blow.

Judging from the political officer's face, which looks like a pigeon that's been shot by a peashooter, our hosts didn't think any of us reporters could speak their language.

She can't very well claim that a colonel in the Federation Army can't understand the Federation's official language.

Her expression definitely went stiff for a second there, but she quickly regains her composure.

She strides over to the colonel, leans toward his ear, pretends to ask him something, and then calmly quibbles appropriately. "...Comrade Colonel says that without a trained linguist, he fears there could be an unintended misunderstanding..."

"So you mean...?"

"Since your mother tongue isn't the Federation language, it's best that we continue the press conference in your native language."

It's an utterly garbage excuse, but from her attitude, it's clear that she has no intention of backing down. The venue fills with sighs once more.

"All right, all right. I understand. In that case, I have a different question." When the political officer gestures for the man from the *Times* to go ahead, he asks, "Why is it we aren't authorized to cover the southern lines?"

"It's mainly a matter of your safety."

"Come on now. We're embedded reporters. As long as we're on the front lines, anywhere we go is pretty much—"

Before he could finish saying *the same*, the political officer cuts him off. "Please understand that security and safety measures are a necessity. I truly regret having to insist on such restrictive precautions, but the fact of the matter is, we're at war. That being said…" She goes on to tell a joke with a straight face. If she intended to kill us with laughter, then it's a smashing success. "While the Communist Party would ideally always strive to facilitate open and transparent news coverage, we'd like you to understand that we can't always follow through on that principle during these extraordinary circumstances."

The true difficulty of this moment is trying to suppress our laughter.

Apparently, there are as many Communists who love freedom of the press as there are gentlemen who hate tea.

Lieutenant Tanechka's remark belongs in the liar hall of fame. The only reason us journalists are allowed to enter the country at all is thanks to the extraordinary circumstances known as war. That's the real deviation from the norm.

I guess the atmosphere finally gets to me, because my hand goes up after all.

"…Can I ask something else?"

The offer must have been music to her ears. The political officer nods happily, looking overjoyed to be free of the previous pain in the neck.

"I'm Andrew from *WTN*. We're authorized to report on this counterattack, correct?"

"Yes, that's right."

"What kind of restrictions will there be?"

Lieutenant Colonel Drake and the Federation Army officer exchange glances; after they communicate something with their eyes, the political officer nods with a tired look on her face.

Is that a sign of some disagreement? Or is there something she isn't in a position to say?

Drake takes a step forward and speaks up. "I'll field this question. To put it plainly, there are three limitations you'll be under while covering this operation, so please listen closely." We nod and wait for him to continue. "First, we don't want you sending any dispatches on the movements of the Federation Army or the multinational unit as they are happening. I'm not so vain that I want my whereabouts broadcasted to the Imperial Army in the news."

Just as the laugh he gets warms up the room a bit, he adds, "If it was up to me, I wouldn't ask this of you, but..."

He continues with a heavy, grave expression, "There will be censors. This will be necessary for the protection of military secrets."

"Will the Federation side be doing the censoring?"

"Communications inspectors from both the Commonwealth and the Federation will be handling it. Before you ask: No, we will not be using personnel shortages as an excuse to slow things down."

They're endeavoring to make the screening process quick and convenient. In exchange, he asks us to make a compromise—for the safety of all involved.

"Secondly, and this is related, but...we want you to report from headquarters. I'm sure there are quite a few brave Tommies among you, but neither the people of the Federation nor the government in the home country has any desire to place you boys and girls in the trenches."

We reluctantly nod. This means there'll be a specific zone where we can report from, and we aren't meant to stray from it. As someone with experience as an embedded reporter, I understand that it's a reasonable request. Ultimately, there will probably be a nonzero number of journalists who strike deals to be exempt or find other ways to slip away. Soldiers have their way of doing things, and we have ours.

Up until this point, Drake has been speaking at a good clip, but he explicitly pauses to clear his throat before raising the last point. "Finally, those with cameras and recorders will be accompanied by Federation Army guides and only allowed to record or film when given the okay."

Urgh. Surely he knew that we weren't about to take this last point lying down. Before the predictable objections start flying, he beats us to the punch and reemphasizes his point.

"The Commonwealth and Federation have agreed to these terms, so... please understand that your press badge hinges on following the rules."

You just had to add that last bit, huh? Getting told our permission to report can be taken away is enough to make all of us hesitate, but it's impossible for any self-respecting journalist to not have strong feelings about these conditions.

Drake pays our voiceless stares of discontent no mind and flashes a smile. "Well, that's all from me. *Was that to your satisfaction?*"

What the hell? The colonel clearly directed that at the political officer!

On the surface, the colonel's attitude seems normal, but can no one from the Federation tell just how incredibly sarcastic he's being?

"Yes, there should be no objections to what Comrade Colonel and yourself have said, Lieutenant Colonel Drake."

"Very good. Then if you'll excuse me, Comrade Colonel."

Playing out the string to the very end, the officer of the Commonwealth Army presents a formal salute and the empty words *Comrade Colonel* to the political officer.

It seems the lieutenant colonel is finding it difficult to hide his distaste for her any longer.

Even when communicating through an interpreter, common etiquette dictates that you should speak directly to the other party. Anyone with any diplomatic experience would know that.

That brazen breach of manners must have been an expression of how unamusing the colonel finds these proceedings. He's the type to make a name for himself in tough situations.

What a mess…

I let a small sigh slip out.

I still owe the man scotch. I'll have to get it even if I need to beg an esteemed friend and colleague from a different firm for a bottle. It'll be exorbitantly expensive, I'm sure, but money is no substitute for trust. Hanging by the shreds of my honor, I have no choice but to go crying to my rivals.

A genuine bottle of scotch from home is unbelievably costly—I end up having to surrender a scoop in exchange—but I secure the goods from *East-West News*. This isn't something I can report back to the news desk, so I just have to swallow it as the cost of doing business; not long after, I give the bottle to Drake.

In the pit of my stomach, I know there's nothing I can do but try to bounce back from my failure, so I explore the compound in search of stories.

But stories aren't so easy to find. After a few days of this, I get so used to it all that I'm basically just leisurely strolling around the base. Still, it isn't as if there are no crumbs, and in any case, this is more productive than lazing around the whole day.

As I begin to wither away in a borderline depressive state, a cheery Lieutenant Colonel Drake strikes up a conversation after approaching me.

"Morning, Andrew. And a belated thanks for the scotch. Can I ask where you got it?"

"One of the other reporters gave me a bottle. It was terribly expensive…"

"Ha-ha-ha," he laughs with a courteous demeanor that's far removed from the straitlaced attitude he showed at the press conference.

It's probably genuine, but frustratingly, he's also the type who refuses to open up during an interview. He's already gotten the better of me once, but I still want to drag some sort of story out of him.

"…Ngh."

"Colonel?"

I ask him what's wrong, but he just starts scanning the area uneasily with his brow furrowed.

Could this be a…?

"Warning! Mana detected!"

The alarm goes off as shouts ring out in the compound, confirming my premonition.

In the same way that tension shoots through a trench line, the Commonwealth mages grab their gear in a panic and rush out. The moment I see that, I know what's happening.

"Andrew, you guys take shelter!" Drake shouts before he races away. I appreciate the thought, but is he joking? I'd be disqualified as an embedded reporter if I ran away to hide during such a perfect opportunity. I gleefully turn my gaze on the commotion.

Evidently, things look bad.

"Shit! They're going to reach us first?!"

The duty officer's cry gets answered by another yell. "We have a code match! They're from the Lergen Kampfgruppe!"

"Get ready! Send up mages to intercept!"

"How many are there?!"

"It's a company of enemy mages! They're closing at speed! A company from the Lergen Kampfgruppe!"

From what I can gather, we've been beaten to the punch.

The besieged enemy has launched a counterattack. These sorts of attacks were a daily event on the Rhine; it's clear that east or west, the imperials are an industrious lot.

"Shit! If they're on the defensive, can't they just sit tight and defend their positions like they're supposed to?!"

"Start putting rounds downrange! Argh, what were the guys on the perimeter doing?!"

"Round up the translators on the double! The Federation Army's—shit—does anyone know what they're saying?!"

Multinational units are vulnerable to this sort of communication breakdown. Unlike on the Rhine, where it was virtually all Republican soldiers, the chaos is being exacerbated by the mixture of Federation, Commonwealth, former Entente Alliance, Dacian, and even Unified States forces.

Even against a small number of mages, this is no good.

They got us right where they want us. I shake my head as I watch the disorganized response. Then I peer up to see what sort of attackers we are dealing with. An enemy mage unit is dancing in the Federation sky. I mostly want to see whether I can get a good look at who the enemy is.

"Hmm?"

I only glanced up out of curiosity, but I catch a glimpse of something flying high above us that doesn't belong there. I have no words.

Unless my eyes are failing me, there's definitely a child zipping around up there.

If anything, it would probably be more accurate to say a child mage.

The flying figure is only a speck, so it's possible I misjudged due to the distance, but I can't help but notice this apparent child is sized very differently compared to nearby combatants.

The enemy mage looks so small.

I reach for my camera and instinctually train the lens on this point of interest.

I can't get the shot in focus...

Right as I am struggling to take the picture that would undoubtedly be my biggest scoop, I feel a stern grip on my shoulder.

"Mister..."

"What?!"

As you can see, I'm a little busy!

"Kindly put your camera away."

It's only then that I finally realize the friendly guides aren't addressing me in their rough approximation of Queen's dialect without a reason. Despite the ongoing battle, they've surrounded me, and I realize very quickly that they're saying please only as a formality.

"...You're saying I can't take a picture of that?"

When I'm met with the stubborn silence of the nodding Federation guides, I sigh faintly. I figure I won't be getting off with a simple *Sorry, I won't do it again.*

As expected, one of them holds out a hand.

"May I have your film?"

"...Okay. But you'll give me a new roll, right?"

"Of course."

Good-bye, scoop.

Good-bye, story that would have covered my debt and then some.

Ah, these sons of bitches.

And so my big scoop is torn from my grasp, the film shredded before my very eyes.

If I get another chance, I'll have to pay careful attention to my surroundings and shoot more stealthily...but by the time I have that thought, it's too late. The attacking imperial troops are already withdrawing. The Lergen Kampfgruppe must have been happy just to harass us a little.

Give me a break.

All I want is to send the news desk a proper story.

Acting on problematic impulses doesn't help in wartime. In a siege that drags on and on without a single interesting development, an embedded reporter like me is worse than helpless. I have no choice but to settle in for the long haul.

With nothing to do, I wind up with too much time on my hands.

After all, there's no leisure to be found in the garrison. Trying to sneak out of the compound in search of a story would only get me stopped by our handlers. Contrary to their courteous demeanors, they aren't the slightest bit open to any kind of bargaining, so my activities are severely limited.

Chapter I

Far from devoting myself to stimulating work, I spend most of my time searching out any sort of stimulation I could scrape together from my daily life.

The logical conclusion of that manifests in all the journalists with nothing better to do regularly coming together for what's supposed to be a "little drink" after perfunctorily picking at our early dinners in the canteen.

The thrill of combat that had been so exciting when we first arrived on the eastern front has become just another part of the background noise. Once things settle down, we slip into routine and soon enough find the daily boredom almost intolerable.

Given the circumstances, the topic of discussion at our gatherings is decided in advance: the war situation and nothing else.

A reporter from the *Times* wonders how the siege battle will play out, and everyone chimes in. Opinions vary, but the most widely supported theory is *Even if the enemy is bold, as long as we have more fighting power, then...*

"They burned Arene. The Empire won't hesitate to do whatever it takes, and that probably goes for the Federation, too."

"...Then this'll be over quite soon, I imagine?"

I disturb the optimistic atmosphere by raising my doubts. "I'm not so sure. This is just my impression, but it seems like there are fewer shells falling here than back on the Rhine."

I'm aware that it's merely my own perspective, but I don't get the feeling our enemy will fold so easily. An unpleasant feeling, or maybe you could call it something like a fearsome energy, seems to waft over from the imperial positions.

Is there some sort of beast lurking over there?

"Everyone who was on the Rhine feels the same, huh?"

"That's only natural."

Though my gut feeling isn't specific enough to lend itself to words or an argument, I can't discount my senses.

A downpour of shells.

The Rhine lines were truly hell. There's no way to describe it but as a land where shells constantly rained from the sky. The unending sound of the artillery barrages on the Rhine was like rolling thunder.

Even with that unbelievably massive amount of metal turning the earth into a pockmarked landscape like the surface of the moon, the lines on the Rhine never moved. Though I'm ashamed to say so as a reporter, describing with words what skulked across those lands is extremely difficult. The moment you give it a label, its horror is diluted, and you become convinced you might come to understand what is in fact an incomprehensible monster.

In the end, I'm not sure what to say to my colleagues, so instead, I tell benign tales of things I've experienced.

"These imperial soldiers can survive even in nothing but a shell hole on the Rhine. I doubt we can eradicate them here."

"Would you bet on that, Andrew?"

"I make it a point not to bet on human lives. Winning a wager that my allies will die would just ruin the taste of my drink."

"Whoa, there. Surely it's not quite that bad, right?"

"Let me remind you that I was there on the Rhine front."

And I covered war in the trenches. I learned about war through the things I saw. I also learned that the only certainty is uncertainty.

"Once you see imperials counterattack after enduring a fifty-hour Republican preparatory barrage, you'll understand, too."

It's easy enough to describe, but having witnessed that very scene myself, the words simply don't do it justice.

"But then... Crap, another alarm?"

It's the siren from the previous enemy attack.

The relaxed atmosphere that has been surrounding the press corps immediately gives way to the sharp desire for a story and ambition; everyone leaps up with their pen and camera at the ready. It's only natural to try to get the jump on your colleagues if a good photo may come from it.

We've got to reach the front line...is what everyone's thinking, but we're quickly met with an unexpected scene.

"Here they come! Just as we thought!"

One of the mages shouts. It's too loud to miss, and when we hear it, we exchange glances.

"...So efficient this time."

Frankly, I feel like they're *too* efficient. The base should have been a chaotic scramble of different languages, but the atmosphere is all too orderly.

Though it isn't business as usual per se, the troops are more "active" than panicked.

That means…

"They expected an attack?"

Someone murmurs what we're all thinking. Evidently, this is elementary encirclement battle stuff. Thankfully, I'll be able to send home a dispatch that communicates some semblance of the tension…but my work here is still undoubtedly lackluster.

I've reached the point where I really need to just drag something out of Drake. I make up my mind to approach him more forcefully. I know it might be rough to approach so directly after we just saw combat, but when things seem to settle down to an extent, I head over to the barracks with some cigarettes and alcohol to meet the man—and what good timing that turns out to be.

Perhaps he was enjoying a modest victory celebration? Because by the time I get there, a bottle is open on his desk. A journalist's best friend is already hard at work loosening the lips of my target.

"Hey, Andrew. I figured it was about time for you to show up."

Letting his confidence peek out ever so slightly, Drake savors a sip from his glass. If he's drinking, he must be off duty. Is he unwinding from the stress of combat?

I figure this is the perfect opportunity and sit with him.

"Did you know ahead of time that the enemy would attack today?"

"It's not as if we're hiding the fact, you know, but yes. We were fully prepared for them."

"Nice work seeing through their plan. How did you know they were coming?"

"Andrew, that's a military secret. If you're trying to interview me, stop it."

"Please. Help a fellow out."

When I insist, he smiles wryly and takes another sip. "If you must know, then I'll say that it's the result of carefully analyzing the Lergen Kampfgruppe and its commander's past actions."

That isn't a real answer. It certainly isn't the kind of answer I should have to struggle for; anyone back home reading my articles by their cozy fireplaces could have guessed that much on their own.

But the word *Kampfgruppe* catches my attention.

"By the way, I've been wondering: What exactly is a 'Kampfgruppe'? I'm not used to the term, so I'd been wanting to ask someone knowledgeable."

"What? It's fairly straightforward... Ah, but you were on the Rhine. I guess it's not so surprising that you don't know." Drake grins wryly. "It's one of the formation types the Empire has started using recently. They gather a jumble of different units under one commander to create a task force. It's a bit like our multinational unit."

"So it's different from a regiment or a brigade?"

Drake nods. "Yes, think of it as something else entirely. The scale is comparable, but the organization is different, even if it seems similar. It's a temporary formation created as needed, bringing together available or suitable battalions of infantry, tanks, aerial mages, and so on, regardless of their original commands."

"And because they're temporary, ad hoc units...they're identified by the name of their commander?"

"That's right. Which means the commander we're dealing with is the Imperial Army's Colonel von Lergen."

"To be honest, that's not a name I'm familiar with."

I'm genuinely confused. I've never been one to brag, but I'm fairly confident I memorized all the names of the high-ranking officers serving on the front lines.

I learned a lot paying attention while on the Rhine front, and right up until the day I was sent to the east, I stayed up-to-date by absorbing the latest reports in the news office's reference room. I studied both enemies and allies, of course.

"Maybe something would come up if I combed the card catalog back home, but I can't say I've ever heard of him. What's the man about?"

"It doesn't surprise me you don't know of him."

"Why do you say that?"

"He originally worked in the heart of the Imperial Army's General Staff. Not the sort of person anyone would naturally have an interest in unless you were already involved with the man. Above all, he's spent most of his time in the rear, so he hasn't had many chances to stand out."

"I see. So his background is in military administration, then? Hmm, I wouldn't expect someone like that to be enthusiastic about taking to the battlefield."

"You may want to brush up on your knowledge of the army, Andrew. These guys are bureaucrats, it's true, but they're staff officers by nature. In other words, these fellows aren't to be taken lightly. Whether or not he was one of the top strategic minds in Operations, there's no doubt that he's a brilliant tactician."

"You say that, but he's a pro from the rear, right? I heard that most of those guys just sit pretty at their tidy desks and are gone as soon as it's time to clock out."

Know-it-alls who spout theories they have no idea how to put into practice—armchair commanders.

Recalling the frank, crude insults the Commonwealth troops often directed at people who were supposedly professionals, it isn't difficult to imagine the type.

"Criticisms you heard in the home country, I guess? Unfortunately, it seems that people from the Empire are different. You can tell just by looking; they're prepared to stubbornly defend their urban centers to the last, but any areas that aren't defensible quickly get abandoned at the drop of a hat. Their defenses are unrefined…and pragmatic."

There's a hint of tension in Drake's voice. He may have simply just been on guard against a mysterious enemy, but something about the way he talked makes it sound more concrete than that.

"You mean they're formidable?"

"The chaps over at Imperial Operations must all be horrible people."

"Can they really be that bad…? Honestly, the Federation Army's official briefing made it sound like it would be an easy win."

I can smell a scoop. I'm aware that the Communist Party is concerned with appearances, but could they be so obsessed, they would allow it to disrupt coordination and communication with the Commonwealth forces that have been deployed here? *That* would make for a compelling story.

…Well, it'd either end up censored or prohibited from broadcasting.

I figure I can at least tuck it away as an interesting tidbit. Maybe it'll come in handy later.

"Do you think this will be a difficult fight, Colonel Drake? Frankly, the way the enemy mages come hopping at us like frogs is enough to make me anxious."

"There's no doubt the advantage is ours. Even in terms of forces committed to the siege, we have three divisions against their lone Kampfgruppe. Adding in the other Federation troops stationed in the area, we completely outnumber them."

Yes, hearing that makes it obvious that, at a glance, our side's combat strength easily outstrips the enemy's. If anything, the battle should end in a crushing victory.

"Despite that, they don't waver."

"...You mean they're expecting relief, Colonel?"

He nods as if to say, *Exactly*. "We're on guard against it. But honestly, I wonder."

"About what?"

In response to my question, the corners of Drake's mouth perk up into a slight smile. "Just so you know, this is strictly between us. I'm not telling you because I want you to blab this secret to everyone."

"I understand, Colonel."

"Good." Drake nods. "The Imperial Army shouldn't have enough reserves to wring out any more reinforcements... If they're already gathering forces in the south while simultaneously planning to break through the encirclement here..."

"Even the Empire must be getting stretched thin?"

"More like 'especially the Empire.'"

When the look in my eyes tells him I don't understand why, he shrugs in disappointment.

Honestly, I feel like I'm being treated like a child... I should try asking, at least.

"Uhhh, Colonel Drake. Would you care to enlighten me as to why you think that?"

"Andrew, have you forgotten why you're here? The Empire, a single country, is waging a war against the rest of the world."

"You mean they've reached their limit?"

"Well, if you get that much, this'll go faster. Setting aside the question of whether we should be surprised that they're capable of waging war

with the world or laugh at them for being stupid enough to attempt it…
listen," he says and continues with a solemn expression. "In the end, it's
an issue of maths."

"Maths?" I wince. "Back home, I was so bad, I made my teacher Mr.
Johan sigh in frustration, so I'd appreciate it if you keep it simple."

"There's nothing that's hard to wrap your head around. All you have
to do is compare populations. No matter what kind of magic the Empire
tries to use, there's a limit to how much of the population can be turned
into soldiers."

"…And now they must be approaching that limit."

That has to be it. Even someone who can squeeze out a win fighting five opponents at once will be defeated if they face six. No matter
how powerful the Imperial Army is, their homeland is failing on the
diplomatic and political fronts. But the most surprising thing is their
response. Even under these circumstances, the Empire seems to want to
continue fighting.

Could it be that war has a harmful effect on the human mind?

"Much more of this, and they'll be using children as soldiers!"

I nearly blurt out that I saw one.

My scoop, including the film I used to shoot it, has already been
scrapped by a Federation overseer.

Furthermore, the replacement film I received is of questionable quality. When I finally got in the darkroom and was able to develop some
pictures, they came out so awful, I wanted to cry.

Sadly, that's what life tends to be like during total war. The Federation's film may be poor, but at least they haven't started resorting to
child soldiers…that I know of. I can't see any fronts besides the one I'm
on, so I can't say for sure.

Still, it has to be better than the Empire, where kids are sortieing with
guns.

"I beg your pardon, Colonel, but if they're that strapped, it's already
checkmate, isn't it? Doesn't that mean our victory is near?"

"That's what you'd think, right?"

"Yes." I nod. Logically speaking, it seems like the Empire would have
to give up soon.

"You really are a sensible guy."

All I can do is nod again. "Mm…"

"But imperials, they're all liable to be crazy. Do me a favor and remember that."

"…On that note, I'd like to interview a sensible Commonwealth soldier. How about it?" When I hold out my notebook like a mic, Drake winces.

"Aside from the volunteer mages from the Entente Alliance, you can question anyone you like. But haven't you been doing that from the beginning anyway? Don't be shy. If you need an introduction, I'll be happy to oblige. Who do you want to talk to?"

"Colonel, if you get it, then…"

"You want me to get you an interview with the volunteers? Could you please not prod the wounds of people who had to witness the fall of their country? There's a direct connection between the mental state of mages and how they perform on the battlefield. You saw that for yourself on the Rhine, didn't you, Andrew?"

There's nothing I can say in response to that.

"Hmm. To point you in a different direction…I'll give you a hint."

"I'd appreciate it. What do you have for me?"

I was hoping for a lead, but the colonel responds in a grave voice.

"Do you know about the Imperial Army lieutenant general called Zettour?"

"Hmm? Errr, I'm sure I've heard the name before. Let me try to remember… I think he manages rail?"

I don't know much about him at all. It isn't that he's unimportant or anything, but he just seems like one of those run-of-the-mill mid-level officers without much else to him. In any case, he clearly didn't leave a very big impression, because the name doesn't ring many bells.

"That's too bad. He's a man you'd do well to remember."

"Okay."

Is that all? I let his words go in one ear and out the other. Flinging some random factoids around is a pretty sloppy way to distract a reporter…

Remembering the past, I smile wryly in the present.

"Telling me to remember that name really was good advice."

…But at the time, my younger self ignored it.

The eastern front was total war in the truest sense.
Have you ever been ordered to take a nap?

—— A veteran of the eastern lines ——

The air in the Federation feels chilly no matter what the season. For better or worse, it's tricky for someone from the Commonwealth to say that the tribe that lives in these parts is friendly. These Communists are a superstitious lot, after all.

My name is John Doe, the man without a name. Sometimes people with good manners lovingly call me Mr. John.

Unfortunately for me, it seems the Commies think I'm a spy—what an outrageous error. Officially, I'm nothing but a simple visa issuer from the Commonwealth who gets sent all over the place in the name of my king and country.

Of course, as a gentleman, I should probably keep the truth a secret.

Having entered the Federation, I toy with that idea in my mind to relax a bit. Even if I'm only a messenger, I feel more nervous than I have been since my very first mission.

It's bad enough that I actually feel relieved when I find the person I'm looking for and finally make contact. That's rare for me these days.

"Hey there, Colonel Drake. What a relief to see a familiar face."

"Why, if it isn't Mr. Johnson. Can't believe you made it all the way out here. You weren't attacked by any savages on the way over, were you?"

"Luckily, I'm playing at being the savages' friend at the moment."

The courtesy offered to diplomatic envoys by Federation officials is legendary—though it goes without saying I mean that in a bad way. So naturally, I expected the entry of a "visa issuer" would attract the attention of the Federation's secret police.

"…Turns out, they're wise enough to be a bit flexible while at war with the Empire."

"Indeed, Colonel Drake. I'm rather surprised myself."

He's being sarcastic, but I've been able to travel safely to the front lines, so never say never during wartime.

"But to be honest, I was nervous. General Habergram works his people to the bone—sending an old man like me all the way out to the eastern front."

"I'm sorry for the trouble but appreciate you coming."

Lieutenant Colonel Drake is another fellow struggling to meet the Intelligence agency's unreasonable demands, so I'm sure that's real sympathy I detect in his voice.

I wish I brought him a bottle of something.

"It really has been nothing but trouble. I don't know how they plan deployments these days, but to think they would hurl me at my age into the evil nest of Communists to serve as a liaison!"

When Drake flicks his eyes, it's clearly meant as a warning. But there's no reason to worry. This is the Federation, and the Federation is providing the garrison space and everything else they need. The troops stationed here are probably being treated to the latest facilities available. I wouldn't be surprised if there are speakers in the walls, recorders in the phones, and a listening gadget or two stashed in the ashtrays, too. On the contrary, it would be stranger to think the whole place isn't bugged. It's not really an issue of common sense.

The Federation's Communist Party's secret police are diligent to the point of borderline paranoia. That makes them a huge pain in the neck.

"Wouldn't you like some insight into what the higher-ups are thinking about now?"

"Are you sure you should be telling me?"

"I'm aware we have an audience, so it shouldn't be a problem."

If it's already out in the open, then might as well go for it. I shrug.

"Truth is, the home country's feelings about the Federation are genuine."

"That's surprising. I thought lots of people in the home country were conservative."

"Not much has changed. But even so, some people are praising the progress of Communism with all their hearts, and many people are extolling the party's wisdom; yes, especially the advances brought to farming villages by the party's agricultural policy—there are even comments that the developments are unbelievable."

"In other words?"

"Communism is just as 'fascinating' as ever."

Anyone from the Commonwealth would frown at high praise expressed like that. Who can say whether colonials would understand, but anyone from the home country would have no trouble reading between the lines. Any bona fide gentleman of the Commonwealth would be at risk of choking on the sarcasm and bile loaded in that statement.

Drake seems to be holding back a laugh as I clap him on the shoulder and invite him for a walk.

"I don't mind letting our hosts hear indoors, but why not use this chance to take in the scenery as we talk?"

"Yes, why not? Let's have a stroll."

Drake readily agrees to the idea and takes the lead; we wander outside on the pretext of me inspecting the outdoor positions.

But there turn out to be hardworking ears outside, too. Well, I anticipated that my presence would draw some attention.

I fully expected there would be some people tailing us. But even so, it's eerie to be stared at so much from all directions.

As a seasoned Intelligence agent, I'm simply stunned by the brazen surveillance state. Everything vividly speaks to the Federation's true nature.

These people are our allies, though...

I feel like I should commit to memory their most prominent trait: their distrust of those from capitalist states, even during wartime.

At the end of the day, the current friendly relationship between the Commonwealth and the Federation is...merely an alliance of convenience. Peeking beneath the thin ice, I imagine it would be quite easy to find a river of suspicion.

You can't let your guard down against what might be flowing beneath the surface. Wincing inwardly, I dare to step forward. Though nothing is stable, the dirt at least is what it appears to be.

What gets built upon the dirt can be one measure of that—which is why I dislike this sad wasteland of blackened earth. Though my family's country house is modest, we're proud of it. I miss the garden there.

Ah, but I'm a public servant, so I should be focusing on work.

"Colonel Drake, I have some news that will put you in an even worse mood. According to the latest intelligence, the Imperial Army is using its current momentum to prepare a major offensive."

"You're certain?"

"I've no doubt. It looks like the participating formations have already been announced. They seem to be splitting the eastern front into sectors: The A Front is the southern offensive, and the B Front is everything else. The A Group will attack while the B Group guards their flank."

If you picture the geography of the Federation in your head, the explanation is simple. The enemy has gathered an unusual number of troops below us—that is, to the south. The intel was confirmed by deciphering and analyzing intercepted communications. It's most likely an accurate prediction.

"It's basic—easy to understand, right?"

"How likely is it that the Federation is able to hold in the south?"

"Good question." I nod, acting calmer than I feel. "It's not hopelessly unlikely, but it's not terribly hopeful, either. The situation is a bit delicate."

People often misunderstand this point. While knowing the enemy's situation is a terrific advantage, it's only an advantage. Just because you succeeded in obtaining intelligence doesn't mean you can automatically parlay that into a surefire plan to overwhelm the enemy.

On the contrary, there's some difficulty in knowing. For example, if you received the uniquely accurate forecast that one hundred trained lions are about to rush you, how would you feel?

"The A Group is apparently comprised of armor, mages, self-propelled guns, and other highly mobile combat elements. If we can find a way to stop them, the outcome might start to look very different, but in a battle of maneuver warfare on a flat field, the Federation's defending forces might be in trouble."

"So an urban battle would give them better chances…?"

Drake seems to realize the situation is unfavorable, and his expression darkens as he groans. "It'll be a bloodbath either way. Contesting control over the cities in the south will be hell. It's awful… We're taking youths with their whole lives still ahead of them and turning them into meat pies." Drake has the black humor typical of an officer who has seen his share of horrors on the front line. "How depressing. If only there was even one piece of good news…"

"…Oh, right. I forgot—there is one thing that might count as good news."

"Anything to lighten the weight is welcome…but the south is in a precarious position. I'd be especially happy if it was something to do with that."

I nod to let him know it is indeed related.

It's become crystal clear that there are signs of an impending Imperial Army offensive, but behind that lies a glimmer of hope.

"We've received political intel that says opposition to the imperial family and the government has intensified. The rumors say that the A and B Group formations reflect an internal conflict."

"It may only be hearsay, but if the enemy is even slightly disordered, that's great."

"Then rejoice. Apparently, things really have gotten quite complicated for our friends in the Empire."

"Ohhh?" Drake seems to find that interesting and lets out what seems like a subconscious whistle.

Frankly, I also welcome anything that might throw a wrench into the imperial war machine.

"Supposedly, a rift has formed between the Imperial Army General Staff and the imperial government. And I also hear that a supply officer in the General Staff who fell out of favor was driven away and forced into the B Group."

"Honestly, that sounds fishy. It's not just something like a lizard cutting off its tail?"

Though Drake's healthy skepticism is admirable, what the Empire's leadership cut off happens to be one of their most important assets.

"If we must labor under the lizard analogy, it'd be like cutting off the brains, not the tail. Though the head of the General Staff and the central office tried to protect the man in question, they were unsuccessful. The deputy director of the Service Corps is getting a 'promotion' to 'coordinator' of B Group."

"A promotion from the General Staff? Which general is that?"

Chapter **II**

"The handful of a military administrator Lieutenant General von Zettour. The specialists in the home country heard it was likely he would be leaving the General Staff and are already shouting for joy."

After listening to my news, Drake seems to fall into thought for a little while, but then he finally nods as if something clicked. "…He's certainly high up enough that I've heard of him before. Is Zettour really such a capable fellow?"

"He is—terrifyingly capable." I nod frankly.

It's too bad I can't explain where I'd gotten the intel. All the reliable info we have shows that this Lieutenant General von Zettour of the Imperial Army is a military man of pure evil.

His skill at continuing to provide logistical support during the Imperial Army's rapid advances always surpassed our predictions. His maintenance of the supply network, the establishment of the Council for Self-Government, and even his procurement of cold-weather gear for the eastern front—everything we learned from the encoded messages we intercepted indicates he's a diligent worker who readily adapts when the situation calls for it.

That's why it's such great news that he's been promoted away from Central.

"Just between us, whether or not he handles the A Group's logistics will make a huge difference in our chances to protect the resource-rich south. The analysts are already anticipating an easier time."

Just as they're about to launch a huge offensive, the military administrator who heads up logistics and supplies has been let go. That's the biggest sign of discord within the Empire.

When operating a large organization, skillfully managing human resources is what decides success or failure.

Has the Empire forgotten that? Maybe their streak of victories has made them cocky.

"Chaos in the enemy supply network on the eastern front isn't bad news, but may I add something?"

"Tell me what's on your mind."

Drake quietly voices his doubt. "You're saying a military administrator has been assigned to this B Group operating on the eastern front. But the enemies we can see are currently establishing defensive lines."

"What of it?"

"That could very well be a sign that the enemy wants a defensive battle! I can't see B Group continuing to build up their defensive positions and interpret it as a good sign."

In my head, I agreed with Drake's keen insight: It's a valid worry. A competent military administrator could function as expert organizational support. B Group having such an officer who could organize the logistical network can affect even the preparedness of their defenses in a big way.

Given the circumstances, it would be a huge problem if the Imperial Army improves its supply situation or strengthens its relationship with the Council for Self-Government.

Then I flash a wry grin. From what I've gathered from the Imperial Army intel, Zettour is tragically being exiled to the countryside and nothing more.

He still has his rank, but one glance at the position makes it clear his new job is a mere formality… This is a bit of an extreme comparison, but it's basically the same as a King of Arms[1] in the home country.

"As a part of the Intelligence agency, I can promise you one thing: He's not coming out here with any authority. This next bit is somewhat speculation, but what we're hearing is that his new position is an empty title."

"That's confirmed?"

"…Personally, I believe it's as good as fact. If I say anything else, we'll start running into issues of how information is evaluated, and classified intel will be involved. But I do believe it's true."

The broken enemy code—that is, the magic—made it clear that the lieutenant general wouldn't be assuming command of B Group. It's unfortunate that I can't tell Drake the source, but the reports are genuine.

---

[1] **King of Arms** I'll explain this! Strangely, there are three Kings of Arms. As for what they do: They decide who gets a coat of arms! They participate in ceremonies! Positions in the College of Arms are honorary, but there is an official salary. Specifically, the top king gets £49.07, and the other two get £20.25. And that's annually, by the way. Whatever expenses aren't covered, you'll have to earn on your own somehow!

Zettour's role will consist of only inspections, maybe providing some support as an advisor at most. During peacetime, it might have sounded important, but during a war, the role of a high-ranking officer with no command authority is limited.

He'll have rank but with none of the power that should go with it. I almost want to pity him.

"It's not bad news, but for those of us who actually have to face off against B Group, it's still a question mark."

I nod awkwardly in response to Drake's shrug. I would have liked to bring some better news, but…that's the best I could come up with.

"The rest is all awful news or top secret, sorry."

"No, no, please give my regards to General Habergram. Of course, I'd have even more regard for him if he'd get certain girls out of my hair."

The emotion coloring his voice when he said that was exhaustion. I can even detect a genuine cry for help in his tired expression.

Drake isn't the type of officer to whine, so he must really be at his wit's end. It must be First Lieutenant Sue. Or at least I think that's her name? He seems to be having a hard time with the volunteer mages who have been deployed as a political and diplomatic necessity vis-à-vis the relationship between the Commonwealth and the Unified States as well as the Entente Alliance.

I feel for him, but Drake, like me, is a poor servant of the state who must fulfill His Majesty's and the homeland's every request.

"I wholeheartedly sympathize. Alas, I can't help you with that. You'll have to ask not General Habergram but his superior."

"Even a man of your position can't help, Mr. Johnson?"

It's terribly regrettable, but that is correct.

Anything involving the volunteer mage units isn't a matter of Intelligence or military rationale but an issue for the absurdly sublime dimension of diplomacy or perhaps even circumstances of the state.

All the colonel can do is nod in silence.

"Reality can be quite harsh… I'll do my best."

"Sorry, Colonel Drake. At least let me present you with this souvenir. I tangled with the Federation customs agent to smuggle in a bottle of scotch from the home country."

"You have my gratitude. I'll be sure to savor it."

"I hope it will be of some consolation to you during your backwater tour of duty. All right, sooner or later I'm sure we'll meet again."

》》》 THE SAME DAY, IMPERIAL CAPITAL BERUN, CENTRAL STATION 《《《

The platform area at the imperial capital's Central Station was brimming with activity as usual, echoing with the intertwining harmony that arose from the sounds of human activity coming from the diverse crowd mixing with the mechanical clamor of the military and civilian trains stopping and departing with every passing minute.

Ever since the start of the war, transport of people and goods by rail had only—and rapidly—expanded. Anyone who tracked the movement of matériel in the Empire would have considered this much traffic as undeniable proof.

This space was both a symbol of modernity and the pulse of the Empire. It was natural, then, that people in military uniform bound for their assignments as a matter of national necessity shook hands and, though loath to part, boarded their trains to begin their journeys.

High-ranking officers were no exception.

"General von Zettour, congratulations on your promotion to inspector of B Group."

"Are you congratulating me on a demotion? I'll respond to that forced compliment with forced gratitude."

The old brothers-in-arms Lieutenant General von Zettour and Lieutenant General von Rudersdorf shook hands and winced as they joked.

"...Zettour, you really got the short end of the stick."

"It can't be helped. I was the one who defied Supreme Command."

Zettour, who in the realm of grand strategy was lower ranking, had snapped at his higher-ups.

The imperial family, the people, the government—no matter what you want to call it, ultimately, a military person was considered subordinate to the wishes of the state. Obedience to legitimate orders was treated as the soul of discipline. There could be no exceptions.

Supreme Command was the master, and Zettour was the servant.

"Honestly, I was prepared to lose my position as deputy director of the Service Corps. What actually happened instead was almost anticlimactic."

"Hmph, the only one who sees it that way is you. That's downright impudent coming from someone being sent away."

"But since my job in the east is a concurrent post and they're leaving my seat open, they must have some sympathy."

Rejecting the wishes of the state was essentially rebellion.

By toeing such a dangerous line, he knew that the worst case would be complete dismissal from the service. In that sense, the relief he expressed to Rudersdorf was genuine.

They must have preserved his position out of some kind of compassion.

Keeping all his achievements in mind, they must have been willing to let him off with exile to the east. Bureaucracy is an agglomeration of cold-blooded organizers, but it can still be considerate enough to treat human resources with care.

Apparently, Rudersdorf had a different impression from Zettour, though.

"...The issue is the lack of parity!" he spat, shaking his head. "You and I both opposed them. So what's this all about? Don't tell me you don't know, Zettour!"

Supreme Command's feelings were revealed in their punishments. On the surface, there was no difference in how they treated Rudersdorf versus Zettour...but in practice, there was a giant chasm.

"I lose out on my promotion, but I stay in my current position. Meanwhile, you're sent to the east. I don't mean to speak poorly of going to the front, but to be sent without any authority? While ensuring you'll have no role in the rear? They're freezing you out."

"I'm choosing to think of it as if I've been given a vacation."

"You never change. But, Zettour, I'm warning you... The higher-ups—no, the whole government has its eye on you."

"Why bring that up now?" Zettour smiled bitterly. "You can't work in the Service Corps without getting blamed for something at some point. We're in the middle of a total war. It's impossible to be everyone's friend."

Groping in the dark for the most efficient way to pile up the bodies of enemy youths while your own are falling to the ground heaving blood in exchange—that's war.

No one was less suited to being a General Staff officer than a person who wanted people to like them. That was incredibly clear, given the lamentations, grief, and anger of the families who had lost loved ones.

"And recall that I was the one who led the initiative. We were meddling in foreign affairs. Even if I hadn't acted on my own authority or opposed Supreme Command...sooner or later I would have been punished."

The person who made every effort with the best intentions had ultimately failed. Given that outcome, the consequences could be considered surprisingly lukewarm.

When all was said and done, Zettour didn't hold any grudges.

"An organization requires rewards and punishments to be doled out accordingly. A soldier interfering in diplomacy, even if their intentions are good, is a soldier who is overstepping their authority. What would happen if we were unconditionally exempt from accountability? It would be against the principles of military command." *So what happened was inevitable*, seemed to be Zettour's point, readily excusing the way he had been treated by looking at the big picture of military administration from the perspective of a single member of the organization. "Restraints are unavoidable. Cracking the whip when the time calls for it is the sign of a healthy military. Shouldn't we be happy there's some punishment rather than none at all?"

"But it's not fair. Rewards and punishment may be the foundation of the military, but when you get down to it, you only stepped out of bounds to make up for the state's lack of a plan. Holding a grudge for the way the General Staff has handled their human resources would simply be—"

Even if there weren't any people around, Rudersdorf was going too far. *This is no good*, thought Zettour as he interrupted. "That's enough."

"Mrph." Always true to his feelings, Rudersdorf's eyebrows expressed his dismay as he held his tongue.

"No matter what, we're still soldiers. And as long as we're soldiers..."

"We have no choice?"

His old friend's discontented attitude gave Zettour pause. "General von Rudersdorf, I hate to say this to you, but...a soldier has to follow the state's grand strategy. At least, that's all I can say right now." He chuckled. "They're probably suggesting that I go honorably to the front lines and cultivate a true warrior's spirit."

Chapter **II**

"Maybe it's a roundabout way of getting the Federation Army to mop you up for them."

"You're overthinking it. If they were sending one of us east as an execution, I think they'd do it a bit differently. They're probably trying to stir my pride so I'll 'volunteer' to be the ceremonial head of a regiment. At least, that's what I would do."

Having been with the General Staff so long, Zettour was familiar with how these things went.

For example, when he thought of how the "promotions" of the higher-ups who pushed into Norden had left the Rhine front in a precarious position...he winced.

"I'm one of the lucky ones, relatively speaking."

"You're always like that. To think that a general is here, groaning like a first lieutenant about how unreasonable the military is. Things have gotten bad, Zettour. Nothing ever turns out the way you want it to when you're a soldier."

"I remember talking about the same thing when we were lieutenant colonels. In the end, your position can change, but things still won't go according to plan—that's life. It just means that the ones at the top of the ladder have their struggles just like the ones at the bottom do."

"You're too philosophical. No one would normally reach that kind of conclusion."

He knew from experience that he had no choice but to be philosophical. And why was that again? Whose mess had he been cleaning up? It was a very interesting question.

Zettour himself had a background in Operations. He understood the absurd requests from Rudersdorf and the other Operations staffers were consistent in the context of their needs and station. Perhaps it had been necessary from the beginning, but he usually went along with their unreasonable demands willingly... *Ahhh.* He had a sudden realization.

"Can I say something?"

"What?"

"The Service Corps is a military organization. Its strength doesn't lie in politics."

Rudersdorf was right to look at him with eyes that said, *Why are you stating the obvious all of a sudden?* But it's important to be reminded that institutions are operated by people.

"I can't have you look at my decisions and misunderstand. So just to be clear: The Service Corps wasn't meant to handle political matters. It's merely a tool. They don't think on their own. So don't expect anything out of them beyond railways to the combat theater."

"In other words?"

"When it comes to negotiating with anyone who isn't the military, sorry, but please lend them a hand."

Flaws in any organization had to be fixed by a person.

It sounded nice in theory, but that sentiment didn't amount to much more than simply putting off the issue with a quick fix. Still, with a war going on, everyone was forced to take measures that were ad hoc, if they were being described charitably. Most solutions were haphazard if they were blunt about it.

Due to the nature of the situation, Zettour often found himself forced to get his hands dirty with political matters…but that deviated from what a staff officer in the Service Corps was supposed to do.

From the perspective of an administrator of supply and matériel, it seemed as if the General Staff was getting lost in a similar yet decidedly separate universe.

"I really think you're too fit for the job. Having you leave day-to-day administrative duties at this juncture…is honestly fine with me." Rudersdorf smiled ferociously. "That said, if instead of Zettour the administrator we had Zettour the Operations man take charge of the secondary fronts…then I would truly be able to rest easy."

"Oh? But I might take such a cushy position as an opportunity to lose myself in philosophical contemplation like the academic I am."

"Ha-ha-ha. That'll be the day." Rudersdorf lightly punched him in the shoulder as he continued laughing. "It's not as if I'm unfamiliar with the kind of Operations man you are. And I can't imagine you've forgotten how things work, so worrying about whether you can handle it is a waste of time."

"Good grief, you're really always ready to thrust some new headache onto me."

Chapter **II**

"General von Zettour, have you forgotten? An industrious staff officer is a good staff officer. I'm not about to let you get away with a nice, long rest for your weary bones in the countryside."

"Hmph," Zettour snorted. "Right when I thought I was being kept on the payroll out of kindness, I get hit with this unexpected request. If you want me to work, you could at least give me a smidgen of authority to make it happen…"

He was being demoted with a nominal rank and nominal position. That was what his superiors intended. Meanwhile, here was Rudersdorf, in charge of things on the ground, rejoicing in his luck and trying to entrust the entire B Front to him.

And if the necessary authority to handle things was unclear, his work would be plagued by incredible difficulty.

"That doesn't sound like the kind of gripe you'd normally make, Zettour."

"Well, I should be allowed a gripe or two. Why should I have to be the only one to suffer? We're talking about holding down the B Front. Anyone 'requested' to do such a thing would normally want to go hide in their parents' basement."

"What are you talking about? If I could have it my way, I would have a much easier time if I could have left all the logistics to you."

"…I know." He swallowed the urge to say, *So I suffer either way.* As he was about to remark that that was always the case, the train's whistle interrupted them.

They had been talking so intently, neither of them realized it was time to go.

"Hey, the train's here. Look, Zettour."

"Yeah, seems that way."

The train that glided into the platform was the usual combination of passenger and freight cars. There had to be a mountain of supplies being sent to the eastern front on those freight cars.

The train's most distinguishing feature was the cheap paint job it had gotten that was supposed to provide a degree of camouflage. The cars were painted a somewhat gloomy color in order to make them hard to spot from the sky.

It reminded Zettour of his future in an uncomfortable way. No matter how Rudersdorf spun it, he still felt anxious.

Before departing, though aware that it was uncharacteristically repetitive of him, he opened his mouth to speak. "About the logistics for Andromeda, to be blunt..."

He had to say it.

He felt he had to make his point clear, but it got him nowhere.

"There aren't enough horses. We'll just barely be ready by forcing everything through with rail. It's all we have left. There are trucks as insurance, but...whether fuel stocks will hold up or not is in the air."

"...Yeah."

If Rudersdorf already fully grasped the main points and understood the most glaring issues, there was nothing else Zettour could meaningfully add.

"I've known that from the beginning. Don't worry about A Group. I'm leaving B to you." With a bob of his head, Rudersdorf pounded his own chest. It must have meant he was up to the challenge.

"I've been going along with your recklessness for so long."

"For better or worse, we're inseparable former classmates. Let's win this thing together."

"And what if we fail?"

Always have a backup plan in mind. That was the nature of a staff officer. Some might have even called it the essence of their being.

They hoped harder than anyone for the operation to succeed. But they also prepared for failures no one wanted to see or think about. It seemed like a contradiction, but it was precisely because they desired success more than anyone that they also constantly envisioned the worst scenarios.

"I'll reorganize the lines and won't hesitate to retreat. I'm not interested in betting on a losing horse."

"...A drastic retreat will affect B Group. If you do plan to fall back, let me know."

He knew Rudersdorf wouldn't screw up the timing. Being nervous about it seemed strange.

But perhaps Zettour was anxious because it was his first frontline duty in a while? He was in a strange mood. He hesitated to bring it up, but something felt wrong, as if he had done his shirt up one button off. He just couldn't verbalize it properly.

Chapter **II**

In the end, he decided to say nothing. It was better not to speak up in the first place if he was unsure.

"I believe in you. And now all I have to worry about is the A Front. You have my gratitude."

"I suppose I don't have to go nuts with it."

"If you say you'll do it, I'm sure you'll do it no problem."

"...I'll do my best. But this isn't an issue that can just be solved with joint responsibility. Allow me to say something, bearing in mind how rough you are with people."

"Let's hear it."

"Colonel Uger and the others I'm leaving behind are excellent officers, but they're good-natured people. They're very cooperative but tend to be restrained when it comes to expressing their own views."

"By that you mean...?"

"You need to understand that when they say something is impossible, it's different from when I say something is impossible. When they say something can't be done, it's most likely because they've already exhausted all their options."

The Service Corps staff officers he was leaving in Rudersdorf's care were too used to working at full tilt. They were incredibly talented at cutting away excesses in the pursuit of efficiency.

As members of an organization, they were the perfect cogs.

The issue came down to how they would be used.

"I hope you'll remember this: All my subordinates are hard workers. You might even say they work too hard. Please keep that in mind when you're making requests of them."

They would never cut corners. They were industrious and unselfish, which was praiseworthy, but...it became a problem when the staff officers didn't get necessary rest. If they pushed themselves to their limits, they wouldn't have the proper reserves of energy in the event of an emergency.

"...I'll keep that in mind. What a mess this has turned out to be. It was much simpler to squeeze resources out of you."

"All the impossible demands from you and the rest of Operations have left my people and me gaunt. At this point, much more squeezing and all you'll wring out is hatred. Our blood and tears have long since dried up.

That's how hard my people work and how much they strain themselves. If only they were blessed with a better colleague."

"Ahhh, I hope you're blessed with a good colleague like me in B Group."

"Ha-ha-ha! If only."

Zettour laughed at how awful Rudersdorf was being, and Rudersdorf shrugged. Though they had grown older, their banter hadn't changed from the time they entered the service together.

"I wish you luck."

"Thanks. I'll see you again sometime."

"You bet. I'll be waiting for your triumphant return, General."

They continued chatting as they clapped each other on the back and shook hands. No matter how much a staff officer was praised, it undoubtedly had nothing to do with how good a person they were.

"Have some pricey liquor and cigars ready. I'm planning on bankrupting you."

"Fine by me. You can expect a welcome back party for the triumphant Operations Zettour. We'll make it a big one. And all the arrangements will be made by Service Corps Zettour, so you can believe me when I say everything's taken care of."

"...I never thought you'd manage to get one over on me. It seems I'm already washed up. Well, time for me to dutifully head to the eastern front. See you again soon."

With those final words, Zettour boarded the train and entered his compartment. Waiting for him there was a batman who bowed low, nervously trembling.

"Excuse me, General! Your luggage..."

"Luggage?"

"Yes, sir! If you'll point me in the direction of your bags, I can take care of them for you right away."

"Thanks, but there aren't any."

The young batman's face went blank. Did he hear that correctly?

"Y-yes, sir... So...you don't require any assistance?"

Zettour almost pitied the poor kid, who had gone white as a sheet, perhaps from the stress of questioning a high-ranking officer.

"Take a look. All I've got is my officer's suitcase. It's not as if I'm moving house, so what would be the point of taking more than I can carry?

An officer has to be ready to move at a moment's notice if the order comes down."

"P-please excuse my ignorance, sir!"

Zettour shook his head lightly and told him not to worry about it.

"How terribly unfortunate if my predecessors gave you the wrong idea. Anyhow, might as well make the best of it. Troops on their way to the east are allowed a free cup of tea, right? As a member of the military, I'd like to take advantage."

"Yes, sir! I'll bring it immediately."

The batman dashed off with impressive speed. He must have been trained well. But the peacetime sensibility made Zettour want to give him a piece of his mind. Etiquette was all well and good, but was that much necessary on a train headed to a war zone?

"...What a handful. He's too polite for field service."

He would probably also have to say something about the operation and usage of the trains themselves. As he was about to make a mental note, he realized something with a start.

This isn't the General Staff Office.

It wasn't the type of place where he could order something to be improved and it would happen immediately. He wouldn't be able to remember everything, so he would probably have to start writing things down at some point.

The right to make requests went only so far.

Sitting in the chair in his compartment, he murmured, "So I've got to wage war while holding the reins of B Group..."

This certainly wasn't what Supreme Command had envisioned. Zettour retained nominal authority, but it was Rudersdorf back at headquarters who was meant to command the operation. The fact that they couldn't have guessed that he, shorthanded for the major operation in the southeast as it was, couldn't handle overseeing both the Service Corps and B Group...made things rather lopsided.

"Thanks to that, part of his work got dumped on me."

The higher-ups didn't intend it, but the labor had been divided. And as a result, he was being sent to the eastern front with greatly limited authority and supplies. Even if the Eastern Army Group and the General

Staff Office hadn't already been on bad terms, he was basically parachuting down on them without warning.

He probably wouldn't be able to take his time and get to know everyone at HQ.

"That idiot Rudersdorf. As if it'll be so simple."

Unable to issue actual orders, only requests. *What a difficult world we live in.* Zettour could already see how his influence on the eastern front would be terribly small.

In effect, he had no pieces to play with.

"No, there is one..."

A single card in his hand. But it was a wild card.

"The Salamanders..."

When conceptualizing the Kampfgruppe, he never dreamed it would be used like this one day. It was a special unit reporting directly to the General Staff with Lieutenant Colonel von Degurechaff in command. The unit wasn't being used very aggressively in the east, but perhaps that would need to change soon.

"If this was going to happen, maybe I should have had the Kampfgruppen currently being formed sent to the east as well? No, that wouldn't have been doable even if I'd wanted to."

There were several experimental Kampfgruppen operating in the homeland for research purposes...but sending them all over the place had backfired. It had seemed fine at the time because of how easy and convenient it was to deploy them.

If they had been held in reserve, they could have been pooled together and sent to the east to give Zettour a decent force to work with.

Instead, he was stuck with hardly anything.

"At any rate, if this is a sign of how everything else will go, all I can do as a field commander is hold my ground as ordered. Of course, it'd be nice to win."

Successfully carry out the objectives of Operation Andromeda on the eastern front—the ideal was clear. And he wanted to do it with as few casualties as possible.

If they could win, Zettour's duties in the east would essentially disappear. If the B Front quieted down, he could snark at the B Group staffers.

"But if we can't win?"

The ominous doubt that slipped from Zettour's lips sent a chill up his spine.

If Andromeda failed? He might be able to handle the aftermath. It would be awfully tough, but he didn't consider himself so senile that he couldn't make do.

But that wasn't the real issue.

At this point, he was confident that the situation was still manageable. They would improve what needed improving, learn from their failures, and plan the next operation accordingly. But what if that one failed? Would they persevere and come up with a third?

They would most likely be able to scrabble together some kind of operation. Though the shortage of manpower had been worsening for a while now, surely the General Staff wouldn't be completely unable to draft a new operation.

The true problem lay elsewhere.

Would the Empire and its army have enough strength left for a third operation at that point? No...would they even be able to recover from failing the second?

Thinking objectively, Zettour had to admit the chances of either scenario going well were hopelessly close to zero. If two major operations couldn't get them over, would the foundations of the Empire still be standing after?

It was difficult to be optimistic about even their chances of successfully defending, much less attacking. It would require an awful lot of self-deception to look away from reality and pretend like there weren't serious problems underpinning the entire situation.

...Vexingly, things appeared to be different for the Federation Army. They endured defeat after defeat, only to stand up again.

"Oh, I see." Zettour finally realized what had been bothering him. "We aren't allowed to make a mistake, but the enemy is... I was just thinking that was rather unfair."

>>> **MAY 28, UNIFIED YEAR 1927, EASTERN FRONT, EASTERN ARMY FORWARD BASE** <<<

When Tanya answers the General Staff's orders to report to the eastern army's forward base, it's under the assumption that Colonel von

Lergen or Lieutenant Colonel Uger—one of the officers she's acquainted with—has come with a message.

Anything too dangerous to transmit in writing, or too important, normally gets delivered by an officer.

Given the market factors of secrecy and convenience, getting called in is surely the going rate for information. And as I'm a lieutenant colonel, the messenger should be no one higher than colonel.

This conclusion should come naturally to anyone familiar with the inner workings of the Imperial Army. Though she happily came along, eager to rekindle an old friendship with the messenger from Central, Tanya is now frozen in place.

Even for a place outfitted as a headquarters…the quarters she had been invited to were much too nice. I should've realized right then and there.

"Been a while, Colonel von Degurechaff."

Waiting in the room the eastern army batman led her to was…not a mid-ranking officer. Raising a hand with a faint smile is a good-natured older gentleman—a general. There's no mistaking him. It's the deputy chief of the Service Corps, Lieutenant General von Zettour, wearing his stars.

The shock from being caught off guard is immense. This veritable sneak attack nearly causes little Tanya's heart to leap out of her throat.

If I had been able to predict the future even slightly more accurately, maybe things would have been different. For instance, if there had been a way to know the next words Zettour would say, maybe it would have been less alarming.

"I've been exiled from the General Staff Office. I'm here to play in the east for a spell…so I have a favor to ask." He went on without hesitating, his tone casual. "To get straight to the point, I've been sent here because I upset Supreme Command… It's not an easy job, pointing out your boss's mistakes."

Lieutenant General von Zettour, who was supposed to be the brilliant string puller in my career plan, has *slipped up*.

To Tanya, who has been proceeding according to her prudent life blueprint, these circumstances are most regrettable. The boss of my faction has failed! This is why I can't stand politics!

Possessing the self-restraint to not grumble like that in front of people is something Tanya can be lauded for. But pride and patience alone won't solve this problem.

By the time it becomes obvious that Tanya has lost the initiative, it's too late. Unlike multiplying positive and negative numbers, multiplying astonishment with astonishment never comes out positive no matter how many times you repeat the function.

Before the stunned Tanya can recover, Zettour begins speaking matter-of-factly without worrying about her status. If there was any hint of him manifesting a Being X–like harmful energy from his entire body, she may have responded differently.

But for the imperial soldier Lieutenant Colonel Tanya von Degurechaff, bound by the norms of society as a civilized individual, fleeing while a superior is speaking isn't an option.

By the time the risks are plain to see, the conversation has progressed to the point where she can no longer retreat.

The General Staff and Supreme Command have clashed.

A major offensive, Operation Andromeda, has been green-lighted for political reasons. Stockpiling for said major offensive has already begun, and the rumored reorganization of the eastern army is already under way.

The forces are split into an A Group that will concentrate on the main area of operation and a B Group that will defend the extensive lines that stretch across the rest of the theater of operations; moreover, most of the armor will be committed to capturing the southern cities...

Tanya is told all these things nonchalantly before she can get a word in.

Having heard this much, I don't even want to imagine how classified this information is.

The next thing Zettour says guarantees it.

"And I'm here on orders to inspect and advise B Group; I'll be aiding in the reorganization of the front lines. In order to properly support Andromeda missions in the south, B Group will have to live with most of their armor getting retasked, but we'll simply have to do our best with what we've got, eh?"

Tanya just stares. Though she should be reacting in surprise, she only listens on while gaping like a numbskull.

Chapter **II**

The eastern front is often referred to as "extensive," but that's actually inaccurate. Put more bluntly, it's *too long*.

And thanks to that, everything is stretched thin and becomes disjointed. That applies to defensive positions and troop formations as well. The ideal logically would be to hold Commie welcome parties from strong points of prepared firing positions and solid trenches like what the troops had on the Rhine. Unfortunately, the positions we're working with are horribly lackluster and worn down.

You could say that one-man operations are becoming a chronic issue.

Though the planners know it's more efficient and desirable to dedicate multiple people to a task, they simply don't have the numbers. The Empire's instrument of violence, its military, can carry on as long as the state doesn't go bankrupt, but it's undoubtedly feeling the attrition of national strength and human resources.

Yet, they're going to take the armor normally saved for emergencies and give it to A Group?

Who could hear that without getting dizzy? And that's only if the unlucky victim doesn't die of shock on the spot.

"I'm sure you must have arguments, objections, and so on, but if we can seize the Federation Army's resource area, we can expect a dramatic shift in our war economy."

"With all due respect, that's only if we're successful."

"That's a very good observation. For the sake of discussion, let's hear what you have to say. What do you think about Operation Andromeda?"

"...I think, considering my rank, I shouldn't..."

"I'll be frank: Give me your unreserved opinion."

Tanya attempts to avoid the question by saying it's not appropriate, but Zettour insists with a gentle smile on his face that doesn't reach his eyes.

I guess I have no choice. Tanya braces herself. Sharing opinions when requested by a superior is part of what an officer gets paid for.

"Overburdened communication lines, a supply network that is about to collapse, a huge exposed flank, barely enough troops to secure various strategic points or hold defensive lines, and to top it off, the tyranny of distance—moving ahead with all these things present"—she almost spits out her conclusion—"is reckless."

"I won't understand if you're vague. Elaborate."

"I don't have any other words to describe it. If I had to rephrase it, I would say that the operation is a gamble that is far too dangerous."

Once you say something aloud, you're obliged to explain it. Tanya offers her view dispassionately, with a professional air that overcomes subjectivity to the greatest extent possible.

"To be frank, under the current circumstances, B Group is a misnomer. Though it's called a group, the only group on the eastern front is A. B might as well be a pile of rubble! We don't even have the minimal necessary troops according to eastern-front standards, much less those found in our textbooks."

"Is that how it seems to you?"

Tanya nods emphatically. "You don't need to have gone to war college to see that; I'd bet even the newest students at the academy can tell. Regardless of A Group's success, if B Group cannot hold, the entire army will be forced to undertake a massive retreat. Under these circumstances, insisting on leaving B Group with little more than a skeleton crew, we'll be risking not only the Andromeda front but the rear as well."

It's clear that these are makeshift adjustments based on creative accounting. The brass can say B Group will hold the line all they want, but there simply aren't enough troops to make that happen.

A Group has secured local superiority, just barely, through the army's efforts to concentrate their forces. They'll probably be able to at least drill an opening in the enemy lines.

The enemy's defenses are thick but certainly not uniformly so; we can consider punching through anytime.

But the biggest question is whether we can exploit the opening.

Unless we have units in the wings with the discipline and leadership to hold that breach open, our pains will be in vain.

"At present, we have no units on standby—not only that but we're drawing off units from B Group! We need to recognize that we're putting the cart before the horse."

"Surely a staff officer's duty is to do something about that."

"A staff officer's duty is to raise appropriate objections as necessary in the face of impossible circumstances. At least, that's what they taught me at war college."

During the staff officer retreat, they emphasized how important it is to honestly admit when something is impossible, no matter how badly you wish it were otherwise.

"A staff officer isn't supposed to brute force things when they can't be done. Even if you can tip the scale, we mustn't forget the underlying laws that govern how the scales work in the first place. We can't put anything larger than a weight on it."

"Colonel, it's not becoming of a field officer to put too much confidence in their academic education. We don't get a blank check. I don't deny that Andromeda is a high-risk operation, but since we've been ordered to carry it out, all we can do is our best."

"I understand what you're saying"—Tanya shakes her head in response—"but I just don't like it."

"You're being awfully negative. It's not like you. Did something happen?"

"I realize my objection is vague and difficult to describe, but if I may be allowed to speak anyway, I don't like any of it. Even the name rubs me the wrong way."

"Oh?"

Tanya catches him smiling wryly out of the corner of her eye. Nothing she's said so far came with the intent to pique his curiosity, but apparently, she has captured his interest nonetheless.

"How unusual."

"Sir?"

The gaze directed at Tanya's blank look is so mischievous. What did she say that could possibly amuse her superior like that?

"I was sure you were my good luck charm… Although I thought you were a bit more logical of an officer."

"Names and natures do often agree."

"Hmm?"

His eyes urge her to continue, so Tanya obliges. Not that I'm a huge fan of structuralism, either, but sometimes there are moments that absolutely call for deconstruction.

"We put too much faith in language. Which is why we tend to forget that our thoughts and imaginations are shaped and restricted by words."

Ultimately, humans are caught in the thrall of words. In Tanya's understanding, names are words, yet the meanings they possess can at times bring about misunderstandings.

"A division from the Dacian Army and a division from the Federation Army are both 'divisions,' but the threat they pose is quite different... Become too used to fighting against the Federation and you're liable to overestimate Dacia, but if you get too used to fighting against Dacia, you might underestimate the Federation instead. The same logic applies here."

"I see. Now that you mention it, that's true."

What an interesting observation. That's what Zettour's expression says as he nods. Well, I'm glad it's a topic that interests a superior scholar.

"So what does the name Andromeda suggest?"

"The Andromeda Galaxy. Doesn't that mean we're reaching a bit too far? To me, at least, it's self-evident. By the time we're endeavoring to ignore the tyranny of distance, it's already clear what we should be worrying about first."

It's almost as if our internal fears slipped out in the form of this strange operation name.

Though I don't know if it was done consciously or unconsciously.

Fascinatingly, this seems a lot like how no companies like the phrases *growth strategy* and *long-term plan* more than those that are about to go under. Put concisely, these are all signs of an organization that's failing to hide how it's already hit the limit.

"There's no need to be overly heroic or overly, odorlessly neutral, but I do think it's important to consider how the name of an operation comes across."

Whether you inspire or stump the members of your organization is a matter of life and death.

"That's a good point, Colonel. I'll be sure to suggest that indirectly to the one who named it."

"Sir?"

"Usually I choose the operation names, but this time it wasn't my choice... I'll be sure to explain your logic in full to General von Rudersdorf."

Yet another unexpected turn. Consistently losing the initiative in this conversation is maddening.

Before Tanya can blink, Zettour takes out a cigar. *Wow, now I have to deal with secondhand smoke?* I sigh inwardly. Today is just a parade of the unexpected. But then after a moment's silent hesitation, he puts it right back in his cigar case!

"I thought I'd have a smoke, but I guess I'm not in the mood."

"Is something wrong?"

"Well, I thought I'd offer you one and we could have a frank conversation, but then I remembered the law. If I gave you a cigar, we'd both be disciplined."

No doubt. Tanya smiles wryly in spite of herself.

Minors are prohibited by law from drinking and smoking. And for an aerial mage, doing anything that could weaken your lungs would violate your duty to devote everything to your job. An underage aerial mage ignoring her duty and smoking? I can't think of a more complete breach of contract.

Putting that aside, Tanya reels her often-wandering mind back in.

What's important here is that the general has something so serious to discuss with her that he would offer a mere lieutenant colonel a cigar.

It must be something totally outrageous.

Even just listening to what he's said so far has been uncomfortable... Any more and honestly, I'd like to turn tail and run. I want to run, but I can't, and that is the rough thing about being an individual in society or an organization—especially the military.

"Today is just full of surprises. But I've decided that nothing you can say will shock me. I'm at your service, sir."

When Tanya braces herself and gives him an opening, Zettour nods slightly. Yet, he still seems to be hesitating, and the silence persists for a time.

It's only a few seconds, but it's a long few seconds.

When he finally looks up, his expression is pained, and he bows his head to her. "Sorry, Colonel, but please lend me an aerial mage company."

"Huh? I beg your pardon... You're asking me to divide up my troops?"

"Yes, I'm requesting one of your companies."

I thought I would be ready.

I knew it would be a difficult order.

But this...

It's such a cutthroat demand that I can't help but be taken aback. Tanya balls up her fists and glares at him.

"With all due respect, please allow me to object. My companies aren't mere companies."

"I know. That's why I want to use one as a command company."

"…It's like you're ripping me limb from limb, but…"

Maybe we aren't quite in standalone operation territory yet, but everyone is shorthanded.

Tanya's precious human resources in the Lergen/Salamander Kampfgruppe can't be described as well staffed, no matter how generous you want to be. Losing more of her subordinates at this juncture would be unbearable.

The recent arrival of a replacement company means we're barely maintaining the head count for an augmented battalion, but only three of the companies can be considered elite. No one with any sense of responsibility could calmly allow one of those three to be taken.

"You should be able to spare one, right?"

"How merciless of you. May I ask what it's for?"

"Reserves. Strategic reserves, Colonel."

"General, please allow me to object out of a sense of duty."

Luckily, he nods and offers to listen. Tanya prepares to do her best to persuade him—she has to protect her people.

"It makes no sense to pull from the Kampfgruppe. If you want to draw troops off, I'd appreciate it if you would consider the Eastern Army Group or B Group instead."

"In other words…you want to say I don't need to take one of your units? Just a moment ago, you were saying that B Group doesn't even exist."

Even if B Group is low on people, this is a magnitude issue. They may not have hands to spare, but taking one person from a hundred is very different from taking one person from ten.

Tanya nearly raises her voice in spite of herself. "The 203rd Aerial Mage Battalion is the core of the Salamander Kampfgruppe. Of our total forces—armor, artillery, mage, and infantry—it's not an exaggeration to call it the keystone. Above all, given the current state of deployments and operations on the eastern front, I strongly oppose this idea."

Receiving a look that urges her to go on, Tanya is happy to continue her rant. "The Salamander Kampfgruppe is under direct control of the General Staff. Shouldn't it already be earmarked for reserve purposes…?"

"Colonel, you're misunderstanding. These aren't reserves for B Group."

"What?"

"They're for me—or more technically speaking, for the General Staff group dispatched to the eastern front."

Even Tanya is lost for words when he says that like it was his intention the whole time.

"Officially, I'm only permitted to *assist* and *advise* B Group...I don't have the authority to give direct orders. It's similar to how an admiral in the navy can't go over a captain's head to steer their battleship."

"Won't you still be providing guidance and oversight to their units?"

"...Nominally. In reality, my powers are greatly limited. It's not much more than a farce. Certain people in the homeland must have been convinced the General Staff would find some other way to handle things."

"So then," Tanya asks without thinking, "why are you here, General?"

"Between conducting a major offensive on the southern end of the eastern front and supervising the aerial battles in the west, handling matériel and playing Whack-a-Mole with the Council for Self-Government, the General Staff is nearing its limits."

"No offense intended, sir, but haven't we trained countless staff officers?"

"We have. But how many of them do you think have a grasp on the actual state of things?"

"Ahhh." It slips out as Tanya understands the root of the problem. Handoffs. Anyone who has handed off a project even once can immediately imagine the difficulty. Even the most dedicated, hardworking, competent individual has an incredibly hard time jumping into an organization and hitting the ground running.

"Since I just happened to be free on the eastern front...the General Staff leaped at the opportunity to shove some work off on me. Thus, if possible, I'd like to have some troops to work with."

Since I do understand where he's coming from, I'm having a hard time coming up with a rebuttal. Certainly, with no authority, his position becomes a formality. But Zettour knows the most about the workings of the General Staff, and he's capable. Given the chance, it makes sense that the General Staff would want to leave things up to him.

That's always how organizations work. Meanwhile, the formality of a position Zettour has been granted is basically removed from the actual work he needs to do.

Which is why Tanya has to ask something. "General, honestly...your explanation only confuses me even more. To be frank, I don't follow."

"What about it?" Zettour tilts his head in amusement while wearing an ever-so-cryptic smile. It's a truly demonic grin.

It's because Tanya is a member of the same organization that she can confidently doubt him: This must be one of those times where there's some outrageous scheme in the works behind the scenes.

"What do you actually want to use these reserves for?"

"You aren't convinced that I simply want to be prepared?"

"But B Group is the relevant party here and should be well aware of their defensive duties on the eastern front, even if they are uninformed of the situation at home. Surely they'll do all they can to deal with whatever may happen."

It's only natural that the unit assigned to defend should give their all. Even when the homeland's political aims or the military's circumstances are involved, I can't imagine anything needs to be added to the job description.

Honestly, for the life of me, I can't understand what he's trying to do.

"General, with all due respect, allow me to ask...the purpose for the reserves."

She stares at his face, determined not to miss a single quiver, and in response he nods with a wry smile. "Colonel von Degurechaff, let's look at a map while we talk."

"Yes, sir."

I'm familiar with the map of the eastern front—I've seen it enough times to be sick of it.

That said, as you might expect when it's a lieutenant general's map, there are new and minute details on it that people at Tanya's level aren't aware of yet.

Still, there isn't much difference from the positions Tanya and the other commanders have been informed of.

Imperial Army units are concentrated to the south along the A Group's positions while B Group's forces are spread thin in the center and north. Though they've scraped together adequate troops for an offensive through extreme concentration, it's clear at a glance that in exchange, a broad swath of the front is vulnerable; the situation is very precarious.

When they were teaching us at the academy, it's likely no one ever imagined conditions as extreme as these.

It's understandable that Zettour would be sent over to nominally advise the defense, and it makes sense that they would take advantage of his presence to throw the whole responsibility at him.

"General, if you're advising under these circumstances, then I feel like reserve troops are…"

"Unnecessary. That's true if I were going about this the usual way."

"You're not?"

"…Colonel, the usual is a luxury. That's what I think."

A sudden murmur.

The complaint is so natural, it must have slipped out by accident. He's practically talking to himself, so that remark could have easily been missed.

"B Group's defense plan is pie in the sky. Supporting the main lines via sustained defense sounds great in theory, but with such a limited number of troops, our defense will be paper-thin; it's utterly reckless… The only solution, though extremely high-risk, is to conduct an offensive defense."

"Are you saying we should target the enemy field army? I beg your pardon, but that sort of move would require mobility."

"B Group has reserves. Most of them have been taken, but there's still an armored division."

"But there aren't enough forces to carry out an offensive."

It's terribly strange that Tanya has to be the one to point out something so obvious. Zettour must know that already.

He has teased her for not acting like herself, but here he is getting unusually timid. Usually Zettour is brimming with confidence… Is this all due to his demotion? None of this seems normal for him.

"…You want to lure them in and annihilate them? That's the ideal strategy when outnumbered, but there's no reason the enemy would fall for that."

As in Austerlitz, as in Trafalgar. Thrashing the enemy when they expose themselves is the most effective strategy. Both Napoleon and Nelson had to work awfully hard to bait their opponents.

"...Take a look at this map. See these railroads? Logistically speaking, the enemy wants to use these rails, right? I want to put out some bait here and nail down this route."

"In other words, manipulating the enemy to act according to our intentions. Of course, that all depends on being able to lure them out."

"True. Basically, if we can lure them out...the rest is easy, right? Maneuvers, encirclement, annihilation. It'll be a classic, quick solution."

His words implying that the Imperial Army shouldn't fight a protracted battle carried an intense desire for a swift solution. There's a grave significance in an officer who is familiar with the situation in the rear doing everything he can to not drag things out.

It means the potential danger is so great that we need to hurry even if it's risky.

"I think I see what you're getting at now. You want the Lergen Kampfgruppe to be the bait? Regrettably, I'd like to decline."

"You decline, hmm? To be frank, Colonel, that's meaningless. While my authority to issue orders to the local troops is doubtful...I still retain my full powers as deputy chief of the Service Corps in the General Staff."

This is what it means for something to be nausea-inducingly sinister. He talks as if I have free will and then flashes his secret weapon—the chain of command.

Tanya serves under the General Staff, which means she reports directly to Zettour, since he's the deputy chief of the Service Corps in the General Staff. I never had any ability to refuse in the first place.

"If it's an order, then I can no longer object to you taking a company. But if we're talking about securing adequate preparations for battle, then I wish you'd give it back."

"But then there's no guarantee I'll be able to mobilize a rapid response force as needed. You'd be wringing your own neck. So I must refuse. Though it's not necessarily a trade, I will, however, take the observer off your hands."

It's true that this offer is better than a simple refusal. Still, it means getting stuck on the front lines minus one company of Tanya's babies in exchange for him removing some deadweight—a pretty rotten deal. Talk about highway robbery.

Tanya replies with an expression that makes it obvious she's fed up.

"So our guest will be sent to the rear. In other words, I won't have any room left to make excuses?"

"Glad you're so quick on the uptake... I'm going to have you get muddy for me."

A direct order: *Wade into the muck.* Apparently, the General Staff loves that mad, black earth. What a ridiculous place to work. If it wasn't wartime, I'd be appealing to the Labor Standards Inspection Office.

"And just to confirm once again, you're going to take a company away from me?"

"Correct." With a tone that said it was an undeniable truth, Zettour declares, "It'll be enough seed money for me to roll the dice with."

"I had no idea you were a gambling man, General. You'll have to excuse me, but I was under the impression you were steadier than that."

"Colonel von Degurechaff, do you ever go to the races?"

"Huh? Y-you mean horse races?"

"That's right."

The question is so sudden, Tanya is bewildered for a moment and lost for words. "No, I mean, I..."

"Ha-ha-ha! I'm sure you haven't. Let's just say your superior ability makes it easy to forget our age difference."

"Yes, sir."

If he's figured it out on his own, then there's no need to prod that snake, so Tanya simply nods deeply.

"...Colonel, horse racing isn't fair gambling. It's not a game that comes down to pure chance but rather being able to peel back the fog of uncertainty after making observations and analyses. In that sense, it's similar to war."

"As someone who isn't fond of betting, I'm not sure if that's true or not, but if you say so, then I'm inclined to visit a racetrack."

"I doubt you'll be able to. Don't even bother."

"Sir?"

"The famous horses are good ones. Sadly, they've all been mobilized as warhorses... I know that for a fact, since—as part of my role with the Service Corps—I'm the one who carried out those requisitions. No exceptions were made. Now, then..." Zettour's expression relaxes into a smile. "To get back on topic, though I detest leaving things up to chance...I have a certain love-hate relationship with bets that I stand a decent chance at winning. Not that the gamble we're looking at now is a particularly good one."

"So you gamble when you think you can win, General?"

"The potential reward is so huge... And it's better to sacrifice personnel with an actual plan in mind rather than simply crashing them into the Federation Army because we must."

"In that case, I'm all out of counterarguments."

After no small amount of hesitation, Tanya makes up her mind.

Either way, the moment the request became an order, she couldn't refuse. In the military, most deviations can be justified by some regulation or another, but it's impossible to rebel directly against a ranking officer's orders or the chain of command.

Thus, since Tanya can't avoid handing over a company, the next best thing is to minimize the damage. Considering pure fighting power, giving up First Lieutenant Wüstemann's replacement company would be ideal. But that's too dangerous, considering how undertrained they are.

Providing troops means taking the responsibility of recommending them, to some extent. In this case, offering the company led by an aerial magic officer who came up through the academy like First Lieutenant Grantz is probably the safe choice.

"...There's a company led by a young first lieutenant named Grantz..."

"You have my gratitude."

He probably means it as a thank-you to Tanya, who has made a distressing choice, but considering the chaos that will soon follow, it's hard to sense any sincere gratitude at all. When going along with one of Zettour's crafty shenanigans, the most important thing to know is what role you play.

"By the way, General, now that my Salamander Kampfgruppe is down an arm, what kind of swindle are we going to be a party to?"

"It's not complicated. While Andromeda is being carried out, you'll be a militarized canary out there helping the army hold the B Front. When the enemy comes, let yourselves get surrounded."

Her superior says something so outrageous with a straight face, as if it was nothing.

Get surrounded?

Unless you've been trained as part of an airborne unit that drops into enemy territory, you're taught *not* to get surrounded. It's obviously a terrible idea for Tanya to direct her openly doubtful gaze at her superior, but she looks up at him in spite of herself. This is abusive.

"Then we'll mobilize units to save you. We'll force a maneuver battle and then turn it into an encirclement. I'm sure it's the only way we can support the main lines."

...That's all well and good, but it's also the opinion of someone who doesn't have to be the bait. For Tanya's sake, there needs to be at least one thing guaranteed.

"Can I trust that we won't be abandoned?"

"I won't abandon you. In the worst case, I'll at least give you back your company. That way, even the most reclusive staffers will come out for the rescue. If I charge in leading the company, everyone will leap into action, worried about what might happen if something befalls me."

"That's a risky move, in terms of how it could affect discipline."

"Setting aside strategic-level discussions, on a purely operational level in a maneuver battle, it's a trivial issue. The enemy in front of you must be attacked."

Even acting on one's own authority can be justified if the achievements are great enough. But that applies in only very specific situations.

"Easier said than done...I think is what they say."

"And that's what wit is for, surely. Basically, your job is to block the railroad. I'll handle the rest."

"Understood," says Tanya before changing the subject. "Please give me the details on where we'll be sent."

They say if you know the enemy and know yourself, you need not fear the result of a hundred battles, but if you don't know the terrain, you can't even start the fight. Even nuclear war requires a map.

"You'll be at a position called Soldim 528. It's suitably urban, at a suitable distance, and most critically, it's right on the railroad. The convenient location makes it an optimal candidate for the enemy to retake."

The point he refers to on the map is indicated with only an ID number.

"Won't they just go around? I doubt even the Federation Army is bored and foolish enough to go banging their head against a stronghold."

The Federation Army has long since stopped mindlessly rushing defensive positions with hordes of infantry knowing full well they'll fail. There were times in the past when they might have taken the bait, but given their recent skill and quality improvements, it's biased to assume they're still just inept Commies.

"Even if the changes are only evident in the enemy's lower-ranking officers, the improvement in quality has been remarkable. While it might be an exaggeration to call them outstanding, they've surely learned the basics after paying the price in blood and bodies by now. Are you sure they'll come?"

"They will. I'm an Operations man with a smattering of logistics knowledge. For a time, I was treated like a logistics man with a smattering of operations knowledge, but that doesn't mean I've lost my touch. The way I see it, it's precisely because the enemy is sensible that they'll aim for the railroad." Zettour's voice is filled with confidence and conviction.

"...That's why you're certain you can divine their intentions?"

"The principle of war has nothing to do with ideology. No matter what you personally believe, ignoring the laws of physics will come back to bite you."

"Yes, I agree..."

"The Federation Army doesn't have much choice, either, especially when it comes to transportation by truck or horse. If they're plotting a counterattack, their options are limited. That naturally means railways take on a life-and-death importance."

The point the logistics specialist Zettour makes has Tanya sinking into thought in spite of herself.

Could the fate of the battle over the eastern front be decided by the fighting surrounding the railroads, unlike in the historical war against the Soviet Union? It's starting to seem like a fairly reasonable hypothesis.

However, the eastern army believes that the biggest risk is the potential enemy armored vanguard advancing over highways or open fields.

"The Federation Army seems to value roads and highways higher."

"I think they care about railways more. Though the Federation Army excels at bringing prodigious amounts of matériel to bear, I doubt they have enough forces available to commit large amounts of armor to deal with A Group and still be able to punch through B Group's defenses with what's left over. That's why our enemy will be tempted to take advantage of the railways as well. They'll want to hold a critical position in order to temporarily stabilize the B Front."

That makes sense.

Limited resources, limited choices, limited solutions.

What a sad war when both sides are scraping the bottom of the barrel. This is the ironic outcome war's extreme consumption has wrought.

Capitalism and Communism fight in the same arena after all.

"I want the Salamander Kampfgruppe to welcome that enemy vanguard. Basically, you'll be defending to the last. Without further orders, retreat will be prohibited."

"...With all due respect, that position is rather close to the enemy lines. If you order it, I'll promise to put up a hard fight, but physical limitations can't be ignored. I'm really not sure a single Kampfgruppe will be enough to hold it."

"All I want is for you to stubbornly stand your ground. Hold Soldim 528 no matter what it takes."

"I'd appreciate the authority to declare a retreat if food, water, or ammunition runs out and there's no hope of resupply."

"I can't allow retreat. Hold until your allies break the encirclement."

The order essentially saying to defend with their lives is maddening. "General?! Surely that's a bit...!!" Tanya replies with military rationale as her shield. If the side that acts most like a fool is destined to lose the war, you would be hard-pressed to claim that assigning the Salamander Kampfgruppe to defend a base is the right move.

"The Salamander Kampfgruppe is by design, fundamentally a breakthrough force! Tying it down with orders to defend a static position should be out of the question. That negates all its strengths!"

"Things are going downhill either way... And the Salamander Kampfgruppe is the only force I have at my disposal. Sorry, but just accept the short end of the stick."

"I'd like to ask...did my unit get the short end of the stick because of some political wrangle?"

"I can neither confirm nor deny that."

In other words, he's not denying it.

In this situation, silence says it all.

"But I'll also promise you this... It'll depend on the situation, but I'll make sure to furnish you with reinforcements. You won't be left to die."

"...I'll do what I can with what I'm given."

>>> **JUNE 9, UNIFIED YEAR 1927, SOLDIM 528** <<<

Shit, so I'm basically Freeman?

Behind some abandoned rubble that was once the outskirts of Soldim 528... With that most excellent cover, Lieutenant Colonel von Degurechaff complains loudly in her head as she peers through binoculars to check enemy movements alongside the other officers.

Surrounded by Commies, unable to withdraw, the Kampfgruppe is currently embroiled in a defensive battle.

If that were describing someone else, I would sympathize, empathize, and praise their ferocity. The heroic struggle of a surrounded unit is sure to grace the pages of history books.

And that'd be great—as long as I'm not involved in a big way.

"Surrounded by Commies, huh?"

If this were the Korean peninsula, heartwarming naval artillery fire would be supporting us from the coast... No, at least in Freeman's fight, they had air superiority.

Meanwhile, I'm an aerial mage, so I have to go get it myself.

I have to do everything. The army is being outrageous. Who takes the foundation of modern society—the division of labor—and just chucks it out the window?

Tanya sighs as she crouches, ready to return to base.

Her adjutant must have noticed, because she asks in a concerned voice, "Colonel, are you all right?"

"I'm just sick of our nasty neighbor's visits."

"...They certainly are a nuisance."

"That they are." Tanya laughs.

You can choose your friends, but you can't choose your neighbors. And as long as our neighbors are the Federation Army, we can't ignore them.

"Damn it all. I'm jealous of Lieutenant Grantz. He's probably enjoying General von Zettour's hospitality right about now."

"You don't think he'll mess anything up, will he?"

"What's there to worry about? General von Zettour is a patient guy. He'll hold off collecting on a mistake or two until a critical moment."

"That's tolerant, ma'am?"

"It's a suspended sentence, so I think it comes from a place of kindness. Now, then." Tanya shakes her head and enters the Soldim 528 encampment like an inspector would. It doesn't take long to make the rounds. That is to say—it's a very small base.

Good grief, thinks Tanya with slumping shoulders as she calls out to the familiar face of her vice commander on watch at the perimeter.

"How are things, Major? What's the status?"

"It seems we are well and truly surrounded."

The comment her second-in-command makes with such an air of importance is actually ancient news. She could call him reliable, but that would be too charitable.

Is there anyone who *wouldn't* notice if they were surrounded by the Federation Army? My frank assessment is that it's highly unlikely. If someone like that does exist, I'd want to have the structure of their mind studied to advance science.

"I can see that. And it's what the general predicted."

If we're going to be hit by a Commie tsunami, then it's only natural that we prepare trenches and a coordinated defensive plan. Traditional wisdom says it's best to have a shelter against every storm, and "prevention is better than the cure" is by no means limited to medicine.

It's important for believers in the principle of a market economy to be sensitive to costs that are difficult to visualize. For people in Tanya's position, it's important to never forget that skimping on risk management could end in tragedy.

Safety doesn't come free.

It's that simple—even a child could understand.

"But I guess I didn't think we really would be…"

"Major Weiss, it's great to be honest, but please have a little more faith in your superiors."

"Well, their estimates are always so optimistic."

"Certainly, when you get good news from above, it's best to take it with a grain of salt, but this was a negative prediction. You should be able to trust that."

They're coming, they're coming, we were warned. That should have allowed us to steel our resolve somewhat.

"If you know it's going to rain, you just have to make sure you have an umbrella."

Anyone shaking in their boots now is the exact type of numbskull who gets rained on because they ignore the forecast. The question is: Did B Group come prepared for the weather?

Given the thin spread of troops, I have my doubts.

"But wow, there sure are a lot of them. What does the air force's recon have to say?"

"Here is the report. They say it's four or five divisions."

Her adjutant hands over the air force's photo analysis. Apparently, they're quite the diligent bunch and sent up an observation unit as soon as we were surrounded.

"The blessing in this curse is that we get air support. But...," Tanya murmurs, "look at them mustering those numbers when all we can scrape together is an augmented regiment."

The Federation troops confronting B Group are suspected to be unseasoned replacements, but...the Federation Army has been known to form new units rather than replenish.

"The issue is the quality of the troops. There's no info about that?"

"I understand your concern, Major Weiss, but no, there isn't."

Lieutenant General von Zettour's predictions are the latest intel we have, but I hardly find wishful thinking such as *Maybe they're exhausted* to be much comfort.

"So we don't have a firm grasp on enemy strength beyond the face value of 'four or five divisions.' That's tricky. If one of those ends up being a guard division or something, we'll be in trouble."

"I doubt it'll be a guard division."

"If you're already feeling that confident, that's a load off my mind, ma'am, but..."

Tanya smiles wryly at her vice commander's strained remark. Officers on the front lines regarding those in the rear with skepticism is typical during wartime, but she can't overlook the fact that he's doubting proper situational analysis.

"Come on now, trust your allies more. The Federation Army's guard divisions are under constant observation. Is Imperial Army Intelligence so inept that they'd miss movement this obvious? I certainly hope not."

"So you trust them?"

"I'd like to do so unconditionally. Sadly, trust is built over time, and our fellows are currently in the rebuilding phase... Don't forget to always envision the worst-case scenario."

Trusting someone is different from overestimating them.

"In any case, our friends in A Group are the ones conducting a major offensive, not us."

Setting aside the outcome of Operation Andromeda, which is now under way, it's a fact the main battlegrounds will be the southern cities. Though the Federation grows people on trees, the Empire has already annihilated them in two different battles. Rhetorically, *nearly inexhaustible* and *infinite* are close, but reality comes through in numbers.

Are they really so confident that they can afford to send a guard division away from the critical battle? If that were even remotely true, they would have repelled the Imperial Army long ago.

"Then what if we conducted reconnaissance in force with mages or armor?" suggests Weiss.

An assertive idea. Perhaps that's how a young major should think, but does even a seasoned field officer like Weiss get anxious when surrounded? Is that what's egging him on?

As an aerial mage, he should be able to relax a bit more, since he can always withdraw via air if push comes to shove. Not that I don't grasp how difficult it would be to propose shamelessly abandoning your comrades.

At any rate, Tanya rejects his idea with a frown. "We're outnumbered, so we don't have the leisure of wearing ourselves out. All we can do is learn what we can passively."

"At least a surprise nighttime raid, what about that?"

As Tanya is about to shake her head and refuse, an unlikely participant voices an opinion.

"It's not a bad idea. We could learn a lot from even a single strike."

"You too, Lieutenant Serebryakov?"

"…Remembering the Rhine makes me want to flex my skills. Taking our shovels on a field trip could be good."

"No, I refuse, you warmongers."

The savage nature of Tanya's subordinates is sometimes worrying. In my previous life, I never would've imagined there would come a day when I'd be living and working alongside the type of people who get a thrill from a nighttime sneak attack.

"Call me conservative, but I'm prioritizing the preservation of our troops."

"Are you sure, ma'am? If you'll excuse my insistence, with your permission, Lieutenant Serebryakov and I could lead a party of volunteers to attack."

Growing tired of her subordinates' refusal to listen, Tanya doubles down. "Whatever you say, no is no. Besides, we're supposed to be focusing on defense."

"But in positional warfare…"

"This isn't a trench battle—it's the defense of a stronghold. Our job isn't a cultural exchange with the enemy trenches, it's preparing to welcome our guests." As the ones surrounded, we're essentially under siege. "Let's be serious—we may not like it, but we know what the enemy is capable of. I mean, they've only just arrived, but they're already fully on guard."

"What are you thinking, ma'am?"

"Today and tomorrow will be dedicated to fending off enemy offensives."

After that, we can play it by ear. I wouldn't say it's a bad idea to strike at the enemy once they've loosened up a bit. After all, some assertive action tends to become imperative in order to maintain the defenders' will to fight. Even my subordinates blessed with plenty of combat experience are itching to move…so I imagine we'll have to sally out and strike at some point.

"This will tempt them to be careless, so…adopt a passive attitude. It'll be a fierce defensive battle with Lieutenant Tospan's infantry in the leading role. We can expect some backup, but it's dangerous to assume the reinforcements will be able to rescue us."

Which means we need to save some energy just in case and somehow cope with whatever the enemy throws at us in the meantime.

"Captains Ahrens and Meybert will play supporting roles as planned. We'll keep them in reserve for the time being. Oh…" Remembering something to add, Tanya continues, "We might send them in as additional forces depending on how the situation plays out. Have them prepare with the worst-case scenario in mind."

That's when Tanya notices Captain Meybert running over, and she smiles wryly at his apt timing.

"Captain Meybert, good of you to come. The enemy is here, but I want you to keep the guns quiet for now."

"Ma'am?"

"What is it, Captain?"

"N-no, understood… I was hoping to be kept for later as well." He smiles, explaining how lucky he feels.

Tanya is utterly shocked.

The artilleryman is worried about requesting to hold back his barrage?! Usually, firing away is all he can think about!

"I never thought I'd hear those words come out of your mouth, Captain! I approve, but what a surprise."

"Well, we aren't receiving any shells. I have no choice but to be conscious of that."

"Welcome to my nightmare. We're literally encamped on top of a railroad, and our resupply is still proceeding at a snail's pace—what kind of joke is this?"

You could have never imagined this situation back at the academy.

We were taught that as long as you held the rails, you wouldn't have to worry about supplies. In the case of a Kampfgruppe being supported by a railroad line…barring the rails being blasted to bits, it should have been impossible to be short of supplies.

Thus, common sense does us no good.

In the ten days since arriving at this position, we've managed to stockpile mainly food from the Council for Self-Government. In other words, we aren't getting deliveries of shells and so on from the homeland. We have to do everything we can to fortify this position in preparation for a defensive battle, but we barely have enough resources—it's bad enough to be cry worthy.

So Tanya racks her brain for ways to increase staying power.

"All right, here are your orders." Her officers await her command with bated breath, and she delivers it in a grave tone. "Prepare your troops for nap time. On the double."

"A-are you serious, ma'am?"

Her vice commander replies, puzzled; he's disappointed. It's such a critical instruction that she wants to snap at him for not comprehending its importance. If her subordinates don't manage their time properly and fail to get enough sleep, that's their own fault, but if they fail to get enough sleep due to the rotation schedule, that's Tanya's error.

No one has time for that kind of mistake when fighting a war.

"Tuck your soldiers in. We need to establish a rotation and give everyone a chance to rest properly."

"...The trick will be securing enough places to sleep."

First Lieutenant Serebryakov murmurs precisely because she's one of the veterans who lived through the demands of round-the-clock interceptions on the Rhine front. Not getting enough sleep is bad for your skin, sure, but first and foremost, it's bad for fighting a war. Exhaustion does a real number on the brain. The drop in mental acuity is unacceptable.

"The troops are already building a half-entrenched position, but we don't have nearly enough beds for everyone. We'll probably have to use sandbags, but still, we can't skimp on water or sleep." Tanya orders her vice commander from experience. "Make sure at least one of every three meals is hot, even if you have to use mages as heat sources."

"That's against regulations..."

"Sometimes a commander needs to act on their own authority. Major Weiss, we're at war, so officers need to take their turn napping, too."

| chapter |

III

Andromeda

The entire eastern front is in crisis. —Imperial Army frontline units

The entire eastern front isn't doing well. —Imperial Army regional units

The entire eastern front is at a standstill. —Imperial Army General Staff

The entire eastern front is contested. —Imperial understanding in the rear

A game of Telephone

"U-urgent message from the Lergen Kampfgruppe! Soldim 528 is suddenly surrounded by extremely powerful Federation units!"

In order to contain their encroaching enemies, the Federation Army
launched an offensive in response to the commencement of Andromeda,
and ensuing movements of A Group to capture southern cities was not
unexpected.

Everyone in B Group Headquarters crinkled their brows and clicked
their tongues in their heads, vexed that their worst predictions had come
true.

As soon as they got the report, several murmured, "Here they come…,"
and swept their eyes over the map, but as they scanned the defensive
lines looking for Soldim 528, they were momentarily confused.

"It's not on the Melting Line?!"

HQ had expected the enemy to advance down the broad, convenient
highway.

For that reason, they had committed all their limited resources to
what they assumed would be the main battlefield, what they had taken
to calling the "Melting Line." The staff officers of B Group were now
realizing that their predictions had been completely wrong.

There was no sign of Soldim 528 along the anticipated route. Instead,
after poring over the map…they could hardly believe their eyes when
they found it in a sparsely defended area far from the main road. It was a
tiny little bridgehead on a barely operating railway.

"What the hell? Shit! Why there?"

Are you serious? The route was that astonishing. Given that the attack
was coming from an unexpected direction, the shock and embarrass-
ment of the B Group staffers were severe.

"Are we ordering the defending group to fall back?!"

"No! It's too late! They're already surrounded!"

All the staff officers had to admit it: The Federation Army had gotten the best of them. They weren't unwilling to admit when they'd been taken completely by surprise. But even so…all the high-ranking officers spat in amazement, "Surrounded?! How is that possible?!"

This was the eastern front.

Not the jungle, not some rugged mountain region, not the Norden border zone with its notoriously poor visibility. While the vicinity of Soldim 528 had a tendency to become swampy, it was flat, open ground typical of the battlefields in the east.

The enemy had done something truly unexpected.

But that didn't explain how the defending unit got surrounded so easily. Whoever was on watch should have detected the enemy's approach. It would have been one thing if the first report had been about the enemy heading their way, but reporting in that they were encircled was bizarre. Could it even be possible for Soldim 528 to be surrounded without warning unless all the troops were *napping*?

It's out of the question for a modern army to overlook the movements of a major enemy force. Aerial recon by plane and observer mages keeping watch over the ground had long since become standard practice, so what could possibly explain this…?

A few of the staffers were of a mind to conclude that the surrounded unit was simply a bunch of idiots, but when they confirmed the name of the unit, they shook their heads in disbelief and had to laugh at the ludicrous situation.

If the seasoned and decorated Lergen Kampfgruppe couldn't be considered competent, then who could? Unable to comprehend the situation, everyone began to yell.

"Why is the Lergen Kampfgruppe surrounded?!"

"Why Colonel von Lergen?!"

"What were the sentries and men on watch doing?!"

"Why didn't the aerial mages detect them?!"

Amid the uproar of crisscrossing shouts, one man looked on with disinterest.

It was Lieutenant General von Zettour, who, it was whispered, had been demoted and exiled from Central. He was the only one present who maintained his usual composure as he stood to address the room.

"Gentlemen, discussion is all well and good. But this isn't a university—we should be debating what to *do*." He appealed to honor and reason to dispel the turmoil. "The enemy advanced down a route you didn't anticipate. As a result, your troops have been surrounded. We have no choice but to act… If we accept the reality of our situation, then we have no choice but to save the Lergen Kampfgruppe." Surveying the eastern army staffers, Zettour emphasized his conclusion. "The only thing to debate right now is how to help them. How should the rescue be conducted? That's all."

Their fellow soldiers were encircled, so they needed to be saved. It was an extremely simple line of thought.

Any soldier, especially any officer entrusted with the lives of other soldiers, would have a hard time openly disagreeing with such a statement. And above all, HQ had to make up for their misreading of the situation.

"Please wait, General."

"What is it?"

"Sending relief under these conditions? I'm sure you know this, but the General Staff gave us strict orders to focus on a passive defense. And more importantly, we don't have any soldiers to spare…"

"That's not quite right."

The B Group staffers tried to argue that it wasn't feasible, but Zettour drove his point home.

"The strict orders the General Staff gave you are to defend the lines. The mission is to hold the lines; it doesn't restrict your movement."

"But please take into consideration how few troops we have!"

"I'm fully aware that our numbers are less than ideal, but without any alternatives, we have no choice… As far as I can see, we should resolve this with a strike of surgical precision. Seems to me like this calls for a concentrated deployment of our reserves, no?"

"Y-y-you mean all the reserves?"

His response to the hesitation was definitive. "That's right. Obviously." He continued, "We can't abandon our troops."

"I think ordering them to withdraw under their own power and supporting as we're able is enough. As long as we lack the troops to mount a major operation to break the encirclement…"

"Is that a roundabout admission that you learned nothing from the staff officer curriculum?" Zettour furrowed his brow as if he'd spotted an insufferable fool. "You would order a unit that has found itself under siege due to their superiors' errors to withdraw on their own? Let me ask you something. What did they teach you at war college?"

This was an elementary concept in basic leadership. Not sending out a rescue when you could has far-reaching adverse effects in the military.

"Are you really saying that after sending matériel to the Melting Line on a mistaken assumption, you're going to do nothing but watch as the troops at the Soldim position get slaughtered? You can't tell me you don't know why the high-ranking General Staff officers who emptied the Rhine front to send the Great Army up north were demoted."

You can't quantify intangible assets such as fighting spirit, morale, or trust in the organization. Human souls are the same. They're not something that can be seen. But can you call someone without one human?

As a group of humans, armies are no exception.

And a blunder made by command is like a nasty flu. It eats away at the entire army. And absurdity is even worse than a blunder. What would happen if instead of rescuing a unit they could save, HQ told them to make it back on their own? Overnight, they'd have an uncontrollable army on their hands.

The issue of whether to leave the Lergen Kampfgruppe isolated or rescue them was the choice between essentially killing the army or fighting through a path of thorns.

"Abandoning them to die amounts to negligence on the part of the commanders. It would cause the trust in the chain of command that makes up our army to rot away," Zettour spat in exasperation.

It had to be one of the two; a choice had to be made. Any fool who would choose the suicide of the military in this situation did more harm than good by being in the army, and the only cure for that was a firing squad.

"Are you trying to turn our disciplined troops into a pitiful, frightened mob overnight?"

The staff curriculum polished staff officers' ability to be vicious, but the assumption was that it would be used against the enemy. They couldn't entertain the option of abandoning a friendly unit that was possible to save.

"…If nothing else, you at least have to act like you're intent on saving them. And in this case, being effective is more important than projecting an attitude. I don't think any of us wants to be known far and wide as the Imperial Army command that abandoned its troops in the east." Wearing an openly nasty smile, Zettour carefully observed the gathered staffers, overawing them.

Abandoning the troops to their fate would irrevocably damage trust. Building up trust again would require time they didn't have, but it would take only a single mistake to destroy it so thoroughly that there wouldn't even be dust left behind.

"I'm sure the Federation Army would eagerly share that news with the Council for Self-Government. Giving them propaganda material is as good as aiding the enemy."

If you join in the Empire's fight, you'll be forsaken. Surely, all the fighting countries would be shocked. They also had to watch out for the Commonwealth whispering to the Council for Self-Government.

If the enemy made the same error—honestly, Zettour wished they would—he would happily use it in the propaganda war.

Most critically, the Council for Self-Government's counterintelligence situation was not great, even speaking generously. If they lost trust in the Empire that was suppressing their unrest, it wasn't logical to expect them to keep a lid on their paranoia.

If Federation moles worked behind the scenes to further exploit that… the Empire would have to be ready for the Council for Self-Government to flip sides. The issue was a serious dilemma.

In order to reduce obvious crackdowns in the occupied territory and maintain public order and stability, the Council for Self-Government tended not to look into the personal history of the people they employed. If they did, their government would necessarily end up being unforgiving. They needed a moderate compromise.

Indeed, given the aim of the policy to secure friendly, anti-Federation territories, there wasn't really an option to remove suspicious individuals. So inevitably, Federation agents would creep in.

Chapter **III**

Of course, they were already exercising the utmost caution under that assumption... Casting a wide net tended to catch some unsavory elements.

It was impossible to be certain with only a couple of pieces of supporting evidence, but...there was even some suspicion that a Commonwealth Intelligence agent had infiltrated the theater of operations.

There was simply too much intel leaking. They had spotted what appeared to be a case of leaked classified messages sent between the diplomats dispatched nominally as a delegation to the Council for Self-Government.

Analysis to determine whether imperial codes had been broken or not came out definitively negative.

Even if one transmission or cipher was broken, as long as they were changing the codes regularly and continually working to improve its strength, the communications security team guaranteed that it couldn't be compromised.

If it wasn't the code, then that left only the people. And sickeningly enough, their enemies in the Commonwealth were unusually skilled at HUMINT. Of course, it was always the case that the intelligence agencies of hostile states wanted to burrow their way in...but there was no reason to give more intel to the fellows who seemed to have mouths only so they could leak more things to the enemy.

Zettour shook his head, clearing away extraneous thoughts, and reemphasized his intentions to the staff officers of the eastern army's B Group. "I'll get straight to the point. Based on political necessity and military rationale, I urge you to take immediate action. I request that we break the encirclement with a maneuver battle."

His comment hit the room like a bomb. It was a request backed by nothing but vague authority. Under normal circumstances, it would be easy to ignore or refuse.

Yet, problematically, his refrain of *We mustn't abandon our troops* struck most of them as extremely logical and valid.

"Oh, and if an inspector's word isn't enough for you...you can add on the voice of the deputy chief of the Service Corps. By the power vested in me by the General Staff, I request immediate action to prevent any negative influence on the Council for Self-Government."

The air froze.

All the staffers locked their gazes on Zettour with eyes that made it seem as if they'd just been walloped over the head. The only thing that kept them from blurting out *Are you insane?* was their last remaining crumbs of reason.

Though shock had shattered their rationality, it could be scraped back together. They were able to barely—just barely—maintain the facade of composure social animals have.

"…With all due respect, General, do you understand what you're…?"

For better or worse, well-trained soldiers have powerful self-control.

That's all well and good, but from Zettour's point of view, they were overly pessimistic and lacked assertiveness.

"You want to call me an idiot, right? Then don't hold back. I'm fairly certain that I'm not inept, lacking self-awareness, or unintelligent enough to not comprehend what I myself said."

Zettour was in the special position of having the ceremonial title of inspector but also retaining his position as the deputy chief of the Service Corps in the General Staff. A "request" from someone with both those titles would require an awful lot of resolve to refuse.

Of course, Supreme Command would be disgruntled. They purposely didn't give Zettour authority so things like this would happen…so if this ended badly, it would become a huge problem.

But honestly, Zettour didn't care. Some wagers are meant to be made regardless of the odds.

"Now then, I think that took care of your hesitation… Was there anything else?"

Zettour must have managed to acquire his reputation as a mild academic due to always being paired with Lieutenant General von Rudersdorf, who was overly aggressive, and Lieutenant Colonel von Degurechaff, whose underlings could rush headlong into battle at the drop of a hat. He smiled wryly to himself to think that ultimately, it was a relative assessment.

Oh, how people change depending on their environment!

Amused, though his expression didn't change, he spoke again. "Put another way, this is a great chance. The enemy is here. They waltzed right into our grasp. Every military man's eternal dream is to annihilate the enemy field army. Then why don't we take advantage of this and pull off our own encirclement to crush them?"

Overpowered by the strength residing in Zettour's eyes as he grinned, the staffers nearly began to nod, but apparently their badges weren't just for show, either.

A few puzzled officers piped up, albeit timidly.

"General, it may be disrespectful of me to say so, but...you seem awfully relaxed. Is there some secret to being so unflappable?"

Implied between the lines was their suspicion that the conversation was proceeding a bit too neatly.

And in reality, Zettour's way of leading them to the answer with no concern for the fog of war stemmed from a trick.

It didn't seem like he had predicted where the enemy would come from and just happened to have a backup plan ready for them.

That could only mean...

But then, if they didn't sense something was off, he would have had to lament their naïveté. An unsuspecting staff officer is immature. Without the superior coordination skills and discriminating intellect of someone like Lieutenant Colonel Uger, a staffer was liable to be disposed of.

"Just experience and preparation."

The word *preparation* caused eyes to widen throughout the room. In addition to the slight tension in the air, a hint of wariness appeared. Apparently, they weren't all timid.

"Could it be that the Lergen Kampfgruppe is...?"

"A pawn to buy time? I won't go so far as to deny it," Zettour answered with a little smile, partially relieved. *Yes, your vague suspicions are correct.*

Let's get straight to the facts.

The Empire had gathered its main forces on the southern edge of the eastern front. The idea was careful selection and concentration, but stripping away units and resources was allowed in the case of scarcity. That's why the rest of the eastern front was supposed to limit itself to nothing but defending what they held. Zettour and the staff of the eastern army were all aware of this.

"General, do you mean to overrule the existing defensive policy on your own authority?"

"That's a nasty way to interpret it."

"But there's no other explanation!"

"While you were all looking to the right, I was on guard against the left—that's all. The Lergen Kampfgruppe got surrounded to clean up your mess!"

"General, how can you say that?"

He had just been posted to the eastern front, and nothing he said had been enough to convince them. His only other option was to force Degurechaff to stake her life on the defense of Soldim 528.

Slightly irritated, Zettour snapped, "Oh, it's not very hard. After all, we've been tasked with defending a vast amount of territory despite being desperately outnumbered. Attempting a textbook defense is a pipe dream. That's why the Lergen Kampfgruppe is out there drawing the enemy attack!"

"S-so you're saying...they got surrounded on purpose?"

"I imagine it's a *voluntary decision* of *self-sacrifice*. I know *Colonel von Lergen* personally to some extent—he's an Operations man."

Strictly speaking, it was a *she* and not at all voluntary, but... When it came down to it, Zettour was sure Lieutenant Colonel Degurechaff would be faithful to her duty. Once he gave the order, he was confident she would work her troops to the bone.

The deception was ridiculous, but it was also simply reality that there were very few people who would refuse to conduct a rescue after being given that explanation.

"The colonel must have felt he couldn't let the vulnerable lines be overrun and made a tactical call. If they withdraw, the enemy will come flooding in. Then we will lose the initiative. He simply couldn't stand by and watch that happen," Zettour said coldly, implying that thinking at the operational level, a passive defense wouldn't be enough. "Now then, gentlemen, I'll ask you again... If the enemy is here, and our troops are in a pinch, shouldn't we go out to meet them?"

"But, General!"

"We don't have the supplies or the troops for an offensive. We've barely managed to fortify the defensive lines as is!"

The high-ranking officers argued back wearing grim expressions.

And Zettour had no trouble imagining how the staffers of the eastern army felt as they voiced their fears.

After all, there *weren't* enough troops. It was too great a risk to sally out to attempt a local offensive. If this were a test on textbook strategy, or as far as was taught at the academy, they would have passed.

But unfortunately, this wasn't a controlled environment.

The prewar education of officers would have cut this out as an "extreme situation" that "would never happen in practice." And thinking rationally, yes, of course, anyone with a proper brain would scoff at the idea of war for the sake of war, continued fighting for the sake of continued fighting.

But at this point, it was impossible to laugh.

"It won't do to spread our troops thin and get skewered by the enemy vanguard. If that foolish move is our only other option, then we might as well gather up what little we have and swing them as a club."

"General…"

"I'll make the request again. The request is for you to consider and come up with a rescue plan. It's fine to be cautious, but I expect you to give me a proposal before our friends get wiped out."

>>> **JUNE 14, UNIFIED YEAR 1927, THE EASTERN FRONT** <<<

In official Imperial Army documents, Soldim 528 is classified as a medium-size forward base. Originally, it was a planned city and a base for the maintenance of Federation rolling stock.

The Imperial Army occupied it during their advance following the successful Operation Iron Hammer, but troops were pulled away during the run-up to Operation Andromeda to take part in A Group's offensive, so the place was practically deserted. Frankly, Soldim 528 was a nonessential base out in the sticks…as it should have been.

If the enemy hadn't shown up, Soldim 528 would've been a breezy posting in the backcountry. Instead, it's currently under siege. The leader of the staff providing the hospitality for this deluge of unwelcome customers, Lieutenant Colonel Tanya von Degurechaff, is woken up from a light nap by First Lieutenant Serebryakov.

"…It's time, Colonel."

Directing her vacant eyes toward the clock, she sees it's time to change shifts.

I would've liked to savor a bit more idle slumber, but that's obviously not an option here.

"Got it. Good work, Lieutenant."

During a siege battle, the commander ends up busy no matter what. Since command can't be left to someone running on no sleep, Tanya has been making time for it as much as possible, but there's only so much she can do.

As Serebryakov burrows into her bed, Tanya rubs her tired eyes and heads for the semi-submerged bunker functioning as their command post.

"Time to swap out, Major Weiss. I'll take command."

"Thank you. No major enemy actions to report. They appear to be positioning units for an attack."

As they have their handoff exchange, Tanya wishes her adjutant wasn't asleep. A cup of coffee would perk me up about now...

She shakes her head and moves on.

"What industrious foes we have. Though I'm thankful for the time to get ready, these guys seem to enjoy picking on the weak—and they seem intent on bullying us with their large numbers. I understand the tastes of the John Bulls all right, but why are the Commies hopping on the bandwagon?"

She meant it as a light joke, but Weiss merely winces politely, maintaining his silence.

"Honestly, these international Communists. They could at least pretend to be pacifists."

"Colonel, you don't really think...?"

"I don't, but isn't it natural that I want them to take their official stance seriously?"

Just as Weiss is about to nod his agreement...

The report of a single cannon rings out in the distance.

It's a familiar sound to us all. Aside from those who drifted off into eternal slumber, who on the eastern front could forget the sound of Federation heavy artillery?

"…Sorry, but prepare for war."

"Yes, ma'am, right away."

"Get everybody up! Here they come!"

Ever since the trench battles of the Rhine, it has been standard to wake everyone if the enemy shows up.

And all across Soldim 528, the troops curse the alarm clock of enemy artillery—*We were just changing shifts!*—jump out of bed, and man their positions.

"…So the enemy doesn't have the resources to rain a storm of shells down on us, either? Good. The battalion will fight for aerial superiority and intercept the enemy mages."

"Who's in command?"

Tanya responds to Weiss's nervous inquiry with a smile. "Don't worry; I'm not leaving you out. I'm going to let Captain Meybert do it like last time. The artillery doesn't have anything to do, so let him take command."

"It's an honor."

Where did that reserved demeanor from before go? Apparently, judging by this warmonger's ferocious carnivore-like grin, he enjoys being on the front lines. I took him out to strike at the enemy position earlier, but apparently, he wasn't satisfied… Frankly, I can't comprehend being happy about learning that I won't be staying behind at the command post.

But this is war.

The front lines need people like him.

"Okay, Major Weiss, you're up. Captain Meybert, keep doing what you've been doing. I'll grab Lieutenant Serebryakov and round up the battalion… If you're late, we're leaving without you."

"I'll be ready."

With a salute, he hurriedly grabs a receiver. Tanya leaves him, dashing out of the bunker to head for the square on the base designated as the battalion's marshaling point.

Everyone is already there. It's impressive no matter how many times you see it.

The absence of First Lieutenant Grantz's company and the presence of First Lieutenant Wüstemann's has already become something familiar. And it seems Serebryakov has managed to make it on time as well.

Setting aside the officers, however... Did some of them literally just wake up? A few of the mages have awful bed head. Tanya always firmly insists that paying minimal attention to appearance is a fundamental part of being a member of civilized society, but it's never clear-cut whether it's best to let this sort of thing slide in the case of an enemy attack.

"All units are present, ma'am!"

"Thank you, Lieutenant Serebryakov."

As they exchange mechanical salutes, I internally fret about how to give this particular advice. Fires or earthquakes are unforeseen, so some slack is acceptable, but during wartime, an enemy attack doesn't just come out of nowhere... It's a serious question whether Tanya should lower her standards or not.

I also have to wonder if this is really the time to be thinking about this sort of thing. But even if "a sloppy uniform betrays a sloppy mind" is a bit of nonsense, neglecting one's appearance is a slippery slope for civilized individuals.

Faced with uncivilized Commies and the anti-civilization Being X, I, as modern citizen Tanya, do ultimately feel the need to say something.

"Troops, I get the sense many of you just woke up. I think our battalion is fairly strict about appearances...but apparently, the enemy artillery mixed up the timing of their morning wake-up call." Aware that snapping at them would be unreasonable, Tanya points out the issue in a roundabout way while making them laugh with a little joke. "Even if a visitor is unexpected, you can't very well go to greet them in your pajamas, right? Take care to dress yourselves like civilized individuals."

Small habits lead to big differences. Heinrich's Law is practically a rule of thumb, but that doesn't make it any less correct. Humans are always haunted by limits. In order to push those limits and achieve a high-average performance, Tanya requires her subordinates to abide by regulations at all times.

Habit is truly the golden rule for success.

"All right, Lieutenant Serebryakov, Lieutenant Wüstemann. Major Weiss should be here shortly, but to fill you in, we're going to intercept the enemy mages. We'll do it just like we did on the Rhine."

Tanya briefs the officers on the situation. Really, it's just a formal confirmation of the notification she got from Weiss...but there's meaning in doing these checks.

Chapter **III**

Deviating from standard procedure often results in laziness.

That said, Tanya smiles at her trustworthy subordinates; I'm sure there's no need to worry about these veterans.

"Lieutenant Serebryakov, this is business as usual."

"Yes, ma'am, business as usual."

"...And as usual, I can rest easy knowing you're here."

This is just praising her accumulated experience. Serebryakov must not be used to getting complimented, and Tanya winces at her puzzled expression.

Her praise not getting through to her people is an oversight.

As a young child reading a biography of Nightingale, I didn't really understand why she said that her last remaining nurse in Crimea was worth more than gold, but now it makes perfect sense. It's just what you would expect from a great reformer who contributed so much to the field of statistics. Human capital has value whether you're a nurse or a military officer—indeed, it has universal value regardless of profession.

In that sense, Serebryakov has most definitely accumulated human capital greater than, as Nightingale put it, the value of her weight in gold.

"...Don't look at me like you find that strange. It may not always seem like it, but I do rely on you."

"Th-thank you, ma'am!"

I should find a good time to arrange a thank-you gift. Tanya makes a mental note to get ahold of some chocolate or something in the rear.

The real problem is... Tanya turns to face the commander of the replacement company who seems to have relaxed substantially since his first battle.

"Lieutenant Wüstemann: Don't overdo it. For starters, just follow me. I'll make sure you come out all right."

"Understood!"

For better or worse, the eager fellow is a green company commander. Though he has combat experience, he's still far from the point where he can be trusted to do things on his own, at least by Tanya's standards.

That said, even the hardheaded First Lieutenant Tospan turned out to have his uses.

In terms of raw materials, it's not as if Wüstemann is inferior, so as long as Tanya makes proper use of him, he won't be worthless.

Young personnel lack experience, but they make up for it with enthusiasm. What they need is the appropriate education. On that point, Tanya has some modest confidence in her results. As the educator who cultivated Serebryakov and Grantz, surely it's her right to be proud of her skills.

All Wüstemann needs is a little bit of time and attention to reason.

"I like that attitude, Lieutenant."

"Thank you, ma'am!"

"Here's something you should know, Lieutenant: War often comes down not to scoring the highest points but having the best average. It's easier to survive if you grind down your weaknesses. That's what you should work on."

"I see—I'll keep that in mind, ma'am."

Tanya nods in satisfaction. It's rare for someone to be so genuine.

"Sorry I kept you waiting, Colonel."

"There you are, Major. We nearly left without you."

I sense a measure of ease in the way he jokingly pleads for mercy. You really can rely on personnel who have experience.

"This'll work out just fine. I'll keep an eye on Lieutenant Wüstemann. The rest are yours, Major Weiss. We're going to intercept the enemy."

It's rough to wage war while needing to look out for your allies. It's reminiscent of on-the-job training for new employees. But in a war, people's lives are on the line. It's fine if I have the leeway to cover for them, but... Tanya is constantly compelled to be miserable.

This is why it hurts so much to lose Grantz's company—to the point that I can't help but complain in my head. With all due respect, General von Zettour, curse you.

"What shall I do, ma'am?"

"Lieutenant Serebryakov, you'll do the same as me. Support Lieutenant Wüstemann." Tanya responds to her adjutant, swallowing her other thought—*You can never have too much backup*—as she guides the battalion into the sky after their skillful takeoff.

The fundamental task of achieving air superiority is about gaining altitude—though ascending isn't so simple when enemy mages are coming to attack.

Is the enemy taking their time for some reason? I can't help but wonder when we're allowed to go up in formation rather than scramble while being harassed.

"...There's too much time between the artillery fire and the charge. Were the guns not calibrated?"

If nothing else, this is a good chance to test the replacement company's combat discipline—something I've been anxious about.

The fact that they're managing, just barely, to operate their Elinium Arms Type 97 Assault Computation Orbs and maintain stable flight makes Tanya emotional.

At the same time, it sends a chill up her spine.

"So it's a war of amateurs against amateurs, huh? We're wasting way too much human capital..."

The poor versus the poor, and on top of that, amateurs versus amateurs. The war is becoming about as total as it can get.

In the prewar Imperial Army, the training for aerial mages met such standards that even a newly minted mage could be entrusted to do artillery observation on their own. Now, as exemplified by nearly getting shot at mistakenly the other day, the situation has deteriorated to the point where we instead have no choice but to entrust newly minted mages with the job.

There's no time for a proper education. The veterans who would provide it have been sent to the front lines. As a result, the baby chicks get sent to the front with their training incomplete and hustled off into a turkey shoot.

The evil cycle of attrition is complete. If there's anything we can do at the local level, it's to secure a decent retention—that is, survival—rate. Yes, I need to do everything in my power to ensure the continued existence of my meat shields. Tanya takes out her binoculars, does a quick scan of the sky, and begins observing the enemy's movements.

"...They're certainly going by the book."

Climb while forming up in midair, then meet the enemy. Both sides will face off, maintaining a certain number of troops on the front.

Compared to our formation, the Federation one seems to have more personnel more closely packed together.

The Imperial Army can almost never compete with the Federation's when it comes to sheer quantity of resources, but in the realm of magic, where the Federation shot itself in the foot, the Empire had managed to maintain qualitative and quantitative superiority for quite some time. Now, though, it seems that the numerical balance is shifting toward equilibrium.

"…The Federation's no slouch."

What a deplorable state of affairs.

I have little distaste for beating on weaker enemies, but competing against an evenly matched opponent is far from pleasant. It's always better if you can finish a job with minimal effort, let alone a war. What a terrible situation this has become.

"Enemy fire!"

In response to the warning, Tanya follows the usual protocol and orders the counterattack. "01 to all units, return fire!"

Since it's extremely long-range, the fire is concentrated optical sniper formulas. That said, the tyranny of distance wreaks merciless havoc on the accuracy and power of the incoming fire.

As we need to pay attention to our remaining formula bullets, both sides are just taking potshots at each other—what a headache.

"Tch! The distance makes this hardly worth th—" Mid-gripe about the wastefulness, Tanya spots a dramatic shift in the enemy movements. "Ngh?! The Commie mages are rushing us?!"

They've broken their battle line, or left formation entirely, for a reckless strike. It's like a runaway charge.

"Did they lose control? How could their discipline get so…?"

Wüstemann's uneasy comment gives Tanya pause. It's too soon for command to fall into disarray and their formation to collapse. She's heard the rumors that long-range firefights grate on the nerves of rookies, but even so, the enemy can't have suffered that many losses yet.

"Did their recruits get restless…? It's known to happen, but…" Tanya is glaring at the enemy, deep in thought, knowing that something isn't right, when she suddenly shouts, "No!"

They began their charge after we formed up in the sky!

This is bad!

"Move! We gotta get out of here!" Tanya shouts without regard for appearances.

"Huh?"

But she's met with Wüstemann's hesitation and confusion. How can you be so dense?! We're above *friendly units*. We did the same thing to the Federation Army, so how could you forget?!

In a rare fit of lost composure, Tanya shrieks at her unit. "01 to all units! Accelerate to full speed! Don't let this turn into a melee over our base!"

It's an abrupt order, but Weiss's company grasps her intentions and begins to charge. Serebryakov follows so as not to let them pull ahead and become isolated.

If they were to get into a scuffle with the enemy above the imperial position, the potential for stray shots impacting below would jump considerably. We can't have someone accidentally blow up our own troops with a misfired formula, and though we want support from below, if our allies down there start shooting now, we're liable to get hit.

In a battle where direct fire support is available, having the enemy swoop in for hand-to-hand combat is basically a nightmare.

So we need to get out front.

"Th-they're headed this way!!"

It's precisely because Tanya feels the enemy got the better of them that she can't stand to waste any time at this juncture. Wüstemann's frantic voice irks her.

"I know! Handle it!"

"Then disciplined fire should…"

No! Do I really need to shout at him again? Trying to fight a war with subordinates who are slow on the uptake is such insanity!

"Don't stop, Wüstemann! They're rushing us! That means we have to charge! Go! Got it? We're going to slam into them and force them back!"

Even elites hesitate when they're taken by surprise, so of course officers and mages with little experience are liable to be overwhelmed.

That's why it's important to give clear orders and show them what needs to be done.

"Charge! Go, go, go!"

It's an abrupt order, but the replacement company just barely manages to keep up with the rest of the 203rd Aerial Mage Battalion on the charge and crash into the enemy.

"Don't get bogged down! Keep climbing and don't let them get near our forces on the ground!"

Keeping in mind that our advantage comes from orb performance at high altitudes, Tanya orders her troops to ascend. But then she's met with something that completely floors her.

The intention was to climb and mock the enemy from above, but we can't shake them.

"The enemy's keeping up at eight thousand?! Of all the— I didn't think they would climb so high!"

This can't be happening. Tanya has to swallow that comment—the scene in front of her refutes it all too eloquently. It's difficult to believe, but the Federation mages, who were always low-altitude specialists, have followed us as a unit up to the same airspace to force us into a dogfight.

They've reached not only quantitative parity but qualitative as well? That's hard to stomach. Nonetheless, these guys who shouldn't be any good at hand-to-hand combat are closing in on us at altitude.

"01 to all units! Climb to twelve thousand! I realize that's asking a lot, but... Wait! I take that back! Cancel that! Maintain altitude at eight thousand!" Right as Tanya is about to order everyone up to their maximum operational altitude, she realizes at the last possible second that it's a mistake and retracts it in a hurry.

Normally, having them ascend would be the right decision.

But not now—not this time.

The replacement company isn't even used to the Type 97s yet; they haven't done the necessary altitude acclimation training. I have serious doubts whether they would physically be able to go that high. This isn't the time to try taking advantage of altitude differences.

"Maintain your current altitude and coordinate to cover one another! 02, you're a trapper! Go after the enemies targeting our newer arrivals!" As she's about to continue with an order to take aim, Tanya notices black specks in the sky. Yes, multiple.

It takes her only a minute to realize what she's found.

"Enemy planes?! Break! Counterattack!"

At the same moment she shouts, the enemy mages who had been relentlessly hounding them begin pulling away all at once.

Hurtling toward the bunched-up mages are enemy aircraft—fighter

planes. I'm not about to let someone shoot at me with a cannon—the concentrated automatic fire of a heavy, high-caliber cannon, at that.

What comes next happens in a flash.

The 203rd Aerial Mage Battalion responds to this unexpected new attack with a promptness worthy of their veteran status.

Each mage performs random evasive maneuvers as they fire explosion formulas to obstruct the vision of the enemy fighter pilots.

This is probably the ideal speed at which a unit taken by surprise can react. No one becomes the General Staff's pet project by bluster alone. It requires the strength to pry challenges open as they arise, pin them down, and break through.

"Casualty report!"

"Minimal casualties!"

Such a pleasant reply from Serebryakov.

Not that the enemy scoring on us doesn't sting, but the fact that we didn't suffer many losses cancels that feeling out somewhat. I can be proud of my successful investments in education and human capital.

Tanya's cheeks are about to relax into a smile as she scans the sky, when her expression tenses all over again.

Standing still would've provided the enemy fighter planes with perfect targets, so everyone resorted to erratic evasive maneuvers and deploying explosion formulas. However, this has left the unit too spread out.

The formation is collapsing!

"Stick with your wingman! The enemy's coming in fast!"

The sight makes Tanya want to click her tongue. The other units are fine, but Wüstemann's company is so slow, she could just die of fury.

"Watch out for fire from below! Shit, what the hell?! The Commies have really gotten good at harassing people!"

"I mean, they're Commies!"

"What about it?!" Tanya shoots back without thinking. And her adjutant's reply is epically witty...or perhaps it's meant completely seriously.

"Didn't you yourself say that's how they are, ma'am?"

"Ahhh, yeah, you're right. I guess it makes sense that they would learn how to do what people hate even in a war." Holding back the urge to click her tongue, Tanya acknowledges the enemy's skill. As her troops scatter, climbing in an attempt to drive off the enemy mages that won't let them get a decent shot off, the Federation fighter planes return to the scene.

The enemy aircraft stick to hit-and-run tactics, emptying their automatic cannons and then swiftly withdrawing.

The altitudes and speeds involved are so different from our own that counterattacking is nearly impossible. What's more, we have company from below—and not just a follow-up attack.

But that's all it is.

As far as I know, there's no logic or reason that makes continued failure inevitable. I never give up. Mistakes simply need to be recovered from.

Tanya takes a small but deep breath.

Steeling her determination, she shouts, "What a bunch of heroes, coming to challenge us to close-quarters combat! These Federation fellows must really love magic blades, so fill their stomachs with them until they've had enough!"

Of course it's Weiss, the practiced vanguard, who volunteers to lead. "Permission to proceed as usual...?"

"Granted. Go!"

He hardly gets out a "Yes, ma'am" before he's zooming off to fight. This is what it means to be on the same wavelength.

"Company, follow me! Charge!"

"Give them support!" Tanya urges Wüstemann's company to move.

"Three rounds of covering fire!"

The fact that they manage to fire properly, despite the rush, probably means they're finally growing accustomed to live combat.

As long as I can trust them not to misfire, it'll be fine to dedicate them to a support role.

"Wüstemann! Keep it up! But no need to fire for no reason!"

"Understood!"

His acknowledgments are acceptable, if nothing else.

No, it's not nice to be spiteful just because they lack experience. Experience can be earned. Failing to distinguish between a lack of ability and a lack of experience is hardly fair. And for Tanya, being fair is a given.

Maybe being on the battlefield for so long has made me combative. It could also be the stress of General von Zettour's unreasonable defend-it-with-your-life order.

"This isn't what I need to be thinking about right now."

Tanya shakes her head lightly to clear out the extraneous thoughts and refocuses on combat. The timing is perfect. The enemy is busy with Weiss's charge…and the rest of us are in striking formation.

It's time. Tanya looks to her adjutant. "Lieutenant Serebryakov, we're going to follow Weiss with our own charge. This isn't any different from usual, but…watch my six. Be especially on the lookout for enemy airplanes that might come barging in."

"Yes, ma'am."

"Okay, here we go. Everyone, on me!"

Accelerate, accelerate, and accelerate some more.

The Type 97 isn't called an assault computation orb for no reason. The designers at Elinium Arms are nuts, but strangely, their technological prowess keeps pace with their outrageous ideas.

It's only natural to give the enemy a thorough beating while they're overwhelmed by approaching at full combat speed—the standard air battle method. After Weiss's unit breaks off, the enemy mages are hanging around in a daze, so we attack all at once from above.

When they notice us, they abruptly raise their defenses, but their reaction is sluggish.

"Hmph, that was slow."

It happens just as Tanya's zeroed in her rifle and is about to pull the trigger to deliver a formula. She nearly licks her lips, eager to score another kill, when an unexpected shot from her flank hits her defensive shell hard, forcing her to change course.

The Commies lured us out?!

"…A trapper?"

Tanya grinds her teeth in spite of herself. By the time it's clear we've been had, the enemy mage blows past Serebryakov's suppressive fire like it's nothing.

Support won't make it in time, but Tanya's in no position to withdraw, either.

"Fucking hell!"

She puts a hard bend in her flight path to change directions. To ward off the enemy coming up on her flank, Tanya opens fire with her submachine gun.

Chapter **III**

Aware that her magazine is empty, she tries to gain some distance and strains the high-precision Type 97 Assault Computation Orb to accelerate as fast as possible.

"Colonel! Are you all right?!"

"Nothing to worry about!"

She comes very close to being shot two times…but it's not bad enough that the Type 95 needs to come out.

If you concentrate, the Type 97 developed by that miserable, obnoxious mad scientist can deploy a defensive shell that's able to take some hits, just like the new Federation Army model.

"Neither we nor our orbs are lousy enough to get shot down like *that*!" Tanya barks at her subordinates, but inside, she feels exactly the opposite.

There's no way to hide the shock from being taken by surprise so completely.

A Federation mage moving faster than her in close-quarters combat is enough to make me consider this a paradigm shift.

What would the enemy mage have done to Tanya just now if she hadn't had a submachine gun that could fire a hail of bullets?

"…Tch. Man, I really hate these guys."

After just barely slipping away, Tanya turns back to observe the enemy.

Between the rapid approaches and interlocking fire, there's usually little point in distinguishing between the faces of the enemy soldiers, but this time, visual input is the priority. After studying the gear, uniforms, and even the race of the soldiers themselves, it hits me. I thought for sure these mages were from a guard unit, but after watching them for a while, it's very apparent that their uniforms are the normal ones most Federation mages wear. I can't spot any difference in their insignias and so on, either.

Still, is it just me, or…? They seem awfully old. The Federation is currently reorganizing the mage component of its armed forces, so it's rare to see anyone over forty.

Are they instructors? Either way, if the Communists are so pressed that they have to deploy personnel who are no longer young, that's a good sign for us. Maybe the reinforcements Zettour promised will take less time to arrive than expected. Being kept waiting is a drag.

"…This is good news. Although that's not something someone who's just been duped should be saying." With a wry grin, Tanya prepares to fire back and pierce the enemy's defensive shell with an optical sniping formula, hoping to increase her score, but…she can't land any hits.

Not only that, whenever she absentmindedly stops moving to concentrate on aiming, the enemy is relentless in obstructing her. What can she do if she gets immediately shot at before she can even take aim?

"Ngh, shit. They're bizarrely coordinated."

Every time Tanya aims at an enemy's back, she ends up finding a barrel trained on her instead. That's the epitome of how two-man cells should work, but she can't believe the Federation's troops might be even more in sync than her own.

Taking another glance, I note the veteran's wingman is another older fellow. Maybe it's two instructors? That might explain why they have such good coordination. The two of them are so in sync that simply shooting at them isn't enough to break their formation apart.

In which case, there's no choice but to respond to their challenge.

As if at this point reckless bravery is a reasonable option, Tanya rushes them, swinging as if she means to crash, and finally manages to down one of them with her magic blade.

"Damn it, this is taking way too long… What the hell?" she snaps as she surveys the area in open confusion.

The 203rd Aerial Mage Battalion, generally acknowledged as elites in the Imperial Army, the cutting edge in terms of mage operations, is practically evenly matched with these Federation mages, who are supposed to be inferior.

In fact, wouldn't it be fair to say that throughout the entire war, my unit has consistently been on the superior side? As the commander of that elite unit, Tanya honestly has trouble believing what she's seeing.

Federation mages shouldn't be able to perform at this level. Having to judge her own troops and the Federation's by the same standards gives her veteran battalion a worse reputation than it deserves.

And while I'm trying to mull over this in midair, the enemy gleefully takes the opportunity to attack.

"Argh, you're so annoying!"

As Tanya fiercely manifests an explosion formula as a smoke screen and tries to take some distance, she notices that her partner, Serebryakov, has stopped moving.

"Visha! What are you doing?!"

"Colonel! Look at that—the enemy's defensive shells!"

"Hmm? What about them?"

"…Your explosion formula peeled some away!"

"What, really?!" When Serebryakov excitedly points at the enemy, Tanya yelps in shock. The whole reason for struggling in this melee was due to her assumption that the enemy had strong shells.

If area suppression is still effective against them, that changes everything.

"Let's give it a shot!"

With formulas that prioritize range over power, Tanya can keep up with these speedy enemy mages to some extent.

Squinting, she tries to make out the results of her shot, but she can't see any difference in the enemy's movements. Just as she's about to click her tongue in disappointment that it didn't work, she notices out of the corner of her eye a patch of red seeping into the enemy's uniform.

"Turns out they're more fragile than we thought."

If the protective film was blown away and the defensive shell sustained damage, however slight, then the enemy orb's defensive performance is far inferior to what she anticipated.

This is good news. Tanya chuckles to herself.

"Weiss, Wüstemann! These guys aren't using the new model. Don't bother with piercing formulas—focus on area suppression!"

""Huh?!""

The officers' confused voices coming over the radio in harmony are strangely amusing. Apparently, Tanya wasn't the only one laboring under the assumption that the enemy had thick defensive shells.

It must have been due to an erroneous rule of thumb. The resilience of the Federation mages made us recoil, so the preconception of Federation mages as tough enemies had a harmful influence on us.

"It's not a problem even if your aim is slightly off! Ready explosion formulas! Fill the skies with fire! Just do not under any circumstances accidentally hit our troops below!"

""U-understood!""

Good. Tanya shouts more orders over the radio. "01 to all units! 01 to all units! Blow up the entire airspace and the enemy along with it! And put some energy into your defensive shells! Open fire!"

An instant later—as if the order had been a literal trigger—explosion formulas blossom all around them.

Perhaps it's a bit excessive to completely obliterate the airspace above friendly territory. But per the *possibility* and *potential* Federation anti–air positions already demonstrated, being determined enough to simply engulf everything in fire and explosions ends up making many things much easier.

The enemy must not have thought the Imperial Army would go that far. The Federation mages are blown away as the air fills with flames.

But their casualties are surprisingly low.

"Tsk, these guys are stubborn. What a respectable retreat."

Caught up in the explosion, they must have flown away from the blast rather than try to endure it; most of the Federation mages are singed, but their numbers haven't decreased very much.

"These persistent bastards… I guess we have to regroup… Were any of our guys stupid enough to get shot down by friendly fire?"

"Zero dropouts! Some minor burns!"

Tanya chuckles at Serebryakov's report. "Must be thanks to the Type 97s… Glad they were able to put up a better defensive shell than the enemy."

Speed, durability, reliability. Once these orbs, which excel in all three dimensions, can be mass-produced and issued across the board, qualitative superiority will be ours again…if we can find enough mages who can operate them, that is.

At any rate, the enemy mages are retreating.

As far as our aerial support objective goes, all that's left is to repel the Federation ground troops, but…it seems the Federation realized what folly it is to send in the infantry when they don't control the air.

Looking down below, everything seems peaceful. The ground units must have been watching our fight like it was one great big show. How nice…

Oh. Tanya remembers she needs to thank her subordinates.

"Major Weiss, Lieutenant Wüstemann. Nice work, both of you.

Lieutenant, you look too tired to even open your mouth. You can return to base and rest with your troops."

"…Yes, ma'am. If you'll excuse us."

Tanya expresses her gratitude to Wüstemann and has him fall back to the rear, then rejoins Weiss's unit to transition them to aerial patrol. Once they confirm the enemy isn't preparing a follow-up attack, then it'll be time to land and have the troops take a light nap. If the chance presents itself, I'll take one, too.

That's my mindset as we cruise in the air. In this state, Tanya naturally finds herself flying alongside Weiss and asking his opinion on the fight that just ended. The perception they share is that their opponent was unexpectedly formidable. Not only their discipline but even their coordination was incomparable to those of previous Federation mages we've faced before.

I wonder woefully how long we'll have to keep fighting these guys. And then there's Zettour with his unreasonable orders, drawing away one of her companies right as the fighting gets tough.

"…This new opponent's a troublesome one."

"They sure are. But wow, what were those numbskulls in the air fleet talking about? 'No need to worry about air superiority!' Those mages were even cooperating closely with fighter planes! What the hell is going on?"

"Calm down," Tanya reproves him. Actually, not everyone in the world loves war so much that they get giddy at the thought of it. If the air fleet had been napping while we were getting dogged by machine gun fire, I might have agreed with him. But that doesn't match up with reality.

"You know, enemy aerial support was technically cut off, Major."

Our fleet wasn't providing direct fire support, but the enemy air force wasn't flying however they pleased, either. So in the end…our allies did their jobs perfectly, depending on how you look at it.

Even if 100 percent isn't possible, if they did 90 percent of what was required of them, then we have to admit they performed adequately. Overemphasizing perfection leads straight to unpaid overtime and harsh labor conditions.

On that point, the air force delivered on what they promised. It may be difficult for hot-blooded Weiss to comprehend, but frontline units are not the only ones who have to make the best of the circumstances they're in.

"Consider how our aerial patrols can afford to be so lax because our forces are constantly fighting for control of the sky and working hard to force the enemy out of it. We're lucky we don't have to worry about securing our airspace. Thanks to that"—Tanya smirks at the enemy position below—"even if we have to pay attention...at least we can just focus on what's at our altitude."

"You say that, ma'am, but it's gotten harder to use altitude to our advantage..."

"I agree. And I'm sure that's the enemy's intention... Would you look at that? Speak of the devil."

Straight ahead are what look like grains of rice. Though the enemy mages have retreated, they haven't stopped watching us. How much easier this would be if we could just squash them like little bits of rice.

"...Wow. They're even kind enough to leave their signals on."

Of course, given the strength of the mana signatures, they're probably meant to function as a warning to us. If they bathe you in them twenty-four seven as if they're proud of them, you have no choice but to notice.

"They say being self-conscious is the realm of the teenager, but when the enemy boasts about their presence to this extent, it makes me feel like they have something against me personally."

"The Federation Army must have some heroes if someone over there is trying to get you to notice them."

"What's that?" Tanya rolls her eyes and glares at her vice commander, but...the effect is not exactly pronounced.

Is it because she's not tall enough? She may be the boss, but perhaps there are limits to how much she can intimidate her subordinates.

Then her bold adjutant floats over to join them. "Wouldn't they have to be heroes to top all heroes?"

Serebryakov enters the conversation with a smirk—she's sure gotten cheeky. But hold on. If I think back on it, I get the feeling she's been quite consistent since the Rhine. Trying to remember how things were back then, Tanya shoots back with a wry smile, "Troops, do you know what the destiny of heroes is?" It's just goofy chitchat. I shouldn't put too much thought into it. "Heroes—without fail—die. So there's no guarantee that it won't happen now. We'll end the legend of the Federation Army's heroes right here!"

"Ha-ha-ha-ha." The three officers laugh together, dispelling the weighty gloom. It's good to not dwell on the rough fight we just had, and this way, we stay determined. It's a good chance to switch gears.

"But they weren't fooling around out there. I have to admit, they have skills. Weiss, what did you think?"

"I'm with you. Their tactics, coordination, and skills were all at practically the same level as ours."

"This is the biggest pain in the ass. Between the new orb model and these new guys, all our strengths are… Hmm?"

"Colonel?" Weiss asks, "What is it?"

Tanya points to some enemies and murmurs in reply: "That."

As she's pointing them out to her vice commander and adjutant, she tries to identify them from their uniforms.

"…It seems like someone familiar is joining up with them… Are their signals in the library? That's definitely not a Federation unit. Who are they?"

A glance at the vice commander makes it clear he doesn't know. Well, when it comes to languages and intel, neither Weiss nor Tanya can beat Serebryakov. Both their gazes naturally fall on the linguistically talented adjutant.

"Probably Commonwealth? No, one moment, please. I'll try intercepting their signal."

"Did you figure it out?" Tanya presses her.

After listening in for a little while, she gives her conclusion. "…It's a mix of the official languages of the Commonwealth and Entente Alliance."

Ahhh. That's when it hits Tanya. She remembers who this could be.

"The rumored voluntary army? Or some remnants of the regular army? I don't know which, but either way, I wish they were a little lazier. Why did they come all the way out here to the eastern front?"

War isn't something you participate in for your health, so why pay your own way out to a remote place like this? Are they that addicted to battle? It's not a sentiment someone with common sense can understand.

Going along with them would entail only unpaid overtime for the body and mind.

"If there's no movement, we'll fall back by group. It's absurd to waste our strength staying in the air."

Though Tanya talks about pulling out, as long as enemies stick around, withdrawing won't be so easy. At the same time, continuing the confrontation is an exercise in futility.

It's a staring contest where we can only watch helplessly as time passes. Ultimately, we stay in the sky for a while, and both sides eventually fall back only after maintaining this standoff for several hours. It's a confrontation that tires everyone out for no reason at all—if the enemy's aim was to exhaust us, they have without a doubt succeeded. There's no point in grumbling that it should have been the amateur Federation side who dropped out first.

Landing and tumbling into her semi-submerged room that apparently used to be a storehouse, Tanya takes up her pen to write her report before she forgets what happened.

If the combat they just experienced is going to be the new standard, the Imperial Army urgently needs a plan to handle it.

The final report is pessimistic even for me.

The qualitative improvement of the Federation's mages will tighten the noose around the Imperial Army's neck. If the Empire loses its edge in the aerial mage realm, where in the world will it be able to make that up?

Reading it over, Tanya sighs. "…Still, there's not even a guarantee anyone will read this seriously."

The Imperial Army's culture allows relatively open communication, but for better or worse, it's also a military organization that closely follows doctrine and its own preconceptions. Just because I sound the alarm about the dramatic improvement in the quality of Federation troops doesn't mean anyone will take it at face value.

The higher-ups will probably be wary or pay attention.

But I can easily imagine a future where they understand with their brains and that's all; they probably won't be capable of *feeling* how serious the situation is.

That's how much Tanya's report is at odds with the prevailing common sense.

I'm the one who wrote it, but even I can hardly believe it. If not for the fact that Tanya personally witnessed it in battle, reading that the threat of Federation aerial mages has rapidly increased would just seem like a mere rhetorical flourish. No one will read this and immediately believe it—virtually everyone will scoff that she's overreacting.

"Argh, how can I explain it?"

Conveying things to other people seems simple but is actually quite difficult. You can write down the truth and call it a factual report, but it takes some finessing to actually get your message across.

Make your point clear, keep your audience in mind, and adhere to an intuitive structure.

"Always easier said than done… This is such a pain. Haaah…" Tanya sighs and takes up her pen again.

Compared to when we burned Moskva, yes, they do have more troops. But improving their quality is in a completely different universe compared to simply having more. If you could immediately get the fighting power of a bunch of veterans by just hiring a slew of part-timers, the word *education* would have to go straight into the trash. In reality, the importance of education has only increased.

And yet the improvement in discipline the Federation aerial mage units have showed is remarkable—like an unnatural burst of instant fighting power. If that doesn't come across properly in Tanya's report, it'll be taken too lightly.

Pointing out the issue isn't so difficult—it's what comes after that's the challenge.

"This is what it means for something to be illogical," Tanya murmurs and begins to review the situation. While gnawing on a military-issue high-calorie chocolate bar, she reads over the reports from each company.

The only commonality she finds among them is the comment that they fought on an equal level with the Federation troops or were slightly superior. Try as she might, she can't locate the key to understanding the phenomenon.

Is it just my imagination?

"That can't be. No matter what lies I tell myself, no matter how I try to gloss it over, the only conclusion I can draw is that the enemy has dramatically reduced their vulnerabilities." Grumbling, she tosses the half-written report into the trash can.

A report requires a concise conclusion. Reporting to her superiors that the Federation units have better discipline now for reasons unknown would only be an admission of ineptitude.

And even worse, this is a job that's been entrusted to her. In the worst case, if she could at least take personal responsibility for everything, things would be less complicated. As long as she was prepared to accept the consequences, she could still send it without too much worry.

But this is an official report from the Lergen Kampfgruppe to the General Staff submitted under Colonel von Lergen's name. Screwing up here would mean dragging his name through the mud.

Surely, there's no better way to brazenly harm someone's career than to cause discord between them and their team. And if the bit about using his name ever came out…the aftermath would be unspeakably awful.

"But what am I supposed to do, then…?"

Turning her attention back to drafting seriously, Tanya begins to get frustrated and grips her stomach as she moans. How should I write this?

There isn't enough information to properly analyze the situation. Conveying only the fact that the quality of the Federation troops has improved and leaving the interpretation up to her superiors would be one way of doing it, but…nothing short of Tanya's best will do.

When you're feeling lost, it's time to go back to basics.

"Let's review the current enemy situation. All I know is that they've dramatically improved, but…what is this weird feeling?"

It's precisely because Tanya whipped the 203rd Aerial Mage Battalion into shape within a month that she knows this level of change is impossible.

Having abused the limits of humanity—or rather, the limits of the limits—Tanya knows that, frankly, qualitative improvements to aerial mage units aren't easy to come by in periods of weeks or months.

Even with the selection process based on which active-duty officers seemed to have the basics down, and even after the live-fire exercise in Dacia, she still had some concerns about discipline.

The concept is even easier to grasp when looking at Wüstemann's company.

Despite giving the earnest, young, inexperienced officer on-the-job training on the eastern lines, he's far from being on Ahrens's or Meybert's level; he might not even match up to Tospan.

The fundamentals make that much difference.

Taking someone from .5 to 1 and taking someone from 0 to 1 are worlds apart.

"...The Federation's progress is too fast."

As someone with her own views on education, Tanya has little choice but to question the dramatic change in quality. "Could an overhaul of their system really have had such a pronounced effect?"

It's a little strange for her to say so, but systemic reform can't happen overnight—even if we assume the Federation has become a more independent organization of military specialists unconcerned with political circumstances. There are limits to what's possible.

Improving how units operate isn't the same as improving their skills.

Logically, it's understandable how perfectly utilizing weak soldiers can allow the enemy to pose a real threat. There's even the classic metaphor of how a flock of sheep led by a wolf is more dangerous than a pack of wolves led by a sheep.

But then Tanya smiles wryly.

"If a company could bounce into the black tomorrow simply by changing one top executive, no one would have any problems. Or maybe that's a bit of an extreme comparison?"

The wolf leading the sheep still only has sheep to fight with. Certainly, it's helpful to train sheep into wolves.

But that process isn't as simple as heating up instant food.

Education takes manpower. Even on-the-job training requires an instructor. Just leading Wüstemann around is already exhausting.

Learning by doing without an instructor may involve less effort, but it must take a stupid amount of time.

"Something's different. What is it? How did they improve so dramatically?"

It's because I have experience working human resources that Tanya can't help but act suspicious.

There's a contradiction here. The strength of the Federation's aerial mage forces has jumped, but results aside, I can't tell how it happened.

Employment, I can explain.

If it's just about getting the critical magic personnel together, they can probably reach head count by drafting every single person who shows the aptitude. Expanding the scope of the draft means recruiting more.

But how exactly has the Federation overcome the issues of teaching staff and time? Recruiting, education, and management are the pillars of human resources; I've never seen a new recruit who doesn't require training. A combat-ready rookie is either a fantasy or a rare exception.

Planning your human resources according to that would be going against statistics—i.e., idiotic.

"...I'm fairly sure the Federation doesn't have the surplus that would afford them a bevy of instructors. Their army was incapable of operating systematically before. Where did they find so many key personnel?"

Comparing the Federation aerial mage forces to the other arms of the Federation military reveals a striking weakness. They must be training up mages at this very moment. If the foundation is fragile, then it's natural to assume that the talent pool they're drawing from is thin as well.

"Isn't that a contradiction? Still, it's consistent..."

To use the metaphor of a company to describe the Federation military, they've simply inflated their employee count by hiring lots of new grads. Liars are the only ones with the patent for thinking they can still conduct business smoothly like that.

Of course, experience in the real world is a great teacher.

I do recognize that soldiers fighting on the front lines will naturally accumulate experience. To some extent, they must be bringing know-how back. Still, it's a question of whether a baby bird can make it out of its shell or not—that depends on their initial average skill level. Even if some of them were instantly transferred to instructor positions, getting results so quickly should be all but impossible.

Questioning this all at her desk in her underground room isn't going to get Tanya anywhere. Standing up for a change of pace, she rolls her shoulders and adds another twist to her line of thinking.

"Normally, this kind of boost would indicate mid-career hires from outside the company. Or maybe a service that provides training or instructors? In this case, it must be the latter..."

When major corporations, worried about being understaffed, do massive hiring rounds, it's not uncommon for them to outsource the training. And here, too, the Commonwealth and Unified States probably have a vested interest in training Federation troops.

Or perhaps they're using former Republic or Entente Alliance personnel as instructors.

"There's demand, and there's supply. That's everything required for a perfect overlapping of desires."

But that logic only works with capitalism. The Federation Commies will stay Red to the bitter end. They may be fighting the Empire out of nationalism, but if people had a chance to escape the ideology completely, there most likely wouldn't even be a Communist Party.

Would that party really want its army to be trained by officers from capitalist countries?

Even if the Commies overcame that conflict of interest, each country has its own doctrines. Can something new be applied so rapidly in the middle of a war?

Even if they resolve all those issues, is it possible to get results this fast?

"No, it's really just impossible."

The enemy is undeniably adaptable, and I'm not about to start underestimating them. Still, the word *reality* deserves some emphasis here. In this case, the only answer is mid-career hires.

But unlike a corporation, the Federation is a country. The state has a monopoly on violence—that is to say, it's the worst sort of monopolistic enterprise.

"Where could they even hire from?" Tanya grumbles as if to say, *You've got to be kidding.*

Does this mean even Commies have the concept of competition on the civilian level? But then it wouldn't make sense that the quality of Soviet consumer products is so consistently abysmal. There's no way the same people who had to recruit specialists from the *lageri* have the redundancy for that.

......*Wait.* There, Tanya freezes.

This is only a theory, a preposterous supposition, but...could they be hiring those guys?

The Federation Army existed before it became the party's army. In other words...there's a pool of mid-career human resources that could potentially be recruited.

"Shit, shit, shit! So that's what they're doing!!"

It hits me only after saying it aloud—I deserve to be shot by firing squad for my obliviousness. What an incredible lack of imagination. How could I think so dogmatically—what am I, a Commie?!

"The *lageri*! Argh, fucking Commies! You should have just killed them all in the camps!"

Apparently, these Communists are strangely talented at holding on to things.

In propaganda, they denounced political prisoners as enemies of their state, as class enemies, as reactionaries, as relics of the abominable past—and yet, they preserved a ton of them in the *lageri*.

Worse, Tanya knows next to nothing about those guys. If they were useless fools, that would be one thing. But having fought them…it's obvious they're skilled.

"…Who would be familiar with Federation Army mage units from the previous era?"

Though Tanya's military career is rich due to the ongoing war, it's inevitably still *commensurate with her age*. Thus, even she hasn't had the opportunity to hear from the generation who knew the Federation as the empire it used to be. After twenty years pass, it's not uncommon for institutional memory to fade, no matter how or why it happens.

"Talk about information asymmetry. Inheriting and passing down knowledge sure is hard. What a nightmare!"

I don't know.

In other words: ignorance.

War is governed by the fundamental premise: If you don't know, it's your fault. *No one told you? So what?*—that sort of thing.

Gentle egalitarians may advise that brandishing knowledge is unfair, but knowledge is power. In a war, the side that can employ more power than a school has the edge.

If you're looking for war without knowledge, you probably have to go back to pre–Stone Age—ape-men level if possible—scuffles.

So I ask myself…

Do you know your enemy?

"…No, not at all."

I've prepped and reviewed with all the available intel. If I still don't know, that means that information on the pre-revolution Federation Army magic units is missing from the official record.

How were they taught?

What were their doctrines?

I don't know a single thing about them.

Tanya is uninformed—to a vexing degree. Basically, no one in the army has any understanding of the current situation. In an age with no Internet, once you lose touch with a memory or record, it might actually be lost forever.

This certainly throws a wrench in things. We can't fight a war if we don't know the enemy. I can't believe I only just noticed this massive gap in our knowledge! Even if the war itself is a waste to begin with, we have to at least win it—argh!

In short, we need to dig up ancient records. Luckily, I'm fairly certain there was contact with them in the past. As far as Tanya can tell, contact means that there should be old data left somewhere inside the bureaucratic system.

"The problem is labor! All I see in my future is labor!"

Data that haven't been organized...

Any member of an organization knows what a headache unorganized data are. Take a mountain of uncategorized receipts, for instance. Or having to find an important document in a warehouse.

How lucky for you if you even know which warehouse it's in.

Oftentimes you don't know where to start looking. That's especially true of documents that aren't handed off properly. No matter how valuable the data, it's hard for it not to be lost in a pile of junk the moment the person in charge of it transfers out of the department.

It's not malice, incompetence, or laziness but simply the reality that unused things are forgotten.

Even if Tanya makes a request, imagining the amount of time it will take for someone to find what she needs is dizzying.

"The library needs to be turned inside out. Those data must be in the General Staff Office somewhere. I have to get them to find them for me."

I won't apply as myself but as Colonel von Lergen. After all, I'm stuck in this situation operating under his name. If a donkey can borrow a lion's skin, who would say no?

I have to get them on it right away. Tanya steels herself.

She rushes out of her room and heads to the duty officer's post. After momentarily scanning for a certain person—there she is!

Seeing Serebryakov jump up and salute like she's spring powered makes Tanya smile to herself in satisfaction.

There's no time to spare returning the salute, but rules are rules. She moves her arm slightly to perform the regulation motion and races through greetings to get down to business. "Lieutenant Serebryakov, this is an emergency. Set up a long-distance call with the General Staff Office. I'd like to send an officer with the message, but the situation being what it is, this will have to do. Use the strongest cipher possible and hurry."

"Yes, ma'am! I'll go wake up the crypto personnel right away. What is it you need exactly?"

"A request in Colonel von Lergen's name to recheck the data we have on the Federation Army. Or rather, I need to get them to dig up some documents that are in the process of becoming history. Naturally, this is of the highest priority."

"Huh?"

Tanya elaborates after seeing her adjutant's blank expression. "The enemy improved too quickly. I can only conclude that rather than training up new recruits, they've begun sourcing an instant fighting force from somewhere else."

If she asks using the name of someone from Operations, the General Staff is sure to process it as an internal request.

It's not good to discriminate based on who is asking and via what channel, but prioritization hierarchies are a reality of bureaucracy.

In order to light a fire under their asses, Tanya needs to exploit every trick in the book.

"I'm fairly certain they've mixed in some troops from before the army turned Commie. In other words, there's a very good chance that some veteran aces are mixed in."

"You'll have to excuse me, but I find that hard to believe. Class enemies of the type that would normally be sent to the *lageri*...? This is the Federation we're talking about."

"Lieutenant Serebryakov, I appreciate your perspective. Your insight and sensibility are valuable."

Chapter **III**

As far as the issue of the Federation goes, it's dangerous to disregard the opinions of those with experience. That said, there's a nonzero chance of reality betraying historical trends.

"And I'm grateful for your advice and assistance. I respect you as a professional, Lieutenant; however, I will give you this warning with confidence."

To know something is to be clad in preconceived notions. It's fundamentally the same issue the army faces as an organization that relies too heavily on preconceptions of what is supposedly common sense. As a sensible person herself, Tanya can sympathize with Serebryakov's misunderstanding.

It's true that if you're familiar with the Commie ideology, it's hard to think that they would simply release people from the *lageri*. But they can sure do it anyway.

"Don't get caught up in the Communists' official position. They can talk out of three sides of their mouths. If they find something that lets them infuriate people, they'll be as diligent about it as religious fanatics." Tanya practically spits the words out in exasperation. "Forget principles. These Commies are driven more by their needs in the moment than their ideology. Authoritarians in the guise of revolutionaries have always used this trick—it's no surprise."

Commies, Commies, Commies.

You could call them an awful societal reaction.

So what's so formidable about them? Tanya knows well. She can't help but understand.

"These bastards steal causes for their own ends. Expect the worst."

"...Understood."

"I'm really getting sick of this. Arrogant ideologues are simple, but patriots? They really get in the way."

What a pain when they operate according to not logic but love for their Heimat. Modernity is the age of love. Unconditional confessions of adoration to a shared construct known as the state.

Blind love.

What a heartwarming, maddeningly saccharine, and elegant poison.

"Truly, what a pain in the neck."

It's extremely difficult to talk of love in Tanya's language. It's absurd. Love is nothing but a bundle of absurdities and irrationality.

But if there's one thing that's clear, it's this:

Love transcends logic.

That much is true. Even if you add the caveat "for certain types of people," it's a major threat. The world is rife with people ready to challenge logic.

It's a world lifetimes removed from Tanya's, but sadly, it exists.

>>> **JUNE 16, UNIFIED YEAR 1927, B GROUP HEADQUARTERS ON** <<<
THE EASTERN FRONT, OFFICE FOR HIGH-RANKING OFFICERS

Though his job as inspector was only nominal, this unexpected opportunity to directly observe the situation in the field was more than welcome.

It didn't exactly compare to leisurely desk work, where he could kick back in an easy chair with a smoking pipe, but it did allow him to see things he couldn't as the deputy chief of the Service Corps back at the General Staff Office.

Of course, you could say the imperial bureaucracy was the best-appointed organization of its era. Details about the situation on the eastern front were collected, analyzed, and delivered along the proper channels to the General Staff Office.

And to be assertive about picking up information himself, Zettour made efforts to stay in touch with and receive reports and advice from mid-ranking officers such as Lergen, Uger, and Degurechaff.

But the world is full of surprises. They weren't kidding when they said a picture is worth a thousand words.

"I'll send relief. That's for sure."

He had promised it, so it was his duty. But faced with reality, even Lieutenant General von Zettour was forced into internal anguish.

This is too awful.

He thought he had understood their plight on paper, but compared to reality, it seemed positively optimistic. The B Front's defensive lines were literally theoretical. It made sense why the B Group staffers were apprehensive.

Logically, one could say that as a conclusion, it was incorrect. But emotionally, he understood the reason for their confusion.

It was clear at a glance when he compared the situation to the Rhine front. Frankly, it was absurd to even call these lines. It was less like units stationed at various points along a contiguous front and more like they were simply defending their individual positions.

The battle to break out Lieutenant Colonel von Degurechaff's Lergen Kampfgruppe would be difficult.

Getting a unit there without overexposing its flank or losing its edge—and most importantly, before it was too late—was going to be… quite a challenge.

The only thing that Zettour felt conflicted about was how relieved he felt that it was Degurechaff he had made the bait. If the enemy hadn't taken the poisoned lure, they would have been forced to halt a real army with defensive lines that existed only on paper.

Thank God and fatherland that the Federation Army didn't commit to a reckless charge.

"…Air force attrition is occurring at three times the rate we anticipated. The drop operational tempo is getting serious; we won't be able to maintain air superiority for long like this."

Though control of the sky was a minimum requirement, the eastern army didn't have much strength to spare in the first place. Even considering concentration of forces in the west to handle the aerial battles breaking out there, the standards here could only be described as poor.

"I thought we annihilated the Federation's air force in Operation Iron Hammer… Does that really mean…?" He murmured and sighed at the photograph in his hand. It was a picture shot by an imperial air force gun camera depicting a fighter plane that looked to be of Unified States's make.

It was pleasant to see it bursting into flames, but the enemy plane was the one on fire because this was the picture in his possession. Plenty of imperial aircraft had been shot down, too. Surely the enemy gun cameras (nice ones with nice film from the Unified States) had photographed the reverse happening.

"What an utter pain."

A murmur of perplexity.

He understood with his brain, but something was still bothering him. Zettour shook his head to try to clear the strange feeling out of his mind and stared at the aerial photo.

"…The colors are awfully faded."

Acquiring aircraft parts was the highest priority, but the quality was still inferior enough that the colors seemed muted. Apparently, the Council for Self-Government was urgently procuring former Federation Army gear.

"Actively using seized gear...? I guess it makes sense that wouldn't be emphasized in the reports. I suppose in the end...it's the same sort of issue as the socks."

Maybe it was different to inquire about. He could clearly recall Colonel von Lergen, back from his inspection of the front lines, relaying the issue of the socks.

He had spoken so hesitantly, everyone thought something horrible had happened on the front, but what it ended up being was socks. All the staff officers were absolutely baffled. But at least it was something they could understand if they listened...

"Bizarrely, until someone explained it to us, we were incapable of understanding. How much of the information the front deems not worth saying are we able to pick up in the rear...? It's concerning..."

The administration considered itself to be working hard to understand the front lines as much as possible. That went for Zettour and every member of the organization.

The socks oversight was due to a difference in awareness or a gap in perception. It was an example of how cultural obstacles regulate group thoughts and actions more than most people imagined. Apparently, old paradigms make their presence felt when you're not looking.

"I thought being on the front lines myself and breathing the same air would give me a different perspective, but...only now that I've seen it do I realize things can't go on like this."

The front lines were captive to their circumstances, and the rear was captive to theirs. He could understand the reasons and the circumstances behind B Group's reluctance, but they weren't being terribly inventive. So did someone in the rear have a big plan to turn things around...? The maneuvers via Ildoa had hit a setback, and the fact that he was even here meant the situation was no laughing matter.

He did let Colonel Calandro know thereafter that he still wanted to stay in touch and strive for improvement, but frankly, it was clear that the Empire had put a damper on Ildoa's efforts to mediate.

Sadly, what Zettour felt keenly standing on the front lines was that nobody fully grasped what was happening out here.

There was Supreme Command, the General Staff, the army, the government, and they all considered themselves strategists, but what they actually decided was the strategic level, and the foundational grand strategy it should have been nesting under had yet to materialize.

"A huge war with no guiding principles... Before the war, I would have laughed in the face of such an idea, saying *How could something so foolish come to pass?*"

...It was a height of stupidity he couldn't have imagined, and it made him sick.

The Imperial Army most likely doesn't have enough combat units. Can the Empire really take on the world like this?

Unfortunately, it wasn't his job to worry about that.

"...It really is concerning."

〉〉〉   **THE SAME DAY, THE GENERAL STAFF OFFICE**   〈〈〈

Though at night they conducted a thorough blackout, the General Staff Office was a fortress that never slept, like the beating administrative heart of the Empire.

So though it was nighttime, Lieutenant General von Rudersdorf was roused from his dozing by the clamorous ringing of the telephone.

"General von Rudersdorf, it's Lieutenant Colonel Uger. Terribly sorry to bother you while you're sleeping, but I have a report."

"Thanks. What is it?" He was used to calls interrupting his light sleep.

When Rudersdorf urged Uger to continue, the lieutenant colonel made his report apologetically. "There was another nighttime raid on the lowland industrial zone."

The aerial war in the west was in a lull, but both sides were doing everything their cunning could come up with to harass each other; it was turning into a spiteful conflict far removed from the sort Rudersdorf preferred.

"...They couldn't stop the enemy planes?"

"The air force was in charge of interception; they're drawing up the report of their accomplishments now. The ratio they managed to down wasn't bad, but if we want to stop every enemy, we need numerical superiority…"

He's serious, thought Rudersdorf with a wince and asked about the important part—how they would respond. "Colonel Uger, what's Zettour doing about it?"

"The other day he coordinated with the Foreign Office to denounce the attacks for violating the law of war. These are bombings on population centers with no warnings, so they're publicizing that fact to third parties and condemning them."

Whoa, hold on. Rudersdorf's mouth fell open.

"…I had heard about it, but can the Service Corps expand their activities so much without running shorthanded?"

"All we're really doing is compiling the damage reports."

It wouldn't do to forget how Zettour had warned him not to work his subordinates too hard when they were already so understaffed.

His intention was to bring up a slight concern, but Uger replied in an unfazed tone that it was nothing…which only made Rudersdorf realize he really did have to be careful how he worked the man.

"I appreciate your diligence. Is our protest and propaganda war having an effect?"

"Formally, not at all. At about the same time as this bombing, we got a response from the Commonwealth via the embassy of a neutral country—stating that the recent bombings are being carried out by *Federation air units; we of the Commonwealth* are not involved."

Rudersdorf sighed in spite of himself.

"You can't get any Commonwealth prisoners out of the planes you're shooting down?"

"They just claim that they're Commonwealth, but they left home to join up with the Federation air force."

"These guys have a comeback for everything, talking out of three sides of their mouths! It's so annoying! How thick-skinned can they be?!" He didn't mean to start shouting, but he realized with a wince that he'd raised his voice before he even realized. *Oops.*

Chapter **III**

It wasn't that he didn't understand the logic of the legal debate; he just didn't see himself ever enjoying these conniving, roundabout ways of putting things.

"...Sorry, Colonel Uger. Please bear with me until Colonel von Lergen gets back."

"No, General von Zettour told me to support you with everything I can muster. I'm at your service. Supporting the front lines is precisely what those in the rear are meant to do."

That may have been the model view, but the fact that he could express it calmly while on night duty...was astounding.

"You're really a no-nonsense guy, huh?"

"Sir?"

The puzzled reply made Rudersdorf wish they weren't speaking over the phone. He would have liked to see what kind of face the colonel was making.

"I'm impressed you didn't burn out serving under General von Zettour. He asks too much of people."

"More than a few of the people I joined up with are on the front lines now. I believe it's my job to do everything I can on my own battlefield to help them. An officer warming a seat in the rear can't complain."

"That's the ideal view for a matériel mobilization officer to have. Very good," he continued, aware that he had taken the conversation on a tangent. He steered them back toward the job at hand. "Colonel Uger. The plan to supply the ongoing Operation Andromeda is questionable. General von Zettour told me that the railways were the magic key, so I want to confirm... There're no problems with transportation itself at present?"

"The public safety operation the Council for Self-Government conducted was a success, so the railways themselves have been freed from the threat of bandits. The issue with track standards is still fairly pressing...but since it's neither winter nor the muddy season, we can squeak by with recovered rolling stock and on-the-spot rail repairs." Uger said he was handling it, but the situation he spoke of wasn't nearly as encouraging. "The bottleneck isn't the supply lines but the supply itself. Since the industrial production zone has been forced to introduce measures against the nightly air raids, production has taken a hit."

"Specifically?"

"Even the blackout policy inevitably has a negative effect when factories are operating around the clock."

That wasn't hard to believe. A blackout hinders efficiency by definition. Having to guarantee continuous operations in the middle of the night during a mandatory blackout must have been miserable.

But without the blackout *and* continuous operations, logistics would crumble.

"…So having our industrial base in the west has become a vulnerability for the Empire…"

The historical how and why that led the Empire's manufacturing to be clustered within range of the Commonwealth's air force was certainly unfortunate at this juncture. The worry of night raids had always loomed, and now that they were actually happening, Rudersdorf just wanted to hold his head in his hands.

"We have to come up with a better air defense plan ASAP. Thanks, Colonel Uger. Keep up the good work on matériel mobilization."

"Yes, sir!"

After putting down the receiver with a *click* and releasing a sigh, Rudersdorf took out a cigar and began smoking to try and buoy his spirits.

Understanding—at this late date—the pains Zettour had been going through with managing matériel was frustrating.

…There are just too many issues to worry about.

If the enemy is trying to reduce our capacity, then we should reduce theirs, too.

Recomposing himself, he held his cigar in his mouth while picking up the receiver he was so familiar with and dialing a number.

"Operations, it's me. Sorry for the late call, but what ended up being the story with that bunch of ships of unknown nationality?"

"According to reports from the Northern Sea Fleet's patrol craft and submarines, the convoy is growing larger. We figure it's the Federation swiftly filling in the losses they sustained at the beginning of the war."

A simple and clear report. It painted a picture of enemy distribution that was only growing stronger, much to his disgust.

"We can't board them? I'd like to stop them if possible."

"The navy says it's difficult. They're being escorted by the Commonwealth Home Fleet, so with our surface fleet, it's…"

The officer from Operations probably didn't mean to say as much, but…*Our fleet can't compete with the Commonwealth's navy* wasn't the sort of report Rudersdorf wanted to hear.

But for better or worse…he was getting used to hearing it. He wished they would figure something out…

"Why can't they use marine mages? Shouldn't the navy be able to think of that?"

"The navy has only a small cohort of aerial mages. There aren't enough to force the issue. And other mages would need to be trained in maritime navigation before they will be able to be of any use keeping an eye out for the enemy."

"So bridging the gap will take time." He grumbled, "Nothing to be done about it now, I suppose."

…Andromeda was an offensive predicated on the assumption that the enemy didn't have much energy left. If the assumption that both sides were hurting was shattered, success became extremely doubtful.

It was irritating that they couldn't grasp the enemy's movements, but depending on how well outfitted their opponents were, the Empire would have to also consider how feasible it was to hold on to their occupied territories.

"Can you get a handle on the influx into the southern zones?"

"The Federation's counterintelligence is frustratingly perfect. That weirdo Loria from the Commissariat for Internal Affairs is a capable weirdo, so he's just all-around nasty."

"Things are that bad?"

"He keeps secrets locked down with unbelievable zeal and a stubborn attention to detail. For HUMINT, we have to rely on the former Federation Council for Self-Government, but for things outside the zones where their people aren't—"

Rudersdorf interrupted, as if to say he'd heard enough. "Hurry up the analysis of our aerial reconnaissance. And what about breaking their code?"

"The crypto warfare section is borderline overworked. Federation Army codes used to be easy to break, but they've been getting a lot stronger."

"It's like being smoke screened at every turn. And we're supposed to keep fighting a war like this?"

Cutting off his subordinate's apology, Rudersdorf got to thinking. *If the enemy is going to skirt the law, two can play at the game… We should follow suit.*

"We have to stop the enemy convoy from delivering those supplies… Isn't there some approach we haven't tried yet?"

There should have been one method for pinching off the flow that they had been considering.

"We had that one plan, whatever it was, right?"

"You mean unrestricted submarine warfare?"

"Yes, that," replied Rudersdorf.

"…There's a large risk of violating the law of war… Are you certain that's wise?"

The hesitation in the Operations man's voice was exasperating. *Laws again?* "We have to avoid possible complications and keep it legal somehow. I want someone researching loopholes in the law."

"The navy's legal division points to the wartime contraband regulations and limitations of the safe sea passage policy. But the specialists in these laws say that the inspection rules weren't made with subs in mind, so that discrepancy could be dangerous."

Rudersdorf wanted to answer, *Why should I care?* but he couldn't ignore the argument.

This was the moment he really resented Supreme Command for banishing Zettour to the eastern front. Rudersdorf wasn't very good at the precise language and grammar necessary for legal interpretation.

How much easier this would be if I could just throw it all at him…

"…Right, thanks. Anyhow, keep looking into it for now."

"Yes, sir."

After hanging up, Rudersdorf smoked his cigar in silence for a time. A few thoughts came and went through his mind, but, rare for a man whose MO in normal times was decisive, quick action…he wasn't sure what to do.

"I'm stuck, huh?"

It's not like me, but it's unsurprising, given the circumstances.

"Apparently, not having him around really throws me off… Guess I'll have to answer my own questions."

Down with overtime.
Workers of the world,
oppose overtime!

——— Lergen Kampfgruppe slogan, from the base at Soldim 528 ———

If I write that fortifying the position at the Soldim 528 position is going slow…is that a contradiction? A position not being a position yet does seem to go against common military sense.

But that's where we're at in reality. There's a serious shortage of materials. As a result, we're having to make do with what's on hand using that creative ingenuity known as the wisdom of the field.

A classic example would be using an underground storehouse as a subterranean trench, perhaps? And that is exactly where Lieutenant Colonel Tanya von Degurechaff has posted herself.

At that moment, about to face a major Federation Army offensive, she is savoring a light nap in her uncomfortable, underground pseudo-bed.

A familiar sound comes closer.

It's always the sound of shell impacts that wakes her.

"…Tch. As usual, it's a bit too loud for a pleasant wake-up call." Jumping up and putting on her cap, she remembers the Rhine, dwelling on the irritating memories. They say memories are beautiful, but there was nothing beautiful about the Rhine.

Tanya shakes her head. Some things are an improvement.

For instance, the environment.

Instead of soaking in muddy trenches, she can go straight to the battlefield from a crumbling, partially submerged pseudo-bedroom; that should probably be celebrated as a cozy work-from-home situation.

"Enemy attack! Enemy attack! All units, prepare for combat! I say again, all units, prepare for combat!"

The belated alarm that rings out and the tension slipping into the voice calling everyone to arms are unmissable harbingers of large-scale combat. Since we've been expecting it, given the increasing pressure from the enemy over the past few days, it's all too easy to realize that this is a major Federation offensive—there's no room for misunderstanding.

"Damn Commies. Working overtime is against your ideology!"

Diligently preparing to attack, getting units into position, coordinating between artillery and infantry—that's not the sort of work that can be wrapped up by quitting time. Even a well-disciplined unit like the Salamander Kampfgruppe would take weeks to finish a job like that working only five hours a day. Commies say they protect workers' rights, but they're swindling labor out of people more effectively than the capitalists.

With rage against injustice, unfairness, and deviance in her breast, Tanya swears to herself that this cheapening of labor will not stand. This unfair competition can't be forgiven. Everything must be done fairly.

Waiting for Tanya when she arrives at the command post bunker in a whirlwind of righteous indignation are reports from Captain Ahrens and Captain Meybert, who were on duty. The gist is that the enemy has come out raring for a fight.

And even while she is being briefed, the command post is a flurry of activity. First, Lieutenant Serebryakov appears with a message from Major Weiss, who is standing by with the battalion for rapid response. At the same time, communications personnel are relaying the info to B Group HQ and requesting reinforcements from the air fleet.

Everything is being handled according to procedure.

Thankfully, that affords Tanya, the commander, some, if not much, time—more precious than gold—to think about their situation.

"If the enemy is coming, our only option is to fight back, huh?" Tanya murmurs to herself.

For a commander on the defense, it's less something that needs to be anticipated and more of a…preestablished harmony. And to be frank, there isn't much room for inventive approaches to countering the enemy attack, either.

"Captain Ahrens, what's the status of the armored forces?"

"They're all still hidden in shelters. No losses."

Without her needing to ask, Meybert gathers that she wants to hear from him as well. "Same for the artillery. Apart from the squad providing sporadic support to the infantry, the guns are being saved for later… although about ten percent of our remaining shells got caught in an explosion."

"That was a tough blow the other day. Getting our food bombed to bits was a frustrating failure."

It isn't clear whether it's preparatory bombardments, harassment, or the Federation just showing off their guns, but their artillery has been causing damage to Soldim 528.

Construction on the position is running behind because of a lack of materials. That's not fatal, but it's enough trouble that it's hard to be optimistic. Compared to the days on the Rhine front, this war is so wretched, I almost want to cry.

Before, it was like materials grew on trees. These days, there isn't even enough space to store what ammo and rations we do have. There aren't enough protected areas. Thanks to that, supplies are basically stored in bivouacs, and stray enemy shots have blown away some of our temporary storage.

Maybe it would be worth it to gather the scorched wheat. But exploded shells could hardly be rounded up and reused. Recycling has its limits.

"All right, if we have enemy infantry on our periphery…are we finally facing an all-out offensive?"

The enemy's movements conform perfectly to a classic assault. The infantry inches ahead and attacks after a few days' preparation. Meanwhile, the side under siege piles up all the ammo it can find and waits. Textbook offense and defense.

Suddenly, Tanya realizes something is missing. To name it: the trumpet calling for the charge, the preparatory bombardment that is the modern-day Gjallarhorn. It's indispensable even for an attack by aerial mages to take control of the sky.

This is the theory.

For a tactical sneak attack, a short, concentrated bombardment is considered a suitable solution, but normally, supporting artillery fire is an essential element of an offensive.

"It's not even a night raid, so it's weird that they're not doing a thorough preparatory bombardment."

"But, Colonel, they probably don't have that many shells, either, right?"

Tanya nearly nods in response to Meybert's plausible remark but resists the temptation; we can't cave to optimism.

As a rule, anything that can't be declared confidently is a hypothesis. Above all, I have a bad feeling about the Federation lately. It's a state blessed with matériel. Even if they're struggling, would the enemy really send in their infantry with no support besides that sparse scattering of shells that landed a little while ago?

"We need to keep in mind the possibility that it's a ruse to make us think that."

Though it's true that enemy bombardments are prone to cutting off. That makes this tricky.

"At present, the enemy artillery are temporarily inactive. We should treat this as a rare opportunity. The question is how much pressure the enemy infantry will put on us. That depends on how long Lieutenant Tospan's unit can hold out…"

We can't expect much from him is what I really think.

In the worst case, Tanya will have to pull a pseudo–command group move like the Federation Army again. She's prepared to go out there, kick the infantry's ass with Serebryakov, and even arrange for a diaper if she must.

Tanya's adjutant, clinging to the comms equipment, interrupts her train of thought with a shout.

"Lieutenant Tospan would like to make a suggestion!"

"What? Lieutenant Tospan? Give it here." She snatches the receiver away from Serebryakov. The hunch that the expected headache has just arrived sends a chill up her spine.

We have enough on our plate with just the Commies. We'll borrow any help we can get our hands on at this point. We've already hit our limits. Just try and pull some stupid shit, Lieutenant Tospan. I may be a sensible individual, but you'll learn that my patience is finite.

"This is Lieutenant Colonel von Degurechaff. I'll thank you to keep it brief, Lieutenant Tospan."

"Yes, ma'am. Then may I have your orders?"

"Orders?" Caught off guard, she merely parrots the word back at him. She's already given instructions for the defensive line. The defense plan has been drawn up, the personnel positioned—everyone knows how things should flow.

At the last minute, surrounded and under attack, what orders could she possibly have for the commander of the infantry stationed on the defensive line?

The only thing there ever is to do is defend. He shouldn't have to confirm that with the commander of the Kampfgruppe back at HQ.

"Sorry, Lieutenant Tospan. What do you mean, orders? I'm fairly certain I already issued them. If it's the plan for directing the defense, you should have received it earlier."

"Yes, Colonel. About that, as a rule, the army would have us retreat when facing an enemy attack of this scale. But if we can't do that, it's possible for the commander of the unit to issue orders to fight to our deaths."

"…Wait, retreat and death? You're citing the infantry manual[2]?!"

"Yes, if you give the order to defend with our lives…"

I take back what I said. I even judge myself for thinking it.

Tanya grins unconsciously.

Moving the receiver away from her ear, she praises him loud enough that all the officers present can hear. "What a guy."

A stubborn fool, in other words, is a useful human sacrifice—someone who will doggedly carry out whatever they are told to do. More sensitive the minds, the faster their gears turn, the more likely they are to flee in a crisis. Even a fool, if they have a tenacious spirit…can be an uncommonly fine meat shield and a welcome asset.

Oh, Lieutenant Tospan. Tanya is of a mind to heartily celebrate his excessive honesty.

I bet I would run away.

No, I have no doubt I'd be long gone. I respect you for willingly holding your ground as if fighting to the death is a given.

Moving the receiver closer to her mouth, Tanya expresses her sympathy as one gear in the machine to another. "I like you, Lieutenant Tospan!"

"Ma'am?"

---

[2] **the infantry manual** All officers are required to memorize this manual approved by top dogs who think they know better—that is, important people with education.

"I'll send over the order in Colonel von Lergen's name."

Doing it in his name is only for show. It's Tanya giving the order to fight to the death. It's only sensible that an action deserves a reaction.

"And you can keep the ones who bring you the orders as reinforcements. I need you to hold firm. Firm! After all, we're surrounded. Where are we supposed to retreat to?"

With First Lieutenant Grantz's unit, which had been originally paired with Tospan's unit, off with Lieutenant General von Zettour, the infantry was operating with reduced firepower. I would rather save First Lieutenant Wüstemann's company, but this is probably the time to use them to fill the gap.

At the moment, I won't be inconvenienced by only having two mage companies at my disposal. If the infantry can hold, keeping Ahrens and Meybert with their artillery and armor as strategic reserves should be plenty.

"Right, Colonel. Just as a matter of regulation, I had to confirm. I hope you understand."

"That's fine! Just fine! I approve! I truly do understand, Lieutenant Tospan!"

Infantry. Independent infantry.

In other words, the cornerstone of war.

You can't build a functioning corporation with executives only. A holding company is basically like a general staff. Without people below actually doing the work, the enterprise can't exist.

In the end, Tanya is forced to demonstrate her cruel management skills and work honest Tospan and his troops to the bone.

"I'll send out Lieutenant Wüstemann's mage company. He's not up to Grantz's level, but, well, do what you can with him."

"Thank you!"

Subordinates who understand their role must be given appropriate performance evaluations. The willingness to defend a position with your life when ordered to is convenient for Tanya.

Certainly, during peacetime, it's an utterly useless, timid attitude. But in wartime, in a defensive battle, there's nothing better than soldiers of that rare nature. It makes sense that a general from ancient times argued that rather than clever soldiers, he preferred stubborn ones who would tenaciously carry out their mission once they got their orders.

They're so easy to use. Human resources who don't whine or complain! That's getting encouragingly close to a manager's eternal ideal. Even setting aside my personal sentiments, if the infantry can be the axle in your plans, it becomes much easier to fight a war.

"You heard that, right, Lieutenant Wüstemann? After delivering the orders to Lieutenant Tospan, you're to support him in combat."

"Yes, ma'am!"

Nodding at his enthusiastic reply, Tanya rotates her shoulders.

The rear, huh? It wouldn't be bad to kick back in a reasonably safe headquarters, or more like that's my personal ideal, but...to someone fighting as hard as Tospan, being the commander issuing the order to defend with your life must sound pretty good.

Meybert is a duty officer, so he has a handle on the overall situation. There won't be any problems if Tanya leaves the rest to him.

Reputation, reputation, reputation.

It is what it is. Humans are political animals. They'll do what needs to be done.

"Captain Meybert, I'm leaving command here to you."

"Yes, ma'am! You can count on me! But where are you going?"

"To the front lines, of course," Tanya declares with a grave expression plastered on her face. Really, she'd like to trade places with him and stay behind instead, but her rank won't allow it.

In that case, she should at least score some points.

"I'm just a little girl. I'm not so thick-skinned that I can order my troops to hold their ground in exchange for their lives and then kick back in a lounge chair—though life sure would be a piece of cake if I were!"

"Ha-ha-ha!" The dry laughter filling the command post indicates that her subordinates appreciate the gravity of the situation and are not in danger of being crushed by it.

The effects of laughter on mental health really are substantial. It'd be great to get a support visit from a comedian, but...if someone's going to come from the Empire, maybe it makes more sense to find a circus? Maybe I should look into it the next chance I have.

Chapter **IV**

"Lieutenant Serebryakov, we're joining the firefight on the periphery, too. Let's make things easy on Lieutenant Tospan and the others. This is what you call that beautiful spirit of solidarity."

"Yes, ma'am! I'll follow you to hell and back!"

Serebryakov's lively reply is a breath of fresh air. Even an annoying job is welcome if I have an eager subordinate.

And so, keeping things voluntary, Tanya heads for line one, where Tospan is commanding the defense.

We're at war, so enemy attacks are expected.

But the sight that greets her when she arrives is despicably hideous.

"...This is unbelievable," she murmurs at the sight of the bodies of enemy soldiers.

Yes, plural. Corpses are strewn all over.

If this were the Rhine front in the early days, say 1923, it would be a different story.

In an era where we hadn't yet learned the might of machine guns, maybe the doctrine of charging so bunched up could still be justified.

But this is Unified Year 1927.

How many years has this war been going on? Or does Federation ideology warp space-time? What year is it here? Did you call up an ancient legion or something? What's with the close formation?

Of course, even the Federation Army has its troops dispersed to some degree. But they might as well be human bullets, the way they're charging at the buttoned-up and fortified imperial firing positions. And it seems like they're bunching up on purpose to make it easier to maintain unit cohesion. Maybe things would have been a little different with a smoke screen, but as it is, they're sitting ducks.

The rhythmic fire of our light machine guns is heartening, but people are being mowed down before Tanya's eyes.

"These damn Communists. Do they value human life at all?"

This squandering of resources can't be justified in terms of humanity, the economy, or the military. Honestly, Communism is the only way of thinking that finds this acceptable.

What do they think human resources are?

As a decent person, I feel sick when I think of these cultists—as sinister as Being X.

"These guys who only give orders are entirely too irresponsible. This sort of thing has to be changed." Tanya voices her righteous indignation in spite of herself.

Come to think of it, how the Federation chooses to waste its human resources isn't something Tanya has to care about.

In fact, I'm happy they're numbskulls.

Still, Tanya von Degurechaff—though she's proud of being a good citizen—must despair. She can laugh off the idiocy of the Dacians—they were foolish because they didn't know any better—but there's nothing to chuckle about where the Federation Army is concerned; they know better.

But Tanya draws a clear line between free thought and her duty.

This is a defensive position on the forward-most line, so if the enemy is rushing them, it's Tanya's job to see how efficiently she can mass-produce enemy corpses and obliterate their will to fight.

They're enemies, so they simply have to die. I do feel for them, dying such pointless deaths, but that's a separate conversation. Even legally, if it's kill or be killed, then it's the plank of Carneades.[3]

"Draw them in! Hold your fire! Not yet!"

Cheerfully mowing them down is an easy method, but laziness and corner cutting are to be avoided on the battlefield. Sadly, unlike on the Rhine, light machine gun barrels and ammo are too scarce to waste on the eastern front.

Since we don't have the resources for unrestricted suppressive fire, the troops can't just let loose with a hail of bullets. Under the current circumstances, the only decent option is to leave the timing of the close-range salvo to the most experienced gunners and wait it out.

It's still irritating to be so short on ammo. We wasted an eye-watering amount on the Rhine. You could even call it a "dim-witted waste of national resources on an unbelievable scale."

But we were also in the grip of a mania wherein the supply network, supported by raison d'état, reliably delivered an unprecedented amount of supplies.

---

[3] **plank of Carneades** A thought experiment about what is acceptable in times of emergency evacuation—e.g., the question of whether it's permissible to shove another person off to ensure you're the one who's rescued if only one person can live.

Chapter **IV**

That said, I'm not sure if it was the sane enabling the insane or the insane enabling the sane.

On the eastern front, something must have run out. We catch glimpses of the limits of our logistics. The supply of things like shells, which should be abundant, is particularly dire—so blatantly that we can't pretend to not notice.

"Heavy artillery incoming!"

The warning shout from her adjutant brings Tanya back to her senses.

So the enemy guns that have been quiet are just now getting down to business? This is the worst possible time for a bombardment. Well, shit. Turns out they were saving ammo.

Just as their infantry is advancing, the artillery pins us down with a barrage overhead. This is the optimal move as long as you ignore the casualties inevitably incurred when Federation infantry are hit by stray Federation artillery fire.

"These vicious bastards. So their infantry is expendable?!"

This is what it means to shudder in response to evil. Do Communists just have no concept of human rights?

"What about enemy mages?!"

"Signals visible, maintaining their distance."

What should we do? Tanya thinks for just a moment. Fighting a defensive battle while enemy artillery forces us to keep our heads down is the worst. Right as she wishes she could order counter-battery fire or a retreat...the field telephone begins to ring.

Having leaped at it, Serebryakov raises her head to report. "It's Captain Meybert. He's urgently requesting permission to return fire!"

"Rejected!"

The words Serebryakov relays with a tense expression are terribly tempting. Tanya wants to shut the enemy artillery up. Any soldier being shot at knows the feeling.

But she immediately shakes her head.

Of course, personally speaking, I would love to let them fire. How great it would feel to say, *Blow away those obnoxious enemy artillery crews.* Sadly, even Meybert, with his duty-focused tunnel vision, can recognize that our stores of shells are strained. We don't have any to spare.

"But, Colonel!" Tanya's adjutant replies, seeming dissatisfied with her verdict. "If I may! I think simply continuing to endure this bombardment will affect morale!"

"I said no!"

"Can't we at least counterattack?"

"No means no! We absolutely do not have the shells for it! Don't tempt me any more!"

It's not as if I don't understand the desperation on Serebryakov's face as she refuses to back down. On the contrary, Tanya feels the same way.

Should she celebrate the fact that she and her subordinate share that feeling? Or should she lament that fate forces her to say the opposite of what she really thinks? Surely the answer is the latter.

Unfortunately, I'm being toyed with by both Being X and organizational logic. Oh, how I must suffer. For a moment, in spite of herself, Tanya weeps internally at her pitiful plight.

"But, ma'am! At this rate, we could be completely pinned down!"

"No problem! We'll have the mages prevent that." She continues, "Call up Major Weiss."

With the receiver in hand, waiting as the phone rings, Tanya has to ask herself if this is really the right thing to do.

Shouldn't we be on guard against the enemy mages?

But the mage unit is currently acting as a distraction. In that case, being overly wary and leaving Weiss and the others idle probably poses a greater risk.

"Colonel, this is Major Weiss."

"Hi, Major. Time to go to work."

"Yes, ma'am. At your service."

How encouraging it is to get such a lively reply even at times like these.

"Knock the enemy's annoying shells out of the sky, Major. I want the mages on defense against artillery."

"You want to protect a position of this scale...with just us?"

Rousing her borderline annoyed spirit, she goes ahead and hits Weiss with a demanding order. If things were slightly different, I would've probably commiserated with him.

Humans are bound to their position down to the slightest remark. Though Tanya would like nothing more than to groan about the restriction of her freedoms due to professional necessity, this isn't an issue that can be solved by complaining. It would only be more wasted effort.

"You've been trained for it. Remember our good times in the homeland. We did it while surrounded by the beauty of nature around the time the battalion was formed."

"Colonel! Our troop density is way too low! We can't cover this huge area with just two companies of aerial mages!"

"Major Weiss, what did I teach you on the exercise grounds? Did past me teach you to whine like that?"

People who keep their subordinates from voicing legitimate objections using a mind-over-matter attitude are hopeless. There can't be any reality less pleasant than the one where I need to employ such distasteful orders.

It's a cruel world.

This is none other than the epitome of middle management misery. First Tospan, now Weiss—glossing things over with empty encouragement makes me want to cry.

"U-understood… We'll do our best."

There's hardly time to debate responding to his stiff reply with a peppering of arbitrary support before the war situation shifts.

"Enemy infantry approaching our zone!"

Is it Tospan or one of the infantry's noncoms? In any case, the warning from a lower-ranking officer causes Tanya to look up.

She's been having them hold their fire, so it makes sense that the enemy is advancing. Before anyone realizes it, the enemy has gotten so close, we can make out their faces. If Tanya has her troops wait any longer, they risk getting charged. Right as she's thinking they should probably fight back in full force, something dawns on her.

It's just a little idea, but little ideas often lead to big changes. Surely there's no harm in trying it.

"Mages, hold up! I want just the infantry to return fire!"

"Huh?"

Paying no mind to the perplexed mages, the infantry begins to shoot. Smiling at Serebryakov next to her, Tanya points out that they're mimicking the enemy's tactics.

"Let's lull them into a sweet dream. We'll pretend we don't have mages, just like our Federation opponents pretended they didn't have artillery."

"Do you think they'll fall for it?"

Tanya responds boldly to Serebryakov's skepticism. "I appreciate your efforts, *Magic First Lieutenant*, but try thinking like a foot soldier."

"Hmm?"

It seems that magic officers frequently undervalue their own abilities, taking them for granted. Since she's not a foot soldier, Tanya can only guess, but she can still imagine how terrified the enemy infantry must be of mages overhead.

We should recognize that they're always nervously looking at the sky, checking for mages. And they tend to split into squads to run for cover when trying to escape machine gun fire.

…Now then, if they're convinced there are no mages, how often will they look up at the sky?

Up… Now, there's an idea. Tanya grins.

It's a universal truth that trouble always comes raining down from above.

"General von Zettour is…being completely unreasonable, too."

"Unreasonable, ma'am?"

Tanya was talking to herself, but her adjutant responds, so she shrugs.

"Are you advising your superior to leak classified information, Lieutenant Serebryakov?"

"N-no." Serebryakov shakes her head, and Tanya lets her know it was just a joke. Continuously shooting at waves of Federation soldiers from behind cover can't be good for a person's mental health.

Seriously, though, this work environment is quite possibly the worst.

"…Shall we blow off some steam by prepping for this counterattack?"

Peering out from behind their cover, Tanya sees enemy soldiers quickly approaching.

Basically, they're focused on the ground, purposely forgetting threats in the sky during their charge. It's an efficient advance, but thinking that war is waged in two dimensions is a mindset that should have been left in the past.

After all, the modern era is the era of three dimensions. Feeling lucky not to have enemies launching formulas at them, the relieved enemy foot soldiers have assumed there are no mages—a weakness Tanya takes full advantage of.

"Did we get 'em? Did we get 'em? ...All right, let's go!"

As if exemplifying how to lead from the front, Tanya leaps into flight.

Soaring into the air, she opens fire on the enemy below with her submachine gun. All she has to do is squeeze the finger laid over the trigger anytime the barrel of her gun lines up with a Federation soldier.

Pop, pop-pop-pop. A pleasant report sounds as the rain of formula bullets falls on the earth below.

No matter how the Federation infantry tries to respond, it's too late. They just barely manage to look up at the sky, but most likely...they can't even tell what's happening to them.

Mana manifests inside the formula bullets, ready to interfere with the world. We control the combustion as much as possible to produce less shrapnel so the explosion formulas we're scattering don't damage nearby buildings.

It's just a single attack. But it's a well-planned ambush.

As the formula bullets burst, elements that were once Federation soldiers spray across the earth; at that point, many of them make up their minds.

"Clear! Clear! The enemy soldiers are losing the will to fight!"

Nobody wants to die. Facing the horror of death, human instinct is to flee. That instinct can only be suppressed with a certain degree of training and discipline.

"01 to my group! Don't destroy too much of the cover! Think of Lieutenant Tospan. If we leave them with nowhere to hide, I'm the one who'll have to apologize!"

"Colonel! The enemy mages are on the move! It seems they're on rapid response duty—they're headed straight for us!"

After nodding a thank-you to Serebryakov, Tanya summons her vice commander, who was on anti-artillery duty.

"Major Weiss, the enemy's here. The enemy mages!"

"So they finally decided to show up!"

"Like kids late for school! Being late for war is human—a fine thing. We should be grateful for their self-sabotage, I suppose."

"You're absolutely right! Shall we punish the tardy children?"

"Yeah." She nods emphatically. "Have fun with them."

"Yes, ma'am! May I borrow Lieutenant Serebryakov?"

"Sure. Lieutenant, go support him."

If she's sending her adjutant away, Tanya needs to find a new buddy. Luckily, defending against infantry on the ground isn't a terribly hard job.

Perfect, she thinks and taps the young guy fighting alongside Tospan's infantry. "Lieutenant Wüstemann, come play tag with me down on the ground. Let's scatter the enemy foot soldiers!"

"U-understood!"

All right. With Wüstemann as her new partner, Tanya sets about mopping up the remaining enemies. That said, chasing away infantry whose will to fight has already collapsed is exceedingly simple. Even a second lieutenant fresh from the academy can do a decent job at it.

Tanya observes how Wüstemann's unit operates, to see what they've got, and mentally notes that they're still very green.

Skill-wise they're not bad, but they don't pay enough attention to their coordination with Tospan's infantry. Certain allowances can be made, since it was such a sudden pairing, and they may not intimately know each other's capabilities yet, but if they're in the same Kampfgruppe, they *should* know.

But at this point, Tanya should admittedly revise her evaluation a bit. Given their education and experience...I suppose this is what you get.

It's not only Wüstemann; all the magic officers are unfamiliar with the way regular infantry operates. It's taught to some extent at the academy, but most magic officers lead mage platoons and companies, not infantry. They just get used to that way of operating.

For that reason, she adjusts her mental evaluation of Wüstemann to *Nearly up to standards*.

"All done here. We've driven off the enemy."

"Nice job."

Having completed their task, Tanya gives the lieutenant a few pointers based on things she noticed. "You put in some great effort, but I want you to learn more about the infantry. Though you still lack experience in leading a mage company, you're coming along. That said, you don't seem to understand how the other arms work, which defeats the purpose of being part of a mixed-unit Kampfgruppe."

"That makes a lot of sense."

"To be clear, I'm not blaming you. I mean, the situation isn't good, but…despite your lack of experience, you're doing all right—that's for sure."

Tanya's way of expressing it is a bit severe, but it's a perfectly appropriate evaluation.

"Thank you for the harsh compliment."

Wüstemann obediently nods; you can say he has room to grow. If all that's missing is experience, education can fill in the gaps. An individual who accepts feedback and is willing to learn can be taught up to a certain level.

Deeply impressed by the power of education, Tanya turns her focus back to work and walks over to the infantry unit.

"Where's Lieutenant Tospan?"

"Here!"

A sooty face capped with a helmet pops out from the edge of some cover.

"Oh, you're commanding from the front, too?"

When it comes to overly frank people and serious idiots who don't even know the meaning of slacking off, it all comes down to how you use them.

Lately, Tanya has felt that Tospan's stock is doing great. Well, part of the problem is that he started so far down.

Anyhow, as long as he's right next to me, that makes things easy.

"Lieutenants, we have work to do."

"Yes, ma'am!"

There's only one reply.

Just Tospan.

"…Lieutenant Wüstemann?"

"Yes, ma'am," answers the young officer, brimming with relief that his job is done. That's no good. You can only let your guard down once work is over and you're drinking your coffee.

I was just praising him earlier, but maybe I spoke too soon. What a handful. Tanya gives him a hearty slap from behind. "It's too soon to relax, Lieutenant."

"H-huh? There are still enemies around?" The way he stiffens up betrays his lack of experience. Only a total amateur changes their level of alert based on enemy presence or lack thereof.

"This is perfect. Reeducation in the field. Let's go get supplies."

"Huh? Supplies, ma'am?"

His perplexed expression shows he wasn't expecting that, but Tanya nods. "We're going to collect lost items—time to show some kindness to the environment by recycling."

You have to be eco-friendly with your ego—that ensures you'll keep doing it.

Being eco-friendly is wonderful, since it makes economic sense. It's lawful and carries economic advantages, and it signifies market equilibrium.

"Lieutenant Wüstemann, it's about picking up what's been left behind. Take weapons, ammo—anything useful—off the enemy corpses. That's one source of supplies." She smiles at him. "Oh, and there's no need to take prisoners for grilling. There's no need to kill them, either, but don't go getting shot because you went too close."

"...It's indecent."

"You think you can wage a decent war? Bullshit." She jumps on his word choice and warns him with a scowl. "Are you saying you throw yourself into the slaughter purely, justly—sane and sober? Don't make me laugh. That's a broken man talking. Going to war after downing some liquid courage with a grimace is much more human."

He frowns for a moment, perhaps thinking to argue back, and then whines, "So are you drunk, then, Colonel?"

Boy, did I overestimate him. I can't have him taking everything literally. Haven't you ever heard of a metaphor?

"How rude. If I look like an adult, you need a new pair of eyes. You know minors are prohibited from drinking and smoking, so of course I'm always sober. Look, it's not like my hobby is torturing my subordinates," she argues, feeling awkward. "It seems that you are misunderstanding me. I'm an exceedingly peaceful, law-abiding individual. I believe that, especially at war, we must follow rules and regulations. And I expect the same out of my troops."

"I beg your pardon, ma'am, but I'm not sure I follow."

"It's utterly simple."

My subordinates tend to be narrow-minded. Recalling the past, Weiss and the other veterans of the Salamander Kampfgruppe used to be the same way, a fact that is vaguely horrifying.

But the reality is we're at war.

It's precisely because we're at war that Tanya makes sure to hold her humanity dear.

"We're soldiers. We shoot because we're told to. Because it's a reasonable order. In the end, we merely pull the trigger because HQ tells us to. Who's out here killing each other for fun?"

"But that doesn't mean..."

"—You want to loot corpses?" Tanya smiles wryly as she instructs him. "Don't be so self-centered, Lieutenant—it's childish. My subordinates and I are merely doing our jobs. The reason I say to get supplies is because we need supplies, and the reason we need supplies is because the higher-ups gave us orders that require them—that's all."

"...So you're saying the army...the army orders it?"

"Lieutenant Wüstemann, did you come to the front lines on a patriotic volunteer trip?"

"I can't say I don't love my country..."

"Haaah," Tanya sighs. Wüstemann may have some aptitude, but his strange way of thinking gives her pause. Tospan, who stays quiet and waits for orders, might be more endearing.

She whirls around to face Tospan and gives him a concise explanation of what to do. "Lieutenant Tospan, I want the infantry to patrol and round up useful items. Recover any souvenirs the Federation Army has dropped."

"Recover dropped items? Right away, ma'am."

An immediate response. No hesitation. So even a person who does only what they're told is capable of this much progress. To Tanya, it's a shining example of successful training. Lately, she's been finding it quite fun to invest in human capital.

"Look at that, Lieutenant Wüstemann. That's the correct work attitude." Telling him to remember that, she turns back to Tospan. Instructing him on how far he's allowed to go out, she also reviews the procedure for the expected counterattack.

Frankly, it's quite an efficient exchange. Taking what we can has become so highly standardized in the Imperial Army that a quick meeting to confirm procedures is enough even with Tospan types.

Tanya should probably rejoice in the optimization. Not that she really wants to think about being forced to be efficient in realms like this.

"By the way, Colonel. May I ask a question about this collecting? If we're sending out the infantry, why don't we consider building an outer perimeter? We can advance if we do it now."

Bewildered, she stares back at him.

A suggestion? From Tospan?

"...You want to advance?"

"Yes, Colonel. The enemy can only offer limited resistance right now."

Logically, he has a point: If we build a forward position, we can use the space we gain to buy time in a delaying battle. But there are too many reasons Tanya can't accept even a decent suggestion from Tospan.

"...Rejected. Your tactical judgment is valid, but we don't have the matériel for it. That's the whole reason we're stuck going out borrowing."

"What a hard-knock war...fighting with supplies people have dropped."

"Truly, Lieutenant Tospan. I'm in complete agreement with you."

Ironically, when we have people, we're short on supplies, and when we have supplies, we're short on people. Tanya vents on her subordinate in a roundabout way.

"I sure miss getting supplies. Lieutenants, put it on a card if necessary, but get me some rolling stock for freight from the Federation Army!"

"...Ummm, Colonel?" Tospan is puzzled.

Tanya shrugs and shakes her head at him. "Forget it. I was just griping—I'm in a bit of a mood."

If she were talking to Serebryakov, who is more familiar with her tendencies, she could expect a little more...of a thoughtful rebuttal to console her somewhat, but it would be too much to expect that out of Tospan or Wüstemann.

"Still," Tanya continues her griping. "Defending this town with a single Kampfgruppe is enough to make anyone want to whine a bit."

By all rights, this should have been a job for a division at least. When you think about it, defending a base with a Kampfgruppe goes against the very purpose of its formation.

"I'm human, too. Now and then, a complaint is going to slip out."

Ah, but they're not interested in listening to their superior's bitching. When they don't say anything, Tanya thanks them genuinely.

"I appreciate the polite silence. Now then, let's be punctual like civilized people. Lieutenant Tospan, I'm leaving collections up to you. Lieutenant Wüstemann, back him up."

""Yes, ma'am!""

The sight of her troops saluting and jogging off elicits both anxiety and hope. If Tanya was forced to pick, she would feel like she needed to count on them. There's no choice but to use the available human resources to the best of my ability, so…having some expectations isn't a bad idea.

Watching them go, these soldiers learning to stand on their own two feet, she celebrates that their careers are coming along. She has no intention of being so inept that she would get in the way of her subordinates' promotions. Making full use of your talented subordinates, the ones you trained, can be said to be the essence of management.

Though it's a bit late for someone who previously worked in HR, I should probably recognize that when I reconfirmed the value of education, a latent talent for cultivating people blossomed.

"They say when you complain about lacking something, what you actually lack is ingenuity… Can't slack off when it comes to cultivating your people. Of course, there's a limit to what you can do in the field, but still."

There's that saying about how necessity is the mother of invention, and a shortage of human resources has spurred Tanya to find new ways to best utilize what little she has. The human infrastructure of the Empire is so fragile that Tanya feels compelled to go out of her way to educate Lieutenants Tospan and Wüstemann despite the costs involved.

What a mess. Tanya shakes her head.

>>> **JUNE 18, UNIFIED YEAR 1927, EASTERN ARMY B GROUP HEADQUARTERS, WAR ROOM**

The officers crowding the war room at B Group HQ all wore severe expressions as they peered at the map spread out in the center of the room.

That part was fine.

Staff officers staring at a map is as natural as human beings breathing.

There was just one problem: The inspector and supervisor nominally in charge, Lieutenant General von Zettour, was glaring around the room, demanding someone speak, but apparently, a cat was holding everyone's tongues hostage.

"Gentlemen, I need your thoughts. The Lergen Kampfgruppe has been surrounded for over a week."

The staffers of B Group glanced at one another, trying to pass off the responsibility of replying.

"The Lergen Kampfgruppe is completely isolated in enemy territory—" When, after taking their time, one of the officers finally spoke up, what he said was awfully trite.

"Gentlemen, apologies for the personal announcement, but you don't mind, right? It turns out I can read maps, too." Zettour decisively cut him off. "If you take into account the enemy unit intel scribbled here, it's clear that Soldim 528 is an isolated stronghold."

In other words, it was also impossible to misunderstand the Federation's desire to recapture the strategic urban rail stop... That said, it was a shock that despite the huge battle raging in the south, they still had enough troops to deploy in such numbers in the central area—which was decidedly not where the hottest action was happening.

Striking at enemy manpower was a necessity—especially now, while they still could.

"I can see that without you telling me. But I do thank you for your kind explanation."

But the response to Zettour's biting sarcasm was silence.

"Why is the rescue plan behind schedule?"

He pressed them again but got nothing. His stare roamed the room—*I can't believe it*, he seemed to be saying.

"You have a fighting force. They should already be positioned in a place where they can deal with the enemy's movements. Though many of B Group's strategic reserves were drawn off, you should still have a unit dedicated to rapid response."

"...General, it's the bare minimum."

"Isn't that plenty?" Zettour shot back at the whining B Group staffers.

Lieutenant General von Rudersdorf and the other Operations staff were partial to the concentration of force, but not so much that they would leave their flanks unguarded. These people had full divisions of armor, mechanized infantry, and regular infantry at their disposal.

"Why aren't you moving them?"

"If failure isn't an option, then we need to take an approach that has the highest chance of succeeding. The state of the Imperial Army forces on the eastern front is, as I'm sure you've heard…"

I knew that already, thought Zettour, staring at the map with a wry grin. The situation was rather far from ideal. Under normal circumstances, the area that each division was defending would have been covered by three divisions, minimum.

In that sense, he could comprehend B Group's hesitation. If they deployed their counterattack and firefighting emergency units, that was all they had; their sense of crisis was valid—if you're waging war according to common sense, that is.

On that point, the Federation Army's inexhaustible manpower and their foreign matériel assistance was a wonder. The Federation Army's military strength and human resources had been deeply underestimated in the existing evaluations of their enemy's fighting power. Or rather, it was all too far beyond the Empire's preconceptions.

It was easy to take out a Federation soldier. Taking out the Federation Army, however, would be a feat.

Thinking of the Empire's current state after they nearly blew it, all Zettour could do was sigh. He would have laughed at the idea that if you couldn't stay on the tightrope, you'd have nowhere to stand, except it currently applied to him. What a horrible corner they'd been driven into.

…But basically…

If failure wasn't an option, then all they needed to do was not fail.

Wishing for all victories all the time was surely too much, but that didn't mean they couldn't win here and now.

"At any rate. I understand the situation and your fears. With all that in mind, I'm still requesting that you come up with a rescue plan."

"General, with so few troops, the likelihood of a rescue succeeding is—"

"Our troops are finite, but remember that time is as well."

As a strategist, Zettour had his worries about the situation, but as a tactician, he knew he could rely on his skills.

After all, he had a better understanding of time and timing than anyone else present.

Strategically, when the Andromeda Operation was poised to capture the southern cities, it would be unacceptable for A Group's attack to be blunted by a crisis in B Group.

"What is it, ultimately, that's causing you to hesitate? If it's already been decided that you'll conduct a rescue, you should probably decide how best to go about it, right?"

"Even if it's necessary, we need to take into consideration the situation all across the eastern front…"

"The objective is to hold the B Front. The target is the enemy field army. It's that simple. Making it more complicated is a heroic first step toward failure." *You don't get that?* Zettour asked with his eyes, but he realized it was pointless.

The hearts and the minds of B Group were at odds.

In their minds, they could understand—that it was unforgivable to abandon their brothers-in-arms. They could see that the only thing to do was for B Group to open a way out for them with a maneuver battle.

If this were war college, they would all undoubtedly choose to wager everything on the maneuver battle.

But their hearts were filled with apprehension. The fact that they were hesitating to act in these strenuous circumstances proved they were thinking with their hearts, not their minds.

He could preach his logic, but regardless of how their minds responded, it wouldn't move their hearts.

…Zettour would have liked to rely on their self-motivation. But if they were this far gone, he would have to give up on utilizing the "bright staffers."

Swallowing a sigh, Zettour fell back into silent thought before the map.

Lure them in far enough and strike before they go on the defensive. The attack needed to punch through the enemy, but it was so vulnerable that any hiccup could be disastrous. It all came down to timing. If they moved too soon, the enemy would be able to get away. If they moved too late, they were liable to get bumped back themselves and lose the Lergen Kampfgruppe in the process.

Determination. That's what a commander's job entails.

If you're going to use your heart, it has to be with unwavering resolve, not hesitation. You're here to make one decision. The lives of your soldiers and the fate of the nation rests on your shoulders.

It comes down to a single person's judgment.

The responsibility is heavy and rough, so if you don't feel sick, you're probably not human. Zettour took out the cigar he'd swiped from Rudersdorf and distracted himself from those feelings to regain some composure.

It was fine to recognize the weight of the responsibility, but if it crushed him, he would be no different from the staffers of B Group. It would defeat the purpose entirely.

If all he did was gaze at the map, the limits appeared on their own. The important thing was what to write on top of it.

Luckily, they had drawn the enemy far enough in.

In that case, the seeds had been sown, so the diligent laborers of the Imperial Army needed to put in the effort to reap. *Is it harvest season yet?*

"It must be time," Zettour murmured and smiled at the sound. The feeling of his doubts melting away and the weight lifting off his shoulders was indescribable.

The certainty that this was the perfect opportunity gave him hope.

Now all that was left was to strike before they missed their chance. Simple, and their target was clear.

It was obvious the enemy was interested in using the railway, so the Federation Army units must have guessed that the Imperial Army would use the rails for reinforcements or escape.

And the reports that were coming in showed that they were keeping their attention on the tracks.

But they were actually too focused. The Federation Army was so concerned with securing the rails that they were excessively concentrating on that one route. They lacked the preparedness to say that the road didn't matter as long as the destination was reached.

So at this moment, attacking from somewhere unexpected would cut deeply.

The enemy wasn't looking beyond the railroad, they weren't keeping the encirclement completely closed, and they were keeping only a rudimentary watch on the tracks…which meant it would be possible to strike despite the power imbalance.

Our chance has arrived.

Not that there was anything wrong with killing time debating, but military logic demanded action. So though he was reluctant to part from them, it was time to take his leave.

Thinking of what came next and what arrangements were necessary, Zettour called the nearest orderly over. "…You, sorry, but can I borrow you for a moment?" He made his order casually. "I need two cups of coffee. Bring them to my office. And can you get Lieutenant Grantz for me, as well?"

To the orderly, it was as if he had asked for the coffee in order to retire to his room. It would be clear to anyone that he had given up on the meeting. But he commented to make sure.

"Well, everyone has their opinions, but it seems to me, gentlemen, that you've understood my request and will respect it. And I understand that the things you want to take into consideration are important to you." He said it in a purposely exhausted tone and heaved a conspicuous sigh. To drive his point home, he expressed himself in a way that could be interpreted as disappointment. "So with the authority vested in me by the homeland, as inspector and advisor, I'm going to take some distance from this debate. Let me know when you've come up with the perfect plan for the operation."

"Understood."

"Very good… I'm expecting a conclusion as soon as possible."

He said it, but he winced inwardly, feeling like a total fraud.

Was this the result of Rudersdorf pulling all the capable soldiers for the aggressive attack operation? It wasn't as if the ones left in B Group had no brains at all, but…they were unenterprising and tinged with cowardice to the point that their autonomy had broken down.

Is the eastern front too worn out?

This wasn't a kind way to put it, but these staffers couldn't be used anymore as a part. He needed to implement a bold change in personnel as soon as possible. These men had lost the soul of a staff officer. They couldn't be treated as such anymore.

Chapter **IV**

Having announced the end of the meeting, Zettour hurried out of the war room.

He had nothing left to do there.

What he needed was people who would act. When he arrived back at the room assigned as his office, he reached for the phone on his table.

The number he dialed was that of the commander of one of B Group's few reserve divisions.

"Commander Cramm, this is Lieutenant General von Zettour."

"Weren't you in a meeting? I beg your pardon, General, but what can I…?"

"It's an invitation to take a walk with me. How about it, Commander Cramm?"

Just as he was about to ask where to, Zettour continued by casually hurling a verbal bomb into the receiver.

"Let's go wage a little war."

"D-do excuse me, but…is that an order, General?" Cramm reacted to Zettour's calm comment by biting, feigning it being in spite of himself.

"No, officially I'm using my authority to advise and make requests of the Eastern Army Group on the division level. It won't bother me if you refuse."

"Sir?"

"The staff officers of the eastern army understand and respect my intentions. To put it another way, they gave me a lot of meeting time." What Zettour said as he continued calmly, or at least in a voice that sounded calm, was inflammatory.

The eastern army staff lacked the nerve to do what was needed. Once you've decided to bring your fist down, war is all about how fast you can take that swing. Consideration should be careful, but action should be decisive—never the other way around.

"I decided to let them enjoy their meeting for as long as they want. Meanwhile, I'm planning on fighting this war seriously with you soldiers."

"…You must be joking."

"It would be great if I was, but unfortunately, this is reality." He denied it simply, in a way that allowed for no misunderstanding, and bowled over Cramm's hesitant voice. "This is war, Commander Cramm. What do you say?"

"...It's to save our fellow soldiers, right?"

"Of course," answered Zettour. "The objective is to hold the B Front. The target is the enemy field army. Our actions will relieve our beleaguered comrades. Of that, I have no doubt."

After a moment's silence and a quiet groan, Cramm's strained voice reached Zettour's ears. "If it's to save our troops...then I suppose I'll at least hear you out."

"You're a model officer—very good. I'll brief you."

He understood honor, so it was easy for a crafty soldier to handle him.

The difference between a staff officer and a division commander is simple. The former is far from useless, but the latter stands out for their passion for assertive action.

Before understanding with their head, they understand with their heart. Division commanders are truly simple, which makes things go quickly.

"The basic idea is bypass, bypass, direct attack. Do you remember the plan I asked you to research?"

"Yes, we're conducting a thorough survey based on the request for consideration the strategic reserve divisions received. I believe it was a classic maneuver battle..."

The energy in his voice was unmistakable even over the phone. It was immediately clear that he was on board.

We'll save our fellow soldiers with a maneuver battle!

Surely no soldier could hate such a plan. If there were such a misguided character in the Imperial Army, they would have to be an enemy spy.

"Have you discussed it with the other division commanders?"

"Per your request, yes."

All it took was one assertive commander to get everyone in order... If Zettour could mobilize them, then his wager had basically paid off already.

"Very good! Commander, I thank you. Now we'll be able to get through this somehow." Zettour made his request in a solemn manner per formality. "By the authority vested in me by the General Staff, I request that you advance our left wing and to the enemy forces' flank."

"So it's confirmed?"

It was only a formal excuse. But soldiers can often be relied on to move as long as they have an excuse.

"Save our troops."

"...I'd like nothing more. Your instructions, sir?"

As Zettour had anticipated as a member of the same organization, they jumped at a justification that allowed them to rescue friendly troops.

Offering an excuse...

That was the only surefire way Zettour could personally move units on the eastern front.

"Encircle them using a clockwise maneuver. Destroy the units of the Federation Army surrounding the Lergen Kampfgruppe. And while you're at it, nip the enemy counterattack in the bud; don't let it become a concern for the main offensive down south."

"Understood."

"Oh, and one more thing. Well, it's not a request, but just to let you know."

"Sir?"

"I'm borrowing a vehicle. Sorry for the ex post facto approval, but I'd like to have your understanding."

Cramm told him that wouldn't be a problem, and after thanking him, Zettour hung up.

"Excuse me, General. First Lieutenant Grantz, reporting in. You wanted to see me?"

Just as he was thinking to ask again where Grantz was, he showed up—what timing. Lieutenant Colonel von Degurechaff's education was comprehensive.

The orderly had even arrived with the coffee. He must have been waiting outside to be polite.

It seemed he would be able to count on these people.

"Thanks for coming. Go ahead and sit down." With a gentle expression, Zettour offered the young lieutenant a seat, as if he was inviting him in to make small talk, and treated him to a cup of the coffee the orderly had brought.

"I'm sorry I didn't ask your preference, but have some coffee with me."

"I-I'd be honored to, sir!"

To Grantz, who excused himself as he reached for the coffee cup with a tense expression, it must have been quite a nerve-racking tea party. Until the orderly left the room, Zettour maintained an amicable smile, but…time was too precious to waste here.

If this weren't a battlefield, Zettour might have been a bit more pure, too.

"Allow me to ask you point-blank, Lieutenant Grantz… What's the condition of the company you've received from Colonel von Degurechaff?"

"No problems, sir! We're on standby for rapid response. As soon as you issue orders, we'll be ready to carry them out."

For Zettour, that was a satisfactory response. No, it was even better than he expected. Considering the average level of discipline among the troops in the east, it was almost jaw-dropping.

But then again, it was Degurechaff's unit, so of course this was the standard. Though it was brimming with the quickness, ambition, and fighting spirit of lower-ranking officers, the soldiers seemed disciplined.

They had been taught well. As officers, cogs of state-sanctioned violence, they were the highest-quality role models. On the eastern front with its mud-water coffee, the aroma they gave off was of the real thing.

"No, I suppose it doesn't make sense to compare them to how awful the coffee is."

"General?"

"Nothing. I was just remembering the dining room in the General Staff Office." He shrugged with a wince, indicating the hardships involved. The General Staff's dining room was truly atrocious. Speaking only of his diet since being thrown on to the forward-most line in the east, he could declare with confidence that his post-demotion meals were better quality.

The young magic officer, Grantz, maintaining a respectful silence, was another quality factor… No matter where you are, there is some sort of advantage. If you can find it, that's a giant step forward.

On that point, the fact that Zettour had this precious pearl of a mage company in the palm of his hand made it possible for him to make daring decisions and take audacious actions despite having been sidelined from the General Staff Office to the eastern army with no authority.

"Lieutenant Grantz, I wonder if I can ask you to bend over backward for me."

"Yes, General!"

He said it with the mild expression of a kind old man. "I need you to go somewhere via tank desant."

"Sir?"

When the youth stiffened up, apparently not understanding, Zettour's eyes crinkled into a smile. *So there's a limit to how well they respond.*

That's fine. I'll just explain.

"War, Lieutenant. Let's start a war."

"A-a war, sir?"

"Oh, well, I suppose I should use my words more precisely. We're already at war, so… To be more accurate, let's call it *our* war."

Even if the eastern army got caught up in it, this was a program that essentially only Tanya and Zettour knew about. It didn't require any pretension to use the word *our*.

Something sacred or perhaps a moment's loneliness.

He couldn't quite describe the feeling, but he rephrased his intention with pride. "Lieutenant Grantz, this is our war. How could you sit it out?"

"General…?"

"What, Lieutenant? If you have a question, ask away. Questions shouldn't be bottled up."

"What is it that we're starting exactly?"

He has the right instincts. It was a roundabout way of asking. He was using language cleverly to appear dense while confirming the heart of the matter.

"Don't be so cold, Lieutenant." Zettour bit on Grantz's response. "It's about Soldim 528. You know the Lergen Kampfgruppe has been surrounded, right? It goes without saying, but we're going to rescue them."

"Oh!"

The open-book response made Zettour deeply envious—that naive joy, or maybe it came from a sense that a superior's words were trustworthy.

Youth that doesn't yet know how to doubt is dazzling like that.

"We're shifting to offense in order to relieve them. We'll lead the way... If we don't, the eastern army...may never get off their asses. I want to believe this is just an issue in B Group... They're only understanding their fellow soldiers' crisis with their minds. Which is why..." Zettour unpacked the reasons the same way he had to the division commander. The idea was to explain, get sympathy, and offer a justification.

Say it was *the right thing* to do.

"They don't have the proper sense of urgency, so we're going to give them a kick in the pants. We'll do a little blocking action."

"Yes, sir!"

However...

Maybe Grantz was too thoroughly trained, given the happy look on his face when told he would lead the fight.

Even if only in name, Zettour's official title was deputy director of the Service Corps in the General Staff. Naturally, it wasn't recommended for him to go riding a military vehicle out to the forward-most line.

To say nothing about how impossible it would be to not stick out carrying a rifle and grenades. Those who would happily go along with the plan, no questions asked, were surely the exception.

And in reality, it seemed that normal people naturally had reservations about it—Commander Cramm, for instance.

When Zettour showed up at divisional headquarters before the sortie with Grantz and company as his escort, Cramm approached, already looking...confused.

"Hello there, Commander Cramm. Sorry to bother you when you're so busy."

"General? What can I do for you?"

"What a strange thing to say, Commander. How's the unit? I hope my vehicle will be here on time."

Apparently, even this most military man became lost for words when shocked. After freezing up for a few seconds, he rebooted and finally seemed to grasp Zettour's intentions. "We'll go! General, please, I beg you—please stay back!" he shouted.

For a man in Cramm's position, his plea for Zettour to stay in the rear was an utterly natural reaction. *But we won't get anywhere that way...*

Zettour needed to fulfill the condition of an elite from the General

Staff standing on the front lines, no matter what. Even the chickens in B Group would hesitate to leave General von Zettour and order an excessive retreat.

"I think you're misunderstanding something." Upon looking into Cramm's confused eyes, Zettour emitted a sigh. "Commander Cramm, you're a newly appointed division commander; have you already forgotten? Seriously? Ever since the formation of the Imperial Army, it's been expected that a commander lead his troops." Zettour drove home his conclusion in an extremely even tone. "I may be the one asking things of you, but I'm also the one who proposed this plan. It's called practicing what you preach. Leading the way is, of course, my right as well as my clear duty."

It took only a moment for the bewildered major general to recompose himself, but in that time, Zettour had hopped into the car and begun checking his equipment.

"General, are you serious? You don't have to do all that—we can...," Cramm said reflexively.

Zettour responded with a sigh. "...Allow me to make one thing clear. I want to fix this misunderstanding." He crinkled his eyes into a kind smile as if to say, *Listen, Commander Cramm.* He could understand that straitlaced field officers were wary of ruses. And he couldn't claim he wasn't going to be tricky.

But right now, he was just another officer in the field.

"You can think of it as a bluff if you like, but I—no, a General Staff officer—should be the one seizing this chance to envelop one of the enemy wings. Do you think I enjoy polishing chairs with my butt?"

"...General, the rescue is your objective, right?"

"Are you asking if I want to give B Group a kick in the pants? Of course I do." Zettour continued, saying exactly what was on his mind, "Naturally, the rescue is at the forefront of my mind. Our target is the enemy field army. We'll hit the enemy and save our friends. Nothing more, nothing less."

There was nothing untrue about the simple words he said.

Personally, Zettour didn't want to leave the troops to their fate. If he had a unit he could send to save them, then of course he would have started the rescue mission already.

"In exchange for that odd job, we'll have to pay by being hated—just a tiny bit, yes, ever so slightly—by the eastern army staffers," Zettour continued in a carefree tone like putting sugar in a teacup. *That much essence was plenty.* "It's a clear rescue action that will merely wipe out the meddling Federation Army in one fell swoop, Commander Cramm. Fewer enemies, assisted allies. I should think that's easy enough to understand. I can't make it any simpler." He smiled. "Gentlemen, we should fight and get muddy, too. I hardly think there are any fools here who are scared of a little dirt."

Zettour declared the debate over and turned to his escort, Grantz. "Take the car out, Lieutenant Grantz. I'll count on you to drive."

"Yes, sir, if that's your order. But, General, are you sure this one's all right?"

"Why not?"

"It's not even armored. As your escort, I'd prefer you rode in at least a light tank."

He was right, but with apologies to Cramm, nodding emphatically next to him, Zettour couldn't heed his advice. The point was to show off the fact that a general was exposed on the front line.

"No. Making requests carries no responsibility. To best announce my presence, I should put my life on the line. This sort of situation is the reason the word *fair* exists."

"It's too dangerous, General. At least allow our division to provide you with a vehicle…"

"Commander Cramm, tanks are too slow. In terms of speed, and only speed, this is the best option. We also have to get into position quickly. Use tank desant or whatever method you like—just get them sent in."

"But the losses…"

"It's not as if I'm telling you to have your troops ride on tanks right into enemy positions and get slaughtered. In order to get the troops deployed swiftly, let tanks be their feet. It's a tight-knit joint operation of infantry and tanks."

This was a lesson learned from Operation Iron Hammer.

Upon further study of the Federation Army operating formation and considering Degurechaff's way of using troops, employing tanks as improvised transports was found to be unexpectedly effective in live combat.

"You mean they should disembark for combat when the enemy is spotted?"

"That's right."

"...I remember the report about how the Lergen Kampfgruppe did that."

"Yes, during that airborne mission. Now it's time to rapidly deploy infantry on tanks and attack the enemy's flank. This is the sort of thing you can only do on the vast eastern front." He nearly continued with a disclaimer but swallowed those words instead.

Tank desant, an enveloping attack, encircle and annihilate tactics. The combination of those three things was clear evidence of an overdependence on mobility.

The Imperial Army's troops were spread extremely thin. They didn't have the resources to consider any other tactical options.

"At any rate, our success depends on speed. Commander Cramm, advance as if you're the main thrust of the entire army's attack."

"Yes, sir."

"All right. We'll advance as well. Oh, and send a repeated request to the other division commanders—not that I think there are any who would still hesitate at this point."

⟫⟫⟫ THE SAME DAY, SOLDIM 528 ⟪⟪⟪

The mind of a unit commander under siege is often torturous. Thus, adequate sleep is necessary to maintain mental health. Sleep is one of the mind's best friends. It's rare to find a person who hates sleep.

Which is why it's a commander's right to request not to be woken up except in case of emergency. Put another way, anytime I find Tanya being dragged out of bed by her adjutant, First Lieutenant Serebryakov, there's good cause to expect trouble.

Yet, here we are again.

"Sorry to wake you, Colonel. It's an urgent message from high command!"

My adjutant has burst in to wake me up again. It's not as if it's

Serebryakov's fault, but when it happens this often, I'd like to express my discontent. Sadly, as a member of the military, I'm not permitted to sleep soundly when high command has an emergency.

"Urgent? Give it here." Bracing herself for another unreasonable demand, Tanya reaches out for the telegram, but the concise text throws her. "From General von Zettour to the 'Lergen Kampfgruppe': 'Colonel von Lergen,' promptly begin the 'designated' actions. What does that mean? This is all of it?"

"Yes, that's the whole message."

If Serebryakov isn't aware of anything else, then this is literally all of it.

The telegram doesn't ring any bells, so Tanya thinks, *Is this meant to confuse the enemy? Am I just taking a dummy message too seriously?*

She wants to laugh it off and believe she is overthinking, but the terseness gives her pause.

It's a message from allies outside the encirclement. If they are trying to tell her something and she misses it, the best-case scenario is that she gets laughed at. But in the worst case, the unit might even be abandoned.

"What are the designated actions?"

Is it some kind of metaphor? Or just a bluff to throw the enemy off the trail? But "designated" actions...

"...Hmm?"

"Lergen Kampfgruppe," "Colonel von Lergen," "designated actions"?

Looking at the parts in quotes, she notices that "Lergen Kampfgruppe" and "Colonel von Lergen" are outward-facing labels. *So does that mean "designated" is the same?*

In other words...maybe the thing to do is consider the message with those parts removed.

"Promptly take action...? ...Action."

When Tanya murmurs it softly, something bothers her.

Action, in the end, is assertive spontaneity.

In Imperial Army staff officer education, you get it pounded into your head countless times that an officer's role is to carry out the mission they're given and to obey not the letter of the order but its intent.

"Intent? ...The issue is the intent. What is this order really trying to say?"

Chapter **IV**

That is, what is Lieutenant General von Zettour determined to do? The important thing is her superior's intention. And Tanya isn't the type who can ignore her superior's decision.

If the boss says white, then everything black in the company is also white. In the most blackened, corrupt cases that won't be able to escape the law, there's no choice but to jump ship. That said, Zettour seems all right, so he scores points there.

Tanya's mind is self-conscious in the manner of a good, modern citizen—she values laws. If she gets an unreasonable order that impinges on her free will, she'll be forced to confront a grave conflict. Lucky for her, the General Staff is admirably law-abiding.

If anything, there have been plenty of orders she didn't want to carry out, but they were all reasonable.

That's worlds apart from the evil of Being X, who thrusts things upon me without considering my free will. Honestly, that's the problem with the devil's kin. No, given how Being X failed to properly explain the terms of the contract, the devil might actually be a more honest guy.

If God can't crack down on this interloper's rampage, he must be dead. As long as God is dead, all I can do is use my modern mind to defend myself from evil in accordance with the laws of nature.

How harsh this world can be.

No. Tanya shakes her head and brings her thoughts back to the present.

She has to deduce what Zettour might be thinking using a thought experiment.

"What would I do in this situation if I were the general?"

A revolving door, decapitation tactics… He's an expert with an exhaustive knowledge of logistics, so let's factor in his career thus far.

His personality almost certainly rules out passively waiting with no plan. Is he attached to seizing the initiative independently? Wait, but then you could say he would favor an aggressive breakthrough action.

"Assertiveness? …Is that what 'promptly' is supposed to indicate?" Tanya raises her head and looks up at the ceiling subconsciously. That's certainly a possibility, or rather, she could see it being true. Zettour may not always look it, but he has a fairly radical side to him.

It appears that the higher-ups want me to take prompt action. If a staff officer is being asked to act, then…?

It can only be an order to begin an operation and choose the optimal action.

The duty is always the same. Use your brain to help yourself somehow. That is, I need to come up with a way to break out of this situation.

The situation? It's the agony of being surrounded.

A light burns in her mind.

In that case, the answer is simple.

It's difficult to accept so abruptly, but it just might work.

"An operation to break the siege. I can't believe it—General von Zettour intends to make an aggressive move, even under these circumstances!"

Once Tanya realizes her superior is planning a maneuver battle, she has no doubt what her role is.

If he's expecting her to fulfill her duty as a staff officer, then this is the moment.

"We'll act in concert with the rest of the troops!"

Having made up her mind, Tanya both promptly and swiftly announces their next move. "We're clearing out! Round up all the unit leaders! On the double!"

"Colonel, will you reply to the telegram?"

Oh. Tanya realizes she is forgetting herself. She was getting so excited that she forgot a simple truth.

Hard work, attentiveness, and success.

The golden rule of being a productive member of an organization is truly simple yet deep.

"You're so attentive, Lieutenant Serebryakov! You're exactly right. I have to reply to General von Zettour's love letter, or I'll be derided as an officer with no honor!"

Okay. Tanya orders an equally concise message in reply.

"From the commander of the Lergen Kampfgruppe to 'General von Zettour': 'Colonel von Lergen' will promptly begin the 'designated' actions. That is all!"

Not long after…

The message was delivered by magic officer to the car Lieutenant

General von Zettour had single-handedly designated as the forward command post.

"Telegram, General. It's a confirmation from Colonel von Lergen."

"Let me see the text."

"Yes, sir, here it is."

First Lieutenant Grantz had received the message with his orb and written it out for the general. After one glance, Zettour gave a short nod. "From the commander of the Lergen Kampfgruppe to 'General von Zettour': 'Colonel von Lergen' will promptly begin the 'designated' actions? This is…fantastic."

The text he received was wonderfully simple.

Clear and concise.

If she didn't grasp my intentions, she wouldn't have been able to reply in such a simple format… That was the moment he knew his thoughts had reached her.

"Everything's going according to plan. This is good news, Lieutenant Grantz. The Lergen Kampfgruppe is ready to coordinate with our operation here. Now we'll be able to pincer the enemy."

"So…" Grantz seemed to have grasped something. He cautiously inquired, "…General, does that mean you and Colonel von Degurechaff set up a plan in advance?"

"No, not at all."

"Huh? But then, this reply…"

"Lieutenant Grantz, that's just the kind of creature a staff officer is."

The young magic officer didn't quite seem to get it, and Zettour patted him on the shoulder with a wry inward smile. *Is it because I hold my subordinates to too high of a standard that I feel he's lacking when he can't immediately comprehend things?*

"Remember this, Lieutenant: No one who fails to understand the necessary matters at the necessary time can be called a real staff officer."

A group of officers who build a shared understanding of what must be done based on shared foundations—that's the secret to the instrument of violence known as the Imperial Army functioning at the greatest possible efficiency. No, it isn't even a secret.

Everyone knows it. Even children know that staff officers are the essence of the Empire. They just don't know what that *means*.

Chapter **IV**

"I hear some people call Colonel von Degurechaff a monster. But if you ask me, she's a fine staff officer."

The strengths of a staff officer...

They lie in decision-making skills but also the ability to sense when to act. Plus, the flexibility of understanding an ally's intentions, or the objective of an offensive, and making autonomous judgments.

A coordinated conjugate of officers who grasp the intent of their orders and can act on their own discretion is exceedingly efficient.

There may be multiple heads, but they think with one brain. All in one and one in all: That is the ideal of the General Staff, the heart of staff officer education, and the fundamental principle of field battle.

"What I mean to say is she's correct."

Given an ideal environment, staff officers are expected to all arrive at the same judgment. With a mutual understanding of what the ultimate aim is, they individually set an objective with an eye on the greater goal and act on their own discretion; the result is organic synchronization and coordination.

The magic officer Degurechaff is a truly exceptional fighter. But more than that, she has vividly proven herself as an excellent staff officer. *It's just so delightful.*

"Ha-ha-ha! Now that we've come this far, we can finally say we're having fun!"

Previously, he had felt a slight pain about using a child for war, but having come this far, he felt a thrill more than hesitation or pangs of conscience.

That's just what she is.

If that's what she is, then that's what you use her for.

"This makes things so much easier than holing up in the rear, dealing with people who can't understand even when you explain every little thing. It's so much more pleasant to work with someone who simply gets it."

Ultimately, even an officer is just a cog in the machine.

If you look at them as merely a part, then all that matters is reliability and performance. In other words, their ability. In a war, anything that isn't ability is nothing but trivial sentimentality.

"A rare breed of officer, an excellent commander—basically, a vicious staffer. I guess we have to watch out for the younger generation."

We must be shouting the same things right about now.

Amused—no, delighted from the bottom of his heart—Zettour raised his voice. Was there anything an officer wished to do more than this?

"This offensive is a go! We advance. Let's get moving."

For the purposes of keeping morale up—much in the same vein as executing an admiral by firing squad—it's best if a handful of generals die on the front lines.

Hans von Zettour, date unknown

On the endless expanse of land, the visible man-made objects were tiny dots. Little grains scattered here and there. From a bird's-eye view, they were probably easy to overlook as inconsequential blips.

But those who approached would surely gasp at their majesty. They were the very definition of massive—the best armor modern technology had to offer: This was the Imperial Army's armored division on the attack.

Leaving ruts in the ground, nothing blocking their path, the group was headed straight for Soldim 528. In the lead was the commander's tank equipped with a large wireless set to keep everyone together, and behind that were several vehicles also fully loaded with communication devices.

That was fairly unusual, but it was a move that manifested the commander's mentality. On the eastern front, where armored warfare frequently took place on a large scale, it had become normal for the unit commander to be there on the front lines in order to make snap decisions; there was nothing rare about that.

But the curious glances from the tanks and infantry trucks traveling around them—from the no small number of seasoned armored division veterans maintaining their formations perfectly—said that something about the commander's cluster was peculiar.

If you lent an ear to the radio, the answer would be clear immediately.

"We've made contact with the enemy. It's a Federation Army defensive unit!"

Ah, but the troops are familiar with that warning voice. The word *enemy* probably made them nervous, but it wasn't out of the ordinary, so...it wouldn't have caused the curious looks.

Chapter V

Nevertheless, for some reason today, everyone was watching for the combat vehicles' reaction with both bewilderment and anticipation.

The reason was the person sticking their head out of one of the tanks. After casting a look at the enemy camp, so focused that it was liable to burn it down, he turned around, shook his head, and shouted. "Notice to everyone in the division; I say again, notice to everyone in the division. This is an order from your commander. Ignore them! Go around! Do not engage!"

He was neither a company, battalion, nor even a regiment commander. He was the commander of the whole division.

Commander Cramm's roar from the front was conveyed via the large wireless set to the other vehicles behind him.

"Don't even think about it—just press onward!"

As he waved an arm fiercely to say, *Follow me!* the figure he cut as he encouraged his troops brimmed with determination. Judging by appearance only, his subordinates probably would have exchanged glances that said, *My old man does the same!*

Cramm had the commander-out-front spirit, and he led the resolute charge after climbing aboard one of the vehicles and saying, "I'm going with you!"

All of this was the fruit of seeds sown by Zettour, who now sat in the rear seat of a military vehicle smiling in amusement.

"Boy, Lieutenant Grantz, Commander Cramm really has us beat. We might as well be spectators."

"General, with all due respect..."

"What is it, Lieutenant?"

"I'm sure from Commander Cramm's point of view..." *It was your desire to go to the front line that brought about this situation, don't you think, sir?* That was the look in the eyes, like he wanted to say something, of the first lieutenant escorting Lieutenant General von Zettour; apparently, he didn't hesitate to express his opinion on the battlefield.

That Colonel von Degurechaff—how in the world does she train her young officers so a mere lieutenant is mentally capable of speaking with no fear, and so unreservedly, to a general? If she wasn't so adept in the field, I'd throw her straight into an education job in the rear... It's actually quite frustrating.

Cracking a smile about what an amusing dilemma that was, he

clapped Grantz on the back. "I see what you're trying to say, Lieutenant. But observing on the front lines is one of my duties in this position—as inspector, that is. So where's the front line? Here, right?"

"Though it may be impertinent of me to say so, do take care, General."

"Of course, I'll be careful once this is over."

Realizing there was no way to get him to change his decision, Grantz flashed a vague smile and kept silent. Disappointed that his joke hadn't gone over better, Zettour turned to look at Cramm's tank.

The way he leaned out of the hatch, paying no heed to his own physical safety, was the very picture of a hero.

"Well! He really is daring," Zettour murmured, swallowing his complaint that all division commanders should be that way.

The group of vehicles driving across the vastness of the eastern front lands probably proclaimed universal order and discipline. But how many people would know that it was actually rare?

The Imperial Army, which had overexpanded due to the massive mobilization, rapidly swelled with new posts, but—not that anything could be done about it—the undereducated officers couldn't replace the personnel lost since the start of the war.

Divisional HR? They were already concerned about regimental HR. Given the mental exhaustion of the B Group staffers, they should have been long since swapped out. The fact that they couldn't even find the personnel to do that spoke volumes to how much the Imperial Army was scraping the bottom of the barrel.

That's why seeing with his own eyes that a critical unit like an armored division was maintaining high standards of both quality and motivation was a rare silver lining.

"It's a bit of a rough situation."

As long as they had to defend such a huge front like the one in the east with limited forces, outstanding, aggressive officers were essential for carrying out missions with the highest degree of efficiency.

"But we don't have enough... We don't have anywhere near enough officers."

After standing on the forward-most line on the eastern front, that was a reality anyone could feel whether they wanted to or not.

The fact that field officers like Degurechaff and armored division

Chapter V

commanders like Cramm were meeting the standards required by the front lines made them...extreme exceptions in the current Imperial Army.

There was no choice but to prepare more people like them. But personnel like that couldn't be whipped up overnight. Cultivating officers who could be truly useful always took time. Even if they wanted to pull from the noncommissioned ranks, the pool of noncoms wasn't exempt from the same attrition and understaffing that everyone else was suffering. Under these circumstances, producing an officer corps that could withstand live combat would probably take a generation.

Zettour wasn't sure whether to be disgusted or depressed; the Empire only realized the value of trained, disciplined, well-educated officers on the front lines after they lost them.

Perhaps most of the country was still living in a fantasy. Maybe they were convinced the Imperial Army was just as powerful of an organization as it was before the war started.

The homeland's wish was for them to push on through the mud of the eastern front. Which is why the army was almost carelessly throwing troops onto the barren earth as fertilizer.

From his rear seat in the military vehicle, if Zettour looked around, he could see the grandeur of nature. If this were a sightseeing trip, it would have been nice to enjoy the great views of interweaving scenery. Though he was no major proponent of a return to nature, this wasn't half-bad.

But on the other hand, it was merely evidence of undeveloped space. To the Empire, this was far from Heimat.

His beloved home was distant, and this place couldn't even be considered a borderland.

"...This is the epitome of a barren battle line."

The words in his mind slipped out in a murmur.

"Something's wrong."

Something Zettour couldn't manage to put into words had been bothering him.

The Imperial Army's current operation objective was to secure a resource area to support the war economy. That was understandable. A resource area was an alluring trophy. If Operation Andromeda succeeded, he had no doubt that the Empire's resource situation would improve. If they succeeded, their victory would be easy to comprehend.

It would probably also have a positive effect on the rear's dwindling will to fight. Of course, that was only if you were looking at the situation from the rear.

To those out in the field, victory in an offensive and expanding their occupied territory was a veritable nightmare. On the forward-most line, anyone who didn't realize what a pointless endeavor this was had to have some screws loose.

It didn't even require an intellectual exercise to identify the problem. It was clear at a glance.

This vast expanse of mud was, yes, marvelously rich black soil. But if it wasn't going to produce any fruit, it really was pointless.

"If we could raise the Council for Self-Government's agricultural yields, we could expect some improvement, surely... Is the bottleneck fertilizer? But we can't stop gunpowder production. There aren't enough resources to go around..."

It would be tricky... Zettour winced as he caught himself considering the balance of things.

That's not my job right now.

For better or worse, I've been uprooted and have no choice but to make my living here on the front lines.

"Hmm?"

Suddenly, the car shook, and tense voices shouted over the radio.

"Enemies spotted! They're at one o'clock...enemy tanks!"

Contact. And armored forces that would be difficult to evade. Enemies with speed always irritated Zettour to his core.

He had been prepared for an encounter battle but had hoped they would be able to avoid it. From another perspective, they could clash with the most problematic enemy in their least weakened state—but the best would have been if they could do it after getting through to Soldim 528.

"Prepare to engage! Watch out for anti-tank guns, and shoot 'em dead!" It was Cramm's rousing encouragement ringing over the radio. Zettour returned to his senses and stared out at the enemy. It was a group of tanks.

When he looked over at Cramm's vehicle to see what he would do...it appeared he wasn't planning on pulling back.

But of course not. The commander's tank must be in the lead. As soon as the platoon jumped out front, the tank regiment began tracing complicated, coordinated maneuvers in order to return the enemy fire.

Cramm's tank had entered firing range, and its main gun began to roar. *Now then, how will they...?* Eager to observe firsthand, Zettour took up his binoculars and opened his notebook, but just then, an unexpected transmission came through.

"General, please fall back."

He couldn't help but be confused by the division commander's voice flowing from the receiver. To put his finger on it, the words were so *boorish*. He couldn't understand at all.

"Commander Cramm? Sorry, but I don't understand."

"What?!"

"Why are you leaving me out? Your vehicle is staying, right?"

The radio immediately barked. "General! I'm in a tank! It has armor!"

Cramm must have been shouting himself red in the face, but...so what? His observation that it was too dangerous to be in an unarmored car was, yes, valid.

It was valid, but that didn't mean anything.

"I appreciate the warning, Commander Cramm. But you needn't worry."

"Huh?"

"I told you I was borrowing mages to escort me, right? They'll handle it. Don't worry about me; go on and wage war."

With that, Zettour took the receiver away from his ear, and Grantz, fairly frothing at the mouth, shouted at him in disbelief. "General!"

"According to Colonel von Degurechaff's report, there's a precedent for using mages as armor in a tank desant—and you were the one who pulled it off."

"But that was on a *tank*! It had armor!"

Cramm, Grantz—are they both only capable of repeating themselves? Zettour furrowed his brow.

Perhaps people these days were too particular about armor, but...it also made him worry about the current paradigm.

"Lieutenant Grantz, armor is important, but it's technology. Ultimately, technology is a tool, not something we can allow to control us."

"One stray shot to this open-top car, and you'll be telling a different story! Armor isn't just for decoration!"

Ah. Zettour gave a small nod. Grantz's opinion was extremely appropriate for someone in his position.

It made sense that escorting a multipurpose vehicle was much more difficult than supporting a tank. Unfortunately, Zettour could absolutely not go along with his advice.

"So? You're telling me if the enemy shoots at us, I should find some armor to hide behind? What am I supposed to do with that suggestion, Lieutenant?"

As the young lieutenant's face stiffened in disbelief, some contempt even for his recklessness probably crossed his mind.

And he was being imprudent.

Attending a tank fight in a mere car essentially made him an easy target. He apologized mentally for making everyone deal with the trouble he was putting them through. But it was necessary.

In military affairs, that one word—*necessary*—was enough to justify anything.

"Lieutenant, I bulldozed the rescue of the Lergen Kampfgruppe through. If the one who proposed the operation retreats, it might make success look impossible and red light the whole thing. If I make an excuse like that, the rescue may not happen."

"With all due respect, General, this is an official military action!"

"That's a dutiful answer."

If he believes it, that is.

Zettour didn't think Grantz personally had all the answers, but he knew he had been trained under Degurechaff. He was experienced enough to be treated as an officer who knew the ropes, and guys like that were well aware of the way the official account diverged from reality.

"Are you saying you don't know what will happen if the one who proposed it flees? Obviously, our response will falter. Without a forceful attack, I doubt we can break the encirclement."

"But... Take cover! Take cover!" Grantz had been about to nod in agreement when his expression abruptly changed, and he shouted. At the same time, the driver's face warped, and he began turning. Zettour noticed a moment later that something was wrong.

Chapter V

"Growing old is such a hassle. Your eyes just can't keep up."

No matter how determined you are to fight whenever you see an enemy, it doesn't mean much if your all-important eyesight starts to go. As he mocked himself, he turned to follow Grantz's gaze…and saw what looked like the silhouettes of enemy tanks with their guns pointed this way.

Debating in the face of the enemy? Apparently, I've been in the rear for too long—I've lost my edge.

"Mages, defend against the bombardment! If you use your shells, the vehicles will be blown away! Don't take the hits head-on—use your protective films to deflect them!"

When Grantz shouted, the mages accompanying him clutched their orbs. Almost simultaneously, a booming sound cut through the air. It was the enemy guns opening up.

"…Ngh?!"

Should it be said that it was the combination of contemporary science and magic that caused a miracle? Or was it always just these moments that God chose to bless him? An enemy shell had been headed right toward him, but its path must have deviated, because it whistled past and flew away harmlessly.

The mages' skill at evading point-blank fire at this range was incredible.

…Degurechaff really gave me some good people. So this is why she was loath to see them go. She might hold a grudge against me for taking them…

"Well done, Lieutenant!"

"It's an honor to hear you say so, sir, but please get to the rear! The enemy tanks are—!"

"I know there are enemies around. But what do I care about that, Lieutenant Grantz? Besides, you're going to do something about them, aren't you?"

"But those are the new model!"

"That's precisely why I need to see them. I need to complete my inspection! An eye for an eye and a tank for a tank…" Zettour's comment trailed off, and the notebook he had taken out dropped from his hand as his eyes widened in shock at the scene unfolding before him.

Though they were in motion, the imperial tanks ferociously attacked the enemy vehicles. The skill of the tankmen, firing their main guns and brilliantly scoring direct hits while on the move, was magnificent.

But there was just one problem.

"…They deflected the shots? I can't believe it."

The imperial tank guns were well within effective range, but the fire wasn't effective. Enduring hit after hit, the enemy tanks were unharmed.

If they managed to destroy the tanks' treads, they could wear them down with focus fire. No matter how proud the enemy was of their armor, once they were disabled, they could be bombarded with concentrated attacks till they burst into flames. Still, that was a result that could only be attained with a massing of firepower against immobile enemies.

…Against the enemy armor under normal circumstances, the imperial guns were as good as useless.

He had read it in reports. But seeing it had a different level of impact.

The scene of enemy tanks fighting on unfazed despite direct hits by the main guns of imperial tanks was difficult to accept all at once… Even if he understood it with his brain, the sight left him shocked.

"Lieutenant Grantz, are those the new types you were speaking of? How often are you clashing with them? Your best estimate is fine."

"They're all over the place. We've taken out so many, yet here we are." Grantz spoke calmly; though his expression said he was fed up with the situation, there were also signs that he had gotten used to it.

"…I understand rationally…and I realize it's a bit late, but I'm reminded how different things *feel*."

Several years ago, 50-70 mm cannons were deemed overpowered and not maneuverable enough, so 37 mm had been recommended for a tank's main gun.

And what about now?!

They would have to start considering 80 mm, 100 mm, or even higher as the new standard!

"So the tanks are evolving like dinosaurs now?"

Could the infantry, cavalry, plus artillery and the small number of mages they had be put to practical use or not? The war General von Zettour had been taught as a first lieutenant was filled with more mystery and honor.

"Things have changed."

Statistical warfare, after all, took an extreme view of humans as interchangeable parts in an intricate, organic violence that moved the machinery of war.

The way the imperial infantry and tanks coordinated to take on the unbelievable dinosaurs of enemy tanks as they roared was a scene that Zettour would have laughed off as something out of an SF novel before the war.

"New enemies! It's a unit of Federation tanks!"

"Federation reserves?!"

"At eleven o'clock, too! Enemy tanks!"

The situation reports coming in over the radio were not good. The Imperial Army was just barely managing to blast the enemy tanks, but they were so sturdy, it was taking an awfully long time. There were no signs they would be wiped out anytime soon. The pace of destruction was too slow.

At this rate, a breakthrough was a dream within a dream.

Even if they wanted to force a maneuver battle, the impact would be too limited. They had no choice but to bypass the defenses here, but doing so right in front of the enemy would basically invite them to cut their communication lines.

They could advance like an amoeba, but if there were creeps on their tail, they wouldn't get anywhere. Everyone knew the advance would be nearly impossible, but they should have at least had some legs. Their speed, however, suffered a greater decline than Zettour had been relying on, and the enemies blocking their path were frustratingly powerful.

If the B Group staffers had been reluctant because they could sense this on some instinctual level, then they had a point. Though sadly, it was only a point and nothing more.

Weakened and facing this caliber of enemy...

How much longer can our army keep up this confrontation?

"...Shit. There's not enough sand in our hourglass. How do we add more?"

If he wouldn't have had the habit of soliloquizing in the car since normal times, the comment would have surely been a distressed shriek. The tactics of putting up brave fronts and toughing things out are all in how you use them. A pinch of salt can hide that something is missing...but if the dish is all salt and nothing else, it's inedible.

In other words, the current situation was awfully salty.

"…The situation is more fluid than I thought. It truly pains me that the data we've accumulated can't be trusted."

It couldn't be helped, but this is why he didn't like war. In the rear, they seemed to be too fond of it; he couldn't keep up.

Ironically, Hans von Zettour, deputy chief of the Service Corps, felt more depressed the more he thought about the rear. He had grown so used to the air on the front lines that he wasn't sure he would remain sane when he returned to the capital.

"More troops! Friendlies are headed this way!"

Someone shouted that they were saved.

It was lucky that the mechanized infantry arrived just in time to counter the enemy reinforcements. Though it was a borderline piecemeal commitment, this augmentation of force would give them more of a fighting chance.

"On the ground! Quick, get ready for combat!"

"Anti-tank commander, hit those tanks!"

The shouts of officers commissioned and not filled the air, and the soldiers who jumped out of the trucks rapidly joined the battle line. The situation was improving. At least, the imperial forces had been strengthened.

Although in exchange, their attack had slowed.

"General, please!"

In response to the pleading voice, Zettour, who (if forced to say so) wasn't exactly eager to die, smiled. At this stage, there wasn't much good holding his ground could do.

If the infantry was mixing it up in combat, then it made sense that he should be running the base.

"All right, all right, I have no intention of being unreasonable. I suppose I'll go with you, Commander Cramm."

A grunt wouldn't have felt out of place as he leaped from the vehicle, and he stumbled as he landed and nearly fell over. He had been polishing his butt on a chair in the General Staff Office for a long time, and it shocked him how much his physical strength as a field officer had deteriorated.

Back in the day, he could have led an infantry charge. He could have fought hand to hand. He was probably that capable up until he became a lieutenant colonel. But now he was hit with the bitter realization that regardless of what he wanted to do, his body wouldn't be able to keep up.

"Times like this, I sure am envious of the young." Grumbling as he took up his gun, he looked out over the area he was sure the troops would take up according to infantry combat fundamentals, and it felt like he hadn't lost his touch; he was relieved that his senses as a commander hadn't dulled. If he failed to understand what was intended by the movements of Commander Cramm and the others as they got out of their vehicles, he would have been a relic of an officer.

Luckily, he could tell what the troops were trying to do based on their position. But there were still some things that made his eyes pop.

One of them was the anti-tank guns all gathered together.

"Huh, that's a rare way to use them…"

"General?"

"Lieutenant Grantz, shouldn't the anti-tank guns…?" He was glad he didn't finish saying, …*be attached to each infantry unit as a tight escort?* The response to the enemy tanks closing in before his eyes answered his question.

"Infantry, don't approach the enemy soldiers! All guns, hit that Federation tank that's sticking out!"

The young commander ordered all the anti-tank guns to fire, and a dozen or so muzzles targeted a single tank. With local firepower superiority, or perhaps simply artillery large-enough caliber to be called heavy, it seemed possible to destroy the enemy tank, even from a distance.

"Concentrated anti-tank fire, entrusting local authority to the commanders… I see. There's certainly no reason we need to fight these things foolishly fair in a one-on-one bout of mortal combat, so that's the right way to do it."

…*Although this is also evidence that without that strategy, we'd have little hope of combating the enemy tanks.* Not so long ago, it was taught that tanks could be destroyed by a close-quarters mage or even infantry assault, but now that seemed rather impossible.

Which is why Zettour asked his field commentator his view with great interest. "Lieutenant Grantz, is that way of operating the anti-tank guns standard on the eastern front?"

"Not so much in our Kampfgruppe. Usually, they aren't necessary because of our substantial mage power, so they're often assigned to assist the infantry against nonmotorized vehicles. But in units where the mage and mechanized forces can't incapacitate the enemy's armored forces and they don't have enough firepower, we're seeing concentrated fire as a stop-gap solution."

"So a desperate measure, then. But it's effective."

Necessity is the mother of invention. Technologies and procedures come into existence when they are needed. And on the battlefield where your life depends on it, creativity probably accelerates without much regard for appearances.

The battlefield was full of surprises. The moment Zettour nodded in fascination, an excited cheer next to them hit his ears.

"...Aerial mages!"

"They came!"

"Best timing ever!"

"Ready signal flares! Send 'em up!"

"Over here, mages!"

He looked up in response to the soldiers' exultant shouts to see three formations. The charge of an aerial mage battalion? ...That was proof B Group was running properly.

If the aerial fleet was supporting them, it meant that at least this operation wasn't Cramm's division operating on its own.

"That's a weight off. So the units in the east are still functioning..."

The comment he let slip out without thinking was how he actually felt. Returning to himself, he winced... *Good grief. To think the day would come when I'd be anxious about our troops in action.* He couldn't very well say that. Which was why he had to swallow his honest feelings.

To gloss over that conflict, Zettour looked up at the sky and praised the incoming mage reinforcements. "Isn't it fantastic to get a mage battalion as backup? Now that I've experienced being rescued by them, I understand how amazing it feels for the troops."

It wasn't the same as banking to wave, but they had their act so together that they barrel-rolled as a friend-or-foe response to the signal flares. Zettour felt keenly what a latecomer layman he was in the field of aerial magic.

Chapter V

It was difficult to avoid preconceived notions, subjective impressions, and misunderstandings.

Actually…one case in point was his utter surprise at the fact that aerial mages in the east were able to fight. Maybe he had just seen too many troops from the east get fooled by optical deception formulas during the 203rd Aerial Mage Battalion screening process.

No… There Zettour decided to suspend his internal judgment. They'd been fighting this war for years. Anyone who had survived this long would have acquired the minimal know-how even if they didn't want to.

"That's a costly tuition, Experience. Couldn't you lower your rates a bit?"

That said, though greedy, there was no denying that it was a fantastic teacher. No one could claim the effects of its education were anything less than outstanding. It was right that he absorb what lessons and wisdom were available while he was in the field.

In particular…he was the opposite of an expert in the realm of aerial magic. He had to admit that he lacked the knowledge to understand simply by witnessing the action; luckily, though, he had a teacher besides Experience with him this time.

This is a great opportunity, so I should ask for his unreserved opinion, thought Zettour as he asked for some commentary. "Lieutenant Grantz, how do you see the situation?"

"Huh?"

Zettour continued his inquiry, pointing to the scene before them. "I want your opinion as an expert."

"Oh? I'm at your service, sir."

The young first lieutenant next to him answered in earnest. Even if Zettour was inspecting his conduct, there wasn't a single flaw, but the attitude felt out of place on the front line.

How was he so calm in the tense frontline atmosphere?

"Give me your unflinching appraisal of their performance."

"You want an evaluation of the aerial mages' combat, sir? It'd be better if Colonel von Degurechaff were here; I'm not qualified as a combat instructor."

It was fine to be cautious, but that was for in the rear.

"It doesn't have to be an official examination. You can curse them out or gush about how great they're doing, either way. Or simply give me running commentary."

"General? What exactly do you mean?"

"You've never listened to that sort of thing on the radio? Sometimes, I'd like it if someone could comment on the battle while I observe, too."

"…The thought never crossed my mind."

This straitlaced youngster was apparently quite strict with himself. He was confronting this god-awful war with too much sincerity.

War leads to destruction.

Even officers need only deal with war itself; if they tried to confront the meaning of it, they were more than likely to get in over their heads. An officer without leisure would have an inflexible mind. An inflexible mind is a fragile mind. If they can't protect themselves except by stiffening up, then they're really in trouble.

"I won't say it's wrong to take things seriously, Lieutenant, but you might want to reconsider your way of thinking."

"I-I'm not sure I understand, sir?"

"You seem to be overly concerned with a lot of things. As far as I can tell, you're a decent officer. On the battlefield, everything breaks down. Yet, you're maintaining your sanity. So save the thinking for when you get back to the rear."

Shells, explosions, screaming, and all the stenches assaulting our noses… How many dialogues in human history have taken place in a setting like this? Zettour found some small amusement in it.

On a battlefield where, just beyond our position, our tanks and anti-tank guns are clashing with enemy tanks, I'm taking it awfully easy. He chuckled to himself and continued, "Worrying is a luxury—because it takes time to worry. So if you flip that, what I'm saying is: Don't worry when you don't have the time for it. Overthinking is the same."

There's no reason to keep going down the same path until it's too late. Zettour remembered the context and cracked a wry smile. This guy was a member of Colonel von Degurechaff's unit.

Anyhow, a superior is a superior. Since she was the type to be demanding of even lower-ranked officers, *Don't think about anything* might have been a bit of a harsh request.

"It must be tough to work so closely with her... Well, I'm just an old man droning on. Feel free to forget what I said."

Re-collecting himself, Zettour lightly wiped his binoculars and pointed toward the imperial mages. They'd gone off on a tangent, but he still wanted to take advantage of this opportunity to hear a critique by someone in the field.

"Let's back up a bit, Lieutenant. What do you think of that aerial mage unit of ours?"

"If we're talking strictly about skills, then they're passable. Their surface attack patterns aren't bad, either."

Lieutenant Grantz was beating around the bush. Though he wasn't disparaging them, the way he spoke was less praise than withholding judgment. Frankly, the nuance was close to completely negative.

"That's not very high praise. How come?"

"Their tactics are too rigid... Well, that might be an exaggeration. But there's evidence that they drilled only certain movements."

"What kind of evidence?"

Grantz closed his mouth for a moment to think.

"...In situations where I would use different approaches, they keep repeating the same patterns."

"Instead of choosing the optimal method on the fly, they select one of a limited roster?"

"Yes, sir," said Grantz with a nod. "Their movements are a bit clumsy, and overall, their maneuvers are too predictable. It's probably due to being drilled in only those things during their accelerated education."

So the same as the aerial battles in the west, then. There was no room to breathe anywhere. That was why they wanted to hurry and at least increase the head count.

As a result, they were finding ways to make good use of under-trained troops...or that was the idealistic hope anyway. In actuality, the abilities of an aerial mage company now were a far cry from prewar units. Frankly, the issue of education duration was too big.

Though the types of missions were diversifying, fully trained soldiers and officers had been scarce for a while now. Reaching head count through shortened, accelerated training due to lack of personnel only made the issue more complicated.

The gap between the abilities of the Imperial Army the operation drafters assumed and the current Imperial Army's abilities was growing too large to gloss over. It was getting so severe that soon there would be nothing they could do to solve it, to the point that headache-inducing risks were involved.

"...If it's all right with you, I'd like to ask you what you think the results would be if we had the 203rd Aerial Mage Battalion and those mages fight a mock battle."

"There wouldn't be any point to fighting with even numbers. We would win with half or even a third of our personnel."

Grantz's immediate reply was the type of comment to be laughed off as overconfidence—under normal circumstances. But on the battlefield, under their protection, Zettour could understand that it was the literal truth.

"Wow." He was wholeheartedly impressed. He had grasped mentally how talented his playing pieces were...but seeing it was a whole new dimension of moving. "Then how about if mages of ours went up against Federation aerial mages?"

"I don't think it would be a bad battle. With identical numbers, they could probably fight evenly or maybe a little better. I definitely don't think they would be inferior."

"...Even or better? You're sure about that?" Zettour's confusion and unease slipped right from his mouth. The idea that imperial aerial mages would have to struggle against Federation mages was absurd.

"Yes, based on the level of the Federation troops we've fought so far, I think so. As long as it's not the rumored guard mages, we wouldn't have to worry about a one-sided trampling."

The lieutenant reassured Zettour not to worry, but he was misunderstanding the situation.

He was leaving out the absolutely critical concern of the skill gap between imperial and Federation mages.

The problem was simple. Though the imperial side was numerically inferior, at least they had been able to boast superior quality; now, that was clearly in jeopardy. To be "even" spoke volumes about what the future held. The Empire's personnel and infrastructural capacities couldn't ignore a kill ratio[4] of one to one. At that rate, even after the Empire had completely dissolved, the Federation would still have units left—and an even bigger advantage.

"Thanks for your comments, Lieutenant. I learned a lot."

Suppressing his expression and emotions, he extended polite yet empty gratitude as he peered through his binoculars. The aerial mage unit ground attack unfolding before them seemed a usage of mages far more polished than anything that had been imagined prewar, but an officer with experience fighting in the east called it "accelerated."

So I'm an old man now. It's extremely questionable whether I'm even managing to keep up with our progress. He harshly mocked himself in his head.

"At any rate, oh? It seems they've mopped them up." He made a point of speaking matter-of-factly. "An anti-tank position, aerial mage tactics, and the concentrated commitment of both armored groups. So we can open up a hole even if it is small."

The moment he had figured that they would be able to break through and retry the encirclement maneuver, those calculations collapsed.

"General von Zettour! It's Commander Cramm calling!"

"Give it here."

"General von Zettour, bad news from the aerial fleet. The Federation Army units are reacting to our presence and changing position."

"Ooh, we have guests?"

"General!"

What a mess. He winced.

Maybe after all that chair polishing at the General Staff Office, he was a little too giddy to be back in the field. The front lines were complex yet simple. He much preferred the atmosphere here to meetings with Supreme Command.

"Commander Cramm, you say there's a crisis, but conversely… couldn't it be considered a chance? I don't mean to be impetuous, but I can't deny that I'm excited."

---

[4] **kill ratio** How many of theirs we can kill during the time one of ours is killed.

201

"A chance?"

"The enemy soldiers who have been holed up in their positions are coming right out. On the Rhine lines, we booted them all the way to the sea."

"Ha-ha-ha-ha, but that was an awfully risky advance. And this time is even riskier."

"That depends on how you're interpreting the situation. Certainly, our flank is at risk, but it'd be a different story if the Lergen Kampfgruppe synced up with our offensive for a pincer attack."

"You're saying the envelopment worked?"

"Not yet." Zettour continued, injecting some slight irritation, "We've only just attained the possibility of it happening. As time passes, that possibility will slip from our grasp... That's why we need to get creative."

"G-get creative?"

"What's wrong, Lieutenant Grantz?"

"No, errr, beg your pardon."

"Getting creative in this scenario could...really only mean one thing, right? It's probably what you're afraid of, but at the rate we're going, I fear the Lergen Kampfgruppe's persevering struggle will only end up a tactical waste."

"What are you planning? I'd appreciate if you would tell me."

It was less a question than a confirmation request. It was clear from Cramm's stiffened expression that he had steeled his resolve.

So, respectfully, he told him.

"We need bait, Commander Cramm."

"Understood, but please allow me to say one thing."

"Which is?" Zettour wasn't arrogant or insolent enough to refuse to hear the opinion of someone in distress.

"If you met with Colonel von Lergen to discuss a pincer operation, you would normally let us know ahead of time."

"I haven't."

""""Huh?""""

Suddenly the object of everyone's questioning stares, Zettour gave them an awkward grin. "Is that strange? I didn't make any specific plan with the Lergen Kampfgruppe beforehand."

"B-but a pincer..."

"I didn't order a pincer. The General Staff's job is to protect the fatherland in the place of God, but who would be able to foresee this situation and give appropriate orders ahead of time? Luckily, it's a staffer in charge over there. I just trust that even in the worst-case scenario, we'll at least get the minimal response necessary."

"What makes you so sure, sir?" the commander asked back, and Zettour smiled at him brightly. *That's obvious.*

"I'm repeating myself, but I'll say it again: There's a staff officer commanding the unit."

They had the same paradigm pounded into them. Plus, she was one of the Twelve Knights at war college.

"So, well, it's a sure thing."

"Wh-what about the message from before?"

"It was psychological pretense, pressure, and an alert. Well, it's pretty easy to toy with both the enemy and our own if all it takes is a single message."

An officer who doesn't require excessive explanation makes a decision immediately, responds instantaneously, and doesn't hesitate to take the necessary action. Sure, Degurechaff may have been broken, but not as an officer.

For the Heimat, that was a competence to be celebrated.

"All right, troops. This is my request. Lure in the enemy—in as flashy a way as you can manage."

It's a tall order, but let's trust that if we lure them in here, the pincer will take shape. This was all a bit too irrational to be called tactics, but since a frontal attack was out of the question, they had no choice.

He was going to push it through with the full awareness that it was reckless.

"Very well, General. Allow me to give you my official reply to your request: 'We will counterattack. I say again, we will counterattack.' That is all."

The concise report of the situation was everything a clear report should be.

And the marvelous way the single line was composed to retain the ambiguity in the chain of command: Taking Zettour's standing and position into account gave it an even more artful essence.

So he's prepared for the worst, too.

"Good, very good. I wish you luck. That is all."

"Yes, sir! All right, General. Then by your leave, I'm prepared to storm Valhalla with you as marshal and general."

"I don't know which of us will be the first to go, but sure, I'll tag along."

Zettour realized the corners of his mouth had relaxed into a smile as he watched them dash off. It wasn't as if he was letting his guard down; perhaps the spirited exchange had simply lightened his mood.

"...I didn't think it would happen, but I've grown sentimental as I've aged."

There was a mountain of things to deal with.

But he had managed to break it down.

Turning it to rubble wasn't just a dream.

Where are you, my means of escape?

"Okay, I can't let them show me up. There's one more job I need to do."

Just as Zettour, gun in hand, was about to mingle with the other infantry and join the defensive battle, a first lieutenant with a panicked look blocked his path.

"General, please fall back! Any more is—"

"Too dangerous? I know that without you telling me, Lieutenant Grantz. Well, this is a do-or-die moment. We're prepared for an infantry battle, and even I can shoot a gun."

"Please stop, General!"

Grantz, standing in his way, trying to bar him from the battlefield, was a good escort. Zettour was grateful that the lieutenant put up with him and, without a single complaint, continued to worry about him.

But withdrawing now was something he couldn't do.

With the enemy approaching right in front of them, how could he be the only one to fall back?

"Lieutenant, this is a critical juncture."

"We'll handle it! Please fall back, General. I have strict orders from Colonel von Degurechaff to protect you!"

"...Is the rest of the division still on their way? Go and tell them to advance as well."

"General!"

Chapter V

"How could I fall back without even getting shot?"

Grantz was trying to argue when he shouted something at the receiver in his ear in spite of himself.

"Commander Cramm has been gravely injured and is being sent to the rear! Brigadier General Schulz is taking over. General, you can't—"

"You heard them! Commander Cramm is the one who should be sent to the rear."

Not allowing any further debate, Zettour gripped his gun and positioned himself on the forward-most line. Sadly, the sound of light machine guns was sparse.

Bearing in mind the lessons learned on the Rhine, the Imperial Army had a love for artillery and machine guns bordering on favoritism...but the prospects for maintaining the necessary supply network on the eastern front weren't promising. While the artillery shells were still being manufactured, they weren't reaching the front line in sufficient quantities. And when it came to light machine guns, chronic ammo and barrel shortages were rampant.

The Empire's faltering infrastructure had been weighing on the east for a long time. But not receiving supplies is all it takes for an army to start writhing in agony. The Imperial Army's ideal of crushing the enemy position via large-scale artillery action became infeasible, and the decreasing density of infantry fire deteriorated the imperial infantry units' numerically inferior combat strength in the extreme.

As a result, all the high-ranking imperial officers were forced to either choose the direct approach of targeting enemy communication lines or make circumvention the goal and bet on a maneuver battle.

That was the fundamental reason Andromeda, Lieutenant General von Rudersdorf's operation targeting the resource fields to the south, hinged on winning a maneuver battle. There was no longer any hope of performing a general offensive according to schedule. As Lieutenant Colonel Uger had nearly spat with a grimace, the Empire didn't have any margin for error left.

Laying the conflict bare was B Group's ammunition shortage. Even working the expert timetable masters to the bone, the army could hardly scrape together enough bullets. That was how grave the situation was for the Empire.

Those who experienced the outcome on the front lines understood whether they wanted to or not.

"Deputy Commander Schulz has been hit! General!"

"No complaints. Have them keep playing it by ear. What officer could complain in front of his men? All we can do at this point is hold!"

"But so many regimental commanders have already been— We can't go on like this! General, please order a retreat!"

"Lieutenant Grantz, quit your whining. The operation is already under way. Just try and retreat now—the entire army would collapse. This isn't the Rhine front."

A plan decided in advance, a stockpile, an adequate railway timetable, and plenty of forces in reserve...were all things the eastern front didn't have.

Now that the maneuver was under way, if they stopped, it could mean the downfall of the Imperial Army. Despite the hardship, they had to carry on.

Even if all they had was a tightrope, they needed to make the crossing—if they couldn't, the only thing awaiting them was death.

...We're at war. If our fate is unavoidable, all we can do is laugh.

"High-ranking officers will die. That's a good thing. Maybe it'll be a wake-up call for those in the rear."

Relying on the creativity of the lower- and mid-ranking officers, plus the skills of the noncoms, the generals were putting their bodies on the line to get the job done.

You couldn't call it a tactic.

A few years ago, he would have laughed it off as a mess, a battle of attrition spawned by a dearth of intelligence. There wasn't enough fire-power left to defeat the enemy. If you didn't have enough supplies, then you made up for it with the right attitude. If your attitude was flagging, then you had no choice but to fill in the gaps with blood and resignation.

...That's an impressive level of foolishness.

"Lure them in! Show them I'm here! Raise the battle standards!"

"The enemy will target you!"

"That's the point! I don't care—just do it!"

But having come this far, the most he could do was act as bait.

Zettour hoped he would be able to lure in the enemy and make the operation a success… Surely, it was terribly childish as a gamble. You would be hard-pressed to call this operation-level intelligence.

Still…even if he died, it wouldn't be in vain. It would shock the nation awake.

If he could inform the rear of the alarming state of the eastern front…

"…It's the best use I can think of for my body. The corpses of soldiers must be employed as efficiently as possible. Heh, have we reached the outer limits of war?"

But that was why all he could do now was fight with all his might.

"Quit jabbing and get busy! Fire back!"

>>> THE SAME DAY, SOLDIM 528 <<<

Military orders, aka the impossible asked of you by your superiors.

Either way, once Tanya infers their fellow troops on the eastern front have begun maneuvers to relieve Soldim 528, she gives up on her leisurely sleep rotation. Overtime is legal during a crunch period if there's a labor-management agreement. And anyhow, imperial soldiers are "public servants," so they're not allowed to grumble.

Being able to peremptorily shift all units into rapid response preparedness is the ideal for a mid-level labor manager. If only there wasn't a war on, things would be perfect; well, no helping that.

First Lieutenant Tospan and First Lieutenant Wüstemann have strict orders to keep watch on the front line; Captain Meybert and Captain Ahrens are on standby at HQ for command and control purposes. Having arranged conditions intently so she can make free use of the subordinates she has trained from the start, Tanya privately gives careful thought to the joint breakout to be undertaken with the mages of the siege-breaking squad. It's fortunate that the rescue Lieutenant General von Zettour guaranteed her is in the works, but it's self-evident to Tanya that the deployment of friendly units doesn't necessarily equal her successful escape.

Frankly, looking back through history, there are plenty of rescue operations that failed.

That's why she listens carefully, making every effort not to miss a thing. She has no intention of getting the unit wiped out because she missed their chance.

"There's been a change in the Federation Army's communications!"

Tanya looks up—*This is what we've been waiting for!*—in response to the communications personnel's raised voice. It's the announcement HQ has been expecting.

Tanya takes hold of the receiver and listens for herself. *Aha, not only has the frequency exploded, but there's a ton going out un-encoded.* It appears less as though they aren't being careful enough with their encoding and more that there simply isn't time.

But she can't understand the critical message.

"Lieutenant Serebryakov, explain it to me. I'm learning Federation language, of course, but…I'm nowhere near native. It's too hard to make out their accents over the radio."

From the way so many un-encoded messages are getting through, she can assume that some kind of major situational change or combat is happening.

But she can't understand the content, which is crucial. Well, how would she be able to?

They're intercepting panicked signals. Not only Tanya but any non-native speaker of Federation language would find it impossible to read the situation on a split-second basis and follow along with the unstable intercepted messages.

Even her adjutant, clinging to the receiver and listening as hard as she can, has sweat beading on her forehead. That's how hard it is to understand.

"Important target? …Command function? Sorry, between the chaos over there and the quality of the interception, I can't get anything clear…"

According to her disappointed adjutant, their grasp of the intercepted info stops at the fragmentary level. But it isn't as if they have proper monitoring equipment; they're doing their best with the communications gear they have.

"But it's possible that the friendly HQ's location has been exposed."

"Exposed…? It's not as if we're the Dacian Army. Did General von Zettour leak it on purpose? There's a very good chance it's fake info. Or maybe a decoy unit has lured them in?"

"I can't deny the possibility, but the word is occurring with high frequency."

What? Tanya peers into her adjutant's face. When she asks if there's no mistake, the timid answer is solidly in the affirmative.

"Ha-ha-ha, ha-ha-ha-ha-ha-ha-ha-ha!" Tanya bursts out laughing.

It was a fantastic moment, when she was sure of it. *Do you—do you really think Zettour would screw up and tell the Commies his position?!*

"'Exposed' is a wonderfully original interpretation!"

I can declare from experience that a specialist in desk work in the rear like a Service Corps man is well versed in not only preservation of intelligence but the art of intentionally "leaking" information. There are all sorts of creative ways to spill intelligence.

"That's the silly talk of someone who doesn't know the general. Ah, but it's such a clear invitation; it's how all lovers should whisper in the three thousand realms… This is the first in a while I've found something so hilarious on the battlefield. It may be imprudent, but it's just so funny!"

Whoever said a person's character is the greatest decision-making material knew what they were talking about!

Honestly, the quality of this laughter is downright bizarre. As far as Tanya knows, staff officers are by and large very cautious. In the field especially, the nastier their personality, the more devious they become.

"C-Colonel?"

"Visha, remember this." She figures she should point out her puzzled adjutant's training bias. "Times like these," she says, smiling ear to ear, "you don't say the HQ's location has 'been exposed' but that we 'exposed it.'"

It isn't wordplay but a problem of subjects. Or probably it would be better to say that what's lacking is an appropriate understanding of the situation.

"B-but in that case…it's such a huge risk…"

"True. Normally, exposing the location of your HQ is too risky. After all, we've demonstrated to the Federation Army how effective decapitation tactics can be."

"I don't understand what General von Zettour is thinking. It seems entirely too futile…"

Serebryakov is probably speaking from her point of view as part of an active service unit. She has some understanding of the Federation Army, hence the apprehensions.

Actually, the Federation Army—and people from the Federation—are extremely sensitive to decapitation tactics against an HQ. Their headquarters are so well protected, Tanya is liable to scoff, *What are you, badgers?*

"You're a respectable person, Lieutenant."

"Huh?"

"If you get a chance, I recommend looking up how staff officers are educated at the war college. Basically, we're taught to take the initiative and try to figure out what people hate!"

You occasionally come across that sort among corporate employees, but the Imperial Army systematically selects people and trains them that way. Essentially, they're a group of human resources whom they can trust with confidence.

…And it's precisely because Tanya understands the way staffers think that she is forced to choose action.

When she looks at the officers around her, it seems that not even the captains, Meybert and Ahrens, have noticed: It's unusual for such a high-ranking officer to put himself in danger.

Frankly, it's so unusual, it strikes her as suspicious. That is, she finds it difficult to discount her serious question as to whether it's being used as a pretense to perform the rescue. Of course, on a fundamental level, she trusts Zettour. She believes in him, but…sometimes the organization's reasoning can blow even a lieutenant general's promises out of the water.

"Anyhow. Flipping things around as you think them over is one of the basic principles of being a staff officer. General von Zettour exposed the location of HQ as a giant lantern."

"Ummm…"

"All right, time for some social studies, Lieutenant."

"M-ma'am?"

With her subordinate's education in mind, Tanya inquires in a light tone, "The Imperial Army's counterattacking unit has exposed the location of their HQ to the Federation Army. What will happen next? Well, what do you think? Be as candid as you like."

"I mean, I think they'll be targeted by the Federation Army..."

"You're exactly right."

The answer is extremely simple, so surely the correct response should be given 100 percent of the time.

After all...the Federation Army has plenty of bitter experiences of headquarters disabling, encirclement, and annihilation at the hands of the Imperial Army. You'd have to be delusional to think they have zero urge to attempt revenge. So they must be thrilled to feel they have a chance to crush an enemy HQ.

And it's probably not wrong to guess that their minds are monopolized by this idea of crushing.

"Now let's ask a different question. What if...the enemy was being attracted on purpose? Then what would happen?"

"They would be perfect bait, but I don't understand the motive. Even if they succeed in luring the enemy in, they don't seem to have the units to take proper advantage."

"Lieutenant Serebryakov, you haven't become a ghost by any chance, have you?"

Tanya lightly kicks her puzzled adjutant's foot, smiling as if to say, *You have legs, don't you?* She exists. Accordingly, she is here. The Salamander Kampfgruppe, done up as the Lergen Kampfgruppe, exists...not that I want to work them so hard. This unit is powerful and too precious to lose.

Also, I have to wonder if the eastern army's strained B Group is even worth sacrificing ourselves for. Under these conditions, the organization's interests—which transcend things like good, evil, and a boss's disposition—could easily lead to a cruel conclusion. Considering the worst-case scenario, innocently waiting to be rescued would be an unforgivable act of folly.

Thus, Tanya makes the same choice as her superior. She chooses what will be great in the best case and allows her self-preservation in the worst case.

It's simple.

"You don't get it? That's such a surprise. There *is* a unit that can sneak up behind those numbskulls preying on the bait and leisurely kick their asses."

Sensing the non-voice filling the office—*Where?*—Tanya sighs. She can set aside the communications personnel and the noncoms, but even the Kampfgruppe officers who went through the academy don't realize?

Everyone needs to have a little more confidence in their existence... Or should I be disappointed that they've naively put too much faith in the military?

Stifling the gripes in her mind, Tanya purposely continues in a light tone. "*Here*, troops." *Tap-tap.* She lightly strikes the floor with a foot, as if performing a dance step, and goes on. "We're here, aren't we?"

Since Soldim 528 is surrounded, the Federation Army must think of it as a static point. Yes, it's hard for an isolated point to pose a threat to their rear. But the troops here include two companies from a seasoned aerial mage battalion. Adding in Wüstemann's replacement unit and that's standard head count for a full battalion.

Certainly, pulling the replacements would be a bit much and cause issues with defending their position, but importantly...taking two companies for self-protection and flying to freedom seems surprisingly possible to justify.

"What say we teach those Commies how sharp the fangs of this forgotten battalion are—whether they're eager to learn or not!"

Realizing what she's saying, the officers gasp.

"C-Colonel! You mean you're going to pull the 203rd Aerial Mage battalion from the position while we're still surrounded?!"

"I do."

Meybert's astonishment is probably warranted. Soldim 528 is an isolated, salient stronghold. And the troops surrounded inside only consist of an understaffed Kampfgruppe.

If the whole mage battalion gets pulled out, their defensive fighting power would plummet. Even if they pushed ahead with fortifying the position, and Tanya stationed Tospan's infantry and Wüstemann's replacement mages there, it must be hard to imagine them holding out against the enemy's fierce attack in the half-destroyed city.

"It'll be rough, Captain Meybert. You can make use of Captain Ahrens's armored forces; they must be bored, since they've been on reserve. Do whatever you have to do to defend till it's over."

It would be such a shame to lose these troops.

Tanya hopes from the bottom of her heart that the defense is a success.

But at the same time, she must prepare herself for the worst case of being forsaken by friendly troops and lead her units on the advance.

If she does that and it goes well, everyone will be saved.

And even if she fails, I'll still be saved.

"Your orders, ma'am."

He must not have a clue. After maintaining a respectful silence, Major Weiss inquires about their orders as usual, and spurred by his request, Tanya gives them.

"…The aerial mage battalion is going on a long-range advance. But we need to keep our signals to a minimum. We don't want our sortie to be detected."

"Huh?"

"Try to do it as stealthily as possible. We'll advance as fast as we can while suppressing our mana signals."

She can't run away, leaving the rest of the unit as bait. This has to be done logically. They need to delay the enemy attack on the position by concealing the mages' absence for as long as possible, or the rest of the troops won't be able to hold out for very long.

She'll save her subordinates, save herself, and show off to Zettour in the process. In order to hit all three birds with one stone, she has to make that compromise.

"Once we've taken some distance, we'll kick the Federation Army in the pants. Our higher-ups have given us this perfectly timed chance! Attack those numbskull enemy soldiers from behind."

If this goes well, some truly great outcomes are guaranteed.

"Got it, troops? Sneak up quietly and destroy their asses. I don't feel the need to repeat myself any more than this."

 THE DAY SAME, IN THE VICINITY OF FEDERATION ARMY SIEGE LINE ONE

To Lieutenant Colonel Drake, the Lergen Kampfgruppe was a powerful enemy to be feared. Tenacious defensive combat, occasional bold attacks, plus a stubborn infantry.

Though he observed their movements, repeatedly scanning for any weaknesses, there were never any holes worthy of the name in their defenses—a fact that was enough to wear him out.

Perhaps it should be said that that was Tanya's intention. Like the Federation Army, Drake was also convinced that Soldim 528 was an isolated stronghold, a static point. He never dreamed that enemy troops could sneak out while surrounded.

But fate is strange.

The order Lieutenant Colonel von Degurechaff gave to her subordinates, to suppress their signals for the breakaway, became a strange trigger. For a sneak attack to kick the enemy in the rear, it was an extremely normal order. No, more than normal…it was straight-up theory.

To put it simply, this officer, Degurechaff, made orthodox decisions. According to the manual, the rules, and even the sense most aerial mage officers had on the field, there was nothing mistaken about suppressing mana signals for stealth action.

But it came with one unanticipated reaction.

At Soldim 528, in order to prevent exhaustion and maintain combat capabilities, they were loosening up wherever they could, as exhibited by the frequent naps taken by the garrison.

Naturally, the mages staying there couldn't conceal their mana signals twenty-four seven.

But because of Tanya's strict orders to cut signals for the advance, their stealth action could be sensed by a sensitive mage as a kind of lack.

So… Let us continue.

The change was big enough for a marine magic officer, Drake, observing enemy movements on the first line surrounding the Imperial Army's position, to feel something was off.

"Tch, they have to be so vexingly impregnable. This is why I hate positions near railways. Coordinated defensive positions with infantry, artillery, and armored troops can fuck right off."

In urban combat, enemy soldiers had plenty of cover to hide behind, which meant they could really dig in. And then to have enemy artillery and armored troops butt in…

"Hmm?"

Drake stopped short at his own words.

Coordinated defensive positions were fine.

Chapter V

Infantry built them, artillery supported them, and enemy armored forces occasionally functioned as the strike axis—these defense positions were meant to be formidable.

But one thing was missing.

One of the enemy threats was gone.

"...Only infantry, artillery, and tanks? No mages?"

It was always his unit's role to chase off the enemy mages attacking their infantry. But bizarrely, for whatever reason today, he was barely conscious of them.

Why? As he was trying to articulate a response, he finally realized what had been feeling off for a while now.

The number of enemy mana signals had...dramatically decreased.

"Where did they go?"

It wasn't as if there weren't any at all. Some were still active. He could pick up a few signals. But it was like a residue of the threat he'd constantly sensed up until the previous day. The feeling...had decreased dramatically.

He would go as far as to say that it was like an empty husk.

"Does this mean that utter pain-in-the-ass mage battalion—they're all gone?!"

It was necessary to consider the possibility that they were suppressing their signal as a ruse. The classic text on ambushes said the way you drew the enemy in was critical. Imperial soldiers were fairly skilled players when it came to the game of deception, so relaxing was not an option.

...But Drake understood this intuitively.

It was like reading the tide.

Rather than overthink things with a chaotic mind, instinct, and intuition, sometimes the heart was far more accurate.

That was especially the case when detecting ill will and threats. Survival instincts were effective for staying alive. This sort of intuition wasn't logical. But it was terribly accurate. Anyone who laughed it off as occult nonsense was either a blockhead who had let their senses as a living thing go numb or a bigheaded jerk who had never been on the front lines.

The intense pressure he should have been sensing from the enemy position under siege had scattered. If he had to describe it, he might say it was something like the void after something had left.

Anyone with a sense for war could guess what had happened. This wasn't an ambush. They—and that monster—were gone!

Without another thought, Drake was off and running. It was extremely irritating that he couldn't make things happen with a single order due to the inconvenience of being part of a multinational unit.

While traveling from the position allotted to the Commonwealth troops all the way to HQ, even Drake, who was treated as an officer, was stopped by the Federation Army—what a pain.

"Colonel Drake? I beg your pardon, but may I ask why you've come…?"

The political officer stopping him with nonsense that had no place on a battlefield was a perfect example of bureaucracy in action. But while he usually felt political officers were only a hotbed of annoyances, this time he welcomed the encounter. If someone with the authority to make calls was around, this would be quick.

"Lieutenant Tanechka, I need to speak to Colonel Mikel immediately."

"Comrade Colonel…? Did something happen?"

Apparently, this political officer was decent enough that she wouldn't waste his time with nonsense at a critical moment. Convinced that's what made her better than most, he kept talking.

"The enemies have made a move. They secretly pulled out some mage units!"

Though the mages had left, the enemy position was still tight as all hell.

The enemy infantry were so vicious, it made him sick; the artillery was disgustingly skilled; and the tank units were thoroughly familiar with urban warfare. But the aerial mages, who had proven limitlessly aggravating at Arene, were mostly gone.

Thus, it's obvious what we should conclude. He continued, "The enemy mages are concealing their whereabouts! Assault the enemy position immediately!"

If they overwhelmed them with matériel superiority, they would be able to push through.

It was brutal arithmetic, but they could expect definite results. The sacrifices would come with returns. At least, it would be better than attacking and leaving his subordinates' bodies behind.

"Let's roll in with a tank desant! Hey, where's the interpreter?! Prepare to sortie! Hurry! Get as much fuel and as many weapons as we can muster!"

"Please wait!"

The words hit him like ice water. Unable to conceal his disbelief, he shot back at her incredulously, "But can't you see? This is our chance! Why in the world would we wait?!"

"Colonel Drake, tank desants on enemy positions are prohibited with the exception of flank attacks! I can't approve an act of barbarism that would expose people's lives to unnecessary risk. Anything that would wear down your comrades in vain is…"

"Are you stupid?!" He knew full well it was extremely rude, but he had to say it. "Look closely! Look with your own eyes!" Pointing at the town's periphery, he continued, trying to calm his voice. "Most of the imperial mage forces are gone! Now is our chance—no, this is our only chance to combine our forces and overcome the infantry and tanks!"

"Do you have definite proof?"

"Definite proof? Of what?"

"Where's the proof that the enemy isn't lying in wait to ambush us?!"

Where would that be?

Who would expect it?

This is the forward-most line!

"If you want the risk to be zero, take off your uniform right now! Bury yourself and enjoy eternal rest! We're fighting a war here!"

In the uncertainty of the fog of war, it's all doubt and hesitation until you seize upon the optimal plan. In the end, you're gambling with people's lives—that always comes with a risk.

But this time, we can strike with confidence, so why hold back?!

"The lack of signals, the operating conditions, and above all, the situational assessment! Take a look at how they're moving, and there's no doubt in my mind! If you call yourself an officer, then make a judgment call!"

"Have you thought about what it would mean if we failed?!"

"It would still count as reconnaissance in force! And first off, there's no way they can hold the line with their mage units gone! We should be able to break through to the urban area!"

"I find it difficult to believe we have a real chance! Did you not get the notice from the party?!"

The way she spoke to him so condescendingly made Drake explode. He was always thinking seriously about the war.

He didn't need this additional hurdle of a political officer's hand-holding.

"You mean about how the cities down south are seeing fierce fighting? Isn't that precisely why it would be meaningful for us to put pressure on the enemy?! That's why we're here!"

"The orders we were given on this front are to be a threat to weakened imperial units and prevent the enemy from concentrating in the south. Therefore, all we need to do is encircle—"

If he interrupted a woman in the home country, Drake would've been slapped in the face with an etiquette manual. But on the battlefield, there was no distinguishing between men and women—a stupid asshole was a stupid asshole.

She was being so dense, Drake's irritation built up to the point that he nearly spat. "That's exactly why securing the railway is such high priority! If we're just surrounding the urban district, we won't get anywhere, but if we get rid of the Lergen Kampfgruppe in our way, we've basically acquired an attack route! If we can destroy them here and now, the effect on the Imperial Army will be massive!" *Why can't she understand? She may be a political officer, but she still wears the insignia of a first lieutenant!* "Isn't the whole point here to have the multinational and other remaining units be aggressive about putting pressure on the imperial lines in order to support the south?!"

Though the fighting was hard, they were apparently evenly matched. He had heard a couple of days ago that it might even be possible to hold out. It was unclear how true that was, but if their allies could really hold in the south… *Why doesn't she understand that a strike here would then be even more significant?*

"That's not our call to make!"

This unbelievable comment rendered Drake speechless. The role of an officer was to make calls. To give orders based on those calls. And then to take responsibility for the outcome.

But she refuses to even evaluate the situation?

Then who will?

"The party's commanded us to lay a siege. Our orders are to keep the enemy tightly surrounded."

"…You're telling me to obey the party?"

"Of course."

The way she declared it as if she had no doubts whatsoever felt a bit chilling on the battlefield. If that attitude was consistent throughout the Federation, then their officers weren't even officers.

"Ma'am, allow me to say something."

"What is it?"

"I'm a soldier of the Commonwealth trained to obey the intentions of an order. I have no plan to follow an order to twiddle our thumbs in a siege when it would mean surrendering the initiative."

Not only military officers but anyone leading others needs to grasp the intentions of their orders and strive to achieve their true objective. That's what officers are for. *Why even have officers otherwise?!*

"Please inform Colonel Mikel that I'm a soldier of the Commonwealth and will only be bound by the operation objective to which we agreed. There's no reason I should have to follow the orders of another country's Communist Party."

"It's unacceptable that you would propose something that crushes our dignity in front of Western journalists!"

"Ma'am, I beg your pardon, but let me remind you: We're at war with the Empire!"

"As you so astutely observe, we're in the middle of a war!"

Shouting matches with political officers were the ultimate exercise in futility. At that very moment, time more precious than gold was passing them by. While they were wasting time debating, their victory was liable to slip through their fingers.

"Then how about just the tanks?! For mages, we'll make do with the Commonwealth's! Send out your army's tanks! We'll coordinate with them to get the job done!"

"I can't do that! Taking action on one's own discretion ruins the army's order and discipline!"

"Fine, then! Sorry, but I need to speak to HQ, not the political officer attached to our unit! Please connect me with Colonel Mikel!" He had been taught at the officers' academy not to get emotional. Had he forgotten the reason why? Or perhaps the eastern front was just that exhausting. "The Devil of the Rhine is among those who have disappeared, you know! We can't let this chance go by! We need an all-out offensive!"

He had let his guard down just slightly and ended up raising his voice against the unreasonable political officer. The fact that he did so without checking who might be listening proved fatal.

When Drake instinctively turned around in response to the strange clatter of something falling, it was the sight of a young magic first lieutenant, face flushed and fists clenched, not at all concerned about the canteen she had dropped, that leaped into his eyes.

Here and now was the absolute worst timing.

"…She's gone?"

It was too late to do anything.

"Lieutenant Sue? Lieutenant Sue!"

Letting Drake's shout to stop ricochet right off her, she ran away. And he was well aware that she wasn't the type to go to her room and sit quietly.

"Shit, that girl's always jumping the gun!"

Spending any more time talking to the political officer was now out of the question. *I have to stop her*, thought Drake as he raced after Sue.

And it was strange how quick she was in this and only this sort of situation. By the time he saw her fly away, just after voluntary mages in full gear who appeared to be on standby tried to restrain her…it was clear that they had failed to stop her rampage. And watching her closely, it was obvious where she was headed. Apparently, she was setting off on a long-range flight, bypassing the enemy position.

"Of all the— Is she really trying to go after her?"

If she just wanted to explode, there were better directions she could have stormed away in!

"She could have attacked the enemy position, but instead she's trying to follow the enemy mages?! Why?!" spat Drake but at the same time bracing himself.

At this point, hesitation is the enemy. I'll have to give up on quietly raiding the enemy position. The rest of the troops can handle the encirclement—it's time to clash with those pesky mages.

In truth, he really didn't want to go. He was wholeheartedly against it. Was it sane to go up against the main enemy defensive force solo?

He didn't even have to ask himself—the answer was clear. It would be the worst. How many bereaved families would end up hating him?

He could already see them grieving. Surely, left before the hearths of the home country, they would ask, *Why did that incompetent superior officer have to go charging after the main enemy force with no plan?*

But from a purely tactical standpoint, it was a great chance to tie up the enemy.

If they had to do what they had to do, then they simply had to do it.

"Notice to HQ! The Lergen Kampfgruppe appears to have sortied on its own discretion, and we're going after them!"

From the spirited letter of the message, some might have assumed he was thrilled for a chance to engage in a pursuit battle. But Drake expected that if Mikel received it, the colonel would understand how he really felt.

"You can leave it to me!"

Drake wasn't a fan of leaping haphazardly into action, but momentum was a factor. He couldn't deny that.

 THE SAME TIME, AIRSPACE OF THE EASTERN MILITARY DISTRICT, AT THE HEAD OF THE 203RD AERIAL MAGE BATTALION

The battalion, flying as stealthily as possible, intends to break through and give the enemy a good beating. We shall be the ones to sneak up on the enemy and kick them in the rear.

But their innocent conviction wavers immediately after sortieing.

"Colonel! The enemy's on the move!"

"What? It's too soon!" Tanya replies with a face that is half-doubt.

The 203rd Aerial Mage Battalion excels at hide-and-seek. Even Tanya, one of the top five imperial mages of the present era, struggles to pick up the mana signal of one of her subordinates if they are serious about hiding.

They've been improving their covert flight skills ever since the trench battles on the Rhine. Even using the twin-engine Type 97 orbs, there's no way mana is leaking.

The idea that *that*, of all things, was the indirect cause of the enemy movement is beyond Tanya's imagination—which is why she's so confused.

"Are you saying they found us even with our magic suppressed?"

We've been operating under the assumption that we had some time until the imperial position would be attacked. Tanya worries that if the enemy has detected the core aerial mage battalion missing, the remaining troops are in danger, but her ability to fret about the issue as someone else's problem ends right there.

"Colonel! Look!"

"They came after us?!"

Her adjutant points at a sprinkling of specks in the distance. The moment they're in the air, they're heading for us. Enemies. Enemy mages.

"This isn't funny!" yells Tanya. "Of all the— They're coming after me? Normally, if the mages are gone, you strike the position they just left!"

Taking mages out of your defensive position is like waving a red flag in front of a bull. It's logical for the enemy to rush the position with zero hesitation—to the point that Tanya had assumed the enemy would mount an all-out attack once they discovered the 203rd had left.

"...I can't believe this. They're really headed this way."

Even the veteran officers Weiss, Ahrens, and Meybert had expressed the same fear prior to departure, so Tanya made sure that the Salamander Kampfgruppe—rather, the Lergen Kampfgruppe was thoroughly prepared for a defensive battle in the mages' absence.

Of course, Tanya isn't happy-go-lucky enough to think they could continue to hide the mage battalion's absence indefinitely, but she didn't anticipate it coming out this soon.

"I was resigned to the fact that our exposure was a matter of time, but...I never thought they would pursue us."

If I were in the enemy's shoes, I wouldn't go after the pesky enemies but the position that the pesky enemies had left open.

Which marbles do you have to lose to decide to charge after us?

"...If I had known the enemy would come this way, I would have done things differently."

Chapter V

She thought she had covered her bases for the worst-case scenario by giving rather final orders to her underlings to defend to the last and fight outside the position.

And though it's an awful way to go about things, quite a few of them have managed to stay alive. Tanya is ready to prioritize protecting herself. Her will to survive is not about to be crushed.

So she should be in a nice position no matter how it turns out, but… if the enemy is in pursuit, her position and premises have completely changed.

Having to join up with Lieutenant General von Zettour's offensive while being pursued takes her out of the frying pan and thrusts her into the fire. She wants to wail about how overworked she is.

—I'll just have to make this work.

This is the battlefield. Sadly, it's an uncivilized world. Worlds where regulated violence carries more weight than civilized debate can rot. Or rather, jerks like Being X can rot.

I need to live, return to the rear, and slap everyone back there with my objections and discontent in the form of a mountain of written complaints.

"Major Weiss, cancel mana suppression. Prepare to enter combat at full strength. Don't hesitate to use the trick up our sleeve—the anti-magic sniping formula rounds."

"Yes, ma'am! Canceling mana suppression and engaging with the pursuing enemy unit at full power!"

I had been secretly hoping that the two-headed chimera of the Federation and Commonwealth armies might help us out by being slow to react.

But I guess I shouldn't have counted my chickens before they hatched.

If I have to do this, then let's get it done.

The one thing we can't do is slow down.

"Major Weiss, fighting back is good, but no matter what, we keep advancing! Deal with pursuers as they catch up to us!"

"We're advancing even while the enemy is chasing us?!"

In response to her aghast subordinate, Tanya nods as if it's only natural. "It'd be worse if we stopped! Forward, forward! Fire back as necessary while maintaining speed!"

If the shock troops supposed to be making the breakthrough get caught up here, we'll have missed the point. And in the first place, mixing it up with the enemy instead of taking advantage of the Elinium Arms Type 97 Assault Computation Orb's speed would be a waste of time.

After giving the order to shake them off and fight with ranged attacks only, Tanya is brought back to her senses by the voice of her adjutant.

"The enemy's in firing range!" The unit in range is an enemy mage company.

I realize it takes a minute to go from suppressing your mana signal to max combat velocity, but they're still fast.

She can't help but be impressed that it's a company that has showed up to cling to her. *They're not even performing evasive maneuvers, just coming straight in—what determined ducks.*

"Baptize these heroes of a bygone era with modern long-range fire! This time we're blasting straight through their defensive shells!"

With one word from Tanya, the two companies return fire. The volley, both quantitatively and qualitatively the best of the age, splendidly slams into the oncoming company, sending enemy soldiers crashing into the Federation earth.

But they don't achieve as much as Tanya expected.

She figured one attack would cut down half of them, but only a few were downed.

The little speck of what must be an officer leading the way should have been on the receiving end of multiple concentrated shots from Tanya's subordinates, but their leader seems fine as ever.

Even taking into account the long-range firing conditions, this fellow is incredibly hardy.

"Tsk, what a stubborn stalker!" Clicking her tongue in annoyance, Tanya tries to manifest a formula that will pierce the enemy defensive shells, selecting an optical sniping formula, but right as she's about to fire, she notices incoming enemy long-range fire.

Did part of the group coming up behind the breakout company stop to snipe? When she looks, it seems like there is another battalion. I don't really feel like going at it with two companies and a full battalion.

But it's clear from this small engagement that these opponents aren't going to give up so easily.

"Entering medium-range and close-quarters combat! This was a very fast move for the Federation. Too fast!"

"Know who you're fighting, Major! They're multinational units. That is, they're not as slow as the Federation. We won't be able to get our job done with these nimble pursuers following us around."

Guess I have no choice. Tanya accepts her fate. Tanya gives Weiss, who nods that he catches her drift, a little smack in the shoulder, then swaps partners to pair with her buddy, First Lieutenant Serebryakov.

The skill on display as the two companies immediately get back into formation to hunt the prominent enemy company is so dreamy.

The mages of the 203rd charge wildly to secure local numerical superiority, and the fate of the enemy company on the receiving end of their strike is miserable indeed. With no time to recover mentally from the shock of going from the hunter to the hunted, most of them die heroic deaths, unable to muster the toughness they had only moments ago.

Obnoxiously, though, the officer who seems to be commanding the breakaway unit is still fine.

"What's with this bastard?"

Is this detachment dependent on that single mage's abilities?

Tanya furrows her brow at this inscrutable arrangement, but there's no reason for her to be concerned with every little detail. She should probably mourn the poor enemy soldiers led by such a lousy officer, but she can do that after staying alive and achieving victory.

For now, she has to get everyone back in formation to meet the approaching follow-up battalion.

"02 to 01, it's urgent! More enemies from the rear! It's the Federation Army!"

"What?!" The alert from her vice commander is earth-shattering. "Of all the—! The Commies, too? What are they thinking?! They're abandoning the urban area and coming after us?!"

With this level of numerical inferiority, it's hard to want to form up and try to outfight the enemy. And more importantly, I'm struggling to understand why they're here.

They've abandoned Soldim 528.

Though bewildered, Tanya can't ignore the reality right in front of her. What a mess. Still, the enemy mages aren't courteous enough to let her consider things at her leisure.

"Let me handle the enemy mages! I'll take them down!"

"Okay. Make short work of them!"

Serebryakov, who had been next to her, flies off to buy some time by counterattacking, so Tanya takes advantage of the opening to review the situation.

As far as she can tell from a glance at the battlefield, the Federation troops aren't terribly fast-moving. These are different from the old ones they had faced the other day. It's dangerous to be overconfident, but it's probably fair to assume these mages are using the slower type of computation orb.

By the time I figure that out, I really want to get out of there.

The enemy's plan must be for the speedy Commonwealth-Federation composite unit to run us down, then have the main forces attack once we've been halted. In that case, playing along by counterattacking would be the height of folly.

Most of the clingy, high-speed enemies have been clobbered. Maybe we should withdraw.

"Major Weiss, restart the withdrawal! There's no reason we have to fight both the John Bulls and the Commies at once!"

"But they're still following us!"

"It's better than getting bogged down in a melee!"

"…Understood!"

He must have been convinced. The way he promptly begins reorganizing his unit is the mark of a real veteran. I don't want to get shown up, but Tanya can leave it to her adjutant.

"Huh?"

But she suddenly notices Serebryakov isn't next to her. No, it's not strange that she's gone, since she volunteered to go intercept the enemy, but…she hasn't returned?

"Lieutenant Serebryakov? Are you still out playing?"

Tanya calls to her over the radio, but there's no answer.

Just as she starts wondering where she could be, a fragmented voice enters her ears.

"Can't...shake this one..."

The hard breathing confirms something isn't right. Tanya's adjutant doesn't lose composure over nothing.

She changes her mind temporarily and orders her forces to shoot down a single enemy. Once the location is confirmed and identification complete, she unhesitatingly attacks with full force.

"Help Lieutenant Serebryakov out! Three volleys of supporting fire!"

Tanya commands her two companies' worth of subordinates to fire simultaneously, and they all shoot in a group.

"Enemy spotted! They're still fine!"

"Get out of there, Lieutenant! Three volleys of explosion formulas! Prioritize suppression!"

"The enemy's accelerating!"

"Drop a formula on their head! Block their path!"

It's difficult to believe, but that isn't enough, either. This mage has been fine after sustaining multiple direct hits—they must have an incredibly thick defensive shell and protective film.

And somehow, they're still so fast! They must be using a different model than the Federation Army. Quick, tough enemies are the worst. And if they're skilled enough that Serebryakov is having trouble subduing them, they're heinous in the extreme. I can't just ignore them, but it's vexing that the options for dealing with them are so limited.

Tanya glances at the Elinium Type 95 she brought as backup and frets. I don't want to use it, but I might have to.

The question of how far one's own mental health should be chipped away at in order to preserve human resources is an ethical dilemma that managers and employers face constantly.

It's a troublesome matter for Tanya, too.

Considering the communications costs she would no doubt incur if she lost her adjutant, some measure of sacrifice must be worthwhile.

"O Lord, banish this enemy of the divine in your holy name and bring tranquility to the world."

Having uttered that irritating mantra overflowing with purity, Tanya manifests an optical sniping formula with unbelievable casting speed. Surely, one would be enough to rip apart the Federation's new models, but she manifests multiple overlapping formulas before finally firing.

First, what should have been a gotcha…misses.

"I miss— No, they dodged?!"

Tanya had been confident in her precision and power, so she feels betrayed. *Elinium Type 95, are you just a piece of junk that eats away at my mind without even getting results?!*

"…O Lord, may my enemy plummet to the earth. By your might, let the land be at peace!"

With her irritation mixed into her tone, she manifests an even more precise and powerful formula. This one is on course to strike a direct hit.

And it does.

Or it should have.

"Ridiculous! That was a direct hit!"

And yet, Tanya's shaking her head mainly in confusion.

Before her eyes is a scene that forces her to fundamentally doubt whether she really scored a direct hit on the enemy or not.

It was a sniper formula specifically using an anti-mana sniping round. It should have gone through a defensive shell like a knife through butter.

It would have blasted through even a Type 97 defensive shell, for sure. But this thing just repelled a direct hit?

"How strong can you be? Even if you wanna joke about it, there are limits!" Tanya spits. But in her head, she has already given up tackling this opponent alone. The only concerns are to save Serebryakov and then hightail it out of there.

She doesn't have even one spare second to waste on tiny efforts.

"Saturation attack! Spatial detonation! Take the enemy out with carbon monoxide poisoning!"

"She'll get caught up in it!"

Loath to take the time to explain to a panicked Weiss, Tanya calls her adjutant up on the radio and gives it to her straight.

"As long as it's not a direct hit, you're fine, right?! Visha, you can hear me, right?! Outta the way!"

"Hold o— U-understood!!"

As soon as Serebryakov's consent came through, Tanya started moving.

"Explosion formulas—burn up the oxygen. Less power, more area of effect. We're going to wreck the enemy's lungs."

Chapter V

The two companies beginning to manifest formulas with zero hesitation are the very pinnacle of closely regulated violence.

"Fire!"

Two companies' worth of explosion formulas fired simultaneously—and aimed solely at oxygen.

"Lieutenant Serebryakov! You're alive, right?!"

"I-I-I'm all right. Somehow, yes."

She has visual confirmation that Serebryakov, who had shifted to withdrawing, is safe, so that must show some sort of concern, right? What they call aftercare.

"Lieutenant Serebryakov, now withdrawing!"

"Then there's no need to hold back anymore—good. Use explosion formulas as a smoke screen and mix in sniper formulas as the actual attacks. This time we'll get them…"

"The enemy mage is withdrawing!"

Sometime later, Tanya would come to regret not giving the order to fire and taking their life. But in this moment, at least, she is eager to move on, so she counts repelling the enemy as an acceptable achievement.

"Shall we pursue?"

"We're breaking off! Who has time to waste chasing a retreating enemy?"

"Understood."

Weiss's awkward grin must mean that even he asked only out of formality; Tanya smiles wryly, rounds the troops up, and begins accelerating to break away from the Federation Army.

"Glad you're safe, Lieutenant."

"Thank you, ma'am. That said, I would have rather you spared me from getting caught up in that attack."

"What choice did we have?"

"What is that supposed to mean?" Serebryakov puffs her cheeks out in a pout, which is surely a sign that she's feeling better.

Then Weiss, who had been flying some ways from the formation, comes over.

"Way to make it back, Lieutenant."

"Thank for earlier, Major… That enemy was…a real handful."

"Yeah, I saw. What was that? They had a defensive shell as hard as the Federation's new models. I can't believe it could repel optical sniper formulas."

"And go so fast at the same time. Honestly, it makes no sense."

Her vice commander smiles wryly in response to her adjutant's sighing and grumbling. If only they could tease First Lieutenant Grantz, then it would be business as usual.

Okay, okay. Tanya shifts gears. Having confirmed a new, pain-in-the-neck threat, she needs to consider how to deal with it—that's only fair.

"Major Weiss, would you be able to take that thing out?"

"...I think it'd be an awfully hard fight." Catching on right away that she meant that mage, her vice commander waves a white flag.

It's because he's capable of viewing a power disparity objectively that his reply sends a chill up Tanya's spine.

Even Weiss, arguably a seasoned veteran, doubts he can win. This enemy is trouble, no question.

"I might be able to keep up and not get shot. But to actually down that one, I really don't know. It would probably be too difficult on my own."

"Right? I have no interest in fighting them, either."

It would be a game of chicken involving either managing to scratch their defensive shell or running out of energy. Definitely not the kind of thing you'd do on purpose for fun.

"Between this and the way the Federation troops are qualitatively improving, we just can't catch a break."

"...Speaking of quality, are they planning on coming after us? Perhaps they've also improved their tactical decision-making skills?"

Weiss inquires about the enemy's attitude, seemingly having his memory jogged by Tanya's grumbling.

"They will. I'm sure of that."

"Because of this crazy, reckless advance?"

Tanya bursts out laughing in spite of herself. "Major Weiss, that's putting it a bit too simply."

"By which you mean?"

"They're basically hunting dogs."

At least, they aren't plain guard dogs. They're war hounds, trained and vicious. There's no way they'll be satisfied with baring their fangs and barking a bit.

"Even if we just suppose they're hunting dogs for a moment—would they turn back when their prey is right in front of them? A cowardly hunting dog who doesn't even try to dig their teeth in misses the point entirely. They're coming."

"You don't think they might take some time to consider their tactics?"

"Do you really think they're capable of changing their plan on the fly? I sure don't."

Just looking at the formation is enough to tell. If it's made up of Federation and Commonwealth troops, that's a multinational unit. In other words, a celebration of diversity! Of course, Tanya won't full-out dismiss the possibility it was an error. One facet of the truth is that rejecting diversity results in deadlocks.

But respecting diversity is an adjustment that takes time.

"It all comes down to time. If the enemy commanders are capable, they'll try to improve the situation by forcing through the plan that was set in advance rather than wasting time bouncing ideas around."

No matter how capable and sincere an individual is, bringing the communication cost down to zero is impossible. The time and energy involved in confirming and deciding on things you already know is considerable. Changing plans is a virtual nightmare.

Even in peacetime Japan, far removed from the ravages of war, communication costs can't be escaped. On the contrary, they were almost excessive. Remembering my time as an employee for a company that had recently undergone a merger and working on joint teams with members from various departments illustrates that concept quite clearly.

A brain made of multiple departments boots up slowly, but changing its mind takes even longer.

To comment on the cruel reality...war, in the end, is about instantaneous decisiveness. As long as quick and dirty is a shortcut to victory compared to slow and tidy, an organ of state-sanctioned violence with a clear, consolidated chain of command will be useful.

Which is why a logical enemy would rather choose the barbaric option than hesitate. Sadly, Tanya is incapable of supposing that the enemy is illogical.

"An enemy unit that has been ordered to chase us down as hunting dogs wouldn't be able to withstand the political ramifications of turning back now. They don't have a choice."

"Even so, they're awfully stubborn. You'd think if we've already gotten this far, they could just turn around."

"I completely agree. They're persistent as stalkers. Makes me sick."

And so by accelerating, accelerating some more, and engaging in some evasive maneuvers, the 203rd Aerial Mage Battalion succeeds in shaking off the enemy.

We're lucky that at this point, the enemy doesn't break away and insist on charging after us.

After scanning the area on high alert and determining that there are no enemies present, Tanya adjusts their flight path toward the unit's actual destination, the vicinity of the friendly HQ.

Then they fly in a straight line, mana signals suppressed.

Thankfully, perhaps because the enemy lost them, there are no further obstacles. They make great time and reach visual range of the rear of the enemy unit their fellow troops are fighting.

"I see them! Twelve o'clock! It's our troops!"

"Lieutenant, radio the position! Major, get ready to assist with anti-surface strikes. We'll get behind the enemy they're facing and—"
Before she can say, *Kick their asses*, her senses interrupt. Bits of gleaming ill will she's seen before.

Argh, these sons of bitches.

"A ton of magic radiation?!"

Detecting it immediately, Tanya sounds the alarm.

"Abort the charge! Break!"

It's them, the jerks who have been following us from behind all this time. Is it an ambush? Did they guess where we were headed? Probably the latter. So they must have taken a stab at where we would show up after we lost them.

What a splendid inference, or should I say *appropriate*. Either way, it's more obnoxious than I can stand.

Chapter V

Enemy mages always show up behind you at the worst times.

If this were a civilized world, we could put this matter to bed in court, but this is the eastern front, and this violent space is hard to call civilized even on the best of days, so we have no choice but to save ourselves. How I miss peace and order.

"Prepare for combat!" Irritation in her voice as she shouts the order, Tanya initiates erratic evasive maneuvers. She's aware that this will mess up the formation and slow down the unit's advance considerably.

But no matter how much she tries to understand and accept it, the opportunity cost always stings.

If we hadn't been bothered by these guys, who knows what kind of productive activities we could have gotten up to! They may not be Commies themselves, but a multinational unit that supports Commies is even worse.

"Tsk, they're obstinate to the point of perversion... Deploy optical deception formulas to confuse them and prepare for a firefight!"

Due to their speed, the unit of mages that appears to be from the Commonwealth is enough of a handful on its own. If the enemy surface units have recovered from their shock, what point is there even of attacking from behind...? Behind?

"Hmm? ...That's perfect!" I just remembered something.

I have a company on the ground, don't I?

We can use that to strike the enemy's rear.

"Lieutenant Grantz, it's me."

"Colonel?!"

He must be in combat on the ground. His background music is a mixture of heavy machine gun fire and reverberating explosions. It sounds like a pretty fierce fight, but Tanya prioritizes her own needs and gives the order. "We're in the process of luring the enemy out so we can annihilate them. After we pass overhead, kick the enemy in the pants."

"Yes, ma'am! But, uh, what about my escort mission?"

Ah yes, using them now could put General von Zettour and the others in danger. Personally, Tanya would like to use them for her own safety, but endangering her superior officer would be the same as endangering her own position, so it is a tricky option.

Just as she is wondering what to do, she is saved from her conflict by the lieutenant general himself hopping on the radio. "I don't mind. Go ahead."

The level, detached way he spoke might have moved Tanya to tears if he wasn't the one who had forced this nearly impossible task on her in the first place.

"...I appreciate it. Now then, I hope you'll watch our art unfold."

"I'll enjoy it."

If your superior is watching, there's nothing to do but give it your all. Even failure at a parlor trick can end up cursing you later on.

"They're so intent on playing tag that they've forgotten to look where they're going. Let's remind them that the world is 3-D, not 2-D!"

We've been fighting as two companies this whole time, so surely the enemy assumes we're two companies.

"01 to all units! Three volleys! Suppress the enemy!"

Formula bullets sparkle, manifested explosion formulas roar, and not wanting to be shown up by the splattering red liquid, Tanya raises her voice again. "O Lord, O Lord, bestow on us shining honor, the iron hammer of providence, and peace and order!"

"Follow the colonel! Prepare for hand-to-hand combat!"

"Supporting fire before the charge!"

When we hold the enemy down and come at them like we mean to confront them head-on, they fire back to intercept. They probably believe without a doubt that a frontal clash is imminent.

At a glance, it appears both sides will collide with all their might.

But that isn't the case.

"Charge! Charge!"

The only one capable of imagining a company would suddenly fly up from the ground to interrupt the fight is the one who gave the order.

"Now! Close in for the pincer!"

The company, led by Grantz, charges up from their position on the ground and into what is quickly becoming a melee.

They return the favor with a rear attack, and the balance of power leans back in our direction.

If you're focusing every last bit of your energy forward right when you get stabbed in the back, it doesn't matter what kind of hero you are; it will be impossible to maintain formation. As a result, the doggedly resisting enemy mage unit, too, finds itself in disarray.

That said, at the moment where they wavered between simple chaos and total collapse, the enemy commander must have tightened the reins. They begin to withdraw with some semblance of unit cohesion.

"The enemy mages are pulling back!"

Serebryakov's joyful news brings a slight smile to Tanya's cheeks. It feels just like getting rid of a stalker. As someone who has experienced being tailed by a degenerate, how could I not feel happy?

"01 to all units! No pursuit! Fix your formations—hurry!"

As they regroup, Tanya doesn't forget to praise the key player. As a superior officer, she keeps in mind how important it is to be considerate.

"Magnificent job, Lieutenant Grantz!"

"Not at all. I appreciate the help."

"That's the job. It goes both ways."

"I can't argue with that."

He smiles, and she claps him on the shoulder; when she judges she's adequately closed the distance between them, she gives him an excessively demanding order.

"You're going back to the ground to support the general."

One must never neglect self-preservation. If she carelessly keeps the escort tied up in the sky, the deputy director of the Service Corps in the General Staff might die an honorable death in battle on the ground, which would result in the brilliant career of Lieutenant Colonel Tanya von Degurechaff dying a dishonorable death in battle.

"Company, on me! We're descending!"

Her subordinate gallantly zooms off. After leaving General von Zettour in his capable hands, Tanya retasks her unit to provide ground support to drive off the remaining enemies.

"All units, switch gears and get ready to help our troops on the ground! We're providing air support! Get into anti–surface strike formation!"

"The main position is—!"

"Enemy infantry?! Shit, on me!"

But there is a shortage of a critical element: suppressive fire. Soldim 528, being under siege, never had an abundant supply of ammunition, and the battalion had been having trouble making ends meet. Participating in a major firefight on the way over decidedly didn't help.

Pitifully, as commander, Tanya has the least firepower at this moment when she needs it the most.

"Tch… Successive engagements are a curse."

She has no bullets left. She despises the limited selection of long-range gear she's stuck with. Just as she is thinking, *Even if I wanted to fight at close quarters…*, she recalls the shovel on her hip. She's wearing it because she thought she could use it during an urban battle, but what's to stop her from using it in a 3-D battle?

When she glances down, she sees imperial positions on the verge of being stormed by enemy infantry. Regardless of how it would go in a normal positional battle, here they only have a makeshift defense without so much as a reserve trench. If our troops get overrun, it won't end well.

I have no choice. I have to put this implement of civilization known as a shovel to practical use.

As soon as she has made up her mind, her shovel glints as she begins her descent. Then, having raised it above her head, she brings it down unhesitatingly on an enemy soldier.

It's a strike landed by an aerial mage without slowing down, boosted by gravitational acceleration, using the same logic of the furious cavalry charges performed in every age and area. Even if Tanya herself is light, she's now a fearsome missile.

A dull crash.

A fallen soldier.

Then instead of braking, she uses her defensive shell and protective film to send the other soldiers in the area flying before finally making landfall. Grabbing a gun off an enemy on the ground, she surveys the area and immediately finds the man she's looking for.

Should she be stunned? Moved by his valor? To her immense surprise, Zettour, who isn't even a mage, is mixed in with the foot soldiers, carrying a personal weapon.

Despite the heaps of corpses, he holds his ground instead of retreating… What a fantastic boss. Tanya doesn't feel she can compete.

"Are you all right, General?"

"The glint of your shovel was mesmerizing."

How awkward that he saw her out of ammo. Beginning to blush, she looks away and apologizes for her bad form.

"Sorry you had to see that."

"On the contrary, Colonel, it was a valuable scene I never could have imagined while polishing a chair with my ass back at the General Staff Office. It was quite an interesting performance."

"It's an honor to hear you say so, sir."

So it's the kind of failure we can chuckle about? Since Tanya did her best, I figure it's okay to feel relieved that the evaluation wasn't too harsh.

"I'll do better next time."

"That'll do, Colonel. That'll do. At any rate, once we clean up here, allow me to invite you to tea."

"How refined, sir." She laughs that it's a strange thing to propose on a battlefield.

"Don't you think that culture is what separates us from the beasts, the normal from the abnormal?"

"I'm not able to be as consistent as you. But I'm exceedingly honored to be invited."

"Good." Zettour laughs, too.

"I have a nice blend our friend from Ildoa left before going home. We should have something other than coffee once in a while. Anyhow, do this right."

"Yes, sir! I'll see you later!"

This is bad.

Hans von Zettour on the eastern lines

The Federation Army units dealt with the charging imperial armored units according to regulations. The reserve forces were assigned rapid-response duty and intercepted the imperial rescue units trying to make a breakthrough.

Though Federation doctrine emphasized numerical superiority, they didn't necessarily have it on the receiving end of Lieutenant General von Zettour's charge. Still, what they lacked in numbers, they made up for with ability.

The Federation Army's handling of the situation, on battle lines ruled by the fog of war, was exceedingly close to perfect. The carefully prepared plan was enacted without a hitch, and the pet they had kept safely in their pocket for just such an occasion—a full armored division—was decisively rushed over.

Even the Imperial Army General Staff was forced to recognize their enemy's organized resistance as something worth imitating.

Without excessive interference by political officers, plus their burgeoning pursuit of military logic, the Federation military organization had built itself a reliable defense. Perhaps it was by the book, but when you have the ability and opportunity, there is nothing more solid than a frontal attack.

If the imperial relief unit had been short on nerves, the Federation surely would have won. Their counter-advance would have shattered the imperial will to fight along with everything else; they probably could have even made a long-range march of it.

If there was one fatal miscalculation the intercepting Federation troops made, it was this: They didn't anticipate wild animals escaping the supposedly surrounded enemy position, baring their fangs, and chomping down hard from behind.

Chapter VI

In a struggle for supremacy, a stab in the back can trigger the collapse of even the most powerful of armies.

Because the Federation Army had unwisely committed its reserve forces and continued choosing the right answers according to the textbook, a single action outside its paradigm froze its brain.

The blessing within the curse was that a sheepdog had been pursuing the animals.

Lieutenant Colonel Drake was forced into the heroic role of saving his fellow troops, which, while not at all what he intended, proved a stroke of luck for the army overall.

Dragged along after rampaging First Lieutenant Sue went rogue, the voluntary mage unit ended up pursuing the enemy, and by slowing down the mage battalion that zoomed out of Soldim 528, the Federation troops just barely managed to contain what would have otherwise been a fatal strike.

But ad hoc tactics would only work for so long.

The Federation Army was aware of the B Group's dwindling will to fight, so the Imperial Army's drive to break the encirclement overturned all its expectations; they were pincered by the mage battalion from behind, and all of their reserve troops had already been deployed.

The commander of any army would have their head in their hands.

But it turned out that the damage to the Federation Army at the point where they were broken through was momentarily localized. The real problem was caused by its organizational structure as they faced this challenge—that is, the issue of decision-making.

What do you do when you can no longer maintain the line?

Counter? Retreat? Defend?

Any of those choices would have been one way to proceed. But the Federation commanders failed to make the crucial call. No one was able to secure the time necessary to reorganize the crumbled formations.

It wasn't that there were no commanders who could make a quick decision.

In fierce battle after fierce battle, Federation commanders were accumulating experience and knowledge, honing their judgment and combat skills at a pace that rivaled their imperial counterparts.

There was only one reason they failed to decide.

Regardless of how outstanding an officer, the Federation Army considered obedience the supreme virtue. Put another way, disobedience was simply not an option on principle. Their organization lacked the culture of acting on one's own discretion, even in an emergency. Not that it hadn't ever been done. But doing so was a heroic decision that took something more than bravery.

Most people would simply wait.

For an order.

Or more precisely, for permission.

That's how they had been disciplined: to fear the party more than the enemy.

Of course, if they realized they weren't going to make it, they might eventually move.

But they didn't go far enough.

So Lieutenant General von Zettour's advance—which went not only far enough but all the way—opened the door.

Was this resolute charge an example of savage valor, recklessness, or a casting away of indecision? No matter how it was described, there was no doubt Zettour had won his wager.

〉〉〉   **JUNE 19, UNIFIED YEAR 1927, THE EASTERN LINES,**   〈〈〈
IMPERIAL ARMY UNIT IN PURSUIT

The rewards of victory are many and various, but one that is guaranteed is the right to chase down fleeing enemies. No matter the era or place, there is nothing that feels better than firing at your enemy's knapsacks.

I mean, you get to attack their backs, you know?

Once a general pursuit is ordered, everyone has to go whether they want to or not.

Among the bravely charging units ordered to hunt down the enemy are Tanya and the rest of the 203rd Aerial Mage Battalion. It's full speed ahead in aerial strike formation aiming straight for the enemy's backs as the Empire's hunting dogs.

Chapter VI

But the face of the commander Lieutenant Colonel Tanya von Degurechaff, leading the troops, darkens for a moment, and she signals nonchalantly with her eyes to her vice commander flying nearby.

He looks worried, too, as he approaches casually. He's a trained officer as well—he gets full marks for considering the watchful eyes of their subordinates.

"My, what a view. Who could have expected a pursuit battle?"

"You said it. The breakthrough is a success. So there was a point to defending Soldim 528."

"Ha-ha-ha." What a cheerful chat as commander and deputy commander laugh together. The 203rd Aerial Mage Battalion may train from scratch, but at least it has commanders it can count on.

So yes, Weiss and Tanya are doing a good job. Probably the only one who catches the cryptic air between them is Tanya's adjutant.

"We're supposed to mop up the rest of the enemies while giving chase in order to secure the area, but…Colonel?"

"Weiss, I'll ask you point-blank…do you really think pursuit is possible, given the circumstances?" Tanya glances at her vice commander with a bitter look.

"We've been ordered to pursue…but it's not what you want? It's true that the unit is tired, but we're still mission-capable."

"Major Weiss, even we're exhausted, and we certainly didn't have it the worst."

Of all the units that participated in the breakthrough operation, the 203rd is probably in the best shape. Yet, Tanya hesitates to take the opportunity to expand their gains via pursuit.

If it were only her own unit, she might have forced them to keep pace with the rest of the troops. Sadly, those other troops, who would be their last hope, may or may not be in any position to move.

Considering B Group's current status, by the time they achieved the breakthrough…the troops were already at their limits.

"So there's no way?"

Tanya gives a small nod in response to Weiss's pained comment. She doesn't have to ask what he's referring to.

It's frustrating to not be able to follow up one success with full force, but neither is there any way to gloss over the complete lack of reserves.

"It's too big a risk to press on with the battalion alone. The best we can do is provide support alongside the air fleet. I'll approve a slight advance as a tactical measure, but I want to avoid incurring any further fatigue."

"If those are your orders…"

"Let's make them strict orders. I don't want to exhaust units that have already been through a hard fight. We had that multinational unit hounding us, too. I can't let this drag on."

"So we should call it off entirely?"

Tanya signals that she wants to consider it and goes over the issues on her mind.

When we met up with General Zettour, he was definitely giving off vibes that implied he wanted to mop up the enemy. He was so amped that he had been personally at the front, gun in hand.

And along with the tea plans, he had made a request: "Colonel, after the pursuit battle, I want you to report in and tell me how it went."

Remembering that, Tanya sighs.

The higher-ups always talk like it's so easy. He said to report in, but does that mean he expects a souvenir? Does she dare to return empty-handed?

I don't want to be the sort of boss who merely hands down her superior's contradictory orders.

"I don't want to be like that, but"—Tanya spots a cluster of enemy mages like tiny floating specks and grumbles—"it also feels like a waste."

If I want to heed warnings from history, then the only practical option is to withdraw. But I also understand feeling, like Cao Cao, that we're squandering an opportunity.

If I could just lay into the Federation and Commonwealth mages who have been following us and causing trouble… Well, it's not something I wish for no reason.

"Colonel?"

"Nothing. I'd like to withdraw, but I also feel like settling the score, since they're right in front of us—two actions that are mutually exclusive. So the only thing to do is to probe them."

Tanya laughs at herself for acting out of character. But this is what happens when you're stuck in a situation with no good choices.

It's awful, but then so much of life is.

Chapter **VI**

Reality is full of absurdity—from Being X, to the sorrows of middle management, or the fool who pushed me in front of the train. Thus do I wish that all those evils rot.

Let's brace ourselves.

Let's stand up against absurdity.

We'll hold our ground and act with tenacity.

"01 to all units! We're going to destroy those enemy mages! Prepare to strike!"

If you're going to do it, abandon all hesitation.

Ordering the charge, Tanya leads her battalion as they swiftly close in on the multinational unit led by Lieutenant Colonel Drake and Colonel Mikel.

>>> **THE SAME DAY, THE MULTINATIONAL UNIT'S REAR GUARD** <<<

Meanwhile, Lieutenant Colonel Drake, on the pursued side, had problems of his own. Or perhaps one could say the thoughts of any member of an organization on a battlefield start to resemble one another. It doesn't matter if you're victorious and transitioning to pursuit or defeated and retreating, your worries will be more similar than some might imagine.

Will it be all right to return empty-handed? It's the first time Drake, magic marine of the Commonwealth and seasoned hero, has had to face the conflict of wondering that while being pursued.

If he had to describe this novel experience in a nutshell: *the taste of vomit.* It was the sort of dilemma he never wanted to go through again.

"The enemy is after us. But I'm not sure what to do. Honestly, what a…"

No, he would hold his tongue, but it absolutely was a shit show. How could he hesitate between counterattacking and fleeing?

Strictly speaking, there was no problem with his own hands being empty, but he had to consider Colonel Mikel and his standing with the Federation Communist Party.

If the multinational unit retreated empty-handed, would Mikel's physical safety be guaranteed or not? Being defeated was already complicated enough.

It was easy to imagine this as a concern shared by all Federation officers—to the point that Drake was forced to realize: *That's why the Federation Army is so fragile.* If he could believe the rumors he was hearing, they were starting to value military logic. But the divergence from a Commonwealth soldier view was still as substantial as ever.

"...So what should I do?" Drake murmured and turned his mind to organizational theory and the Federation's internal logic. If it were only about clobbering the enemy in front of them, things would be much simpler...

But as it was, they were basically being pincered.

"Does it bother you so much to bring up the rear of a fighting retreat?"

"...No, it isn't that. I'm worried about what excuse to make..."

"Colonel Drake?"

He was having a frank conversation with Mikel, who gave him a puzzled look—minus the usual interpreter. It was a risky move, but if neither the political officer nor loose-lipped First Lieutenant Sue was around, he didn't have time to waste on useless formalities.

Risk, risk, risk.

They were only waging war alongside the Federation, so why was there so much to take into account?

"Please allow me to ask you plainly. Are we allowed to retreat without achieving anything significant? I'm especially concerned about any difficulty you might experience in your position. Do you think you'll be let off the hook without punishment?"

"I'm making it a point of not discussing politics. Could you do me a favor and not make me leak confidential intel?"

In other words, politics were involved. If politics were involved, he wouldn't get off easy. Drake responded to Mikel's implicit answer with a hollow laugh at the sky. "...Got it. I understand the Federation's culture and wish to respect it."

They needed to return with a souvenir as a matter of political necessity.

He had always believed that politics was a nasty business, but with this, he confirmed anew how truly, hopelessly rotten it was.

"So we need something to show for all our effort, but we're the rear guard fighting fiercely as we retreat. I hate to admit that Lieutenant Sue's rampage saved us this time, but in retrospect, we were able to provide effective support for our fellow troops as a result of her actions."

Chapter **VI**

They had been able to avoid the collapse of the army when the imperial pincer attack threatened to destroy them completely.

"Let's hold out at the back of the pack. We'll stay with you and fight."

Mikel's apologetic thanks was lost to the wind.

Drake didn't hear what he said. It wasn't the sort of thing that should be said between brothers-in-arms. A man doesn't need a reason to stand firm beside a fellow soldier.

There's my friend.

And there's me.

So like Horatius, I've got to protect what I've got to protect. In the name of the homeland, one man makes loyalty his duty. What was there to be afraid of?

"At least tell me this...how many of your subordinates...?"

"Thirteen."

A company's worth of people had been lost.

Without Sue's rampage—no, there was no point in thinking about that.

I killed them—the unit was under my command. I should apologize to their families. I should be punished. It should be my shame to bear.

"...Dear God and fatherland, may you know their glory," Drake prayed quietly, faintly.

"Colonel, they did die fighting the enemy."

"By which you mean...?"

"...It's good that you're not used to your troops dying. And they were able to die in battle against the enemy. That's a relatively blessed way to go."

There was a story Drake had been taught as a boy. A heroic tale of a brave and just knight. He would have to add to it the contributions of his subordinates who made the ultimate sacrifice so far from home.

What we're doing has meaning.

He wanted to believe that.

At least they had fallen fighting the enemy of the homeland they believed in. There were few times he felt as proud to be a citizen of the Commonwealth as he did now. *Oh, beloved Commonwealth, may you delight in our peerless adoration.*

Well, that's enough sentimental musing for now.

For now, just for now, he had to force this unromantic reality to make sense.

"Well, it seems I've been comforted by your words, so let's get down to war, eh? How serious do you think their pursuit will be? That mage battalion is charging after us, but do you think it'll end there?"

He had to admit that the charging Imperial Army was handling things quite nimbly. The imperial mage unit and the Devil of the Rhine had a lot of fight in them despite giving chase right after flying out of the heavy encirclement and harsh conditions they endured at Soldim 528.

They could have gotten a little tired, but instead they were coming at the multinational unit as if their adrenaline was blasting on full power; it creeped Drake out in the same incomprehensible way Sue did. Why not get worn out like a human being?

"The answer is obvious, Colonel Drake. There are few things as amusing as seeing your enemy's knapsacks."

"What?"

"Is this a generational gap or something? Shooting at the packs on the enemies' backs is good old fun. You could say that it's an officer's dream to see the enemies' knapsacks."

"I was a little boy with status, so I've always preferred chasing foxes." He held his rifle up as he mimed hunting.

The customs of his hometown. How nostalgic—the scent of peaceful civilization. In warlike style, the tradition of hunting was extolled for making sure men had a gun at the ready in case anything should happen to the home country.

Harkening back to those memories from a battlefield was especially nostalgic. What a clear and simple thing it was to innocently take up your hunting rifle and chase your quarry.

"So it's a cultural difference, hmm? Anyhow, now then, we're about to greet the war-loving imperials. We've got to prepare a splendid welcome party."

"Can we expect anything out of the fighter planes? That political officer guaranteed support, but it's only her guarantee after all. I'd like to hear your opinion, Colonel Mikel."

"…Colonel, your dislike of the political officer has gone a bit far. I've told you repeatedly that she's one of the better ones."

"And no matter how many times I hear you say *better*, I don't understand what you mean by it."

He wasn't unaware that his hatred of politics was growing, but given that he was being forced to fight as a rear guard for the sake of politics alone, he would have appreciated some tolerance of his griping.

"The worst is far beyond what you can imagine. She's more—how should I say? She's like a good little lamb pretending to be a wolf."

"She may be good, but she's a wolf in sheep's clothing. It's no wonder good sheep can't get along with her. That said, I'll leave off here. It's time to party."

He had just lit a fire under his subordinates' behinds with gruff orders to get into formation so they would be ready to confront the incoming enemy when he received a rare bit of good news.

"Colonel! Lieutenant Sue reports enemies in our path of retreat!"

Good news from his man carrying the communications kit.

While it may have been unfortunate that enemies were sighted, Drake and his troops were being pursued—of course enemies were coming after them. It was as natural as rain falling from rain clouds.

The important point was that Sue, the entirely too willful lieutenant, had carried out her orders properly and reported in.

"The imperials could have taken their time, but oh well. Engage immediately—no, wait. Order her to break through and secure our path."

"Yes, sir! I'll order her to secure the path of retreat."

Even Sue would obey him if the order entailed rescuing her fellow soldiers. Perhaps you could say she had purehearted concern for her allies? But she was still a newly minted first lieutenant.

She wasn't a bad person at her core; on the contrary, the trouble was that she acted only out of good intentions. But for once, that would work to their advantage.

"And tell her that there are lives depending on her support of the Federation Army! Under no circumstances is she permitted to go charging off into some random imperial troops. Don't loosen the reins!"

"Understood!"

After giving his old wingmate instructions over the radio for how to handle Sue, Drake emitted a small sigh.

He was glad the wild girl could be somewhat controlled.

After being showered in concentrated imperial mage fire and nearly getting shot down, she seemed to be learning to hold back a little from her reckless charges.

He was glad that the imperial troops had given her an education. Though he was furious that the tuition cost an awful lot of his subordinates.

But perhaps the issue lay more with Sue's command ability.

"Okay, troops!" Drake shouted in borderline desperation. "We're getting back alive. And when we arrive, I'm breaking out my entire stash of drinks. The catch is that the dead don't get any. If you don't want to be robbed, fight with all your might!"

>>> **THE SAME TIME, THE IMPERIAL ARMY'S 203RD AERIAL MAGE BATTALION** <<<

"Enemies spotted—two battalions' worth of mages."

"Yeah, I see them."

It's too bad that the number of mages her adjutant counted is correct.

"...Once again, the response is awfully fast for a Federation-Commonwealth composite unit. I guess I just can't describe them with 'for a' anymore."

It would be great if the two-headed organization would get confused about who's in charge, but somehow they either unified the chain of command or the commander of the Commonwealth troops is a Commie—however they did it, a Communist army and a capitalist army were marching in step.

"What an unpleasant thing to see. Really horrifying."

"Then leave it to us. You can watch as we attack and scatter them."

First Lieutenant Grantz's eagerness as he reacts honestly to her complaint sure is something to behold. He looks delighted to be liberated from his position as Lieutenant General von Zettour's bodyguard.

Well, I understand that between accompanying a VIP and doing your own work at your own pace, the latter is easier, but...that said, determination needs to be used judiciously. Grantz is getting a bit carried away at the moment.

"We can't assume that the enemy is poorly disciplined. So no, rejected."

Any normal day, her subordinates would stand down after a declaration like that. But—if he isn't looking back at her with eyes that say, *We really can't?*—today she's astonished.

She wants to scream at him to ask if he's a child.

"Lieutenant Grantz, a no is a no. Are you really going to make me repeat myself?"

"N-no, ma'am. Understood!"

When Tanya hardens her eyes and demands he understand where she's coming from, he's quick to consent. While on the one hand, she wants her people to be bold, it's also important for them to listen to reason.

Though if the enemy camp were to fall into disarray, she wouldn't object to guaranteed gains.

"What a pain these enemies are who won't fall to pieces."

Before them, enemy mages adjust their formation as if they're about to engage. They've been called two battalions, but they're too tightly coordinated to really resemble survivors fleeing a lost battle.

Strange. This was supposed to be a pursuit battle, so what's going on?

Pursuit means shooting at the enemies' backsides. If the enemy has this much fight in them, it's more like an encounter battle. Talk about bad luck.

Here! This is where an indirect approach can be handy.

"Split into two groups and target their path of retreat. If their way back is threatened, they should…"

"They're coming this way!"

In response to her adjutant's yell, Tanya shouts in frustration. "This ploy again?! What do they take us for?!"

This was supposed to be a pursuit battle, but they're turning around? That takes guts, but it's also an awful lot of screwing around. We've already been on the receiving end of a coordinated feint attack like that once before. It's terribly upsetting that they think we'd fall for the same trick twice.

"Watch out for enemy planes and…ngh! Aircraft spotted at three o'clock! Identify it!"

"Seems to be the enemy, ma'am. More than one headed this way!"

"Good work, Weiss!"

It's as if all has been revealed. Aerial tactics that combine mages and air forces are interesting, but once you know the trick, it's mere prestidigitation.

We have the ability to learn. We'll show them that rehashing and trying to reproduce the same success over again are clichés we understand!

"Maintain distance between formations and shower each one in bullets!"

Preventing erratic evasive maneuvers and the scattering of formations, Tanya orders defensive barrages in the form of interdiction fire. The battalion's rapid response is nearly perfect as it works to turn the enemy planes into expensive scrap metal.

But their fight ends anticlimactically.

"Huh? Where are they going...? Crap!"

Having interpreted the enemy flight path as a charge, the battalion was ready to counterattack, but right in front of us, the enemy leisurely turns away.

It's not even a hit-and-run, more like "no hit."

Having been faked out, the battalion fires a splendid barrage at the air. And to make matters worse, enemy mages basically begin bullying us with long-range sniping fire in the spaces between the formations we'd split up to counterattack.

Good sense really does hold back a good modern citizen like myself. Limeys and Commies, is it something about that *mee* sound that imparts the powers of an evil deity? Should I be proud of myself for not being as adept at becoming the object of hate as these two great evils of the world, the Commonwealth and the Federation?

Or should I lament that they got me?

"The enemy mages are turning around!"

At First Lieutenant Serebryakov's report, Tanya lets a tongue click slip out.

Vexingly, the enemy's conduct is clever enough to be put in a textbook. When I look, the supposedly charging enemy mages have already gotten away. They gave up so fast, it's a letdown.

"So it was just a feint...? They tricked us again. The enemy isn't performing half-bad, no, sir."

At this point, the idea of all firing at once, swooping in, and finishing the pursuit battle in one go might as well be a fantasy. Even if the damage is negligible, my will to pursue has been largely drained. Frankly, going after an enemy with that much organized energy left on our own is out of the question.

Chapter **VI**

Enemy mages who flaunt their ability at us and then make a flashy retreat are a dangerous threat, which is why I want to have nothing to do with them.

"We could get additional pay, and it still wouldn't be enough for this..."

The labor union, where's the labor union? No, military officers are public servants, so...we probably don't have collective bargaining rights. I guess we'll have to hope the labor standards supervisor will do something.

The labor standards supervisor, where, oh where is the labor standards supervisor? Commissioned officers around the world eagerly await your arrival...

"Take out the fighter plane unit! Spatial area suppression with explosion formulas! Let's at least get rid of those guys!"

"No, Grantz!"

"Huh?"

Suppressing the urge to cradle her head and sigh, Tanya checks her subordinate.

It's not as if we get paid enough for this, and more than anything, performing anti-aircraft combat as mages will throw our formations into disarray.

The enemy mages may be keeping their distance, but we don't need those speedy fellows to linger right outside of engagement range. I'm not saying it's the same as a fleet in being, but having a threatening presence that nearby severely curtails our freedom of movement.

"Ignore them. That Federation mage unit is too close. And in the first place, even using the Type 97, you'll wear yourself out accelerating to a speed that matches the fighter planes."

The enemy may be harassing us with long-range fire on their way out, but they are leaving of their own accord. And we engaged enough to call it a proper attempt to pursue them. We can say we met our minimal obligations. Now if we just support the ground troops and mop up the rest of the stragglers, those achievements should make a nice souvenir for Zettour.

All that being said...take the initiative to do things people hate.

We were taught in compulsory education that that's the way people are. Having learned the same in Japanese schools, in the Empire's staff officer curriculum, and in my experiences on the battlefield, perhaps I should consider it a universal law.

"Still, there's no reason we have to let them escape unscathed!"

Apologies to my eager subordinates, but there will be no swooping.

Unlike more dynamic officers like Grantz, Weiss, and Serebryakov, Tanya isn't a fan of bothersome things.

Labor is a product. Selling yourself short amounts to dumping founded on sincerity. Honestly, it's criminal.

"Ready formula bullets! We're casting long-range optical sniping formulas! Hit 'em in the ass as they go! We'll give them something to remember us by!"

Instead of giving our enemy a helping hand, we'll give them a helping of lead. The ground is the perfect partner for them. I would be delighted for some of them to take a precipitous turn and share a passionate embrace with it.

But unfortunately, it seems that neither the Federation nor Commonwealth mages feel like deepening their loving relationship with the ground. The Ildoans are legendary for their amicability, so perhaps we should try to persuade them into that tender hold if the chance ever arises. Thankfully, our allotment of peace means we shouldn't have that opportunity for a while.

Either way, launching formula bullets at speck-like enemies at long range doesn't achieve very much at all. After a few dozen volleys, the enemy aerial mages exit our range in an orderly fashion and continue their leisurely withdrawal.

It should have been a simple pursuit battle consisting of firing at the enemy as they retreated, but the results are poor.

"This is enough, though." Tanya indicates to her troops that the fight is over by leaning her rifle back on her shoulder. "We can't catch them. Any farther than this, and the risk is too great. Weiss, Grantz, we're pulling out!"

"But if we act now—!"

Grantz is such a lover of knapsacks that she's used to him pointing at the enemies' backs and pleading impatiently with his eyes for pursuit.

"Lieutenant Grantz, are you really doing this again?!"

"The ground troops fought so hard to catch them! Please!"

"…We can't."

She knows that their fellow troops made sacrifices. From a cost-effectiveness perspective, it's clear that their kill ratio needs to be improved.

But Tanya hates gambling. When investing, she prefers steady trust funds and building wealth over a lifetime to day trading, or even better, investing in her own human capital.

Pursuing the enemy isn't a bad choice, but…the divide between profit and loss has long been crossed. Continuing any further carries too high a risk. What the idiots who mock turning back as defeatist need is intelligence. According to Tanya's self-analysis, she shouldn't be desperately short of that.

"If we leave now, we still have the strength to make it back."

What's important is safety.

Safety, peace, and certainty.

Based on her clear policy, Tanya declares, "As long as I'm in command, I won't ever back down from this. I won't let my troops be exposed to pointless risk. Do your part to remember that."

"…Understood."

It's a rather quiet reply but clear, so Tanya nods in satisfaction. She'd like responses to be a bit snappier, but she has discovered as an educator that as long as humans have emotions, asking for 70 percent is a surer thing than trying to get 100 percent.

According to my keenly observant eye, Grantz seems to have recognized his inadequacies when confronted with Tanya's confident declaration. It may well be that after facing her sound argument, he's feeling ashamed of himself.

That's not surprising.

Tanya expects that he'll learn from this mistake and put his knowledge to future use. Mistakes are human, and anyone who can learn from them with a calm, open mind is a decent human resource.

"As an educator, I'd like to turn this expertise into a book someday."

"Is everything all right, Colonel? You seem to be in a strangely buoyant mood."

"It's nothing. This is just an interesting experience, even for me. I was thinking I'd like to write a book about education, that's all."

Just as she's about to continue with, *It's about the importance of changing your point of view*, she realizes she's in need of some self-criticism. It won't do her any good to focus only on her workplace. She nearly misses a major resource that can only be seen from a broad, overhead perspective.

No, rather than *miss*, perhaps the better verb is *overlook* regarding things *below*.

"Look at that, Major."

"Hmm?"

"Our enemies left all that stuff behind. It's a mountain of treasure."

The enemy mages' conduct was exemplary, but the confusion of their ground troops was exemplary in the opposite meaning. If pressed, I'd say it could be used as a textbook example of a rout.

It's the same scene we saw when we trapped the François Republic's army in the revolving door. You can only call it the perfect example of how much a company, an army, even a country—probably any human organization—weakens when the person in charge fails to provide a clear direction.

Most of the enemy ground troops, unable to take decisive action in response to the swiftly changing situation, ended up choosing the foolish plan of defending whatever position they found themselves in and rapidly deteriorated into a chaotic mess.

Even if a couple wise, brave officers ordered a retreat, the difference between an organized retreat and individual heroes retreating is huge in terms of the resulting confusion and losses.

As a result, they dropped a lot of things.

"Let the rest of the troops know. Tell them to send out some trucks to seize the abandoned Federation artillery gear. And invoice them for our discoverer's fee."

"Enemy artillery gear? Shovels I've had Grantz and those guys collect before, but I'm not certain we can even put heavy equipment to use..."

"It's called diversifying your procurement channels. The supply process is in dire shape, you know."

Chapter **VI**

The Art of War mentions this, too, but goods procured in enemy territory are cheaper, whether in terms of shipping or price of acquisition, than those from the homeland. In my Japan days, what Sun Tzu said was such a fundamental principle that I couldn't grasp it, but it can't be denied that he was cost conscious. Regrettably, current international law prohibits a formal plunder economy...

We can't break the rules, but thankfully the laws don't ban seizure. And to come at it from the other end, it's just a fact that we aren't able to carry everything from the homeland like the American Empire.

"...What a drag," she grumbles before she catches herself. "At this rate, we may have to rely on the enemy for rifles, too."

When Weiss begins to chuckle—"No way..."—Tanya shakes her head slightly.

"Major, right now may be the only time you're able to snicker like that."

》》》   THE FEDERATION, SOMEWHERE IN MOSKVA, OFFICE OF THE   **《《《**
COMMISSARIAT FOR INTERNAL AFFAIRS, WHICH
EXISTS TO SERVE THE PEOPLE

In the plain office, the commissar of internal affairs...the devil in the guise of a human, Loria, was cocking his head in surprise.

"We lost?"

Across the desk, a career soldier, with the rank of colonel in a uniform with no wrinkles, flinched as a chill shot up his spine; he broke into a cold sweat as he nodded in silence.

"Against the Imperial Army's B Group?"

"...Yes."

There was fear in the voice he had to squeeze out. This colonel had known Loria for some time and was able to speak his mind to a degree... but having witnessed firsthand the commissar's severe reaction to failure, he was probably having a hard time relaxing.

To put him at ease, Loria gave a casual shrug and put on an intentionally cheerful expression. "...Well, I don't mind. We managed to win in the critical cities down south."

"You're counting this as a victory?"

"Comrade Colonel, I'm surprised. You're a soldier, yet it seems you lack common sense for a military man. From a military standpoint, we can surely call this a win."

Even if it's better to be feared than loved, binding people with fear alone is for fools.

"Comrade, I'll be frank. Our comrades-in-arms are doing a good job."

Fear is like a medicine you administer as needed. The right amount keeps the organization functioning smoothly, but the side effects from too much are extreme.

"But…"

The Federation Army officer was still hesitant, and Loria delivered his conclusion matter-of-factly. "We bore the brunt of the imperial attack in the south. The resource-rich regions are unharmed."

The Imperial Army's attack had been ferocious, but it eventually ran out of steam. Even the imperials were stopped by the combination of the tyranny of distance and nationalism.

Yes. There, Loria added something in his head. The large role played by the material support they were receiving from the capitalists was indeed *material*.

Either way, the thwarting of enemy intentions had a decisive psychological effect on the party leadership. Being able to resist the Empire… was better proof than insulting reconciliation struggles that the Federation could forecast bright prospects.

"We not only prevented the enemy from achieving their aim but wore down their armored forces at the same time… One lost city is a small price to pay."

Even if the fallen city's name was taken from their general secretary's… they had only lost a city with a symbolic name. That was all. The impact on their ability to continue fighting would be extremely limited.

The party leadership was so terrified of losing the southern resource area that the types of people who would make a fuss about losing one city when they stood to lose them all were *no longer around*.

Come to think of it, the party had felt well ventilated of late.

"The army judged that they wouldn't be able to defend it successfully and retreated. I'm not about to go back on my promise to accept the comrade generals' decisions unconditionally."

"B-but...the city we lost is Josefgrad."

That those below should fear the disfavor of the general secretary made sense, but the commitment to use everything available was now long in the past.

"I'll inform our comrade general secretary personally as well—that the troops did a good job. And I'll arrange a little something for our comrades in the field."

"I—I appreciate it!"

As the color returned to the colonel's face and he relaxed his shoulders with a sigh of relief, Loria smiled like a loving, understanding father.

"The problem is the enemy's B Group."

The central lines should have performed a checking attack, tidied up the lines, and achieved a modest victory; that they were instead repelled was unexpected.

To the Federation anyhow, it should probably be said.

To Loria, it was also a surprise, but he could see how it was possible.

"That what-do-you-call-it, the Devil of the Rhine? I saw a report that she was there raising hell. There aren't any further details?"

Her...

My adorable, mischief-loving fairy...

My little devil brandished her fury.

This is what it means to get suddenly hot between the legs.

Ahhh, I had no idea my fairy was right there, so close.

"We're going after her unit, since they're the ones who caused trouble in Moskva..." Suppressing the heat that threatened to creep into his voice, Loria maintained a nonchalant air to the greatest extent possible. Falling in love at his age struck him as embarrassingly pure.

"Due to the failure of the offensive, nothing is certain. At present, we have the unconfirmed report that the multinational unit engaged with the Empire's most capable unit."

"With Comrade Colonel Mikel commanding, was it?"

"Yes, it's Colonel Mikel from our side. A magic marine by the name of Drake is the commander from the Commonwealth. Though apparently, this lieutenant colonel has ties to their intelligence agency."

Having been asked implicitly if that was a problem, Loria smiled. "That's probably fine. We're good friends with the Commonwealth.

Friends don't need to worry about each other's backgrounds, and there's nothing we need to hide."

If there were, they would never have let in even the limited group of journalists they had. They needed the West to see only the good points of Communism.

They weren't about to show problematic elements to outsiders. Of course, if the Commonwealth Army's intelligence agency made some kind of egregious slipup, he would be more than happy to condemn them in front of the journalists and lament the infidelity to their alliance...so they always stayed ready.

"At any rate, we can recover."

It was actually huge that they had managed to stop the invasion at the cities and protect the resource-rich areas. He could live for love, but if he suffered a setback at work, he wouldn't have time to tend to his affections, so he was grateful to the army for doing a good job.

"It was the enemy's Operation Andromeda, yes?"

"Yes, that's what the code said."

"We'll just laugh at them for being overly attached to such a fantasy operation. The winners will be we who are supported by scientific Communism. We shall claim victory!"

"Yes, sir!"

The colonel straightened up and saluted—he was a good career soldier. These comrades of Loria's would be quality pawns who would bring his desires to fruition.

"Then, Comrade Colonel, if I can trouble you to tell the General Staff, I'd like them to take the measures that are necessary from a purely military point of view."

"I'll be sure to let them know."

"And one more thing. That Devil of the Rhine really is a problem. Do you agree?"

"Of course, she's a dangerous presence..."

Loria nodded that she was a special sort of danger.

This devilish fairy was making off with his heart.

The things that welled up in him when he so much as thought of what her panting and gasping might sound like...

He wanted to know so badly.

Chapter VI

What a tempting danger of a monster.

"On that note, I'd like you to ready a unit specifically to track her."

"...Is that an order, sir?"

"No, just the suggestion of one Federation citizen. Do be so kind as to consider it. Though if you're up to it, I'd like you to pursue her jointly with the Commissariat for Internal Affairs."

>>> B GROUP ON THE EASTERN LINES, PROVISIONAL FORWARD COMMAND <<<
POST, THE POSITION PREVIOUSLY KNOWN AS SOLDIM 528

"Lieutenant Colonel von Degurechaff here."

When she enters the room, her sense of smell is confused by an unexpected stimulus. The entire space is filled with a mellow fragrance. After a moment's hesitation, Tanya's brain remembers that it's the long-lost scent of black tea.

Ohhh, right. This is the smell of real tea.

"Hello there, Colonel. Yes, I've prepared us some tea as promised. Take a seat."

"Thank you."

This is a source of caffeine often interrupted due to the John Bulls' maritime blockade. Eager to partake, Tanya happily accepts Lieutenant General von Zettour's invitation.

"The orderly will bring it right over. Now then, Colonel von Degurechaff. Let's have a little chat while we wait. How's the pursuit battle going?"

The moment she sits with a cheerful expression, the question hits her like a ton of bricks. Chuckling inwardly at his brilliant command of soft and hard manners, she answers her superior's question with the very definition of a sober look on her face.

"...We weren't able to catch them. At least, it's not possible with my troops alone."

Maybe it would be possible with an augmented mage battalion?

Nah, that would be tough. We need to face the fact that the Imperial Army can no longer guarantee qualitative superiority. Just by discovering that the Commies can compete with us in quality, the future of the Empire has gone pitch-black.

"Really, the entire army is short of manpower."

"Well, that's no surprise. As long as we're lacking reserves, hoping to increase our gains in a follow-up attack is an awful lot to ask in the first place."

"...Can we even say we've won in a situation where we're unable to properly run down our enemies?"

Being unable to even go after withdrawing enemies is tantamount to allowing them an opportunity to recover and organize a retreat. It may look like we successfully took ground or broke through the encirclement, but really, we dropped the ball.

"What do you think?"

"You're asking my thoughts, sir?"

Tanya is bewildered when he nods the affirmative. She thought he might ask her opinion, but she wasn't expecting him to be this direct.

But he's asked. If she doesn't make good use of this opportunity, she's nothing but a mooch. She hesitates for just a moment and then speaks what she has felt for a while now.

"We're failing to annihilate the enemy field army... If we don't even have the wherewithal to chase them as they retreat, this is truly a disaster. At this rate, it'll become a battle of attrition. That's what the Imperial Army needs to avoid more than anything." This is Zettour she's talking to. She figures that rather than dress things up, she should get straight to the point. "With all due respect...despite that, I fear we're already getting ourselves trapped in that situation."

"I welcome your honesty. But I'll amend one point."

"Sir?"

"We're not 'getting' trapped—we're in up to our necks."

He grumbles that things are abysmal and sadly shrugs. The murmur, stripped of Zettour's usual calm, even carries a whiff of powerlessness and frightens Tanya.

"...It's that bad, sir?"

"I was in the Service Corps, you know? Well, no, I still technically have a position there. And I'm also here dabbling in leading troops on the front lines."

This is the analysis of someone well versed in rear echelon matters who has taken a dive into the field. Basically, he should have the best understanding of the current situation.

"I'll give you my conclusion, having seen both sides. Colonel, things are horrible. To call them 'too horrible' wouldn't be overstating it."

When he glances at her, Tanya realizes how precarious the atmosphere is. Not that she's overly concerned, but she doesn't want the mood to be bad. Discretion is the better part of valor.

She searches for a way to change the subject and—*Oh!*—grins. "...Ah, how rude of me. I completely forgot. Congratulations on your victory, General."

"...It's hard to be genuinely happy about it. Oh..." He smiled wryly. "I can't forget my manners, either. I appreciate the rescue, Colonel. You saved me from a dangerous spot. I mean that."

"Hmm?"

She's confused by his last few words. She thought she had dodged a bullet, but this conversation seems to be heading off in another strange direction.

"What is it, Colonel von Degurechaff?"

"I was sure you leaked the location of the headquarters on purpose to act as bait... Was that not the case?"

"You're right that I meant to be bait." He continues in a bitter monotone, "I never believed I would be saved, though—there was no guarantee."

He risked his life to lure the enemy? Tanya can't relate at all. He acted as bait without even thinking about his own safety?

"...That's a bit difficult for me to comprehend."

"I'm sure it is. I never imagined we'd be so hard-pressed that we'd have to use HQ as bait. I knew this would be rough, but I guess I underestimated things."

Zettour spoke so simply. Tanya considered him logical, had never doubted it. She even specified in her mental evaluation of his character that he was a pragmatist you could talk to. Yet, he's capable of self-sacrifice in the heat of the moment...? That's a grave oversight on my part.

If you follow someone unconditionally, you risk being led into danger; the warning echoes in Tanya's mind.

"That's why I'm grateful to you. You did a great job commanding out front during both the pursuit battle and the defense of Soldim 528. I'll have Colonel von Lergen pull some strings to submit a medal application."

"All I did was have my troops form a meat wall to be bludgeoned. It had nothing to do with my abilities."

"So you're saying the one who ordered it should be responsible? That's an interesting way to comment. Or are you saying it was terribly irresponsible?"

"I think in my position it's best to keep things formal and remain silent."

"Hmph." Zettour smiles wryly. "You always do stand your ground, Colonel von Degurechaff."

"Yes, I believe in myself."

You can only lie to other people. Trying to deceive yourself is sheer folly. In an era when all things are uncertain, you should at least be able to have unconditional trust in your loyalty to yourself.

I go my own way. Rather than leave my fate up to randos like Being X, I've decided to put my faith in my modern self's determination.

That's why people with no sense of self-preservation frighten me.

"Perhaps you're making too much of self-determination?"

"It's more productive to act and regret it than to regret not acting. I prefer taking responsibility for myself over leaving my fate up to someone else."

"…That must be why, then."

I don't know what it is that he saw, but Tanya sincerely expects that Zettour will accept her ideals.

Especially in this sort of era, getting to probe the leader you're following is a precious opportunity. Given that she and Zettour have had some communication hiccups in the past, whether they are able to gain a solid common understanding here or not could very well determine my future.

"Oh, the tea showed up at just the right moment."

"Thank you."

The orderly delivers properly brewed tea poured into a cup warmed to just the right temperature.

Chapter **VI**

She had almost forgotten this rich, blossoming fragrance. Though amber in color, tea is nonalcoholic; having some after finishing a job on the eastern front makes her almost obscenely happy.

"The friendly Ildoan or whoever has great taste."

"Biting commentary from a neutral country, perhaps. No…I doubt our mutual friend is that sort of man."

Setting aside the character of the supplier, there's no doubt about the fact that he knows his stuff. Understanding the temperament of the supplier—that is, Colonel Calandro—it was a social gift presented half-kindly and half-calculatingly.

Tanya would also do well to remember that Zettour is the type to bring tea leaves to the forward-most line on the eastern front. Is that half-eccentricity, half-sophistication? It's definitely revealing of a civilized temperament.

"Kindness is truly delicious."

"To be sure. But goodwill can also be awful. And sometimes ill will does the most good."

"Oh?" Tanya raises her head and observes Zettour's expression. "You're saying that bad intentions are sometimes better than good ones? I beg your pardon, but if you're saying that from the purview of your position…I fear I might read into it and get some strange ideas…"

"You're free to think what you like. Use your common sense to decide what's right."

"You mean sense that is common in the homeland will apply on the eastern front?"

Tanya is laughing as though she's heard a fantastic joke.

"Watch what you say, Colonel. Surely that's going a bit far."

"Yes, sir—I'll be careful."

"Do that. I think nothing of it, but words of that nature are liable to get twisted and find their way into unexpected places."

I don't know what the goodwill of the homeland looks like, but I should probably be grateful for the ill will Zettour has shown me. Honestly, as someone in the field, he's been a great help. Although in the long term, he may affect things in other ways…

Furthermore, Tanya didn't expect to be given such candid advice. What is compelling him to reprove me more than I expected…?

"I had no idea it was so careless."

"There are reasons… Once you hear the bad news I received just prior to our meeting, I'm sure you'll agree with me."

Tanya braces herself, and Zettour lobs the word bomb at her so simply.

"I don't mean to rain on your victory parade, but it's not good… Andromeda's hit an impasse."

The bomb explodes smack in the center of Tanya's mind. She just barely manages to remain calm but fails to hide her shock.

An impasse? So it failed?

"W-we couldn't get past the southern cities?"

"We didn't even get that far. After advancing to Josefgrad with blinding speed, the offensive ground to a halt due to supply line chaos. As a result, Federation defense tightened up, and there's no way to advance any farther… The troops are too busy trying to protect their vulnerable flank at the moment."

"So"—it's not a question as much as a confirmation—"the resource area?"

"We can't reach it, Colonel."

The news is disappointing enough for an *argh*. We've failed to secure the resources that are the foundation of a war economy.

All I can think is that this mistake is—like dissolving what little money you earn in the forex market—one of those that you should absolutely not make, yet the Empire has done so on a national level.

"I'm surprised. It's not like General von Rudersdorf to slip up."

"Matériel mobilization not happening in time must have been the main factor. Lieutenant Colonel Uger is in charge of that; it's unusual for him to make mistakes, but…"

"But?"

"If you take another look at the situation, a new answer appears on its own. If the supplies can't be transported, then part of the responsibility must lie with the railroad people."

"So it has to do with the rails?"

The Empire and Federation have different rail gauges, so we can't simply jump tracks, which results in a bottleneck for traffic in several places. That's a well-known fact.

If anything's problematic, it must be that.

"The issue of unifying the standards is difficult, but Colonel Uger and his team are no slouches."

Zettour snaps off the update that the technical issues have been solved. "It's quite the juggling act, but they're working magic to convert the gauge on part of the trunk line and, in the meantime, keep supplies moving with captured rolling stock."

In other words, though it was a problem with the railroad people, it also wasn't a problem with the railroad people.

"So the distance was too great, then? Or did the Council for Self-Government fail to preserve the rails?"

"No, the council is doing a good job. It has even developed its internal administration to the extent that it is in the process of organizing the self-governing bodies at the village level."

"In that case, only the worst-case scenario is left…"

"Yes, it's the absolute worst."

The significance of Zettour affirming her fear is tremendous.

…There's a path.

But supplies aren't coming down it.

The reason is simple.

"We're short of supplies themselves?"

"We must be."

"Excuse me for asking, but how did you make things work, then?"

"I was scraping the bottom of the barrel and committing limited resources in a concentrated way to maintain production volume. And as the chief coordinator, I knew how to apply the right kind of pressure on the correct places."

And now he's been flung to the eastern front.

He doesn't have to say it; even someone with paltry powers of imagination could easily grasp what kind of confusion that would cause at the working level.

The organization is learning through experience that coordinators earn high salaries because without their leadership in overseeing smooth unified operations, the organization can't function. Only an idiot who has no idea what work on the ground is like would take that leadership away, throw everything at the working-level personnel, and expect operations to continue without a hitch.

"Allow me to say one thing." Tanya chimes in with an awful headache gnawing at her. "Even if we're talking about a capable guy like Colonel Uger, isn't that a bit too much to put on him? This is a lieutenant colonel versus a lieutenant general. Those ranks have different authority, jurisdiction, and powers of intimidation."

"The military organization should be made up of people who can stand in for each other...or I suppose I should say 'should have been.' Now then, Colonel, I've done enough learning on the eastern front."

"Yes, sir."

"This won't work."

Tanya nods.

"We can't go on like this."

It's impossible to deny, so Tanya nods politely in response to his soliloquy.

"My conclusion is simple."

"I'm eager to hear it."

"...This...at this rate, our current path is no good."

"Sir?"

"Somewhere in my mind, it's possible that I...thought that maybe if we kept following this path, we might find a way out." Zettour wears an expression of regret as he shakes his head, which has noticeably more gray hairs. "It was a fleeting dream."

The Imperial Army has stabilized the vulnerable portion of the eastern lines. On the surface, that's a great step forward that makes up for the offensive's setback in the south.

But for anyone aware of the full domestic situation of the Empire, a different side of things comes into view... Even if you don't want to see it, you can't help it.

We step forward, we extend our legs, we even stretch out our arms, but they don't reach anything we want them to.

But what exactly is the general referring to?

"In our current situation, the setback in the southeast is fatal. We need some propping up... Eventually, I'm sure your unit will be sent down there to fight."

"We're going to leave this delicate balance and concentrate all our forces in the south? That doesn't sound sane to me. Launching a direct attack on Moskva while we tidy up the lines here would be more realistic."

"*The General Staff* would probably agree with your view."

Tanya's spine stiffens at the words that seem to imply too much.

"I heard recently that our nice chat with Ildoa didn't go so well. Was that also…?"

"On the army's orders. Do you understand now, Colonel?"

She stares back at him, astonished. *On the army's orders?* So the army intends to do the opposite?

Does that mean…? Wait, the Supreme Command is the only entity with the authority to give orders. Is the army under attack by some formal rubber-stamping gone wild or the monster known as public opinion?

"The fatherland has become dependent. Colonel, it's sad how bad it's gotten."

"Dependent on victory?"

"Exactly." He nods, expressionless. "'All our problems can be fixed with victory.' In other words, we're sorely addicted. If we can't envision tomorrow without a victory, we're simply doomed." He says this with a quiet but clear tone of voice as his eyes crinkle in a smile. "The fatherland wants to dream. It's a grand dream. Everyone hopes for a great victory for the great Empire to be reality."

"Then our only choice is to shatter that dream. We've got to throw out their comfortable bathwater and open these idiots' eyes with ice-cold reality."

"That sounds like treason, Colonel. Are you calling the fatherland a bunch of idiots?"

"Unfortunately, I'm a soldier. I was taught in academy that anyone who can't see reality for what it is should be called an idiot."

In an army at war, it's utterly natural to call an idiot who can't face reality an idiot.

One of the nice things about the army is that you can call a son of a bitch a son of a bitch. It's wonderful to not have to say things in a roundabout way.

"Most importantly," she says, "I love the peaceful days in the fatherland. If a bunch of blind, reckless patriots or whatnot are going to destroy that tranquility, I can't even consider them real patriots. We've got to string them up like pigs and obliterate them."

Tanya von Degurechaff is a utilitarian pacifist to her core. She's against war on principle. She's especially against any war that isn't an easy win and won't end with their finances in the black.

If it isn't a winnable, low-cost war with guaranteed returns that can be obtained in a safe way, then there's no way she counts it as a viable investment.

Basically, anyone who recommends that sort of venture is either a crook or a numbskull—in any case, criminally inept.

"Patriotism has nothing to do with taking bad advice. In the first place, if you love your country, you should be protecting its peace—and to go a step further, it's precisely a patriot's duty to prevent their country's ruin."

"Certainly. That's the definition of a true patriot."

His amused murmur makes Tanya realize their conversation is veering into strange territory. *I didn't mean to act so patriotic… Why did he take it that way?*

"So, Colonel von Degurechaff. As a patriot in this situation, how do you define victory? Is it a victory for the Empire? Is it the victory the Empire dreams of?"

She's not really a patriot, but she knows that denying it will offend him. Only a numbskull would declare to an officer—a high-ranking officer at that—that they haven't got so much as a milligram of patriotism in their heart.

Not saying things that don't need to be said is like a little bit of lube to keep society running smoothly. Silence is an expedient for suggesting friction to the whole of society.

Which is why Tanya thinks for a moment about what the appropriate thing to say as a patriot would be.

It's not as if I intend to share the Empire's fate, so I don't really care whether it wins or loses, but if my life and assets aren't protected, I'll have problems. Major problems.

"I don't acknowledge any difference between the former and the latter. How could I? Military regulations don't allow it."

She seems to have tapped Zettour's funny bone; he grins slightly. It's amazing he's able to smile in the middle of this exchange.

"That's quite the honor student outlook... I've given up on the old ways."

"You gave up? That's surprising."

"I'll do whatever's necessary. In the end, you can't compensate for poor strategy with superior tactics. We have no choice but to chime in on the strategic level, don't you think?"

There's no way Tanya can say she thinks that. Her face starts to cramp up, but she interrupts with self-preservation in mind.

"General, I think you know this, but...we're soldiers."

Career soldiers—that is, officers. In other words, our job descriptions are set out clearly in the associated laws and regulations.

The bare minimum requirement for control of the instrument of violence is civilized use of force.

Deviation would surely be harshly punished, and it'd be a breach of contract, so it's hard to even bring up an objection.

"The role of a soldier, who is subject to military orders, is to do only that which is clearly defined as military service. Our jobs don't include politics."

"In an ideal world, perhaps. I see no flaws save the one issue of it being sadly unrealistic."

I'm starting to really hate this debate, sighs Tanya internally. It's not that she has *no* idea what Zettour is thinking, but...if she shows that she gets it, she might end up being pulled into the same boat as him.

"Colonel von Degurechaff, ultimately, morale is like salt. Without salt, your only choice is to die, but neither can you live on salt alone."

He speaks with so much gravity, but what he says is the most banal common sense.

Tanya doesn't understand what he's getting at.

"Do excuse me, but that's pretty much self-evident, isn't it? There aren't any dishes you can cook with just salt. Even a child knows that. There's no reason for us to get all excited about it."

"Colonel von Degurechaff, don't you know the upcoming trends? In the imperial capital, alchemy using salt is all the rage."

"...Everyone in the capital wants to transform salt into gold? Like trying to make a philosopher's stone?"

Unable to hold back, Tanya bursts into mocking laughter. Alchemy! It's not as if we're some unenlightened society from the time before the science of magic was standardized into the system we have today.

Frankly, even if it's a metaphor...it's not a very good one.

She wonders if she should swallow her unnecessary *What kind of fool would do a thing like that?!* remark or blurt it out.

"Some think it's possible. Yes, they have a blind faith that no matter how great a fortune they wager, they'll make it all back."

"Is there a chance of succeeding?"

"None. They're going to fail disastrously and pickle the whole Empire."

Sodom and Gomorrah, the city of salt.

Horrible words cross Tanya's mind, but she dismisses them at once. She's not living in the unenlightened world that begot mythology. Though it's vexing that I can't completely deny that, having confirmed the presence of an evil deity like Being X... Was it careless to be relieved that she hasn't been interfered with lately?

"...General. Is Supreme Command in the rear so useless?"

"Extremely sensible people are being *ruled by the dead*."

The words appear so suddenly, Tanya fails to grok the context. She asked about the situation inside high command, and he replied, "Extremely sensible people are being *ruled by the dead*." Tanya doesn't have enough info on what's been going on in the rear to grasp his meaning there.

"Colonel von Degurechaff?"

"Huh? E-excuse me, sir, what do you mean 'ruled by the dead'?"

How uncomfortable it is to honestly admit you don't understand something. It's the painful moment that, vexingly, she realizes she's been on the front lines for too long.

"Have you heard people talk about 'the sacrifices we've made so far'?"

"A bit. From Colonel Uger."

"That'll make this quick. What did he say?"

I remember, at a table in the homeland, insisting that we cut our losses. Uger's counterargument was that we'd already made too many sacrifices, so the desire for reparations would be too strong. It's a sentimental argument that reeks of the Concorde effect, and frankly, it's difficult for me to comprehend. After squandering so much sacred human capital, choosing not to minimize further casualties is practically tantamount to murder.

I'd like to ask them what they think a human life is, exactly. To be told such a thing by someone who should know better, like Uger, makes her want to shout that it can't be.

"Honestly, I don't intend to slander Colonel Uger behind his back."

"Ha-ha-ha. He probably claimed that a powerful, unreasonable, emotional argument had taken hold, right?"

"Yes, sir."

Tanya failed to understand what Uger said.

Or rather, she felt he was exaggerating. *Surely, he's not that idiotic!* Though she's perfectly aware that some people become idiots, she's not so sure about turning into super-dreadnought-class idiots.

Does that actually happen?

"As someone who has seen the innermost workings of the Imperial Army, allow me to state with certainty: Colonel Uger is speaking the truth. If there was any issue with what he said, it's that he may have been underestimating the situation."

"...I find that extremely hard to believe. We're at war!" she yells, so shaken as to be visibly upset.

To Tanya, a pacifist, peace has a value that can't be exchanged for anything else. Human capital is the hardest thing to rebuild.

"We're sitting here feeding logs of human lives into the fires of war like idiots!"

If the economists at the World Bank saw the way we're carelessly gouging into the educated working population, they'd faint for sure. This is just like Ebola and AIDS. If you let something go unchecked because the cure is expensive, society will eventually pay an even greater price.

No matter if it's bitter or costly, if there's a prescription for a cure, it must be accepted.

"After hemorrhaging precious human lives, they can't even make the call to cut our losses? I don't think that's how intelligent people would act."

Peace is an investment that generally pays reliable dividends.

Ah, but perhaps start-up costs are high. Still, it's certainly wiser than carrying on with an enterprise that's constantly bleeding out into the red.

In response to Tanya's shriek-like rumination, Zettour wears a vague, dry smile. There's no refutation, no persuasion, no denial, just a mute silence.

I would prefer if he said something.

If a logical General Staff officer was joking, there was still a possibility. But having no words carries a significance that...

If there isn't anything you can say, silence is correct.

It's the limit of words or perhaps of reason.

"...After putting us in the red with all this waste, the rear is trying to escape our unproductive reality?"

Still mute, Zettour takes out a cigar and abruptly cuts it. Then he strikes a match, and the way he slowly begins to puff at it makes him look, at a glance, like he would on any normal day.

"Maybe the romanticists looking for honor and prestige out of war have finally died off. But the desire for revenge and gains that match the sacrifices we've made are a whole other issue. Public opinion is birthing a chimera-like hodgepodge of a monster."

"It should be mowed down with sweeping machine gun fire. Iron and blood will fix it."

Physical laws demolish silly talk.

No matter how strong your belief, the world will never move exactly as you predict. Perhaps it's an inconvenient truth for guys like Being X, but the world just does its thing. Interventions don't just work because you want them to.

"If everyone and their mother thought the way you do, that would be convenient. But we've got to accept that we're the hopelessly tiny minority."

"Like the majority that believed in the geocentric model and the minority that believed in the heliocentric theory, sir? I feel like a trail-blazer who'll teach dimwits some truths about reality. In order to win, we'll need to reform our awareness."

"Colonel von Degurechaff. As a practical problem, your opinion is worth considering... I should accept that we need to overcome our internal challenges."

Though she was the one who said it, Tanya finds herself bewildered by the bad feeling that has beset her.

"A soldier achieving victory in domestic affairs? Is there a chance you can seize the initiative?"

"Problematically, I've only ever worked as a faithful military bureaucrat. Regardless of how I fare within the military organization, I know nothing of how to make things happen in politics. I'm an inexperienced amateur without a single trick up my sleeve."

"So you're going to start now?"

"It's time to study, Colonel. Let's learn some nasty tricks. For starters, I want you to be one of my accomplices."

Tanya flinches slightly.

I don't like that word.

"An 'accomplice,' sir?"

"...Yes."

"I can't help but feel bewildered."

This is an invitation that the normative, modern citizen of good sense and abundant law-abiding spirit, Tanya von Degurechaff, has a very hard time replying to with a nod of acceptance.

Crime is not my style.

Laws, yes, are merely for hitting people with. That is, they're a useful blade, but that doesn't mean they should be your own death sentence like some sword of Damocles. When you consider that trusting in the law is what secures the market's reputation, then breaking a law on purpose is unacceptable.

If there's one thing ten thousand people in modern society agree should be taboo, it's "breaking the law."

"...You're one of our most experienced frontline commanders. And you have the right abilities for a staff officer. I hardly think you don't understand our situation."

"General, with all due respect, it's precisely because I understand that I hesitate."

The Imperial Army General Staff has been an exacting boss. The quotas they impose are brutal, and they don't give your feelings one iota of consideration when deciding where to send you next.

But that's the fate of anyone stuck in a normal job.

You have to go where you're sent and do what you're told—anything goes, as long as it's a lawful order.

But that's based on the premise that the higher-ups understand the way things ought to be.

Any member of society who has to cover for a nincompoop manager on top of doing their own work would want to throw up their hands. But when you find out the leadership has abandoned reason during a war, are you willing to consider illegal countermeasures?

To Tanya's sensible nerves, that's intolerable.

"Forgive me, sir, but please keep the gap between our ranks in mind."

"Hmm?"

"I'm merely a member of a military organization whose duty is to obey lawful orders."

Even if it's for work, I'm not about to cross during a red light.

Tanya reveres the life of a law-abiding citizen; it's not as if she's interested in deviating from the norm, and she definitely doesn't want to get dragged into being someone's accomplice and made a bona fide gangster.

Laws are for getting other people to break, not for breaking yourself.

She understands that Zettour, this important man, is implying all sorts of things between his words, but once you touch that guilty business, that's your life. Everyone knows that someone who gets their hands dirty is tainted forever.

Well, or maybe it works a bit differently from how the Nikkei corporations did it.

Maybe personnel doctrine in the Reich is kinder toward underground business… In other words, could it be set up so you can be ordered to ignore the law as necessary?

To Tanya, a proudly justice-loving individual, that makes the world a very sad place.

"General, allow me to say once again: I'm nothing but a soldier bound by lawful service. No matter what the intention, any deviation from legal norms would mean betrayal of the imperial family and the fatherland."

Of course, that applies only to the letter of the law, not its spirit. Anything not written down is nonexistent.

"Very good. Incidentally, your duty is to defend the Empire, is it not?"

"It is, General."

Her nominal duty...

To Tanya, it's simply to devote herself to what her work is according to the contract. Perhaps it should be called a stipulation against side jobs, but pursuing anything besides imperial victory would be a contradiction of the idea of a contract.

"Then sorry, but I have an order for you. Colonel von Degurechaff, find the way to do that which you deem 'best.'"

"If that's your 'order,' sir..."

"Good. Well, yes. I'll just give the order."

Wondering what the command will be, Tanya is frightened, but Zettour smiles to relax her.

"It's an all-new initiative. A new way out. It's unorthodox, but it might be a soldier's greatest ambition."

"I'd appreciate if you'd tell me what it is."

"Sure." Zettour nods benevolently. "Are you fond of preventative surgical measures, Colonel?"

In this context...

In this conversation...

Preventative measures.

Surgical?

In this ever-so-pregnant string of words, Tanya discovers the source of the dangerous vibe she has been getting from Zettour since the start.

For a high-ranking officer to come out and say this openly sure is a sight.

"...Not to be insolent, but I'm *an imperial soldier.*"

Official stances are wonderful.

Official stances are safe.

Thus, Tanya resorts to the model answer that Magic Lieutenant Colonel Tanya von Degurechaff is supposed to give. Emphasizing that she is a soldier and will fulfill her duty as an officer while simultaneously declaring her firm refusal to deviate.

She's so desperate that Zettour cracks a smile.

"Fantastic. If you had answered with anything else, I would have had to shoot you. If you understand that much, then I have faith that you'll be able to take the appropriate surgical measure."

"…What in the world are you planning to do?"

She doesn't want to ask, but the risk of not knowing is greater.

"In order to give our undivided attention to the east, we need to win our war in the west."

"You mean the western air war?"

She realizes that's wishful thinking, but it's a hope she can't give up on so easily.

"A little more toward the east than that."

Ahhh, damn it all. She sees what he means. *So it's come to that?*

East of west could only mean the beautiful place Tanya has been wanting to return to so badly: the dear homeland. As a rule, falling back to the rear is a happy thing; however…this particular instance makes her hesitate.

"Rejoice, Colonel. It's a peaceful type of war. We'll have a grand time back home."

"If that's an order, then of course I'll do what little is in my power."

Tanya repeats that she's a soldier, a member of an organization. Implicitly informing your boss of your position is essential for self-preservation. Although I'm not sure how effective it will be here.

After all, the man staring her in the face, Zettour, is a specialist in military administration. If a pro at formalities gets serious, they'll find a way to do whatever is needed.

"Great."

"Yes, sir."

"Let this be a golden era for the Reich… Even if it's a twilight, we've got to show them that the sun will rise again. I'm counting on you, Colonel."

"We shall…make this a golden era for the Reich."

"Good! Very good! Let us steel our resolve. We don't seem to have much of a choice."

"…Yes, let's prepare ourselves just in case." Tanya murmurs a reply.

I'm sure this order will be awful. I'm sure it'll be justified as necessary, but it's terribly upsetting to be forced to go along with it.

Still, if running isn't an option, then there's no choice—Tanya needs to be ready no matter what comes next.

(The Saga of Tanya the Evil, Volume 8: In Omnia Paratus, fin)

Appendixes

Mapped Outline of History

Mapped Outline of History

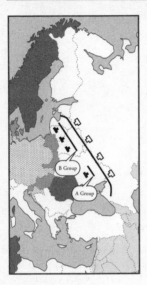

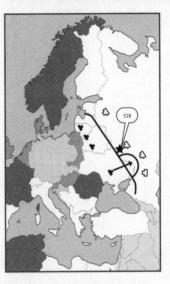

Beginning in Late May, Unified Year 1927

1 The rift between the Imperial Army on the eastern front and the central government's foreign policy grows beneath the surface. The conservative Lieutenant General Hans von Zettour is promoted to inspector on the eastern front (while retaining his position as deputy chief of the Service Corps). He sets about leading the reorganization of the front lines.

2 The Imperial Army General Staff launches a major offensive aimed at the Federation's resource-rich south in Operation Andromeda.

3 The Federation Army carries out a plan to strengthen their coordination with their allies. They also take steps toward international conciliation by accepting members of the press, and so on.

The Lergen Kampfgruppe Is Deployed to Soldim 528 on an Emergency Basis, Begins Building Field Fortifications

1 The Imperial Army commences Operation Andromeda, and A Group begins the offensive in the south. In response, the Federation Army mounts a counterattack all along the eastern front to contain the imperial advance. There are also clashes with the Imperial Army's B Group.

2 B Group desperately searches for a way to relieve the Lergen Kampfgruppe, which is isolated and besieged on the front lines. The position itself is protected by the seasoned Kampfgruppe, but the encirclement is closing in.

3 Meanwhile, Operation Andromeda is running into difficulties. The pace of attack is slower than anticipated, and success begins to look doubtful.

General Commentary

Pincer by the B Group rescue team and the Lergen Kampfgruppe

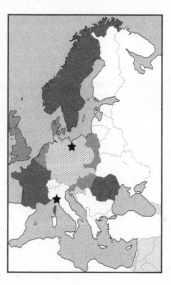

❹

Though the Imperial Army reaches the limits of its advance, it manages to hold the line.
Meanwhile, the counterattack coordinated between the Federation Army and government starts to take effect, and Federation troops begin to evenly match or best the imperials.
The Empire finds its hourglass running out of sand.

June 18, Unified Year 1927

1 Group A captures a city that is one of the operation's strategic goals but reaches the limits of its advance. On the same day, B Group begins an operation to rescue the Lergen Kampfgruppe.
2 The rescue units and besieged units coordinate via a witty exchange and crush the enemy encirclement. Some of the forces quickly go from partial envelopment to attacking to a pursuit battle.

June 22, Unified Year 1927

1 The Imperial Army and Federation Army both cease major maneuvers. The Imperial Army abandons Operation Andromeda. But given the limited change in the front lines and successful defense, Supreme Command declares it a major victory.

Afterword

Are there any heroes out there who bought the books in one fell swoop after seeing the anime? I've heard rumors that I only half believe, but in any case, please mind the difference between bravery and recklessness.

Nice to meet you, hello, or perhaps long time no see. This is Carlo Zen (@sonzaix).

Soon the manga will pass the novels in terms of number of volumes. How in the world did this happen?

When I consider the reason, I feel it must be that working on the anime took up some time, but if I think about it harder, I also get the feeling I'm just slower these days. Thus, I truly appreciate you comrades who always wait patiently for new volumes.

Perhaps this is wisdom of the crowd, but in the sense that many people have discovered various ways to enjoy *The Saga of Tanya the Evil*, I think we can say that the anime has achieved favorable results. I am indebted to the anime staff, as I relied on them a great deal. Now I simply have to carry on the extremely easy work of releasing more volumes at a constant pace.

Strangely, my only worry is that I don't seem to be staying on schedule; in that sense, manuscripts are kind of like summer vacation homework. That said, I vow to do my summer homework according to a plan.

I have the feeling I made the same vow every year of elementary, middle, and high school, but looking at it another way, that means I've held fast to the idea all these years, so I hope you'll acknowledge my tenacious integrity, if nothing else.

It's thanks to all of you that a guy like me can continue

writing and making books. I really owe the designers at Tsubakiya Design, the proofreaders at Tokyo Publisher Service Center, my editors Fujita and Tamai, and illustrator Shinotsuki.

And thank you as always to you, the readers who stick with me. I hope to keep seeing you around.

June 2017 *Carlo Zen*

To learn about the structure of guns and their history,
I spoke with Chicago Regimentals Co., Ltd. about
deactivated firearms. I want to give them a big thank-you.

Burn up the last of your desperate efforts...

When logs need to be added to the fire, how many people would demolish their house for fuel? That's what it means to be trapped in total war.

...and stare into the darkness beyond.

THE SAGA OF TANYA THE EVIL

Omnes una Manet Nox

[STORY BY] Carlo Zen   [ILLUSTRATION BY] Shinobu Shinotsuki